SLEEPERS BOOK SERIES

SLUMBER
-BOOK I-

By
Ted Cummings

Dearest Nena,

Thank you so much
for such incredible work.
It means the person
to me. You are the
Book signing
that my very feast
happening. May God
you Always.
Bless and increase

Ted Cummerlos

Dedication

For Traci, Solomon, Zoe, Christian, Leri, Khristian & Pharaoh in all of whom lay my future and my legacy, and for the Children yet to come.

For all of the Men who have gone before me and paved the way: Shade, Daniel, Joseph I, Joseph II, Herndon and Robert.

For Christine, Andrea and Rebecca who encouraged me when I needed it the most and edited my work to keep me going.

For Darrius who carried the Light to take me to see what the end will be.

For Dr. Joan Payne who gave me my start and always pushes me to be my best.

SLEEPERS BOOK SERIES
SLUMBER – BOOK I
TABLE OF CONTENTS

SLEEPERS BOOK SERIES

By Ted Cummings

PROLOGUE

Two years before our story begins.

It is another sleepless night for Jerome. He looks at the legal pad filled with numbers. His eyes are blurry from fighting a sleep that he dares not fall into. He has to figure this thing out. The mortgage is due. The car note is due. The twins' tuitions are due. The lights are about to be cut off, and his family still needs to eat.

When Jerome lost his job with the State of Ohio a few years ago, he and his wife still decided that Elena needed to come home to care for the kids, their twins. They knew that it would be tight but believed that Jerome would be able to get another job to take care of them. Elena, his wife, had reassured him that, with the Lord's help, everything would be alright. At the time, Jerome could not see nor feel the Lord's help. He decided, though, to trust his wife and to hold on for her sake. As it turns out, she had been right.

*   *   *

1

Dr. Krauss checks and re-checks his results. He almost can't believe what he sees.

"Emily!" he calls out to his assistant.

"Yes, Dr. Krauss?" Emily replies.

"Have you seen these results?" he bellows.

"No, sir. You forbade me or anyone from looking at the overnight results of the testing until you saw them first. You said something about not wanting them out before you had an opportunity to massage them."

Dr. Krauss sighs in relief. He is nervous for sure. Usually, he became nervous about producing bad results that would have to be communicated to the board, which could ultimately lead to his firing or worse.

These results, Dr. Krauss thinks, would not have to be massaged, he sees. His theory had worked. His methodologies had worked, and soon his results could be widely shared.

"Emily," Dr. Krauss intones, "don't share these results or the fact of their existence with anyone. We'll need to do rigorous testing first to confirm what I'm seeing here."

"No sir, I won't," Emily says. "But Dr. Krauss, what do the results say?"

Dr. Krauss looks at her thoughtfully and clears his throat. "Emily," he says, "I think that we may have just discovered," he pauses, "the fountain of youth."

*　　*　　*

Current Day

　　Dr. Alexandria Taylor, or Alex as she prefers to be called, glances furtively down the hallway of her company's main building in Chicago. The coast is clear, she thinks. She knows that she has one, and only one shot to get this right. The computer virus that she is about to install in Pharmatech's mainframe should work, but will only work today, and only for a few minutes. Today is special because all of Pharmatech's mainframe computers are scheduled to run their maintenance software at the same time. Why the computer engineers at Pharmatech had designed the system to operate that way, Alex swears she will never understand, but such poor engineering affords her this singular opportunity for a bit of strategic anarchy, she hopes. As a disgruntled employee turned industrial spy for Pharmatech's chief competitor, disrupting the roll out of their newest miracle drug is the next best thing to having the formula for the drug itself. Since she couldn't get that, her bosses had instructed her to ruin this new drug's coming out party. She is happy to oblige.

Alex knows that if she is right, careful and a little lucky, her computer virus will cause a major, but temporary calamity at all of Pharmatech's main drug testing facilities. This calamity will assure, she thinks, Pharmatech's set-back for years, and possibly decades. Having intimate knowledge of Pharmatech, she had helped conduct the tests for the new drug and seen its failures, and especially the ones that Pharmatech had kept hidden and lied about to the press and government.

At thirty-six Alex no longer considers herself to be a young woman. Though her bright eyes continue to show much of the hope and ambition with which she started her career at Pharmatech, she is now tired. In particular, she is tired of the racism that she constantly experiences as the only Black person in her department and the sexism that also pervades it.

She does not know which is worse, the racism or the misogyny, but Alex also no longer cares about either. All of it is bad and had taken their toll on her. Pharmatech, she fiendishly thinks, will pay for every missed promotion and every neglected complaint that she had made to HR, and today will be the day that they start to pay, she thinks.

Alex applies her thumb to the thumb print scanner. She waits for the light on the door to go from red to green. At the door's beep and green light, she pushes through into the room that holds the mainframe computers for the Chicago facility. It is empty as expected. Alex walks to the end of a long line of mainframes. She finds a keyboard connected to a mainframe at the end of the row. Alex then slips a USB card out of her front breast pocket and connects it to a USB outlet in the keyboard. A screen connected to the keyboard registers the presence of the USB drive.

Alex pulls up a command line on the screen and types "run freegen1." As the program runs, she muses about the impending results and wonders to herself if she's covered her tracks well enough. Aside from having her thumb print entrance registered, she knows that she has not otherwise been recorded. Pharmatech's security is lax on this level since no R&D occurs here. The company spares no expense to create and protect its R&D, but had done a less than admirable job of applying such protection in other departments, namely in its computer mainframe security. There are no security cameras on this floor except the one in the main hallway which Alex easily avoids, and none in this room.

After the program fully uploads and Alex runs it, she walks back to the door to leave, she thinks again about calling in sick tomorrow, but decides that would look too suspicious. She hopes that the calamity that she's causing will not be detrimental to her, as they hadn't been previously. Regardless, she considers her coming to work the next day a necessary risk to allay suspicion. Besides, she thinks, she would pay good money to see her boss and co-workers knocked out on the floor for a few hours or days as Pharmatech scampers to cover its tracks. Closing the door behind her, she chuckles at the thought.

CHAPTER I

Sabrina awakes with a violent shake that almost knocks her out of her seat. Something is wrong, terribly wrong. Her seat belt digs into her torso and causes the left side of her hip to ache. She looks forward down the long aisle to the front of the plane, and sees that her own personal chaos has spread to every row. She had fallen asleep, she thinks, for just a moment. She takes this crazy red eye flight once a month from L.A. back to New York to spend time with her fiancé. Anything for love, she thinks. Right now, she wonders just how bad their plight might be. Suddenly, the plane lists badly and turns almost a full ninety degrees to its left side.

She expects to hear someone, anyone, over the intercom, but nothing is said by anyone official, nothing. She smells smoke and sees it coming from the pilot's closed cockpit door. She sees one of the flight attendants slumped over at the pilot's door. She is a pretty blonde with blue eyes that smiled a lot when Sabrina boarded the plane. She hadn't caught her name, but now she just looks dead. Sabrina isn't certain if that's true, but the thought of that possibility puts her into a near panic.

Suddenly, Sabrina feels the plane dive. They're diving! Where are the pilots?! Is this a terrorist attack?! Are we going to die?! Sabrina thinks all of these in rapid succession as most of the

plane's occupants scream at their collective terror. She joins them

and screams at the top of her lungs. Taking a momentary break for

air, she looks to her right and sees that her neighbor is dead! No,

not dead, Sabrina realizes, but rather sound asleep. How can he

sleep through this? She wants to shake him awake and would have,

but sees that the ground will soon meet them. She closes her eyes

and crosses her arms over her chest. Her last thoughts are of her

mother, her fiancé, and the life she would never get to live.

*　　*　　*

Donnie Hernandez thought that if he spent a little more on

a high-end car that somehow his daily commute to work would

be a bit more bearable. He is wrong. He should have opted for

a brand new affordable car or a bus pass. Being twenty-seven, a

recent MBA grad and more than a little cocky, Donnie feels that

he is entitled to a sports car. He is at least owed, he thinks, a starter

sports car before he gets the Porsche that he really wants. This

BMW will do just fine until then, he thinks. Rarely at a loss for

confidence, Donnie sees himself shooting up the corporate ladder quickly. This is a ladder that he had been well-groomed for by his parents, his family, his alma mater and his fraternity.

Donnie bristles at the nickname, "Flamingo," that his college frat brothers had given him. He couldn't honestly say that it hadn't fit. He had always been known to be a bit flashy. Besides, he thought at the time, "If they're going to call me a *pink bird*, I'll just have to be a pink bird of prey on their bamma asses!"

Chicago is even colder than usual this morning, but at least he has heated seats and a heated steering wheel. The latest polar vortex could do nothing to touch him, Donnie thinks as he smirks. Though leaving at 7 a.m., he knows that his earliest possible arrival time to work downtown will be about 8:30 a.m.

He checks the mirror and sees his hazel brown eyes staring back at him. He also sees his sun-deprived light brown skin, his winter yellow he calls it. He hates it because his close friends and frat brothers are more than happy to remind him of his lack of melanin. All of his beach color had left him for this dreary February sun.

Driving along Interstate 55 during the morning rush had never been fun. This morning, though, seemed to be pretty smooth. Donnie notes that he's been able, for the last forty minutes or so, to keep it moving at pretty close to sixty miles per hour. It is not nearly as fast as he wants to drive, but it is better than being stuck in a parking lot. He knows that feeling all too well.

Donnie passes into the far left lane to begin to try to speed up a bit more. His new car feels precise and certain. Its throttle response is excellent. He presses the gas a little more to see if he can push his car a little faster.

Feeling it more than seeing it, Donnie slams onto his brakes as another car careens at full speed directly at him on his right side. He stops just short of the car hitting him at full speed, crashing into a concrete retaining wall to his left. Donnie clutches his steering wheel in a death grip. His heart pounds fiercely and he begins to sweat. He has a nanosecond to process his physical response, as he watches the car that just missed him hit and then flip itself over the concrete wall.

Donnie then hears the familiar screech of rubber behind him. He checks his rear view mirror and sees another car, seemingly out of control, come barreling up behind him hitting multiple cars in its wake. Smartly, Donnie decides to test the acceleration claim of his new car to see if the commercials tell the truth. Ultimate driving machine? Donnie is about to find out. He has no idea what in the hell had gotten into these people today, but he is not about to let his new toy or himself be the victim of any crazier I-55 drivers. Donnie takes off at maximum speed and leaves all of the traffic behind him in his wake. He can't wait to get to his office to read and hear about all of the accidents that had nearly claimed him as one of its victims.

*   *   *

Raheem stretches out as much as his bed would allow his six-foot, five-inch frame to stretch. He had learned years ago that prison beds aren't built for tall men. Really, he learned that prison isn't built for any man.

Raheem reminds himself that today is set to be a good day. His girlfriend Candace and their three kids, Pharaoh, Angel and Jaret are coming to see him. He lives for them, and they keep him focused. He had served three years on an eight-year sentence. He is due to be out in the next six months on good behavior. Nothing and no one is going to come between him and his family. Candace had remained faithful and held it down for the family while he has been locked up. He loves her for that, and promises himself that he will soon make an honest woman of her. Raheem looks forward to the day that he can call Candace his wife.

Raheem knows that his sentence had been unjust in the first place, though he blames himself for even getting caught up in the predicament. Still, he wonders again, as he had often wondered, who gets eight years for knocking out an asshole boss who makes racist comments against his employees? Raheem, that's who—the big Black dude who had been trained by the Special Forces and had an exemplary military record. Candace had always told him that his temper would catch up with him. She had been right.

The judge had given him the maximum sentence for assault, and justified it by saying that his combat training in the Marines and his expertise in martial arts made him a deadly weapon. That is ridiculous, Raheem thinks. If he had wanted to kill the guy, he wouldn't have punched him. He would have done something deadlier and much less obvious. None of Raheem's many character witnesses could convince the judge to decide otherwise. Raheem received the toughest sentence possible.

Thoughts of that fateful day come easily yet painfully to Raheem. He had held his tongue on the first fifty "niggers" and "boys" that he heard his supervisor say either to him or to his fellow Black work staff. They all needed those jobs, and his supervisor knew it. However, today Raheem was done being the object of that man's scorn and racial derision, so he punched him as soon as he let a racial epithet escape his lips. It wasn't even that hard. It was more of a slap than a punch. His manager hadn't even been hurt. He just got woke up as Raheem would later describe it. Regardless, his whole life had changed in that one instant. Like most bullies, his supervisor had dropped like a sack of wet potatoes and crawled into the fetal position. Punk that he is, he ran to HR, who then called the police. Raheem had been arrested and was escorted from the premises. He was soon after fired.

That's okay, Raheem thinks at the time, it was worth it. He soon learns that it had not been worth it in the least. As Raheem stands at his arraignment and listens to the long list of charges being read against him, he wonders whether his now former manager had died. It is simple assault at most, but he is being charged with aggravated assault, terroristic threatening, kidnapping, and false imprisonment! The prosecutor wants to make some sort of example out of him. After his conviction, Raheem goes to prison with a lengthy sentence hanging over him. Raheem's girlfriend, Candace, is understandably devastated.

With the separation from his girlfriend and kids, he comes to later acknowledge, that one punch had not been worth it and had done far more damage than he could have ever calculated or imagined.

Cracking his neck for the third time, Raheem feels the hairs on the back of his arm stand up. His military training, reinforced by his prison stay, has made him nothing if not a man of routine and discipline. This morning, that routine is off. He should not have been able to get a second neck crack in without hearing the first of the three morning bells commanding him and his fellow inmates to wake up and get dressed. He gets up and slips on his jumpsuit. His cell mate, Carlos, is still fast asleep. He shakes him roughly. "Carlos, wake up man, something's wrong," Raheem says. Carlos murmurs something about "Five more minutes, Señor," but Raheem does not relent. He shakes him again. "Carlos! Get up man, I don't see any guards!" At that, Carlos shoots out of bed nearly slamming into Raheem. "Sorry, Rah," he says in a thick Spanish accent, "did you say no guards?" he squints as he asks.

"No guards!" Raheem repeats as he notes to himself that there is no sound of any guards either. In fact, he thinks, there are no prison sounds at all except that of the stirrings of his fellow inmates. "Listen, Carlos, it sounds almost like," Raheem pauses, disbelieving his next words, "that we're here all alone." That couldn't be possible, Raheem knows, but now he sees that other inmates across from him notice the same thing.

"Open up on cell 236!" they hear. Cell 236, is Raheem's cell. It creaks open, and Raheem and Carlos step out. Looking left and then right, they see no one. "Raheem, what's going on?" Steven, another inmate housed next to him and Carlos' cell asks. "I don't know, bro. We're going to go check it out. Let's go."

Over the intercom Raheem and Carlos hear "Prisoners Raheem and Carlos, please come to the guards' pod ASAP!" Please? Raheem thinks, since when does a guard say please?

Moments later, Raheem and Carlos arrive at the guards' pod, which is the location where the guards watch the inmates. They control the doors from the pod also. The door to the pod is slightly ajar, something that never happens due to standard prison procedures. The guards usually enforce strict separation between themselves and the prisoners. "Come in," they hear from inside, "and shut the door behind you." Walking into the pod they see something that they aren't expecting to see; three guards laying on the floor next to one another. Each guard is as still as stone. They look dead, but Raheem and Carlos see that their cheeks are still flushed with life. They also sees that they are each still breathing by the steady rise and fall of their chests.

"What the hell happened, Roscoe?" Raheem asks incredulously. Roscoe is one of their guards and the only one in the pod, apparently, that's conscious. Roscoe works the graveyard shift every day until 8 a.m. His crew is responsible for the wake up and inmate transport to breakfast. He has been a steady fixture in Raheem's life for the last three years. He seems pretty affable, but he and Raheem have had little interaction recently. Raheem is a model prisoner and trustee and is usually still asleep by the time Roscoe starts making his rounds. Raheem knows CO Roscoe well enough to know that he isn't the head-cracker kind of corrections officer. Roscoe is a long time veteran. He comes to work, punches his clock, does his job, clocks out and goes home. Raheem had never heard Roscoe's name in connection with any revenge plot against the guards or in any injustice perpetrated against the inmates. Roscoe has always seemed like a regular dude, Raheem thinks.

"Damndest thing, Raheem. About 4:00 a.m. this morning, all these guys either just slumped over in their seats, or fell where they were standing. I tried to wake them up. No one so much as budged. I've been sitting here for the last three hours trying to figure out what to do next. No one in the warden's office is answering my calls, and I haven't heard from anyone else in any other part of the prison. It's like we were just left here all alone, but all the inmates are still here." Raheem and Carlos look at each with the same quizzical look. No guards? They seemed to each be thinking and communicating in their respective looks. "If there are no guards," Raheem speaks up, "what does that mean about what's going on outside the prison?" he asks.

"Honestly, Raheem," Roscoe says, "I have no idea. My phone gets no reception in here, never has. I can't connect with anyone on the outside either. The phones in here don't dial outside of the prison. They're for internal communications only. But here's the thing, fellas," he continues, "I can't release everyone to breakfast. It's just me. I don't know who else will or will not show up today. So, I need your help. I don't trust more than five of you in this cell block, so I'm not releasing you all at once. Until I get reinforcements, you two are going to be in charge of distributing breakfast to the cell block. And we're going with dry cereal and milk on that. Nothing hot. Go to the cafeteria and load up the pallets with two-hundred and forty trays. Report back to me what you see along the way and in the cafeteria. I need to know how alone we may or may not be."

"CO Roscoe," Carlos breaks in, "what happens if no one comes by lunch time? Are you going to keep us locked down for the duration? That could cause a lot of problems."

"Noted, but what choice do I have? I'm taking a risk letting you two goons out. It's either this way or everyone stays in their cells with no food. I'm not delivering and watching by myself. I've got the watch. You two have the delivery. If lunch comes up, we'll address that then. Clearly, I can't leave my post even though my shift ended fifteen minutes ago. We're all in this together for now, fellas. Dismissed."

In any context, military or civilian, dismissed means dismissed. "C'mon, Carlos, let's get to it. We've got a lot of food to gather and deliver." Quickly walking to the cafeteria, Raheem focuses on the task at hand. He wonders whether he'll get to see his family today. With the strangeness at the prison, he isn't sure. Regardless of how that turns out, he would treat today like any normal day and remain focused on his time drawing up.

*　　*　　*

Captain Jill Williams awakes with a start. Her co-pilot is slumped over in his seat and the plane is beginning to list badly. They aren't scheduled to arrive at LAX for another two hours and she has left Jimmy awake to catch about thirty minutes of shut eye. Now, she is awake and apparently the only one in charge of a plane that is badly off course.

She checks the gauges and sees that they had traveled five-hundred miles off course and are rapidly losing altitude. Grabbing the controls, she pulls back to take the plane back to 50,000 feet from the 25,000 feet at which they were currently. Checking the fuel gauge, she sees that they did not have enough gas to turn and make it to LAX. Looking at her unconscious co-pilot, Captain Williams clearly understands that she has two issues: first, waking Jimmy up if possible and second, avoiding an in-air collision since they are now in occupied commercial airspace without permission and she is receiving no guidance from air traffic control.

"Jimmy! Jimmy!" she calls out. Jimmy doesn't so much as flinch. Reaching over, Captain Williams vigorously shakes him. That does nothing. This is more than odd. Jimmy doesn't drink, do drugs, is a work-out fanatic and had basically converted to veganism over two years ago. At twenty-eight years old, her junior officer is the most fit post-college kid that Captain Williams had ever known.

Captain Williams had liked Lieutenant James "Jimmy" Langston from the day they first met. They had become flying partners over two years ago. Jimmy had been assigned to her after she had been promoted to full Captain for Eagle Airlines. Jimmy is 5'10," red-headed and still retained some of the freckles that he had as a boy growing up in Cleveland, Ohio. Like Captain Williams, Jimmy had received all of his flight training in the Air Force. He is a top notch pilot who takes fastidious care of his mind and body. What then, Captain Williams wonders, could have caused him to be rendered so unresponsive?

Giving up on trying to wake him, Captain Williams then turns to the next problem: finding a suitable airport at which to land. They had just enough gas to make it to about five different airports, but four of the five were too small to accommodate her big jet. The only other one, San Francisco, is large enough, but she'd be interrupting their flight plan with her emergency landing and that by itself could cause major problems. Captain Williams is not certain that she can even gain permission to land at the San Francisco airport given how busy it normally is.

Realizing that she has little choice but to try to land there, Captain Williams turns the channel of her radio to the frequency that the San Francisco's control tower uses.

"Mayday! Mayday! This is Captain Williams on Eagle Flight number 1908. We have an emergency landing request at San Francisco and seek immediate assistance."

For several seconds, Captain Williams listens. There is no response. She calls out again. "Mayday! Mayday!" There is still no response. "San Francisco, where are you?!" she yells. Still, there is nothing, just static. A buzzer sounds in the cockpit that lets her know that a flight attendant is trying to reach her. She immediately answers it.

"This is Captain Williams," she says.

"Captain Williams," says Felicia, her most senior flight attendant, "Monica, Kelly and Ronald are all unconscious! I've been trying for the better part of an hour to wake them, but they're not responding! As far as I can tell, nothing's happened! One moment we are serving breakfast, and the next, they are on the aisle floor collapsed!"

Now, Captain Williams' head begins to spin. What she describes is exactly what had happened to Jimmy. "Felicia, how are the passengers?" she asks.

"That's the thing, Captain, hardly anyone is awake except for a few. Everyone else," Felicia pauses, "is asleep, not dead, asleep. I checked almost all of them."

Now, Captain Williams knows that she has three problems. Heaven help them all, she thinks.

*   *   *

Dr. Krauss had thought that he had just one small issue. Correction, he thinks, he has a massive, stupendous problem. What's worse, it's his fault. Whether what had occurred was done by accident or intentional, for now, did not matter. The alarms blaring at his Dallas headquarters rattled the fillings in his teeth. These alarms mean only one thing—loss of containment. If he'd lost containment in Dallas, he may have also lost it in Chicago, Charlotte, Boston and San Bernardino.

The data does not lie. The viral material in his new drug Zoesterol had regenerated. When it regenerates, it changes and mutates. When it mutates, it turns nasty and is aggressive. It is, by all appearances, communicable by air, touch and through bodily fluids. The only good news is that it could not survive, they had found, for more than forty-eight hours outside of the body. Animals are immune to its effects, but they can act as carriers and incubators.

When the first near break-out happened six months ago, Dr. Krauss believed then that they had successfully contained it. Six months later and the virus, now in a highly lethal, even more virulent form, had come roaring back, defying every conventional method at containment. It is almost as if the virus has a mind of its own: it wants out and it wants to be free. Worse than all of that, it wants to change. That thought chills Dr. Krauss to the bone.

In the first near outbreak, they had lost ten scientists. That strain of the virus had not merely put them to sleep, it had killed them. Their deaths had been painful and gory. They learned from that debacle though. Dr. Krauss believed then that they had to keep the truth of the scientists' deaths a secret, and away from prying government eyes. He had blamed their deaths on an explosion; a convenient excuse, since Dr. Krauss ordered the burning of the scientists' bodies. When FDA officials examined the bodies, they found only what he and his staff had intended them to find— charred remains and no trace of the virus that had killed them.

Reports coming into him are different than the last break out. Infected persons aren't dying as in the first outbreak, but they are becoming unconscious. The infected persons' unconsciousness is so deep that they cannot be revived. Dr. Krauss thinks about the implications of that to the populace at large. What might happen if everyone just fell asleep? Who could possibly survive that? he thinks.

Dr. Krauss carefully considers his next move. He is now in the middle of a major health crisis affecting large portions of the United States. The only thing that he can do is what he should have done months ago: the responsible thing. Making his choice, Dr. Krauss slips on his specialized yellow bio-hazard suit and leaves his office to board a private jet to Washington, D.C. He had specifically requested his pilot for this trip, so he knows that he will be safe. He needs to speak with the one person who might be able to do something to help them all—The President of the United States.

*   *   *

Jerome looks at his watch: 6:06 a.m. They are right on

schedule. Rounding into their first neighborhood on their Monday morning run, He is pleased to see that in spite of the previous night's dusting of snow, the streets had been salted and were therefore passable. He rides point, as usual, on the truck. He and Darryl make their morning run on a too cold day in Cincinnati, Ohio. It couldn't have been any more than twenty-eight degrees out. The wind chill makes it feel like it's about ten degrees. Thankfully, Elena, his wife had been listening to the weather report and made sure that he wore his thermals underneath his trash jumpsuit. Thank God for that woman, he muses, as he recognizes that she is always thinking about him—especially when he isn't thinking about himself.

In Jerome's current line of work as a sanitation technician, his fancy way of saying trash man, Mondays are always the worst. The cans tended to be heavier than any other day of the week, and they were sure to get some kind of strange weekend surprise. Besides all of that, it is the toughest day on which to work after a restful weekend.

Since losing his job during the last recession, Elena had been a great encouragement to Jerome to keep going: "don't give up, don't lose hope, the Lord will see us through." She really never stopped encouraging him. Truthfully, Jerome believes only a little bit of what she says, but he is grateful that she's had the faith that she has. He believes enough of what his wife says to listen and keep it moving. When this job came open, he all but jumped on the first trash truck that he could find.

Jerome is a college-educated man with a degree in social work. He once had a good job with the State of Ohio until the cutbacks started happening. With budgets shrinking federally and at the state level, his position became expendable. "Jerome the Expendable," he used to think when his humor felt as black as he is. Now, he is a certified, trained and well compensated trash truck driver. He is good at his job and takes a certain albeit reluctant pride in it. Ultimately, he feels no shame in his current occupation, but had always seen it as something temporary. As the years began to tick by, what once felt temporary now feels much more permanent.

"Jerome!" he hears Darryl shout. Darryl is his partner on the truck, and had been for the last three years. He is also one of Jerome's best friends and Jerome's kids know him as 'Uncle Darryl'.

"What's up, D?" he replies.

"We can't pick up these two cans right here. They're a clear violation of the weight restrictions."

Darryl knows the union rules backwards and forwards, and he never fails to remind his fellow trash men thereof. Too heavy meant too heavy, and Darryl isn't going to handle it or let Jerome handle it either.

"Okay. Leave a note on the can reminding the Johnsons of the weight rules." Jerome, of course, knew it was the Johnsons. They violated the known trash rules more than any other family on this block. It had become a joke between them.

"Third one this year, and the year's still young," Darryl reminds Jerome with a tinge of admonishment in his voice. "They'll be upset that we didn't pick it up again."

Truthfully, this was the part of Darryl's job that he loved the most; saying no to homeowners about what he would and would not do. Jerome likes that part a little too, but he would never admit or, God forbid, relish in it like Darryl does.

Trash is dirty business, but it had been a good job to Jerome. Monday through Friday, he wakes up by 5:00 a.m. His days are mostly complete by 2:00 p.m. Though not loving the early hours, he loves being able to pick up his son and daughter, who are twins, from school. He enjoys debriefing with them about their day at school, and attending their games and practices. Both kids, Micah and Sarah, are academics, but also athletic. In fact, Sarah had become known all over the city as its best sixth grade girl basketball and soccer player.

Micah is equally as athletic, but his passions are football and track. He had stopped playing soccer once football fully kicked in (and once Sarah had routinely begun to outperform him in front of their friends and classmates). Together, they represented everything and more that Jerome and Elena had prayed for. They are not perfect kids by any stretch of the imagination, but they are smart, down to earth, good looking and had both seemed to internalize their parents' values of hard work, personal responsibility, faith and fun. Like their mother, the Middleton kids had been solid during all of Jerome's work issues.

Jerome is excited to be leaving work at 12:30 p.m. today, since he and Darryl's Monday run has been assumed by another trash crew in training. Their boss, Robert, is riding with that crew to show them the ropes. Jerome's excitement is palpable.

"The hell's the matter with you?" Darryl says after watching Jerome walk around with a goofy smile for about five minutes.

"Wrong?" Jerome replies. "Me? Nah, bruh, I'm good. Everythang is everything!" Jerome says in a faux Black southern accent that he knows Darryl hates.

Darryl dutifully responds with a blistering eye roll that signifies his derisive displeasure. Darryl can roll his eyes all he wants, Jerome thinks. He is happily going to meet his wife and hopefully get some one-on-one husband and wife time before he has to pick up the twins from school. Elena had been feeling sick for almost two weeks and in that time had been all but inaccessible. She spent time recovering from something that looked like a mix of the flu and a series of migraines—she had truly been miserable. Thankfully, Jerome thinks, she is finally healthy.

Back at headquarters, clean-up is pretty much automatic: disrobe in one room; shower in another; and dress in the locker room. Bam. No problem. Occasionally, a few of the newer guys would forget to leave all of their soiled clothes in the first room, and track something into the locker room. The veterans like Jerome all hate that, but not as much as the poor worker who transgresses the rules. The offender is required to wash all of the uniforms for the week if he so errs. This had happened to Jerome once, and once had been enough for him to learn the lesson.

Quickly clocking out after a fresh shower, he scrambles to his car, happy to be leaving so early. He drives in joyful expectation of his time with Elena. The radio blares a commercial, something about Pharmatech FDA trials, blah, blah, before Jerome quickly turns to the local R&B station. Now this is more like it, he thinks. Marvin Gaye croons one of his famous baby makers, exactly matching Jerome's mood.

The Pharmatech commercial triggers an unpleasant memory. They had been blasting their ads on television and radio for the better of a year seeking participants in their drug trials. Jerome had known better than to sign up. He had done a drug trial in college to earn some extra money. What a big mistake, he remembers. The three-hundred and fifty dollars earned in that trial could never properly compensate him for the blurred vision and diarrhea that he had experienced for a week. He swore after that experience that he would never again do another drug trial. If he needed extra money, he would give blood or plasma like every other self-respecting college student had done.

Whatever drug they manufactured, it is supposed to be the next big thing, but when Jerome had done a Google search on its name—Zoesterol—he could find few details. There was very little information about it and Pharmatech's website said almost nothing about it. Out of curiosity, Jerome had even called the 800 number to get information as a prospective participant, but even then he could not get a straight answer as to what the drug actually does. A friend of his, Barney, participated in a trial for it. He was instructed to record any ill effects. Barney recorded bad breath, a stomach ache and loose stools. He was paid pretty handsomely for his service too, about one-thousand dollars for each trial. Jerome had considered joining the trial but remembered the fiasco from college and had decided that a one-thousand dollar check was not worth any of the symptoms that Barney had reported or any other side effects that he hadn't heard about yet. Of course, Pharmatech told Barney nothing about what the drug was supposed to do. He was literally a human guinea pig. No thanks, Jerome thought at the time, and hadn't considered it since.

Quickly casting such thoughts out of his head, Jerome hurries home to his waiting wife. She had promised him a special treat when he got home since he had been so patient and helpful to her during her recuperation. To Elena, this constituted consistently doing the dishes, tending to the kids, taking out the trash and taking care of her while she had been sick. Jerome had indeed been a good husband and was excited about enjoying his wife, and her enjoying him.

Arriving home, he finds Elena in her come-and-get-me robe, yet her face says anything but that. "Honey," she says, "I think that we may need to go get the kids from school." The television is blaring, something she routinely forbade. The screen shows serious looking reporters in split screens, all seemingly in different locations around the country. Some sort of major catastrophe is happening, and it didn't seem to be localized to any one place. Jerome keys into the announcer on MSNBC who is describing a series of plane crashes in the United States, about twenty. Wait, twenty plane crashes?! Jerome thinks, what the heck is happening?! Is this another terrorist attack? he wonders.

"Elena, what the hell is going on?" he asks her.

"Shhh, Jerome!" Elena says. "I just turned this up to hear. Something very bad is happening, Baby! All those people!" she exclaims.

These are commercial airliners that had been full of people. Their planes are crashing indiscriminately all over the country, seemingly without pattern except that the crashes are occurring only in the United States. Even some of the planes that had safely landed crashed into other planes on the ground that had taxied onto runways, but never took off.

Elena turns the volume up as the video switches to the White House press room. A very austere looking Black man with graying temples stands behind the White House Press Secretary's podium and begins to speak.

"Good morning. My name is Michael Casey. I am the acting press secretary. Press Secretary Jay Carney will return as soon as he is able. As you may have seen reported, there have been multiple airline crashes in the air and on the ground. The President has put the nation on high alert. Terrorism is suspected but has not been verified. Currently, these attacks, if they are indeed attacks, do not seem to be following any sort of pattern other than the planes have been crashing since early this morning. We've grounded all domestic and international flights. We are estimating twenty planes have crashed at this point. We do not have the exact number yet, but we are working hard to clarify that now. Neither the NSA nor the CIA have been able to ascertain what it might be.

DOD Intelligence is also reviewing this, as well as the NSA. We hope to have some answers soon within the next few hours.

We do know that none of the plane crashes were international.
They were all domestic flights. Regardless, we're not taking any
chances until we find out more. We don't yet know who may have
died in these tragic accidents. Families of the deceased will be
contacted, and their names revealed at that time. We also know
that there have been many car accidents reported this morning.
This morning's rush hour seems to be even more disastrous than
our air travel has been. We are asking everyone to stay home and
off of the roads. If you're at work, stay at work until we know more.
Accidents are being reported in the many, many thousands and all
over the country.

There is no casualty count. State and local emergency
responders are, at least for now, responding. As I've said,
wherever you are, please stay there unless children are involved.
If you have kids at school, please get them home as soon as
possible. Homeland Security is on high alert as well as the
Pentagon. The President has canceled all military vacations
and all reservists are ordered to report to their command posts.
We're sorry to do this, but until we know more, everyone in
government and the military is on high alert. We'll be reporting
new developments as they occur. You can consider this a rolling

interview that will remain open for as long as it takes. I'll now take
questions."

At his conclusion, Mr. Casey is barraged with a cacophony of questions from the reporters assembled in the room the first of which is a question about where Press Secretary Carney is. Elena turns the television down to a much lower din. Jerome stands there planted. He is thunderstruck. Since the events of 9/11, nearly every American had remained alert to the possibility that terrorism might strike the U.S. again. The scope of what is now happening is far beyond anything that all, but the most paranoid, could have suggested would happen.

Pulling himself together, Jerome looks at his wife and says "Elena, get dressed. We're getting the kids from school. Meet me in the car in five minutes. I'm getting my gun."

CHAPTER II

President Douglas sits in the Situation Room looking at his generals and all of his high level staff. Two hours ago he sent his sons off to school. His thoughts are with them now, and whether they should be retrieved. He couldn't help but worry, even though he knows his wife, Helen, is on top of it and that he needn't be overly concerned. Soon, his thoughts shift to what is before him. As he looks at the multiple screens around him showing the carnage from around the country, he wonders whether the previous seven years have adequately prepared him for this dreadful day. This is an unprecedented tragedy spread out from one coast to another.

"Generals," he says, "your *best* assessment, please."

"Mr. President," General McCarron, the most senior of his generals begins to speak, "our intelligence assures us that no bombs went off on any of the planes. As of now, about thirty-three planes have either crashed while in flight, or were crashed into by one of the planes that fell from the sky. There were, we believe, five to seven mid-air collisions. We don't know the actual number yet. We're still trying to sort through all the information. Most others, though, simply dropped out of the sky. Five of those

crashed in some highly-populated areas causing massive damage-
-Houston, Denver, Nashville, Detroit and," General McCarron
pauses rifling through some papers, "Phoenix. The last city is
Phoenix, sir. Tracing the flight paths of the planes, it appears that
each plane simply stopped being flown, almost as if the pilots
weren't there anymore. There was one plane that managed to land
safely, but not by its pilots. A passenger named Max Hollister
noticed that the plane was listing and dipping left, alerted a flight
attendant who then tried to speak to the pilots. Getting no response
and finding the pilots unconscious, --more on that in a moment--
Mr. President--she asked for a pilot. Mr. Hollister stepped up and
with help from one of our control towers, landed the plane safely
about a hundred miles or so off course at an alternate airport."

"In addition to all of this, Mr. President," White House
Chief of Staff Barbara Smith says speaking up, "we're starting
to get reports on the extent of the car crashes that occurred
during morning rush hour. It's truly unprecedented, sir. First,
it's countrywide, the heaviest damage being concentrated on our
highways in our largest cities: Chicago; L.A.; D.C.; Philadelphia;
Atlanta; Dallas; San Francisco; and more. Sir, the casualties are
in the thousands, perhaps as many as a few hundred thousand

or more. There are, however, no reports of bridges, roads or buildings being blown up or otherwise collapsing. There have been explosions, but mostly at gas stations after fuel pumps have exploded due to collisions with autos or fuel tankers on our highways that have crashed. This has elements of terror activity, but it seems to be much broader than that, and is missing an essential ingredient," she pauses, "terrorists. There don't seem to be any terrorists involved, at least not directly. Plus, given the highly individual nature of the car accidents in particular, it seems extremely unlikely that any terrorist group could inflict this much damage over such a widespread area in such a short amount of time. Something else is at work, sir. We just don't know what it is yet."

The President leans back in his seat clasping his hands together in front of his mouth with his index fingers extended upwardly in an expression that his staff had termed the "thinking pose." His wife calls it the "worry pose." He inherently knows that his next words are critical to untold numbers of American lives and begins to speak slowly, yet purposefully to his senior staff.

"I want all flights grounded until we can assess how far this goes. I want teams shipped immediately to the crash sites. I want

Congress placed on high alert and ready to generously allocate funds as necessary. Contact Homeland Security and advise them to ramp up their efforts now." "Diane," he says to his personal assistant, "I want to be on the air in twenty minutes. The American people need to know what's going on and how we're handling it. I want our military placed on high alert. If this is a domestic attack, I want our forces in position to be able to counter it. Have our reserve forces up and active in our twenty most populated cities. I'll be back in ten minutes to check status." With that, the President stands and exits the room moving quickly to the private residence to change suits for his upcoming camera time and to check on Helen and their sons.

*   *   *

Captain Williams sees the runway from the cockpit. Guiding the plane to San Francisco International airport had not been the problem. The problem had been getting directions from the airport's control tower on where to land and when to land. Her fuel gauge is close to empty. She calculates that she has maybe twenty minutes of flight time left before her airplane crashes.

Angling toward the main runway, Captain Williams' dark face becomes ashen. What she sees befuddles and alarms her. A violent crash has occurred on the runway, and at least two more large planes like hers sit upon it. Nothing seems to be moving, and she still has heard no communication from the control tower.

Captain Williams takes a moment to review her choices as she speedily approaches the front of the runway. She considers her choices: try to land and attempt to avoid the other planes and debris, or, with only twenty minutes of fuel left, find another suitable place to land, an empty highway perhaps. These are all bad ideas, she thinks, and all with bad and potentially tragic results. Their best case scenario, she thinks, is to land her plane here at the airport, avoid at least two of the parked planes, hit a third parked plane only partially losing, maybe, a wing at most, she hopes. She'd have to do some nifty flying and landing to get that result. The worst case, though, is almost unthinkable. It would be total destruction of her and all of her passengers, plus any number of occupants on the ground. If she dies, her wife will not be amused and will probably *kill* her, she muses darkly.

Making her choice, Captain Williams looks at Jimmy, who is still unconscious, for what she hopes is not the last time.

"Whatever this thing is, Jimmy, let's hope that we both survive it, dude." Pointing the nose of the plane down, she angles for the landing strip. She believes that if she changes her landing point on the strip, she just might avoid two of the planes that are stopped near the front of it. It would be very close, Captain Williams knows. She'd have to fly in at a much lower angle than what is common or allowed by FAA regulations. *FAA regulations be damned*, Captain Williams thinks. She sets her will to save these people and try her best not to kill any of the people on the ground.

"Felicia," Captain Williams calls into the passenger cabin's speaker for her one conscious flight attendant, "buckle up. We're going down. It may be hard. You may want to pray. Please secure the passengers." It may be hard? That's the understatement of the year, Felicia thinks as she pulls harder on her strap and wipes away a tear from her cheek. She hadn't been to Mass in years. In this moment, she promises God and herself that if she survives this flight, she'll give up men, alcohol and not going to church.

Captain Williams feels the strong tug of turbulence on the plane's body as a violent wind from the San Francisco Bay buffets the plane. Her speed gauge tells her that she is coming in too fast due to the angle of her approach. She drops her landing gear and all of her flaps in an attempt to slow down. She sees that her angle

of approach will have her nearly clip one of the planes as she

attempts to hit the next closest spot to land. The crash that she sees

most clearly is at the end of the landing strip. Two planes burn

brightly, and are irretrievably tangled together in a brilliant ball of

fire and metal. There's no way that there are any survivors from

that, she thinks. She fervently hopes that once they land, she can

apply the plane's brakes in time to avoid crashing into the bright

tangle at the end of the runway.

Taking a deep breath, Captain Williams makes her final

approach. So far so good. She is now about twenty seconds from

touching the plane down. Miraculously, it looks like they're

going to make it. All those flight simulator hours had been worth

it, she promises herself, just hold her steady. Passing no more

than ten feet directly over the first plane and five feet over the

second, her 747 bumpily touches down onto the runway and then

bounces up uncontrollably, the plane tilting at an awkward angle.

Captain Williams corrects for the bounce and the tilt and lands all

the plane's wheels solidly onto the runway with just a few more

bumps. But they are still moving way too fast, she sees. The crash

at the end of the runway rushes to meet them much faster than she expects. She has to quickly adjust, or the entire plane will become part of the fiery, tangled mess ahead. Captain Williams sees that there are only a few yards between them now.

Doing all that she knows to do, Captain Williams applies all of the available brakes and feels the plane turn to one side. If she is going to avoid crashing into the blaze ahead of her, she has one and only one shot: drive the plane off the runway directly toward the Bay and risk a slide into it. It occurs to her that water isn't much better than fire, but she knows that fire is sure death whereas water at least gives them a chance.

With all of her remaining strength and training, Captain Williams turns her controller to the right. Because of a cross wind pushing the plane toward the crash, the controller resists her mightily. The plane wants to maintain a straight line. Captain Williams desperately needs it to go right. Straining until the veins on her neck are visible and she feels the joints in her legs and arms crack, she wills the plane to move to the right, slightly, just enough to point the nose and body away from the fiery crash that was no more than twenty-five yards away from them. They are going to hit it, no matter what, but at this angle, they might just walk away from this crash with their lives. At least, there is no more fuel left in the plane, she reasons, so they shouldn't explode or catch fire immediately upon impact.

Exactly as she hopes, the nose of her plane rides right by the crash. The left wing, with a loud sound, crashes into the ruined planes and is ripped apart from her plane's body. The force of the crash further slows her plane down, and halts what remains of the plane mere yards away from the Bay. Captain Williams takes a deep breath and mentally counts all of her fingers and toes, not to mention her blessings. No training could ever really prepare her or anyone for this kind of landing. She is relieved that her family will not have to cash in her life insurance policy just yet. Now, to the passengers.

*   *   *

As Elena quickly dresses, the television in her bedroom blares an interview of a woman of about forty-five years old, Captain Jill "Wilson" or "Williams," she hadn't fully caught her last name, who had just emergency landed a 747 at the San Francisco airport. Elena sees that she is a pretty Black woman who looks ten years younger than her years suggest. She speaks in measured, calm tones that are dead giveaways to her military bearing and training. She records how her co-pilot had become unconscious, and how most of the passengers on her plane had been unconscious as well. Due to her quick thinking and piloting skills, no one on her plane died. They are all fully alive, yet most became unconscious and unresponsive prior to the tricky landing. She did not know whether they had been revived yet.

It is clear from all of the activity in the background of Captain Williams' interview that state and federal personnel are on the scene and moving quickly about. The San Francisco airport is a mess as several other planes had crashed there. Authorities say that it is closed indefinitely. Elena wonders whether Cincinnati's airport is also closed. She has not yet heard anything definitive about that.

Elena hears a voice off camera shout that three of the flight attendants are likewise unconscious. Unconscious? Elena ponders what that means. She does not understand the use of that word in this context. Are they asleep, knocked out, or something worse? As these thoughts race through her mind, she finishes dressing.

Though home full-time with the kids now, Elena had spent the first seven years of her marriage with Jerome working as a nurse. She remembers that there are varying states of unconsciousness and that most of them require some sort of outside stimuli to cause them. A few such states, of a rarer variety, can be induced, but she does not know what kind these are.

Closing the front door behind her, she sees Jerome dutifully waiting in the car for her. She feels suddenly overwhelmed by her love and affection for him. Since high school, she had borne his every success, setback, his children: their twins, Micah and Sarah. Marriage to him for the last twelve years had not always been easy, but it had been well worth every hill and every valley that they encountered together. They had gone through it together, hadn't they? she thinks. No matter the obstacle or terrain, they had always walked hand in hand together, always coming out on the other side whole if not a little bit bruised.

Sitting next to Jerome, he smiles at her and grasps her hand. "Baby, everything is going to be alright. I called the school and told them that we are coming. Apparently, other parents had the same idea that we do and are pulling their kids out too. The school had not told the children yet what is happening. I think that's a good thing." Elena nods her head in agreement. She turns the radio on to the news channel they most often listen to and hears an unfamiliar voice.

"Hello, again, folks. I'm Monique LeBeach reporting the news to you. Rick Smart, our regular anchor, is currently unavailable, but we're still able to report the news." Elena notes that Monique sounds young, very young, and also more than a little unsure of herself. "Several car crashes in and around metropolitan Cincinnati have occurred. Drivers are asked to avoid I-75 and I-71 stretching from downtown to West Chester and Mason. Also, 75/71 into the city from Northern Kentucky has been blocked off given the high volume of crashes that are still being sorted through. Emergency response teams are experiencing uncanny delays and seem to be short staffed. Emergency responders from other municipalities have been contacted to help, but they seem to be short staffed too."

Just then, two police cars with sirens blaring speed past Jerome and Elena with such speed that Jerome's car shakes and momentarily swerves before he regains full control of it. "Jerome, what direction are they heading," asks Elena. "Don't worry, babe, it's not the school. See, they're turning left. We're making a right at the next corner."

"Elena, please call the school and tell them that we'll be there in fifteen minutes," Jerome says. As Elena dials, Jerome thinks about the route that he should take. They live on the west side of town along Route 50. The kids' school, Hyde Park Day, is also along Route 50, but is located on the east side of town. Normally, they would take Route 50 and be there in less than fifteen minutes. Jerome thinks that if accidents are clogging up the highways, there might also be some happening along their normal route. Listening to the radio they hear that there are indeed "multiple lanes along Route 50 that are clogged up—avoid!"

Going through the city, they decide, is the only way to reach them. It will take longer, but Jerome and Elena believe that it will be safer. Slowly but surely, Jerome wheels the car through the Clifton neighborhood first, Walnut Hills next and then finally into and through Hyde Park, where Hyde Park Day school sits. Along the way, they see some strange sights. There are multiple accidents along the streets too. It is far worse than what they had expected. They see dozens of people collapsed on sidewalks and not moving. Especially around the University of Cincinnati in the Clifton neighborhood, they see dozens of college students still strapped into their backpacks collapsed on the streets surrounding the university.

In all of the neighborhoods that they cross on their way to

their kids' school, they see wrecked cars and pedestrians collapsed on the street and on the sidewalk. At first blush, there hadn't seemed to be a pattern amongst the collapsed people. There are young and old, college students, young professionals, male and female, White and *Bla-*, no, Elena stops herself in mid thought. She had not seen even one collapsed person who is Black. Everyone that they see laid out is White or appears to be White. Wait, Elena thinks, that isn't right. They had seen some non-White people in a few cars that had been in accidents with other drivers, that is, White drivers that were slumped over their steering wheels. And hadn't the Black drivers seemed either awake and coherent or else unconscious due to injury? Elena thinks again. Clearly, her nurse's eyes miss nothing. She can still spot the injured and their injuries from a mile away.

Arriving at the school, Jerome and Elena find a zoo of activity and fear. Parents hastily run into the school. The school's parking lot is nearly filled with cars of parents seeking to retrieve their children. As Jerome and Elena get out of their car, they notice that several of the parents wear surgical masks. Walking quickly to the front of their kids' school, they come upon Delores Fuentes, the principal.

"Principal Fuentes! Where are Micah and Sarah?"
Jerome asks.

"Right here. In my office," Principal Fuentes responds.
"I pulled them out of class as soon as we got your call." Delores
had been a friend of the family for many years and is the chief
reason that Micah and Sarah attend Hyde Park Day school. She
started speaking to them about it since before they could talk.
By the time Micah and Sarah could talk, there was no question
about where they would attend school. The education there was
excellent and perfect for their kids who are also athletes. Outside
of school, Micah and Sarah called Principal Delores *Auntie D*. She
is unmarried and has no children of her own, and so welcomed
them and treated them as her own kids. They visited with her after
school often. She had been a Division I soccer player in college
and had also coached the twins since they could walk and play.

"Delores, what's happening? We saw some of the parents
coming into the school with surgical masks. Has there been some
sort of outbreak?" Elena asks.

Delores bites the inside of her cheek. She looks down at
the ground with her hands upon her hips before raising her head to
speak. "There are a lot of wild reports out there. Some say that this

is a terrorist attack. Some say the government has released some harmful chemicals into the environment. Nobody really knows. What I do know is that I've got several staff members who did not show up to work today. In fact, I've got two teachers who did show up, but who are now unconscious in their classrooms. An ambulance picked them both up about an hour ago. I can't make sense of any of this. The kids seem to be okay, but a few of them started to look a little sick. They're in with the nurse now. Since we spoke, I sent an email to all of the parents asking that they come and get their children. At first, I thought that this was merely a school issue, but then I watched a little of the news and saw the car crashes, plane crashes, and accidents. There are too many unknowns. My advice? Go home. Batten down the hatches, and I'll be over to check on you guys just as soon as I get the school cleared and locked up. Okay?"

Jerome and Elena hug Delores, thank her, and grab the twins. "Let's go, kids," Jerome says when he retrieves them from Delores' office. Heading for the car, they notice that almost all of the parents coming to retrieve their kids are Black or Brown-skinned. Some White parents to be sure, but an overwhelming majority seemed not to be White. Hyde Park Day is a racially balanced school being about fifty percent White and fifty percent non-White, but today the parking lot does not reflect that. Jerome makes a mental note of that and plans to bring it up to Delores later. He wonders to himself what, if anything, has happened to the White kids.

On the way home, they take the same circuitous route that they took to get there, avoiding all major streets and the highway. They see more cars crashed into one another and into fire hydrants, parking meters and retaining walls. They even see a car smashed into the living room of a house. They also see dozens more people collapsed on the sidewalks and in the streets. To Jerome's untrained eyes they all look dead, but to Elena, they look unconscious or asleep.

They are tempted to stop and help some of those who are unconscious, but decide not to stop in case this is some sort of sickness or communicable disease. Jerome and Elena pray for every victim that they see, and resolve to make it home as safely as possible for themselves and without injuring anyone else.

Arriving home, Jerome instructs his family to get in quickly and make sure that all of the doors and windows are locked. If there is something in the air, he wants to ensure that it does not get into the house. "Elena, do you still have a box of those old surgical masks that you brought home on your last day?" he asks.

"Yes, and I know exactly where they are," she says.

"Good. Let's get those on ourselves and the kids until we know better."

"Agreed," Elena responds.

Being inside of their own home with Sarah and Micah makes them feel safe. Jerome grabs the closest remote and turns the television on that hangs on a wall in their living room. "Continuing reports coming in are that in addition to the plane and numerous car crashes nationwide, power outages have begun to occur across the nation as well. Here in New York, we've experienced five such outages since about 8:30 this morning. Other cities are reporting similar outages, but most have managed to regain power. Dallas, Houston and New Orleans are still dark. News is being reported from those cities by MSNBC, CNN and FOX field offices thanks to their backup generators. Key personnel at power plants in those cities are said to be missing, dead or unconscious. We will report more news as we are updated."

What is happening is nationwide, Jerome now knows. This catastrophe looks, from his perspective, far larger than the terrorist attack on 9/11. If this is as a terrorist attack, Jerome thinks, he wonders what might happen after this and how the government is responding. He also wonders how they might all survive it.

*　　*　　*

This day had really begun to wear on President Douglas. Sixty minutes after his press conference, he sits behind Resolute, his desk in the Oval Office. Truly, there is little that he feels very resolute about in this moment, except for figuring out what is happening in his country and reversing it, whatever *it* is. His closest advisors are here along with his top intelligence officials. The Joint Chiefs and all attending military commanders are in the Situation Room monitoring the military's actions and all that they had been commanded by the President. He now wants sitreps— situational reports—of everything happening in the country in fifteen to thirty minute intervals.

By now, there had been many reports of what sounded like a couple hundred thousand car crashes or more and related accidents nationwide. There are so many hurt and killed people on U.S. soil that emergency responders are totally overwhelmed.

Those that had been operating vehicles or riding as passengers and not killed persisted in strange, unalterable states of unconsciousness. What's more, many emergency personnel had themselves gone missing in great numbers including firemen, police officers, paramedics and even doctors and nurses. It's not that these folks had vanished into thin air. Many were being found, often at their jobs, in their homes or on the streets. Mostly, they are being found and reported to be unconscious. There does not seem to be any rhyme or reason for their persistent states of unconsciousness, no one who is unconscious seems to be waking up.

The President asks question after question regarding the nature of these unconscious states amongst the populace. Was there a gas leak? Is this chemical or biological? Where is the most damage? Had there been any explosions caused by a terrorist, domestic or otherwise? What is the intelligence community saying? Terrorist or other cause? How in the hell are these incidents happening across the entire nation instead of being localized to one or two places? The President peppers his staff with question after question until he believes that he has as much of a handle on the best known facts. What he comes away with is a profound sense of the unknown. In this moment, the facts are few

and the President's options even fewer. At best, he can only hope to

contain what is happening, and even such containment is dubious

and problematic. How exactly does one find or rescue thousands,

potentially millions, of unconscious Americans with such limited

resources? How do we wake the unconscious up? Each question

that President Douglas considers causes the pounding over his left

eyelid to increase in intensity and volume.

The President's briefing session goes on and on like this

until an outline of what is happening on the day begins to emerge.

In spite of all that the President and his staff did not know, they

begin to grasp some of the more salient details. First, terrorists

are not believed to be involved. Their presence might explain

the plane crashes but not the thousands of car crashes especially

with no terror-induced explosions or bridge collapses. Second,

top scientific and intelligence officials had ruled out any sort of

gas leak. Perhaps that could be the cause for a localized outbreak

but a nationwide outbreak like the one that they are seeing is not

probable and probably not possible. Third, there may be a biologic

cause, but it had not yet been isolated and is currently unknown.

Last, large amounts of the population seemed to be unavailable because they are unconscious, many of whom might be dead due to injury or exposure to the elements, given that it is still winter.

Director of Homeland Security, Janet Taros, creases her forehead as she looks down at the iPad in her lap that gives her real time updates of events happening across the country. The President asks, "What is it, Janet?" "It seems, Mr. President, that power grids across the country are going down. Still, there's no indication that this is terrorist-related or even cyber-related. Personnel at key sites are simply unresponsive. We have teams going to each major power plant to determine the cause. If the cause is the loss of personnel due to unconsciousness, then we'll have to either put those plants on auto pilot, if possible, or replace with personnel that isn't susceptible to whatever this is. And not knowing what this is doesn't help. I've got all my people in biohazard suits, Mr. President, until we know what's happening."

"Mr. President," the White House Chief of Staff says, "all of the persons who are being rendered unconscious seem to only be," she pauses, "very fair-skinned people," she stumbles, "White people, sir." This news makes the President's head spin and throb even more. He thinks that he might get sick, which of course will not do. Before speaking, President Douglas clears his throat "You mean to tell me that the only people being affected by whatever this is, this unconsciousness, are White? Are you sure? Are there any non-White persons that have been found to be unconscious?"

"There have been non-White persons found dead, Mr. President, usually due to a car crash or from one of the plane crashes, but none found in this state of sleep or unconsciousness," Barbara Smith, the Chief of Staff replies.

President Douglas takes a moment to consider the implications of what he has just heard. He looks upon his mostly White staff and thinks what this crisis might look like without them. "Barbara, seal off the White House. Nobody White or extremely fair-skinned goes home tonight. Declare a national state of emergency. I want, at least, all critical fair-skinned staff in bio hazard suits. Janet, have your office send over two-hundred suits immediately. In the field, I want all critical white or fair-skinned staff in biohazard suits until we figure out whatever this is, and whether it's in our food, water, air or all three. These measures may sound crazy, but we cannot afford to be shorthanded as we sort this out. Tell the generals too. All essential fair-skinned military personnel are to be masked and dressed accordingly. Understood?"

"Yes, sir, Mr. President," his top staff responds.

The President gives a signal to his Chief of Staff which means that he wants the room cleared of everyone except himself, the NSA Chief, Valerie King and the head of Homeland Security. "Ladies and gentlemen, may we have the room," Barbara Smith says. It is an order, not a question as the President's Chief of Staff looks into the faces of the President's most key personnel, a look that commands all others to leave and only a few to remain.

Once the room is clear, the President addresses the group. "Okay, contingency plans for a worst case scenario. What are they? And by worst case, I mean our inability to contain whatever this outbreak is. What happens if we lose a significant portion of our population and how do we recover?"

"Contingency plans, Mr. President, are that we continue to operate government at all levels until we know something different", NSA Head Trevor Campbell says. "If by worst case scenario," he hesitates, "you mean that a majority of or all of our fellow White citizens become unavailable due to this unconsciousness, there's really no contingency for that. White Americans make up sixty-three percent of our nation's population. They're in every part of our government and civil institutions, not to mention corporate structure. There's no way to replace them in an emergency such as this. If they are all or nearly all to become unavailable, that means that two-hundred and twenty-one million of our fellow Americans are unconscious and therefore, unavailable."

Two-hundred and twenty-one million people. The President understands this number and what it means for the rest of them, those who are not unconscious. He had already worked it out mentally before Trevor said it. What he hadn't noted yet was that while White Americans made up sixty-three percent of the population, they probably made up, easily, at least seventy to seventy-five percent of the population of all essential services and possessed at least that much of the expertise to run the country. The implications are staggering. If the majority or all of White and/or fair-skinned Americans became unconscious, how will they function? What will happen to the country in the near term?

"Mr. President," Barbara chimes in, "what you may be looking for is a sure way to keep government running and afloat should we go away. We don't know enough yet, but it may be time to consider, and pardon the pun, sir, a shadow government that can quickly slip in and control its levers should the rest of us become unavailable." The President grimaces. What his Chief of Staff had just suggested is unconstitutional at best, treasonous at worse. President Douglas, though, had long been known to be a very pragmatic man. He takes the world as it is, not how he wishes it to be.

He takes a moment to consider not only Barbara's suggestion, but all other possibilities as well. What might a shadow government look like? How would it function? Would it merely be one made up only of persons of color? Any other day, the mere consideration of such a thing would be more than absurd. Could such a thing even be formed? Are there enough non-White persons with the requisite expertise to help maintain the day-to-day structure of the United States, at least in the short term? The President is nervous to even consider the weight of this crisis operating long term. And what would the public's reaction to this so-called shadow government be when the unconscious citizens awake? The Republicans had been trying to impeach him for "high crimes and misdemeanors" for years. What he is considering would most certainly give them all the ammunition needed to do just that. Practically, though, the President considers that this is his seventh year remaining in office. He has one more year left that is more ceremony than substance. He is a lame duck, and he knows it. Even if his enemies awaken to find him acting as a dictator, he is gone in a year no matter what.

The President then asks, "But what about Congress? Are there any unconscious members of the House? The Senate?"

"Congress, Mr. President, is about fifty percent accounted for. All of the non-White members have been accounted for, but many of the White and fair-skinned members are either missing or have been found in states of unconsciousness," his NSA chief says. "About a half-dozen Congressmen and women are overseas. We know which ones--they're all White. We've instructed them not to return to the United States until we know more."

The President and his top staff continue to discuss their options as they receive updates every half hour. As time progresses, it has gone from bad to worse. Though all air travel had been halted, continuing reports of accidents, casualties and deaths mount. There had even been reports of some looting starting to occur in a few of the largest cities.

Now the evening, the President looks up from his latest report and rubs his temples. It is about 7:45 p.m. The President's head hurts. His stomach growls too, having not eaten since about 7:00 a.m. that morning, but food is nowhere on his agenda. He can only think about the gigantic implications of millions of Americans being impacted by this, whatever it is, and its impact on the country. He asks the nearest butler to bring them another pot of coffee so that they can all keep going. He plans to go back on television to address the nation. His stand in Press Secretary has performed a yeoman's job all day and evening. He's steadfastly answered all questions thrown at him. Tellingly, the complexion of the reporters changes throughout the day going, literally, from light to dark over the course of about fifteen hours. No one had noticed the change at first, but by the evening, there are whispers. White House staff are being found, more and more, in the same states of unconsciousness afflicting others in spite of the President's "lockdown" order. The bio-hazard suits seem to be hit or miss.

"Barbara," President Douglas says to his Chief of Staff, "here's what I need. I want all available resources to find and lock down all conscious members of Congress, the Senate and the Supreme Court. I want them quarantined and suited up to avoid this illness in the air, water or food chain. I want our top scientists, those we have left, to confirm that this issue is contained within our fair- skinned citizens and is not spreading outside of that group. I want every fair-skinned member of staff in the White

House to give blood and to have that blood tested in order to identify a possible pathogen. The Secret Service says that I have to move underground just in case, but I'm not going. I do, however, recommend that all of you in this room move to the underground residence now. It's isolated and probably remains untouched from what's causing the unconsciousness."

"Mr. President, that's all well and good," Barbara speaks up, "but no amount of isolation or biohazard suits may be able to help us if we've already been *infected*." As if on cue to her last spoken word, she falls where she previously stood and suddenly convulses upward arching her back. Her eyes roll to the back of her head and she shakes violently. "Barbara! Barbara!" The President yells as he attempts to hold her down while she shakes. "Margaret, get the doctor in here now!" the President yells to his secretary. But just as suddenly as Barbara's attack begins, it stops leaving her strangely, placidly calm. She is, they all see, unconscious. Bewildered, the President looks at his Chief of Staff intently. He shakes her gently and then more vigorously. She does not respond. She does not wake up.

Dr. Murray, the President's personal physician runs into the Oval Office. He leans over the Chief of Staff. Grabbing her wrist and looks at his watch, he checks her pulse. "Steady. They're all steady, Mr. President. This is the fifth case that I've seen today in the White House."

"Fifth case? Dr. Murray, are you saying that my staff is being affected by this, this sleep disease?"

"That's exactly what I'm saying, Mr. President, and the bio-hazard suits don't seem to be helping, at least not for long" Dr. Murray says.

Turning to Valerie King, his top advisor, the President looks somber, yet determined. "Valerie, you're my new Chief of Staff until we get this thing figured out. I want everyone from the Congressional Black Caucus and every non-White member of Congress and the Supreme Court in the White House by nine tonight. We have to meet immediately."

CHAPTER III

Sabrina awakens with a scream. Her last thought had been of her soon-to-be missed life as her airplane plunged to the ground. She takes several big gulps of air and feels its cold sting against the back of her throat. Her head hurts and her body feels like it's been put inside of an industrial sized dryer and spun on high for a few hours. She hurts everywhere. Sabrina also realizes that she must have blacked out right before the expected impact. Fighting to gain her bearings, Sabrina sees that she lies on a gurney and is in restraints. The gurney sits on a runway. Her scream is stifled due to an oxygen mask fitted securely to her face. Sabrina is further irritated because the straps holding the mask down are too tight, and seem to cut into her cheeks. It is also loud, and cold.

Sabrina looks furtively to her left and to her right. This is not L.A., she thinks. In fact, it looks like San Francisco to her, but she is not sure. She begins to piece together some of what may have happened—a near plane crash, an emergency landing, and somehow, they were put several hundred miles off course from L.A., only to land safely in San Francisco. In this moment, Sabrina cannot believe that she's alive. The pains in her body and head confirm for her that she is indeed still in the land of the living.

"Hush, now, Miss, and stop struggling against your restraints, they're just a precaution," an older lady says to her in a Jamaican patois. "You've just been rescued from that airplane over there," she says pointing to a plane that looks to be half on and half off the runway. "My name is Patty, and I'm here to help." Patty loosens Sabrina's restraints and helps her to sit up. Sabrina looks at her plane and sees just how lucky she had been.

"Ms. Patty," Sabrina says, "what happened?"

"Oh girl, you're lucky to be alive! We all saw your plane come down! It was fast and almost hit a few planes along the way! I think that someone caught it on video. The pilot is doing an interview for one of the networks right over there," she says pointing to the pilot who apparently guided their plane in. Sabrina sees the pilot, a slender mocha-colored woman of about forty. "That's her?" Sabrina asks. "It is indeed," Patty replies. "But for her quick thinking and expert flying, you'd all be dead now, the wake ones and the sleep ones."

"Where are we?" Sabrina asks though her voice is muffled behind the mask.

"You're in San Francisco. At the airport. Lots of craziness today, Miss," her Jamaican handler tells her. "Look, I don't even do this. I'm a ticket agent at the airport, but it's all hands on deck. We're short a lot of staff today."

Just then, an emergency responder jogs up to Sabrina's gurney. "Is she awake? Good. Not many like her. She doesn't appear to have any injuries. Let's get her up and onto the bus," the responder says. Sabrina doesn't agree that she's not hurt. Her head pounds ferociously, her vision is blurry, and her body aches terribly, especially her lower back. From her days of playing lacrosse in high school and college, Sabrina is pretty sure that she has, at least, a low-grade concussion from being knocked around on her airplane. Patty releases Sabrina from the restraints of her gurney and gingerly helps her to sit all the way upright. Sabrina is thankful for the help as every movement causes a new sharp stab of pain that shoots across her forehead and through her temples. Her lower back feels like a raging forest fire. Ugh, Sabrina does not need this. The pain makes her feel nauseous. She wonders if she'll be able to walk unassisted.

"I know you're not feeling all the way right yet," Patty says. "Let me walk you to the bus. We're putting all of our awake folks onto the bus to go back to the main terminal" Patty says. Awake folks, Sabrina wonders, what does that mean? Before she can ask, Patty puts a supportive arm around her to help put two feet on the tarmac of the runway. "Up you go now, Miss. Lean on me. I can take it. Patty is strong."

Sabrina gratefully nods her head in agreement to proceed, and Patty, a stout shorter woman, takes Sabrina under one of her arms, puts an arm around her waist for support. Patty walks her to a bus that sits waiting about twenty yards away. As they walk slowly to the bus, Sabrina sees a number of gurneys on the runway just like the one that she had been on. She also sees that nearly all of them are filled with a person strapped to each. She wonders whether these folks are alive or whether, like her, they are unconscious. Sabrina also notices that the sun has come up, because it hurts her eyes as she walks towards the bus further adding to her head's misery.

Boarding the bus, Sabrina finds about a dozen people sitting upright, but all seem to be in a state of shock just like her. "Good bye, Miss," Patty says. "I hope that you're well and that you get to where you need to be. I couldn't find your purse, but someone at the airport will help you with your next destination." Patty steps off the bus and Sabrina watches her walk quickly back towards the plane that had been hers and the field of gurneys surrounding it.

The bus doors close and it pulls slowly away. It drives toward the airport's main terminal. As it moves, Sabrina sees airplanes scattered about the runway. She sees at least a half dozen planes parked awkwardly, two of which are on fire with fire crews attending to them. The bus creaks by carefully to avoid them and the fire crews working on them. She sees another plane cocked at an awkward angle in a large grass section between the runways, one wing half buried in the earth with its other wing pointed toward the sky. Its nose is also partially buried in the ground. That plane looks like it had landed badly, run off the runway and crashed into the grassy area. Thankfully, it was not on fire or looks like it had ever been burning. Sabrina hopes that all of its occupants had survived as she has.

Looking around the bus, she sees weary travelers like her. No one is speaking. All seem to be either entranced within themselves, or entranced by the sight of the near carnage around them. Many emergency vehicles flash brilliantly on the runways of the San Francisco airport as dozens, if not hundreds of emergency personnel move frenetically to attend to the landed or crashed passengers of the ten or so airplanes on the ground. Sabrina doesn't understand what has happened, but she is happy to be alive. Before she blacked out, she believed that this would be her end.

Sabrina's thoughts soon turn to her fiancé, Michael, who by now would know what had happened to her. He is probably undone with worry for her, at least he better be, she thinks, given that she almost died in a fiery plane crash. She and Michael met in college in Washington, D.C., at Howard University. Like many Howard couples, they had met during freshman orientation, locked eyes and hardly let each other out of eyeshot or earshot since then. Their pairing had been unlikely, given where each is from, and their respective backgrounds. Sabrina is from Los Angeles and comes from a well-off Black family. Michael is from New York and from the "Boogie Down" Bronx, as he often pridefully proclaims.

Michael's family is dramatically less well off than Sabrina's. In fact, he is the first and only person to have ever attended college. Sabrina is the fourth generation of her family to go to college. In New York, he had been a highly-recruited high school student given his grades and test scores. All of the Ivies had accepted him, but he famously chose Howard above all others because he believed that this experience would give him something that none of the other schools, save Morehouse, could give him.

He had been right. He'd met Sabrina and made irreplaceable friendships with similarly-situated young people like him who were prime to make their mark on the world. At Howard he soon realized that his status as New York's most sought-after Black honor student was nice, but not that special. In college, he studied with the best and brightest from around the world. New York is part of the world, but it's not the center of it, Michael quickly learned.

Sabrina had liked Michael's calm, reserved and unfazed manner. She had been instantly attracted to him. Being no fool, she realized at the time that her parents and grandparents might look askance at Michael's background. The fact that he is pre-med and makes her heart sing are mitigating factors, but still. During their sophomore year, Sabrina decides to bring Michael home to L.A. to meet her parents for Thanksgiving break. She is beyond nervous and attempts to prep him about what to say, what to wear, and how to speak, all in an effort to enable her beau's acceptance with her family.

Michael, of course, would hear none of it. "Babe," he says, "I love you and would like to be accepted by your fam. But if they choose to hold my background or my family's background against me, there's nothing I or you can do about that. It is what it is. So, if it's all the same to you, I'm gon' be me." Sabrina reluctantly agrees as she bites her lower lip and nods her head, the anxiety of their impending meeting written clearly on her face.

Sabrina's father had always been stern and strict with her about her dating choices. She is the third of three children, the youngest and the only girl. Her brothers had been very protective of her, over-protective she thinks. Over the years of her growing up, her mother had barely helped to balance out all the raging testosterone in their home, though their mother is no shrinking violet.

Walking up to the front door of her home in L.A. with Michael, Sabrina is floored when she sees the door swing open, her father standing there with a wide grin, his right arm extended in greeting to Michael and his hearty greeting rendered: "Hiya, Michael! Welcome to L.A. This your first time here? Come on in, you must be hungry!" Her father quickly ushers Michael in while Sabrina, comically, is left to fumble with their luggage. Her brothers soon come to her aid, both giving her sloppy kisses on her forehead and mumbling quiet threats and comments about "some random dude coming into their house." This is her normal, and she is strangely thankful for it. Her father's super positive attitude had been off-putting. This wasn't like him at all.

It is Thanksgiving of Sabrina and Michael's sophomore year at Howard, and all are looking forward to their normal Clayton household traditions. Sabrina's mother grew up in the South and had brought all of her Southern sensibilities and cooking prowess with her. Their holidays are always filled with authentic New Orleans style Black Southern cuisine. Such food is unlike any that Michael had ever tasted. Sabrina knows that he will be well-satisfied. After their Thanksgiving meal Michael asks, "Sabrina, can you cook like this because holy moly, I'll marry you right now!" They both laugh at his food-fueled exclamation, but Sabrina remembers how her mother and grandmother had always told her to get and advance her cooking skills. It seems like old fashioned advice and archaic at the time, but attending Howard had taught her that with so many beautiful women at school and around D.C., differentiating oneself from all the others is not a bad thing.

Sabrina understands that at some point "the conversation" will be had. This conversation is the one in which the right young man at the right time will sit down with her father, and possibly her brothers, to discuss what his intentions are and why he is here.

Sabrina does not know when it will happen, but she is confident that it will happen soon. About an hour after dinner as the family and a few friends recline and sleepily watch a football game, Sabrina's father calls Michael into his study. At his call, Sabrina tenses up and looks at Michael anxiously. He smiles back at her confidently, but not cockily, and rises to meet Sabrina's father.

The conversation seems to stretch on for many long minutes. To Sabrina, it seems like an eternity. In truth, their conversation takes no more than twenty minutes. She hears muffled and, at one point, loud laughter coming from both her father and Michael. She wonders what the hell is so funny. Soon after, the door to her father's study opens and they exit. Her father has one hand on Michael's shoulder as they walk out and he is smiling, genuinely smiling. She cannot believe it. She looks over at her brothers and they're smiling too. By some miracle, she thinks, Michael passes the test. Her brother Xavier leans over and whispers to her "I still don't like him," but there is none of the edge in his voice that she expects, and he even sports a goofy grin.

Though she asks often, Michael refuses to tell her what he and her father discussed. She tries many times to address it, but he remains as secretive as the Sphinx. Sabrina drops the issue once they return to Howard, but soon after, she notices that his discussion of their relationship takes on a greater urgency and tenor of permanence. They had always discussed the possibility of a future beyond college, but something about their trip had sharpened Michael's focus.

By the time that graduation arrives, Sabrina and Michael are one of the "it" couples at H.U. When he receives his medical school acceptance letter, he asks Sabrina to marry him. She accepts, but with conditions. Her career as a future business executive is important to her. She wants Michael to be just as supportive to and for her as she is committing to be for him. He quickly agrees, desiring her success as much as his own.

They live together during his med school tenure, but after his graduation, their careers place them on opposite sides of the country. He must complete his residency in New York, while her career demands that she remain in L.A. for now. Their wedding day is quickly approaching after which she plans to be in New York with him full time. She thinks about all of this as she continues to wheel slowly to the terminal on her bus. Sabrina soon remembers that she is without a cell phone, as well as her purse and luggage. She needs to call Michael. He'll be worried sick by now. She hopes that he knows that her plane survived the crash and that its passengers are all alive.

Looking at the passengers on the bus with her, she peers to see if anyone has a cell phone that she can borrow. Seeing none, she begins to dive deeply back into her own thoughts, but then abruptly stops. Observing the passengers again, she wonders why they seem to be so few in number, given all of the airplanes on the runways. There is something else strange about this assembly as well. Her head still hurts, and she still feels more than a bit concussed. Her thoughts aren't moving at their normal break neck speed, but she's clear enough to register that their group seems to be missing something other than just more people.

Finally arriving to the main terminal, Sabrina and her fellow passengers are met by more emergency personnel who help them off the bus and direct them inside. They are told that there is no public transportation and that some of the roads into and out of San Francisco are closed, including the Golden Gate Bridge into Oakland. Sabrina marvels at this. Up to this point, she thinks that her near crash had been an issue for her plane only. That changed when she sees all the other planes in distress at the airport. Of course, landing in San Francisco in the first place is a major tell.

She needs, somehow, to get back to L.A., her home. Staying here is not an option, she thinks. But first things first, get a cell phone, call Michael, and assure him that she's alright.

Once inside the terminal, Sabrina finds a ladies' room and goes inside. She walks in front of the big mirror that sits atop a bank of sinks and looks hard at herself. No one has told her, but she is a mess. Her light brown hair is disheveled, almost beyond recognition. She has several small cuts on her face, neck, and upper torso. Thankfully, none of these are too serious, she sees. She also has a large black eye firmly tattooed onto her left eye. Ah, she thinks, something or someone had hit her pretty damn good. Her mind thinks back to the large gentleman that she had been sitting next to who was unconscious. She wonders whether he or one of his limbs are to blame for her injury. Sabrina remembers thinking that the large man was not dead but also wondering how he could sleep during any part of their near collision. Sabrina remembers that she had blacked out too, her brain mercifully shutting down right before the expected impact.

Sabrina is dressed in her business attire because she had planned to walk off her plane and go directly to work. She wears a blouse, now missing its top two buttons, and a skirt that looks

78

mangled. Her shoes are a pair of comfortable flats that she put on for the flight. Her work shoes, heels, are in a bag that she may or may not ever see again. Turning on the water, Sabrina cups her hands under its cool flow, bends over and brings them to her face. The water refreshes her and takes a bit of the edge off of her head ache. As her head begins to clear, she realizes that she has several needs: information, communication, and transportation. She needs to know better what happened to her and is happening to others. She also needs to get her hands on a cell phone to call Michael and her family. With no money and no I.D., this will be tricky, she believes. Next, she needs transportation to get out of San Francisco and make her way back to L.A. Sabrina hopes in that moment that whatever is happening here has not spread to L.A. If it has, she knows that getting back to L.A. with no money and no I.D. will be extremely difficult.

Stepping out of the ladies' room, Sabrina looks out into the main terminal. She sees pockets of recently-liberated passengers sitting, most looking as shell-shocked as she had first felt when she boarded the bus. Sabrina spots a later than middle-aged Black man who looks like he could be her father's twin. She walks toward him and sits in the seat across from him. "Excuse me, sir," she says.

"My name is Sabrina, Sabrina Clayton. I was just rescued from one of the planes outside. I lost everything, my phone, purse, bag, everything. I need to call my people. Would you happen to have a cell phone that I can use?"

The man looks up at her slowly. He attempts a smile, but it falters. He is in shock, more so than what Sabrina had been. Without uttering a word, he hands her his cell phone and looks back down at his chest. Sabrina thanks him, takes the phone and begins dialing. Her first call is to Michael. When she dials, she hears several clicks and whirls, but the call does not connect. She attempts this several more times with the same result. She then calls her parents. Sabrina does not expect a connection, but miraculously, her mother picks up. "Hello? Who is this?" she asks. "Momma," Sabrina replies, "it's me, Sabrina."

"Baby, speak up! It's really hard to hear you," Mrs. Clayton responds.

"Momma, I'm in San Francisco. My plane got diverted. I don't know what happened. We had some trouble. I didn't think I'd make it. I'm surprised that I'm alive." Sabrina hadn't meant to say all of that, but she is so relieved to hear her mother's voice that she says more than she intends. She hopes that she has not frightened her.

"Oh, baby, I'm just so glad to hear from you. We're watching the news. We didn't know if you were on your usual flight or not. Michael has been worried sick. We can't speak with him. All of the cell service on the East Coast is out. But we've been able to email. I'll email him to tell him that you're okay."

"Momma, what's going on? I haven't gotten any news yet. What's been happening," Sabrina asks, the anxiety clearly rising in her voice.

"We don't know, Sabrina. There's a lot of speculation out there. Your father thinks that it's terrorism of some sort. All we know is that a lot of planes have crashed today, starting late last night. We also know," Sabrina's mom hesitates, "we know that a lot of people pretty much everywhere are turning up unconscious and some dead, more than a few actually" Mrs. Clayton says emphasizing her last phrase spoken.

Unconscious, Sabrina thinks, a realization suddenly dawning on her. "Momma, that's exactly what happened on my plane. I woke up to it almost crashing and saw that most of the people on the plane were asleep or unconscious. The guy right next to me was out cold. Only a few of us seemed to be awake. Even the flight attendants, except for maybe one of them, were out. What is this, Mom? Are we sick? What's happened?" Sabrina's breathing becomes labored as she speaks, and her head begins pounding again. She puts her left hand over her heart and tries to slow down her breathing and regain control.

"Baby, I truly do not know. Neither does the news. All we know is that it seems to be affecting the entire country at once."

Sabrina takes a moment to appreciate this important fact. The entire country, she thinks. Now she knows that her travel back to L.A. will be more difficult since, presumably, all of San Francisco, all of L.A. and all of the area in between is stricken with whatever this as yet unknown catastrophe is.

"Momma, do you know where Michael is?"

"Yes, baby, he's at work, at the hospital. He said it's all hands on deck, and he'll be there for the foreseeable future. There are a lot of casualties there as there are here. Lots of traffic and public transportation accidents. Lots of injured and, unfortunately, lots of dead folks. It's all really bad. Michael had already been at the hospital on a shift, so he hadn't needed to travel when all of this happened. He's okay though," Mrs. Clayton says reassuringly.

"Okay, Mom, thanks for the update. I feel a bit better. I still need to get home to L.A. though. I lost my purse and my luggage. I'm using someone's cell phone. I'll get it figured out," Sabrina says.

"Honey, I can send your brothers to come get you, if you like," Sabrina's mom says.

"No, don't send them. I'll get home. Let me check here first, and I'll call you back."

"Okay, dear, but be very careful." At that, Sabrina and her mother hang up.

Sabrina soon realizes that she sounded more confident to her mother than she actually feels about her prospects on getting home. Looking at the gentleman who loaned her his cell phone, she sees him staring intently and directly at her.

"Isaac," he says. "My name is Isaac. I need to get to L.A. too. My wife is dying. She's there. I need to get home. I can help you if you help me. I don't think that I can manage it by myself."

"Isaac," Sabrina says, "I would be happy to help you, but I have no way to pay."

"I do," Isaac says. He pulls out his wallet which is full of credit cards and full of cash. "I think that these will do," he says with a grin.

"Yes, sir, they should. Let's get to a car rental, Isaac."

"Dear, what is your name? I don't think that I can manage the walk. I'll need you to find me a wheelchair. Then we can go," Isaac says.

"Okay, let me go find one. I'll be right back." Sabrina walks up the terminal and soon finds a sign that says 'CUSTOMER SERVICE' in large scripted letters, leading to a large room. The room is empty of people, but there are about ten wheel chairs there. She grabs the nearest one, quickly walks back to Isaac and helps him into it.

"Alright, Isaac, we're all set. Let's go! By the way, my name is Sabrina. I'm very pleased to meet you."

With Isaac in tow, Sabrina begins the long walk through the terminal as they walk and roll toward the car rental counter. Like most modern airports, it's located away from the main terminal and there is no running bus service to it today. Sabrina then rolls Isaac the next quarter mile to the rental car station. Upon arriving, she and Isaac immediately see two things that startle them. First, there are a number of apparently unconscious people in the rental car building, and there are no employees in the building other than the three employees who are collapsed and unconscious behind the counter.

"I think that we have a problem, Isaac," Sabrina says. "There doesn't seem to be any available employees. Everyone is unconscious, or sleep or whatever" she says exasperatingly. In that moment, Sabrina feels a torrent of emotion well up within her. It is the result of her shock, her near death, her fear and her near total lack of understanding of what is happening. Her knees buckle, her shoulders shake, and she lets out a heart-wrenching sob. She goes on like that for a few minutes. The task before them seems overwhelming, and she sees herself too small for it.

"Sabrina," Isaac says, "this is a bad situation, it's really bad. I don't have any good answers. You're young and I'm old. We're both far from home. I've got a sick wife who I need to see before she passes. You've got to get home, I'm sure, to some people who really love you. But as tough as this is, I need, we need you to pull yourself together, and stay focused on our objective. We've got to get home. I can't get there without you, and, I fear, you can't do it without me. Sabrina, pull yourself together, find us some keys there behind the counter, and get us a car. We've got to get going." Whoever Isaac is, he has the same kind of military bearing that Sabrina's father has, she thinks. She takes his advice, and in a few moments, straightens herself up.

Sabrina allows herself a few more tears before wiping them on the sleeve of her blouse. She stands upright, looks at Isaac sitting in his wheelchair with a firm, determined look and kisses him on the top of his nearly bald head. Isaac chuckles and comments that it's been a long time since a woman so young and pretty had kissed him, other than his wife. Sabrina smiles at the compliment.

Looking behind the counter, she sees a panel on the opposite wall that is partially open. Peering inside, Sabrina sees a couple dozen sets of key fobs for rentals in the parking lot out front. Since there are no available employees, she helps herself to a key fob of a large SUV. She feels a slight twinge of guilt at taking the key fob and ultimately, the vehicle itself, but knows that this is an emergency and that she'll turn it in once she gets them to L.A.

"Okay, Isaac, I've got it. And I see the row of SUVs. I'll just click the open button until we see some flashing lights. That'll be our truck," Sabrina says.

"Fine by me, just make sure that it's full of gas," Isaac advises.

Wheeling Isaac into the parking lot and along the row of

SUVs, Sabrina feverishly presses the open button on her key fob. A large black SUV flashes its lights obediently in reply. It sits in the third parking space on Sabrina's left. It's a bit bigger than what she expects, and Sabrina hopes that she can, without hurting herself or Isaac further, place him into the passenger seat. He is a large man and she is petite. This will be a heavy lift, she thinks.

"Oh, I like that one. This reminds me of one that I used to have. Yep, we're going to be okay," Isaac says cheerfully.

Sabrina sighs and wheels Isaac to the front passenger side door. She opens the door and helps Isaac get out of his wheelchair. Isaac takes a step onto the truck's side rail and almost nimbly hoists himself into the seat. "See, not so bad, huh?" He says grinning at Sabrina knowingly. "You thought 'ol Isaac wasn't gonna make it? Pishaw! I was all state in football and basketball back in my day." Sabrina cracks up at that and Isaac does too. Their laughter breaks the heaviness between them and lightens her soul. She has a reason to hope. Michael is okay. He knows or will soon know that she's okay, and her parents are expecting her. With a renewed sense of purpose, Sabrina fixes her gaze to getting out of San Francisco, getting Isaac home, and getting herself there too. "Okay, Isaac, it's you and me. Let's see what this big boy can do."

Sabrina wheels out of the rental car parking lot and sets

the truck's GPS for Los Angeles. She hopes to be home before the

next day. The trip is normally only about six or seven hours by car,

but she understands that this calamity could make it much longer.

Sabrina remembers that she has just survived a plane crash and

whatever is causing so many folks to become unconscious. She is

suddenly thankful. "Isaac, we'll get there. You and me, let's go,"

she says, and off they drive.

*   *   *

Donnie eases his car into the underground garage of his

office building in downtown Chicago. His mind continues to reel

about what had just happened to him. Surviving multiple collisions

will do that, he thinks. Finding his parking space, he parks, gets out

and begins to walk toward the elevators of his building. Because

he arrives earlier than usual, the parking garage is fairly empty.

He is heartened by that. A mentor in college once told him that

successful people are also early risers and early arrivers. Donnie

had taken that advice to heart. Donnie considers his financial

analyst position to be temporary, as he plots his rise to the top. His

company is one of the largest securities traders in the world. He

hopes to one day be CEO of this company, or another large firm like it.

His building is one of the largest in Chicago. His company doesn't own it, but leases ten floors in it, a mere fraction of the eighty or so floors in the building overall. Donnie's office is on the 55th floor, the main floor, the same one on which his CEO resides. As the door to his elevator opens, Donnie walks out and heads toward his desk. It sits in the middle of the floor in the main section of all the financial analysts like him.

At his desk, Donnie begins to settle in and turn on all the various electronic equipment on it. His company has a strict policy of turning off all computers, printers, and fax machines when an employee leaves for the evening. They, like many others, have had many problems with hacking, both internal and external. Random audits were routinely held to ensure that employees followed this strict guideline. Donnie had even seen a few well-paid analysts and junior executives suspended or fired for violating this policy. He plans to never be named among them.

As his machines whirl to new life, Donnie sees that a desk lamp of a fellow analyst is on. That's Samantha's desk, he thinks. Samantha sits opposite to him and three desks down to Donnie's right. "Samantha?" he calls out. She is known as a late-stayer. It is pretty typical for Samantha to stay later than all of them, but she had never been known to pull an all-nighter. "Samantha?" Donnie says again. Not receiving a reply, Donnie stands up to walk over to her work station. He sees that one of her computer screens is still on, and thinks to himself "oh, crap, she's going to get into a lot of trouble if she's not here."

Donnie walks to her workstation, but then stops suddenly at the edge of her desk. Samantha is here. Her head and torso are laid out awkwardly on her desk. All her electronics are on. She looks as if at some point in the evening, she fell asleep and never woke up. Donnie and Samantha are not friends, per se, but they are friendly. Donnie decides to try to gently wake her. He doesn't want to see her get into trouble or to be seen in the same clothes that she'd had on yesterday. "Samantha," he whispers. She does not respond. "Samantha!" he says now with a bit more urgency. "SAMANTHA!!" he now fairly shouts. She doesn't respond at all. Donnie begins to wonder if perhaps she's been drugged. She is clearly alive as he can see and hear her breathing.

Donnie decides to a lay a hand, gently, on her left shoulder to see if she will respond. She doesn't. He then shakes her, gently at first and then more vigorously when he sees her lack of response. Samantha still does not wake up. Just then, all the lights on his floor spring to life. They are set on a timer to turn on and turn off every day. As the lights on his floor turn on, all the televisions that hang from the walls and pillars also turn on. Each television is set to either a financial news channel or to cable news. They are all on mute. Donnie is distracted from Samantha for a moment by the lights and TVs. One television that is set to cable news hangs right above his work station. Though silent, the images are unmistakable. Something devastating is happening. From where he stands, it looks like a plane crash, no, multiple plane crashes. Donnie walks over to this television and un-mutes it. There are several reporters stationed in different locales who report a number of plane crashes, highway crashes and unexplained explosions occurring all over the country. One reporter cuts in to exclaim that there are unconfirmed reports of people being found unconscious or asleep everywhere. The reporter explains that these people will not wake up or cannot be awakened.

Donnie looks over at Samantha. He begins to wonder, is she part of what's happening, is this a terrorist attack? Another reporter chimes in to say that though terrorism is suspected, there is no evidence of that yet. Donnie's mind begins to spin. He had already tried to wake Samantha up a few times. She is not budging. He does not want to leave her where she is but cannot think of a good alternative. He then remembers that there are some couches in their break room. Donnie thinks that placing her there, whether a part of what's going on or not, is better than leaving her where she is. He walks back over to Samantha, checks her one more time to see if she'll wake, then picks her up and walks into the break room. Donnie lays her onto one of the couches, but makes sure that she's in a comfortable position before leaving.

It is just past 7:00 a.m. Though Donnie is technically the first person in the office today, he knows that many of his colleagues like to get early starts as well. They should start to arrive in a few minutes, he thinks. Donnie places his television back on mute, but continues to watch its images. They are horrific. It is clear that whatever is happening is spread far and wide. He next wonders what the impact on the financial markets will be when they open. That depends on the cause, he thinks. If this is natural, the hit would be lessened in comparison to a terrorist attack, especially one as large as this one seems to be. Financial markets all over the world are sure to be impacted. To confirm, Donnie looks at this computer to see what is happening overseas in Asia and Europe. He sees right away that word of their calamity has gotten out. Both markets are down significantly, several hundred points each.

Donnie looks at his television and sees someone in the White House being interviewed. It's not President Douglas or the press secretary, but someone that Donnie doesn't recognize. He prides himself on being a politico and very well-informed about current events. He knows all the names of the major political personalities in and around Washington, D.C. and is able to recognize almost every important person in that world on sight. He does not, however, know who is speaking at the press secretary's podium. Donnie turns up the volume on the television to hear the new speaker and the questions being asked.

The stand-in press secretary makes clear that the current calamity is nationwide. He calls for calm and restraint. He lists out the places, including several cities, in which the damage is the worst. To Donnie's horror, Chicago is one of those cities. The speaker says that multiple planes have crashed in and around Chicago, and that the airport is closed until further notice. He also recounts the many accidents on Chicago's main highways and warns all to stay off of them. He then notes that scores of people are being found unconscious or seemingly asleep and that this seems to be the cause of much of the calamity. Donnie thinks about Samantha at that moment and the fact that none of his colleagues have yet arrived.

Donnie again looks at his watch nervously. It's now about 7:30 a.m. Chicago time. By this time, at least a dozen of his colleagues should have arrived. Glancing at the elevator doors of his floor, he sees no activity. Donnie wonders if they've been in any of the accidents that have happened. That seems unlikely given their numbers. He then wonders if they all might be unconscious. If true, he wonders to himself, why aren't I unconscious? What had happened to Samantha that hadn't happened to him? Fearing the worst, Donnie rushes to the closest men's' room and washes his hands vigorously. He has no idea if this will help, but he knows that he held and moved Samantha and was in close contact with her. If whatever this is, is communicable, he thinks, he'd rather be safe than sorry.

By 8:00 a.m. the office is still empty except for Donnie and an unconscious Samantha. All of the cable and financial news channels say that none of the U.S. financial markets will be opened today. Donnie wanders over to the main executive suite on his floor and pokes his head in. All of the offices are empty. He walks the length of the suite to verify that. He could have missed someone, he thinks. The executives enjoy their own private elevator. One of them could have arrived without his knowledge. When Donnie sees that the entire executive suite is empty, he returns to his desk flustered. He now knows that he's all alone, and may be for a while.

Donnie notices that the office is eerily quiet. It is devoid of its usual activity and clamor. The phones are quiet too. None ring. Donnie checks in on Samantha and sees that she is just as he had found her. Donnie wonders whether he should call an ambulance for her though she appears to be in no immediate danger. Dialing 911 is fruitless, he soon discovers. He receives a persistent busy signal for each of the ten times that he dials it. The guy in the White House was right, he realizes, when he said that emergency services everywhere were stretched to the breaking point. Donnie next considers taking Samantha to the hospital himself. He decides to go there in a little while. He wants to wait a bit longer to see if someone shows up. He needs to compare notes and get more information about what is going on in his city.

At 9:32 a.m. Donnie's office is still silent, save for the now blaring flat screen perched right above his desk. It's clear now that no one is coming to the office today. It's just Samantha and him. He's a bit afraid to leave his perch, but his concern for Samantha outweighs his caution. Donnie puts his winter coat back on, finds Samantha's coat, which is located on a coat rack near her desk, and puts it on her. He then picks her up and holds her in his arms. Walking to the elevator he considers for a moment how strange they might look to an onlooker: a tall skinny Black man carrying an obviously out of it red-headed White woman. Maybe they'll think she's drunk, he muses. But no, he considers, it's too early in the morning for that and I'm probably too Black for that kind of benefit of the doubt. Donnie chuckles at the bitter irony of their situation.

He reaches the car garage with Samantha and walks them toward his car. Normally he wouldn't be able to see it from the garage elevator, but today, the garage is ghostly in its emptiness. He sees it right away as soon as he steps out of the elevator: fourth row back, six spots down on the right. Thankfully, he thinks, Samantha is not heavy. She's easy to carry and her deep unconscious state keeps her stable in his arms. Donnie has no idea what could have caused this to happen to her and so many others, if the news reports are to be believed. Whatever this is, Donnie sincerely hopes that he does not get it. Whatever has afflicted Samantha does not seem like a terrorist attack to Donnie. He worries that it could be biological or chemical or worse.

Donnie gently places Samantha in the back seat of his car and puts a seat belt around her. He tightens it to make sure that she is secure. Her head droops down to her chest. She does not stir the slightest bit. As Donnie drives out of his garage, he faces a bright, chilly Chicago morning. He puts on his favorite pair of shades to take the edge off the sunlight. Reflexively, he turns on the radio to his favorite hip-hop station. He hears an announcer blaring an urgent message:

"YO FAM, THERE'S WHITE PEOPLE PASSED OUT OR DYING IN THE STREET! WE'RE GETTING REPORTS THAT THERE'S SOMETHING WRONG WITH ALL THE WHITE PEOPLE!! CNN WON'T TELL YOU THAT SHIT, BUT WE THINK IT MIGHT BE TRUE! WE'RE SENDING PEOPLE OUT RIGHT NOW TO TAKE PICTURES AND GET BACK WITH US. SO STAY TUNED!"

Other than having their broadcast certification snatched by the FCC for using profanity on their station, Donnie thinks "White people, what the heck?' He looks back at Samantha and then considers who all the missing folks at work are. They're White, all White. Donnie is the only man of color who does not work in the mailroom or maintenance. Donnie can't believe what he's just heard. It makes no sense. But then he remembers the stand-in press secretary from this morning's White House briefing. He had been a man of color, not White. The Press Secretary, who has been in President Douglas' administration from its beginning, is White. He had never been known to skip any sort of major briefing. He's as dependable as the mailman, he thinks.

As Donnie continues driving to the closest hospital, he looks around intently to see if there is any evidence of what the radio announcer had just said. Downtown is pretty deserted. He sees no one, unconscious or otherwise, until he rounds the next corner into the hospital's main entrance. He slams on his brakes to stop his car. There is an unconscious person laying right in the entrance. If Donnie had not seen him in time, he would have most certainly run him over. Donnie puts his car in park and gets out. He drops down to examine the person, an elderly man, and sees that he is alive, but unconscious just as Samantha is. Donnie decides to pick him up and put him in his car. He'll be delivering two people, he thinks, one he can identify, and one that he cannot.

Once he places the man into his car, Donnie wheels around to the emergency entrance of the hospital. There are multiple emergency vehicles there and many gurneys filled with people right outside of the entrance. There appear to be at least fifty emergency workers there as well, doctors, nurses and assorted others. When Donnie gets close, someone in grayish green medical scrubs waves him into a lane and tells him to stop.

"What'ya got, sir?" He says.

"Two people," Donnie responds. "One male, one female. One I know and one that I don't know. I found one unconscious at my job and one right at the entrance of the hospital. I almost ran him over."

"Yeah, we've seen a lot of that today. Wherever the unconscious drop, they've tended to be part of other accidents, either in the street or behind the wheel. That's what's been causing a lot of the car accidents today."

Donnie nods his head knowingly. He thinks about the two accidents that he narrowly avoided coming into downtown today. "Are you a doctor?" Donnie asks.

"Nah. I'm just a maintenance guy. But it's all hands on

deck. A lot of our doctors and nurses have either not shown up yet or have taken to" the man hesitates "this unconsciousness. Somebody told me to put on these scrubs and receive folks out here. The hospital is already full. We're trying to find room for everyone. Every hospital looks like this one."

"Sir, how can I help?" Donnie asks.

"For now, use your car to find as many unconscious people as you can, and bring them here or to the next closest hospital. We need to get these folks out of the elements. My name is Steven, Steven Clarke, by the way. If you come back here, look for me or ask for me. I'll be here all day."

At that, Steven calls for two gurneys from two other workers. He and the workers delicately pull Samantha and the older unconscious man from the back of Donnie's car and place them on the gurneys. Donnie watches them get checked in at a make shift check-in station before they are wheeled inside. His mind spins at the sight of what's before him. He thinks about what he'll experience next, and sets himself to do just as Steven had said. He will drive about the city looking for the unconscious and getting them to a hospital. He can load at least three people in his car, and four, if they're small.

Donnie faces east and says a quick prayer. He prays for strength, guidance and safety as he slides in behind his wheel. He knows that he'll need all three if he is to be useful on this strange day. He decides not to go back to his office today. He doubts whether anyone will show up for a good while.

CHAPTER IV

Jerome feels the familiar pins and needles of pain in his back assert themselves as he stretches lengthwise, the hallmark of a bad night's sleep. His rest last night could not reasonably be called sleep. It was more sit-on-the-couch-stay-awake-all-night-watching-cable-news-dozing-in-and-out, which is exactly what he had done. He and Elena put the kids to bed hours ago, but neither could retire without knowing more. The President had spoken at about 10:00 p.m. last night, but it was clear that neither he nor his staff knew exactly what was happening, or, they weren't being fully forthcoming with all that they knew. Jerome could not tell which. The one thing that the President had been able to do was to assure the country, that to the best of their knowledge, what is happening is not a terrorist attack. Great, Jerome thinks sarcastically. That provided, however, little comfort and almost no information as to why people are dropping like flies in the street.

Planes had crashed. Lights had gone out in some, but not all cities. There had been thousands of car accidents. They had heard that some major highways were now impassable. In Cincinnati, south bound Interstate 75 had been completely shut down. The main bridge from Kentucky leading into Cincinnati is itself a wreck due to a hazardous chemical spill from a tanker that had crashed. Hopefully, Jerome thinks, a hazmat crew is on the scene and providing relief. He isn't so sure though. With all of the disappearances of people, emergency relief services seem to be very hit or miss. It seems impossible to know exactly how many people had been injured or killed. Jerome suspects many more than just a few thousand, which itself is hard to fathom. Many people had become unconscious right where they stood or drove, but they aren't dead, at least not from becoming unconscious.

Jerome and Elena suspect that some sort of disease or virus had inflicted almost everyone, at least those with white or very fair skin. That infliction caused them to become unconscious or something similar to a deep sleep state. It isn't death, Jerome thinks, but there also does not appear to be a way to safely wake anyone up. Between the President's comments, those of his officials and their own eyes, Jerome and Elena arrive at these conclusions. What they did not know is what might happen next, and whether they too might become similarly afflicted.

From the living room couch, Jerome clears his eyes and looks up. He squints as his powers of recognition begin to gather. Looking at his television, he sees the President at a podium preparing to speak. He shakes Elena who lays right next to him on the couch. "Honey, wake up. It's the President. He's getting ready to say something." Elena gets up slowly and sits fully upright once she sees the President for herself. Jerome notes that the clock next to the television reads 6:38 a.m. That's early, he thinks.

"Turn it up, babe," Elena whispers.

Complying, Jerome turns the volume up and hears the rustle of papers that the President shuffles before beginning to speak. He looks tired and exhausted as if he is sleeping less than even Jerome is sleeping. The thin layer of make-up that is placed around his eyes barely conceals the obvious rings that lie beneath it. Clearly, the President has been devoid of sleep in the last twenty-four hours at least. He looks like Jerome's back feels—old, rickety and in pain. Jerome and Elena watch and listen intently as he begins to speak.

My fellow Americans. The last twenty-four hours have been unprecedented in our country. Never in our history have we faced such a crisis. Not since the Civil War has the fabric of our nation been called into such question. I know that many of you are worried about loved ones. We are too. We know that there are many wild rumors out there. Let me dispel some of them now. First,

104

this is not a terror attack. None of our enemies are responsible for what has happened. We suspect some kind of viral outbreak or a pathogen of some sort, but we just don't know. We don't understand why some folks are unconscious and others are not.

Many of our fellow citizens have taken ill because of this virus. They may appear to be dead. They are not. They are asleep. They cannot, however, be safely wakened from this sleep. Many of those who fell asleep were in accidents or may have caused them. This has been purely accidental. While we are working on a cure for them, we implore you to remove them from harms' way if you see them, and in no case do no harm to any of them. Again, I repeat, they are in something akin to a deep sleep, but you cannot safely wake them up. Anyone caught harming another person who has fallen asleep will be prosecuted to the furthest extent of the law. We are establishing procedures as I speak to gather and secure our fellow citizens and move them to safe locations. Anyone found unconscious can be brought, for now, to your local hospitals. There will be medical and military staff there to handle them.

Before speaking this morning, I signed Executive Order #1906 that federalizes ALL police departments at the local, state and federal levels. Until we find a cure, the maintenance of order is our top priority. The military has been put on highest alert and all reserve military personnel are being activated and called in to serve. Our highest priorities are to our fellow citizens who are unconscious, and the safety and security of our nation.

This is an incredibly serious and daunting problem. Its resolution will require all of our efforts. But as in all hard times before, we shall come together as Americans and resolve it. We shall overcome. God bless you all and God bless the United States of America.

Jerome looks at Elena who has tears in her eyes. The President hadn't said it, but they know who is being afflicted—their fellow WHITE Americans. All last night, the news broadcasts had talked about how White and very fair-skinned people seemed to be the only ones found unconscious. Others had been hurt or killed by the accidents as well, but it is now clear that the non-Whites hurt had been caught up into the events inadvertently caused by their fellow White and fair- skinned citizens who fell unconscious.

"We have to call all of our friends to see how they're doing," Elena says. She of course means our White friends, Jerome thinks. Of course, she is right.

"Okay. Who do we call first?" Jerome says. "We've got our church group, friends from our kids' school, your book club, your dance studio friends, a lot of folks to check up on, Elena," Jerome says.

"I'll call everyone from church. You call the school and then work your way down the school list. Let's let the kids sleep in. Chances are that they've already started this process themselves using their phones," Elena says.

"Elena, before we begin, I just want to say that I love you and that we'll get through this. I've got about an hour before I have to go into work, but I'll make these calls first, and I'll keep my phone on me while on route today." Jerome pulls Elena close as he speaks words and kisses her lightly on her cheek. She nuzzles into his chest and holds him tightly. They exchange no further words during their embrace and let go only when they each feel a small measure of comfort and hope.

*   *   *

At work, Jerome's main route includes coverage of the Hyde Park neighborhood in Cincinnati. Hyde Park is a tony enclave of the well-to-do and corporate professionals that make up the main part of Cincinnati's professional class. The houses here are beautiful and most are quite large. It is prime real estate and highly sought after in the city. Houses here do not stay on the market long. It is also very expensive for most with houses averaging around $500,000. It also comprises mostly White people. No neighborhood in Cincinnati is legally segregated, but there are some, like Hyde Park, that are inaccessible due to their high cost of entry, a kind of socio-economic segregation, Jerome thinks as he has many times while working this route.

Thinking about the events of this morning before he reported to work, Jerome is disheartened. He hadn't gotten through half of his call list before he realizes that no one is answering his urgent calls except for his brother Steve. Steve is Black with four beautiful children, every one of them a product of his marriage with his wife Susan, who is a pretty White woman from Philadelphia. They met in college, at Virginia Tech where Steve also played football.

They both studied in the business school and majored in finance. They were study partners, best friends, and ultimately a couple. Predictably, Steve is distraught as he relays that Susan had been at work when he found her. By 7 p.m. when she hadn't come home and wasn't answering his many calls and texts, he went to her office and found her amongst an entire floor of other people seemingly dead, but unconscious at her work place. He couldn't wake her or anyone else up. He picked her up, put her in the car and brought her home. She's been in their bed ever since—totally unresponsive, but safe, Steve tells Jerome. Jerome tries his best to console his brother.

Steve and Susan live in New York City. Jerome assures him unconvincingly that everything will be alright, that Susan will recover and that he and Elena will be to see about them as soon as is possible. Hanging up, Jerome does not know if any of what he had just said to his brother is remotely true. He has a sick feeling that everything, in fact, would not be alright. Jerome is determined to remain brave and hopeful in the midst of this adversity.

When they had gone into work today, none of their White co-workers had been there, just the Black and Hispanic ones. Russell, their city manager, who is Black, tells them that they might not be picking up much trash today. Instead, their jobs would be to run their regular routes and identify as many of the unconscious as is possible. Once found, rescue them from any precarious condition, if possible, but in every instance identify where each is by marking their location with a big fluorescent "S" for *saved*. Russell gives them each a bottle of spray paint with which to mark whomever they find. He tells them not to enter any homes, but any unconscious people that they find on the streets should be identified and removed, as much as is possible, from the elements. It is February and winter in Ohio, and it's cold outside almost every day.

As Jerome drives his truck, he sees what looks to be a ghost town in Hyde Park. The streets are deserted. That isn't fully accurate though, Jerome thinks. He sees that there have been several car accidents in and around Hyde Park Square, the main gathering area about which Hyde Park is built. Several pricey late model sedans and SUVs are tangled up around each other, or light poles, or fire hydrants. Some unfortunate person had run his SUV right into the wall that rimmed the pedestrian portion of the small park in the center of the square and tipped over. Upon closer inspection, Jerome and Darryl see that the SUV is still occupied. The driver is White, male and unconscious. A deep gash indents the right side of his head. Jerome and Darryl notice where the blood had been flowing. Luckily for the driver, the blood had hardened and was no longer spilling out of him. He is still alive, barely but asleep like so many others.

"Let's get this guy right side up, Darryl," Jerome says.

Jerome and Darryl unbuckle Mr. SUV from his car seat, being careful to slide him out slowly. They lay him a few feet away from his truck. Jerome spray paints a large fluorescent "S" on the sides of the overturned vehicle while Darryl verifies that he is breathing and alive.

"He's definitely asleep, Jerome. I'll take his picture and send it to home office. Did you find his I.D.?" Darryl asked.

"Yeah, D., it's right here. His wallet fell out of his coat. 'Ryan Fitzgerald,' it says here. His home address is right off of Edwards Avenue. Here, take a picture of this too." Jerome handed Fitzgerald's driver's license to Darryl to take its picture.

Jerome looks up to see two Cincinnati police cars approach him and Darryl. Their lights flash, but their sirens are silent. There is an officer in each car. One is Black, the other appears to be either Arab or Hispanic, but Jerome can't really tell which. "Hey, Officers," Jerome says, "What's up?"

"I was about to ask you the same thing," the first police officer, Officer Johnson says.

"I'm Jerome and this is my partner Darryl. As you can see, we're not exactly doing our normal occupation today," Jerome says pointing to his trash truck. We've been assigned to this and a few other neighborhoods to find folks like this one, by our manager. We're assigned to make them safe if they're in an unsafe condition, mark wherever they are and then get that information back to our headquarters," Jerome explains.

"Right," Officer Johnson replies, "we got the memo. We've got similar responsibility with the added feature that we're supposed to go house to house and see who's in there."

"Lots of houses in Hyde Park, fellas," Darryl chimes in, "of lots of folks who don't look like us."

The two officers look at each other knowingly. "So you figured it out, huh?" Officer Johnson says more than he asks.

"What's to figure out?" Jerome replies. "We haven't found one Black or Brown unconscious person. We've seen, what, at least a hundred people out in various states of distress or unconsciousness, and not one of them had been a person of color. Not one. This problem," Jerome says hesitatingly, "seems to only be impacting White folks."

"That's correct," Officer Johnson says. "So far that seems

112

to be the case."

Just then, the two officers receive a loud message on their walkie-talkies: "BE ADVISED! BE ADVISED! THERE HAVE BEEN REPORTS OF LOOTERS DOWNTOWN! DO NOT BREAK OFF FROM YOUR PRIMARY ASSIGNMENTS TO HANDLE! CONTINUE CATALOGING SLEEPERS AND SEND THEIR DATA TO DISPATCH. OVER."

As their walkie-talkies squawk into silence, Jerome realizes that if looters are hitting downtown, they could soon come up north to neighborhoods like Hyde Park, Kenwood, Indian Hill and more. Jerome wonders how CPD will be able to perform their search and recovery mission without the help of all of their officers, including the unconscious ones, he presumes.

"Sleepers?" Jerome asks. "Is that what you're calling them?"

"Yes, we are. It's bad, I know, but it is descriptive. That's the word that the feds first started to call them. It fits," Officer Johnson says. "Jerome," he continues, "we're going to be more than a little stretched with all of this work. As you may have heard, CPD has been 'federalized,' Officer Johnson says with air quotes around the word federalized. "Our Captain also gave us orders to find and deputize fit men and women to help us perform our tasks. Consider yourselves deputized."

"You say that like we don't have a choice in the matter," Darryl says accusingly.

"You don't. Trash is secondary to the security of our city. Take this card. Report to Captain Hinton in District 2. Get a change of uniform and report back to me in an hour or less. And no, you won't be getting any guns," Officer Johnson says pointedly. "At least, not yet", he continues. Having said that, Officer Johnson and his partner silently ride off to begin their sweep through the neighborhood.

Jerome and Darryl look at one another dumbfounded. When Jerome gathers his thoughts, he looks at Darryl and deadpans, "okay, I guess that we're cops now. Let's get down to District 2 and get to it." Darryl looks at his card again, but then nods his ascent. They then jump into their trash truck and drive to the District 2 police department.

At District 2, Jerome and Darryl meet about thirty other deputized new officers like themselves, about half of whom are women and the rest men. Captain Hinton herds them all into a briefing room for some instructions and warnings:

"Good day, all, I'm Captain Hinton. This is District 2, your official headquarters. You have all been deputized and now work for me and the federal government. Yes, there will be government pay for all of your work. Your jobs, until further notice, are to assist the police officers that you're assigned to. Whoever told you to come here is the police officer that you're assigned to. I know that they gave you instructions to report back to them after I see you, so do that. For purposes of everyone outside of the police force, you are police officers in every way but one—guns. We are not giving you any and you're not allowed to carry guns or weapons of any kind. But you have all other police powers—the power to arrest, the power to stop, and the power to investigate. With each of these you are to follow the instructions of your supervising officer to the letter. Is that understood?" A chorus of "yes sirs" resounds. "Good. Most of your assignments will be to aid your officers in search and recovery of the Sleepers. As most of you know by now, the Sleepers all seem to be White or otherwise very fair. You'll be entering their homes and places of business. You'll be finding them among their belongings. Steal nothing, take nothing. For all intents and purposes, everything that you see still belongs to the Sleepers. We have no idea when or if they'll be re-awakened any time soon. And that's another thing, don't try to wake anyone up. We've had reports of Sleepers dying from the effort of someone, usually a loved one, trying to awake them. If your uniforms are too small or too large, please be patient. You're probably wearing the uniform of a Sleeper officer. We'll get you right fitting ones in due time if we need to. Any questions? Good. Go report to your officers."

And with that Jerome and Darryl are released to report back to Officer Johnson in Hyde Park. They arrive at about the place that they had last seen Officer Johnson. Officer Johnson is in his car with his lights on as before, but the other police officer is nowhere in sight. "Alright, guys, I see that you've been properly deputized and uniformed. Great. We're going to hit all of the homes starting on Erie where it meets Madison and work down from there. We're going into the houses after knocking and identifying. You two will work together. You are to go house to house cataloging every one that you find there. When you find them, move them out of harm's way if necessary. If on the floor, move them, carefully, to a couch or bed. If you find anyone in a tub or shower, make extra sure that they're still alive and breathing. Cover them up and make sure that they're warm. If you find any cold bodies, put them someplace accessible, call District 2 and give them the address of the body and identity if you have it. This could become gruesome work, fellas, so hang in there. I'll be available by walkie-talkie and shouldn't be more than a hundred or two-hundred yards from you at any given time. Now come on and jump in. I'll get you started. Oh, and for every locked door, knock it down. These are exigent circumstances. Don't worry about the house alarms. The power has been shut off for this neighborhood while we're combing through. Once done, mark the door with your spray paint. Put the number of occupants in the house on it and circle the number. Any questions? Yes?"

"What do we do about any pets?" Jerome asks. "A lot of these homes have pets."

"Great question, Jerome. First, don't get bitten. You may come across some angry, afraid, confused animals. Second, you may have to coax some of the bigger dogs outside. We need to get on the inside to see what's going on. If it's too crazy, call me and I'll come handle. I've got some pet grade mace that you can use, here, take this."

Reaching the first house that Officer Johnson wants them to inspect, Jerome and Darryl get out of the police car. Officer

Johnson lets them out on the left side of Erie facing Madison. The first house is on the corner, their first quarry. Jerome looks at Darryl encouragingly and motions toward the house. "Let's go," he says.

Walking towards the house, Jerome wonders what they might find. He hopes that there will be no dead bodies, of course. At the least, he hopes there will be no angry BIG dogs to meet them. Knocking on the door, they do not expect an answer. Pressing the door bell is of no use because the power is out. Knocking again for good measure, Jerome readies himself to kick the door in. Just as he is about to kick it in he feels it give way a little on his second knock. He pushes it in without much effort, and they were inside. The house is a duplex with, undoubtedly, a basement underneath. Most of the houses in this neighborhood are built like that.

"Darryl, I don't think that there are any dogs in here. Why don't you take the upstairs, and I'll search the first floor and basement?" "Deal", Darryl replies. As Darryl ascends the stairs, Jerome wonders if he has given his friend the harder job of the two. He feels slightly guilty as he makes his way into the dining room.

The decor of the home is modern but also modestly appointed. The furniture reminds Jerome of some of those ultra-modern furniture displays at IKEA, his wife's favorite store. But this furniture is not from IKEA. Some of it looks custom-made, and all of it is made from whole wood, not the pressed stuff that is in his house.

Jerome's sweep through the dining room turns up no inhabitants. The living room is clear too. A room attached to the living room, a den, still needs to be searched. Jerome stops in his tracks as he approaches the den. He sees a small foot on the floor behind a wall and the slightly frayed end of what are clearly pajama bottoms. Stepping fully into the den, Jerome finds a little boy of about four or five year's old unconscious on the floor. He looks no worse for wear, Jerome thinks. Jerome picks him up to closely examine him for any obvious bruising or injury. There is none. He then gently places him on a couch in the den. Jerome puts a cover that had been on the back of the couch onto the boy. This should keep him warm, Jerome thinks. Since cutting the electricity, the house feels unnaturally chilly. Jerome expects to see his breath at any moment. Jerome takes the boy's picture, and texts it and his address to the number provided by Captain Hinton.

Moving on, Jerome finds no one in the kitchen, back porch, back yard, or first floor bathroom. He walks to the stairs going to the second floor and calls up: "Darryl, how's it looking?"

"I found a mom and a daughter who looks to be about nine or so. Mom was slumped next to the bed. Daughter was on the bathroom floor. No one looks hurt. I put both back into their rooms. Thankfully, everybody was dressed," Darryl says.

"Okay, did you take and send their pictures?" Jerome asks.

"You know it," Darryl replies. "That felt weird as hell, though, Jerome."

Jerome nods in agreement. Weird indeed, he thinks.

"Okay, D. I found a little boy in the den. Put him on the couch. I'm about to hit the basement. Meet me on the first floor in five minutes," Jerome instructs. Even though Jerome is not Darryl's boss in their new jobs, he still acts like his boss. Darryl doesn't seem to mind and follows his lead.

Walking into the basement, Jerome observes that it is not finished. This house, Jerome sees, had been built at least eighty years ago when stone foundations were the norm. This family had done a good job of preventing moisture from coming in, he could tell, due to the white sealant that covers the foundation from the basement's ceiling to its floor. At the bottom of the steps Jerome turns right. At the right corner of the basement he sees a solidly built man lying on his front. He hears the man gently breathing. The man is easily identifiable to Jerome as the 'man of the house' dressed in standard issue corporate khakis, loafers and a starch pressed white shirt. He lays directly in front of an open safe. Ah, Jerome thinks, he had been about to either close or had just opened his safe when he was stricken. Jerome peers inside of the safe. It is a solidly built four-foot gun safe that contains two types of handguns and a shot-gun. He also sees two stacks of cash and what looks to be some pretty expensive jewelry.

Jerome steps over the man, closes the safe and turns the tumbler several times to make sure that it's locked. He turns the man over to get a good look at him. He is easily two-hundred and twenty pounds or more. Jerome has no intention of moving him. Looking around, he finds a stack of folded towels. Grabbing two, Jerome puts them behind the man's head. He then covers the man up with an oversized beach towel and blanket that he finds to keep him warm in the drafty basement. Jerome takes his picture and sends it and the man's address to the number provided by Captain Hinton.

Walking to the steps he calls up to Darryl, "found one more, D., the husband/father. I catalogued him. He's too dang big and heavy to move safely upstairs. I made him comfortable though. I think that we're good."

"Sounds cool by me," Darryl replies, "let's get to the next house."

Jerome slowly climbs the stairs after one last look. What a tragedy, he thinks, but he knows that they had done all that they could do for this family. It's on to the next house and the next set of folks to find, hopefully alive, and help and catalogue.

*   *   *

Most of the day and evening had gone, for Jerome and Darryl, as it had during their search of the first house. Most inhabitants had been stricken in the morning of the day before. It was not yet clear what the cause of the Sleepers' unconsciousness was. They had probably been to two-hundred fifty houses or more throughout the Hyde Park neighborhood. Officer Johnson had been in close proximity to them for the entire day. Jerome and Darryl worked fourteen hours on this, the second day after the Sleepers, had been made unconscious.

Jerome and Darryl are used to hard work, but this work had taxed them mentally and emotionally, as well as physically. They usually do not walk any steps in their regular trash jobs. But today, they had each walked twenty-thousand steps or more, all in order to search houses and find unconscious people. Jerome notes that they aren't just finding unconscious White folks. They find people of different ethnicities who happened to be very fair-skinned. Jerome quickly reasons, by his observation, that the common thread amongst the stricken is the lightness of their skin, not their race or ethnicity per se. And of course, Jerome further reasons, Mother Nature doesn't care about race at all, since race is a social construct and not a biological one.

Jerome and Darryl discover two unfortunate persons who had been killed in their homes by accident. One had been cooking and knocked a scalding pot of water onto herself when she passed out. The water had severely burned this poor woman's face and upper torso, almost beyond recognition. She died from her injuries. Hopefully, Jerome thinks, she had not experienced any pain due to being asleep. Another person, an elderly gentlemen, is found by them at the bottom of a steep flight of stairs in his house. A cane lay next to him. This poor gentleman's neck had been broken. Right away, Jerome recognizes that his head was twisted at an impossibly unnatural angle, and his entire face had turned blue. Jerome and Darryl had seen their fair share of oddities on their trash collection, but this new job is very strange and gruesome.

Jerome is nowhere near as dirty doing this work as he typically is at the end of a shift in his usual job as a trash man, but he feels unclean nonetheless. Going in and out of peoples' homes, mostly at the end of his boots, as he kicks their front doors in, had felt highly intrusive. It is necessary, Jerome acknowledges, but being a private person himself, he respects the privacy of others. Walking out of their last house for the day he wants nothing more than to crawl into his trash truck, retrieve his car and go home to Elena and the kids. He doesn't yet know how he will feel about sharing his day's experience with his wife, their normal ritual. Right now though he just wants a hot bath and some warm food. Between the two of them, Jerome and Darryl find and secure over a thousand people, all of them White or otherwise very fair-skinned.

"Good job today, guys," Officer Johnson says. "I know that this is tough work. You have both been exemplary. I told Captain Hinton an hour ago how much work you have both done, and I can see that neither of you got sticky fingers. Good. You're in a tremendous position of trust. We really don't understand what's going on. Until we do, we're the thin blue line."

"What happened with looting downtown?" Jerome asks.

"Nothing. People looted. With our numbers there was virtually nothing that we could do to stop them. All the stores got robbed blind. Our focus, as I'm told, is to keep as many Sleepers safe as possible. We've got a large team of cops and conscripts like you two cataloguing them left and right. We warned the folks downtown not to come uptown to any of these neighborhoods. The Chief of Police has given us orders to shoot on sight anyone who attempts to hurt, kill or otherwise molest any Sleepers."

"Wow," Darryl says, "what are we supposed to do if we come across anyone trying to hurt a Sleeper?"

"If they're armed, nothing, call for back up. If they're not armed, stop them and put them in hand cuffs until they can be transported," Officer Johnson replies. "For now, go home and get some rest. My relief should be here any minute. Tomorrow will be another long day. We won't be done until we've catalogued the entire neighborhood, which could take at least another week. By tomorrow we should start to see transport of all the catalogued

Sleepers out of their homes and into the hospitals. Be ready to keep working. Bring a lunch. That's all that I can say. I'm glad that I found you guys when I did."

In silence Officer Johnson returns Jerome and Darryl to their trash truck. It is parked near Hyde Park Square. Neither says a word along the short ride back to their sanitation headquarters. On the way home, Jerome prays silently to himself, hoping against hope, that Elena has reached any of their White friends and family members. The idea of losing any one of them is almost too much to bear. Once in his car, he pulls it over to catch his breath. He feels a slight panic attack coming over him. He needs to get control of himself before he can continue to drive. He hasn't had one of these in years. Today would not be the day to break the streak.

Jerome works hard to control his breathing and center himself. He thinks about all that he loves--his wife, family, and friends--until the shaking in his hands ceases and the voice in his head is one of peace. Feeling in control again, Jerome travels on.

Eventually reaching home, he trudges up the steps to his front door with none of the verve or vigor that he had just one day ago when he had been so looking forward to seeing Elena for their scheduled couple time. Opening the front door, he sees her sitting on the couch rocking back and forth to what she is hears on MSNBC. Kendra Smith, an anchor on the network, speaks about all of the events of the day. The President, apparently, has been quite busy. In only day two of this crisis, he had closed our borders, halted all non-military air and sea travel, contacted all of the major world leaders, halted all U.S. based securities trading for the foreseeable future, and re-staffed his cabinet including his Joint Chiefs of Staff. The Vice-President had been found in the Vice Presidential residence with his wife, both unconscious. Every White or fair-skinned member of Congress and the Senate had been stricken. Except for those who were abroad outside of the U.S., the government consisted essentially of the President, a few members of Congress, one Senator and two members of the Supreme Court. Justice Abercrombie is said to be distraught over his wife's unconscious state.

"Hey, babe," Jerome says, the fatigue clearly showing in his voice and written on his face.

Elena looks up slowly. Her eyes are red and moist. She had been crying a lot, Jerome sees. He sits next to her and places an arm around her for comfort.

"You don't look like a 'sanitation engineer' anymore,

honey," she says.

"Oh this? Yeah, well I've been conscripted by the Cincinnati Police Department, which itself has been conscripted by the federal government. Speaking of the federal government, do we still have one of those?" Jerome asks in a half-joking, half-serious tone.

"For now, we do," Elena replies. "The President has been on television no fewer than three times today since you left. He warned us that state and local police departments would be conscripting able-bodied men and women to help them with the identification and cataloguing work of the unconscious. I knew that as soon as CPD saw you and Darryl, that you'd have yourself a new job. I'm proud of you, honey. How did it go?"

Jerome takes a breath to gather his thoughts. He muses, how had it gone? Well? He wonders and determines there is no right answer. He and Darryl performed their new jobs which are incredibly hard, disconcerting and heart breaking. Also, horrifying, this job is horrifying, he thinks.

"Elena, today ranks up there as one of the worst days of my life. We saw whole families in their homes unconscious and unable to do a single thing about it. Most, thankfully, were unhurt. Maybe a bruise here or there from a short fall. But we found two DOAs who died because of their forced unconsciousness—an elderly man and some poor woman who burned herself in her kitchen. We probably walked through two-hundred and fifty houses or more. And when I say 'walked through,' I really mean broke into."

He pauses to catch his breath. Jerome's heart had begun pounding wildly again. He needs to calm down before he loses control. His anxiety is back in full force. The events of the last forty-eight hours had severely unnerved him. Being thrown off of his usual work routine hadn't helped. Elena senses his anxiety and lays a gentle hand on his until he begins to breath normally again.

"Jerome," she begins, "today has been hard for us too. Of course, I've been very worried about you. The kids have been downright distraught. They're old enough to understand what the news is saying. They haven't been able to reach most of their friends—only the non-White ones. There's been lots of crying and hand holding today. I've been glued to the television trying to get every bit of information possible. It almost seems as if the only person left in the country with any authority is the President. Most of Congress has been afflicted, and you know that the Senate only had one African-American Senator and two, maybe three others considered to be persons of color. They're okay but everyone else is," she pauses, "unconscious. Unfortunately, a few of them were found severely injured from accidents that they sustained when they became unconscious, and they died. As much as we've seen the President today, he has no answers on when a cure might be found or when this affliction might subside. No one, including the President, seems to know whether this is viral, biologic, in the food, the air or the water. We still don't know." Elena now sounds strained. She tries to choke back a sob but it springs forth like an old country dirge.

Now it's time for Jerome to comfort her. He does the best that he can, given his own down spirits. He holds her close and lets her nuzzle and sob into him. She does so for many minutes until she cries herself to sleep on the couch. Jerome knows that she is as exhausted as he is. He releases her gently and lays her out on their couch. He then quietly gets up intending to hang up his new uniform, get a shower, some food and then to bed. First, he wants to check on the kids.

Micah and Sarah share an adjoining bathroom, Jack and Jill style, with their bedrooms on opposite sides. They had stopped sharing one bedroom two years ago when Sarah's body began changing. The twins, though a boy and a girl, are as close as two siblings can be. Sarah is every bit the sportsperson that her brother is, and had often out done him on their soccer and baseball teams. Now, as Micah has gotten bigger and looks more like a young man, the spitting image of his father, he is starting to consistently outstrip her in their teams in every way except for speed. She is still faster.

Like many other twins, they love and help each other in every way possible. Micah is a math genius, so he often helps his sister with her math homework. Sarah is a reading fiend, so she helps her brother in reading and language arts, and especially in their written assignments. And no one ever bullies them. Everyone in their neighborhood and their school knows that she fights for him and he fights for her. They are each other's best friend.

Jerome pokes his head into Sarah's room. "Hey, Kids, what's up?" he says trying to sound casual, which is the exact opposite of how he feels. Sarah and Micah sit next to each other on her bed. She grips an iPad that is tuned into a news report. They listen to the estimated numbers of people found in states of unconsciousness all across the country. The number is in the many millions. "Turn that off for a second, please" Jerome requests.

Sarah hits the pause button and looks up at her father. Her almond eyes glisten just like her mother's do. At twelve years old, she is already showing the form of the woman that she would one day be. She is a beautiful combination of both parents. Her hair is long and natural, and just now tied into one pony tail—her soccer look, as she calls it.

Micah had been growing taller and taller in the last year. By Jerome's estimation, he had grown four inches in the last year alone. He has also developed that musty teenage smell that made their laundry come alive prior to its washing. Elena, having grown up with a brother, now deceased, knows those smells well and detests them. Her brother Lionel, who had been four years her elder, routinely tormented her with his sweaty, stinky garb after his football practices. He would chase her around their house as she moved as fast as she could trying to avoid his touch. They had loved one another fiercely. His death due to a motorcycle accident had left Elena and her family devastated. As bad as that time had been for Elena and her parents, in many ways, this was much, much worse.

"What have you heard, kids?" Jerome asks his children.

"The same things that mom has heard, Dad," Sarah says.

"But it's what we haven't heard that is so bad. We haven't heard from most of our friends. We have no idea what's become of them. We have no idea who's helping them."

Jerome looks away sheepishly. He knows what "help" looks like, and in his estimation, it isn't really help—at least not yet. Help, real help, would be the revival of all of these people. Real help looked like a cure for this affliction. Real help, Jerome thinks, has to be more than breaking and entering the homes and offices of others to identify and catalogue Sleepers. Only day two into this thing, and real help did not seem to be on the immediate horizon, he thinks.

"Dad, why do you have a police uniform on?" Micah asks.

"It looks like I'm the police now, Micah, at least temporarily that is. Uncle Darryl and I were deputized today when we were out on our usual route. We're working to identify all of the afflicted and to get them catalogued for further help." That last word stuck in his mouth like generic peanut butter that had missed a step or two in its final processing.

"Kids, I don't know how long any of this will last. I do know that there are good people out there trying to help. Uncle Darryl and I personally identified and protected over one-thousand

133

people. We're going out again tomorrow, the next day, and the next until we get everyone that we can identified and protected, at least until some sort of cure is found." Jerome speaks much more confidently than he feels. He wants to give his own children some confidence so that they do not give in to despair. Jerome wonders, though, who will give him confidence. Elena? He muses, no, not his wife. They are both wrecked and barely holding on. Jerome consigns himself to playing this game until something changes, and they get word of a breakthrough.

"One thing that I do know is that the Lord is with us. He'll never leave us. If nothing else, let's hold on to that fact. This is hard for your mother and me too. We are yet holding on. Would you like to pray?" Jerome asks.

"We've been praying today like we never have before, Dad," Sarah says. "And we'll keep praying. Right now, I just want to sleep. We stayed up waiting on you to get home. Mom told us that you might be late. We're just glad to see you."

That warmed Jerome's heart. He knows that he has the best kids in the world. They are his frick and frack. He'd be lost without them.

"Okay," he says, "I'm going to hit the shower and get some

food. I'm exhausted. The next thing that I'll hit is the sack. It's a new day full of more work. You're obviously not going to school tomorrow. I don't know how I feel about you missing school all day again, but I guess that it can't be helped. I want you both to keep your mother company tomorrow. She's taking this very hard. Okay?"

Sarah and Micah immediately give their assent to their father's request. He closes the door and leaves them sitting on the edge of Sarah's bed listening to the latest news pouring out of their iPad. Thirty minutes later, Jerome is washed, fed and in the bed. He asks Elena to join him. He has no intention of letting her sleep all night on the couch watching the news. It is too dang depressing and she needs real rest too, he thinks. She gratefully acquiesces to his request and lays next to him as they both drift off to sleep, embraced against whatever tragedies or calamities the new day might bring.

CHAPTER V

In the last few days when Sleepers began to appear,

President Douglas all but stops sleeping. Fifteen minutes here,

thirty minutes there, but overall, he cannot rest. This is patently

obvious watching him during his many television interviews. After

getting his unconscious Chief of Staff to the hospital, meeting

with all the non-White members of Congress and the Supreme

Court, and teleconferencing with all of the remaining members

of Congress who are outside of the continental United States, the

President is exhausted, yet remains unable to sleep. His worry does

not allow him rest.

Though he is highly stressed, a plan beings to form in

his mind about how to proceed. Congress, or what's left of it,

will temporarily hand the President some expansive powers to

deal with this crisis through an official state of emergency. The

financial markets will not open until some stability is regained.

All police, local and state, will be brought under the military's

umbrella, temporarily, and will be federalized. General Phaylen

Martin, a Black man of Jamaican decent whose parents immigrated

to the United States before he was born, will head the Pentagon

in place of the now unconscious General Schultz, who was found unconscious in his home two days ago.

The President knows that he needs to address the American people, and the world community at large about what has happened and continues to happen in real time in every major city and small town in the country. There are more reports of widespread looting, power outages and general societal upheaval. A rumor circulates that only White people are being affected by this crisis when, strictly speaking, that is untrue. They are all being impacted by it, President Douglas thinks, and very fair-skinned people of all ethnicities are being physically impacted by this disease, if it even is a disease. Every emergency response department across the country, including the police, is being strained as their fair-skinned and White members are either disappearing, being found unconscious or worse. Where do we go from here? President Douglas wonders.

The President sits at his desk in the private residence of the White House. He has typed out his thoughts for his prepared remarks this morning. He reviews them carefully to make sure that the facts are right. He knows that he must not only inform, but also encourage. Neither he nor his staff can or should say everything. It would not be wise, he thinks, to say all that they know or don't know. He needs to preserve calm and not send his nation nor the world into a greater panic.

The breadth and width of this crisis is astounding. Perhaps two-thirds of the population is in real physical jeopardy and unable to regain consciousness. The President realizes that as the leader of the free world he balances on the edge of a razor. If he says too little, he could send the world community into a panic. If he says too much, same outcome Thanks to social media and its penchant for snap judgments, the world is already at a fevered pitch of panic. Even worse, he knows that his words could well incite some of his country's enemies to commit some reckless act that attacks one of the country's allies, or the United States itself. This is not the time for the United States to be perceived as weak. No matter what he says, President Douglas thinks, the world markets are going to take a hell of a beating when they open, whenever that is.

What truly frightens President Douglas and his staff is how vast the problem is. Simple math tells them that White Americans make up roughly about two-hundred and sixty million of the country's population. They are also the country's dominant cultural and ethnic group. They control and operate all of the nation's most important institutions—financial, educational, military, and commercial—pretty much everything. This, they know, presents a thorny practical problem for the nation: What happens when you remove the most knowledgeable, best-educated two-thirds of the country? The President has no more time to ponder this question. He and the nation are knee-deep in it, and it will soon be moving up to their elbows, and then up to their necks threatening to drown them all.

There is non-White expertise in all of the key areas needed for running and maintaining the country, but those numbers are far less in comparison. Theirs, the President realizes, is an issue of quantity of those holding the requisite knowledge. For example, the United States has about one-hundred and twelve nuclear power plants throughout the country, and every single one of them must be continually maintained and regulated hour by hour. In this crisis, who will and can man them? Perhaps some or all can be maintained on auto-pilot, but that is not a long-term solution. It's short-term. President Douglas and his remaining cabinet recognize that this is but one example of what they must consider and soon provide an answer to. Also under immediate consideration are the nation's military, water supply, oil supply, electric grids, and food production. All are exposed without their core demographic to help run them.

The President's head begins to hurt when he considers all of the possible outcomes and ramifications of running a country such as theirs short-handed. He recounts these details as he tightens his tie in the private residence. It is 5:00 a.m., a little earlier than his usual check-in time, but given the obvious circumstances, quite necessary. Leaving the residence, President Douglas feels a certain sense of gratitude knowing that Connor and Grayden, his sons, are okay, home, and out of harm's way. They will not be going to school today or any day until this crisis can be averted. His wife would have them on a steady diet of reading and school work until that time.

Honestly, they had no idea what state their school might be in and who could even show up that had not been affected. The kids' school is an elite private school in Washington, D.C. that teaches the sons and daughters of the nation's Congressmen, Senators, foreign ambassadors and federal judges. It is not diverse in an American sense, nor is it economically diverse. At $60,000 plus per year, only the most elite could hope to attend it. Most of his sons' classmates and teachers do not look like them. They are, by and large, White or European. If they have been affected by this unconsciousness, there would not be any school for the President's children for the foreseeable future.

Walking into the Oval Office, the President stops in his tracks. He sees Trevor Campbell, his NSA head, Valerie King, his now Chief of Staff, and a very odd looking figure dressed from head to toe in a canary yellow biohazard suit standing in his office.

"Mr. President," the strange figure says, "I am Dr. Josef Krauss, the CEO of Pharmatech. I am afraid, Mr. President, that this whole awful business is my fault, that is to say, the fault of my company."

"Mr. President," Trevor says, "Dr. Krauss contacted NSA late last night and insisted on meeting with you personally. After he shared his story with me, I thought it prudent for him to share with you what is happening and why. He may be the key to this whole matter and for finding," he hesitates before taking a deep breath, "a cure if possible." The President immediately reacts to the word "cure" as it parts Trevor's lips and wonders just what exactly Dr. Krauss knows, and how he came to know it. They would all soon find out.

"Mr. Campbell is quite right, sir. This unconsciousness, as you call it, is actually a deep sleep which is a viral-induced coma. Let me explain. It is an unnatural consequence of a drug that my company has been testing in humans for some time. The drug, we call it Zoesterol, was created to extend the lives of its takers. It promises to extend life by slowing down some of the key metabolic markers for aging. We figured out how to slow down human aging at a metabolic level. Our animal testing was highly favorable. We form Zoesterol from formerly active viral material. Our earliest testing shows that it worked wonderfully in mice and primates. We began our human trials, under FDA approval of course, two years ago."

Dr. Krauss hesitates before continuing. The suit that he wears is hot and he begins to noticeably sweat. "Mr. President, when we started our human trials under FDA approval," he stammers, "the viral material that we used began, almost immediately, to mutate. The mutations reformed into fully- formed viral material and reproduced rapidly. We lost control of it and could not stop its reproduction phase. The mutated virus had no discernible effects whatsoever on our highly melanated human subjects, but when it was given to those subjects with little or no melanin, we found that it either killed them or put them into deep, un-revivable sleep—comas essentially, Mr. President. As closely as we can tell at this point, the drug slows the metabolism of some subjects to a point at which they become unconscious, seemingly irreversibly so. Because it happens at a metabolic level, only a metabolic or genetic response seems likely to be able to revive them. We have no cure at the moment, Mr. President."

President Douglas looks at Dr. Krauss with a mixture of horror, anger, and disgust. He really wanted to know, how had he allowed this to happen? "Dr. Krauss, how did the virus get out and why did you continue your trials with these kinds of results? Did you even notify the FDA of what was happening?" the President says, his voice and agitation rising with each question.

"Mr. President, we're not exactly sure, but given the aggressive nature of the mutated virus, we know that it's airborne, waterborne, and may even pass by touch. We contained our affected subjects immediately, but we have evidence that the virus has become airborne. If that's true, then nearly everyone within our borders may already be affected and have the virus in their bloodstreams. The only good news, if we can call it good news, is that it's best transmitted through body fluids. Though it is airborne, it doesn't seem to like that environment for long and cannot live outside of fluid for more than, say, forty-eight hours. But it's so aggressive that once you have it, you have it. We're calling it, internally, the Sleeper Virus. Right now, there is no cure."

"Also, Mr. President," Dr. Krauss continues, "we think that we may have been the victims of industrial espionage. We don't know who yet. But it could have been done by one or more disgruntled employees or a competitor or both. The virus was released at almost the exact same time on the same day at all of our facilities across the country that house it. This was no glitch, sir. This was a well-coordinated attack that took advantage of a lapse in our internal security. And, no, we did not notify the FDA of our initial bad findings. We hid those, I'm sorry to say. We thought that we could contain it, and well", Dr. Krauss stumbles, "we thought that if we told the FDA, the entire program would be canceled and the company would lose billions."

The President again looks fully at the strange little man before him. He looks to be in his late sixties. He measures no more than five feet seven inches tall. He stands slightly stooped over in a manner that suggests that he is older than he really is. He wears big glasses that are bifocals. He speaks with a slight accent that sounds, perhaps, German. His hair is white and thinning, and his strained face shows the lines of too much worry too soon in life.

The President has at least one million questions to ask this man. But the most important question presses forward and asserts itself.

"Wait a minute," the President says, "are you saying that we've ALL been infected?"

"Yes, sir, Mr. President. At this point, it is reasonable to believe that every single person within the physical boundaries of the United States has been or will be infected. Of course," he continues, "this does not include any of our citizens who found themselves outside the country on the day of the outbreak. The first day of the outbreak is so significant because the virus is airborne but also passable by human touch. Also, we monitored heavy outbreaks in each of the cities in which human testing occurred-- Boston; Charlotte; New Orleans; Dallas; San Diego; Chicago; St. Louis; San Francisco; Pittsburgh; Seattle and Philadelphia."

As Dr. Krauss says each city's name slowly, methodically the President folds his arms about his torso and allows what he hears to settle upon him like a weighted blanket from which there is no escape. He has the peculiar sensation of shortness and loss of breath--the kind of shortness that one might experience when submerged under water for thirty seconds or more--the feeling, he thinks, of almost drowning.

"Mr. President", Dr. Krauss continues, "at this point, we should divide the population into two distinct groups: the 'Sufficiently Melanated'--SMs--and the 'Insufficiently Melanated,' IMs. There may be a third group, Sir, but we have not had proper confirmation of them yet. For now, these are the technical terms that we're using. They're crude, I admit, but it helps us to talk and think about this problem a bit more", he pauses, "scientifically." At this point, the President is decided. He, in fact, does not like this man.

*   *   *

Candace awakes with a tremendous feeling of anticipation. She has barely been able to sleep due to her excitement. She gets to see Raheem today, and she has a surprise for him. He is expecting to see her and their kids, but she has worked it out with the warden, John Smith, to have thirty minutes of alone time with him in a private room. This is definitely not standard procedure for the prison, but Raheem has been an exemplary prisoner, and Candace was fortunate to have hired the warden's daughter for her first job at the retail store that she manages. Candace had had no idea of the young lady's identity, but that changes on the day the warden comes to visit his daughter while Candace is there.

The warden is very appreciative of his daughter's hire and introduces himself to Candace, recognizing her right away. Raheem is a killer chess player, and the warden sets aside one hour per week to play him. Being ex-military himself, the warden appreciates Raheem's heavy military background and how he carries himself with military bearing inside of his prison. The warden knows that Raheem is a great example to have inside the prison. The other inmates seem to fall in line whenever he is around. The warden instantly recognizes who Candace is because Raheem had, of course, spoken about her often and had often shown him her picture.

Warden Smith had even confided in Raheem once that he thinks that he received a raw deal from the judge, especially since the prosecutor in the case had not requested the maximum prison time for him. He and Raheem understand exactly why the judge had placed him there, but Raheem resolves to do the best with a bad situation. When Raheem first arrives to the correctional facility in Lorton, Virginia, he promises Warden Smith that he won't make trouble, will follow all of the rules, and will not use his skills and training to intentionally hurt anyone. Warden Smith appreciates Raheem's forthrightness and assigns him to jobs that intentionally steer him away from trouble spots in the prison.

Candace, the night prior, places their kids with her mother. She needs a full night's uninterrupted rest before she sees her husband-to-be, as she thinks of him. She is well aware that Raheem fully intends on marrying her soon after his release. They both rejoice through their many letters and phone calls that he will soon be free. Today, she thinks, will be a lovely precursor to the love they will get to enjoy as a married couple. Chuckling to herself as she rises from her bed, Candace mischievously thinks that she will put Raheem on restriction from her right after he gets out so that he makes good on his promise of matrimony. That is a trick that her mother had taught her.

Thinking about their future together, Candace muses that she does not want a fancy or big wedding. They already have two children, and she wants two more. Instead, Candace considers, she would be happy with a small service in their quaint home. That is good enough for them, she thinks, and then on to the honeymoon.

Candace picks out a pair of jeans that nicely hug her hips and buttocks, and a sheer white blouse that fits well but does not cling too tightly. Leave something to the imagination, she thinks. Her hair is naturally straight, but she curls the ends and wraps them up the night before with hair rollers. When she releases her hair from the rollers, she is pleased with what she sees. She thinks that Raheem will be too. Before putting her clothes on, Candace selects a matching pink bra and panty set, Raheem's favorite color for her. Almost ready, she thinks, almost. None of this will go or look right without Raheem's favorite fragrance, she knows. "Chanel No. 5 or nothing, baby," he had once told her. She sprays the fragrance over her liberally, but not too liberally.

Donning her outfit, Candace checks herself in her bedroom's mirror. Perfect, she thinks with a wry smile. He's going to love it, she knows. Feeling a sudden and unmistakable gush of happy anticipation, Candace grabs her winter jacket, car keys and cell phone. The prison is a short fifteen minute drive from their house. At this time of day, there is little traffic. She will arrive at 9:30 a.m. and then they can have their date. Candace is thankful for Warden Smith's favor to her and Raheem.

As she drives to the prison, Candace avoids the highway so as to avoid any remaining rush hour traffic. The streets seem particularly empty this morning except for a couple of car accidents, but Candace does not stop to inquire, given her tight timing. Arriving to the prison, she parks in its visitor's parking lot. Strangely, she sees that what would normally be a full or nearly full parking lot is almost completely empty except for her car and one other. Candace looks around to make sure that she was in the right parking lot. She had been here many times before, but this emptiness is new to her. Verifying that she is indeed in the right place, Candace parks and gets out.

The entrance for visitors is to her right. She walks briskly to its door, trying to avoid the chilly air and wind pushing the air toward her. Because of her many visits to see Raheem, Candace knows all of the admitting corrections officers, and they all know Raheem. She has been treated, she believes, very fairly and cordially by them all except for CO Robinson, who had leered at her one time too many. One complaint to Warden Smith about him, and CO Robinson no longer works at that prison.

Walking into the facility, Candace sees a strange sight. The check-in room is empty except for one correction officer who is slumped over the x-ray machine. Candace recognizes this CO, but does not remember his name. Candace looks around before moving toward him. Not seeing an immediate threat, she slowly walks toward the CO to determine his state of duress. Touching his arm, Candace feels its warmth and sees that it's flush. He's alive, she thinks, but what else, she wonders. She hears his soft breath exiting and entering his lungs and understands instantly. He's asleep. This was obviously a break in all possible protocol, but Candace touches his shoulders to try to wake him.

"CO!" Candace whispers softly at first. "CO!" She whispers more loudly and urgently. The slumped over CO does not move or stir. Candace walks around to his side of the x-ray machine to see if he is injured. No injuries, she observes. He's just asleep, she surmises. Seeing a chair directly behind him, Candace gently but firmly shoves the CO into it. Once in the chair and facing her, Candace sees that he is in a deep sleep. Now, she yells loudly directly at him, "Wake up!!" but still, no response. She snaps her fingers by his ears, but again no response. She even gives two or three gentle but firm slaps to his cheeks. Again, no response. Frustrated and starting to become more than a little fearful, Candace looks around to see if anyone else is around.

A short hallway lies between the check-in area and the visitation room, where she expects to see Raheem. Seeing no one in the hallway, Candace walks slowly down the hall knowing that this action could easily cause her to lose her visitation rights. At the end of the short hallway sits the visitation room. Candace peers inside and sees an even more curious and frightening sight. Each of the correction officers that normally man this room for visits are slumped over and, she realizes, are asleep just like the first CO she encountered.

Candace's mind now races. What has happened? Where is everyone else? Where is Raheem? These are just a few of the questions that race through her mind as she works to sort out all that she has witnessed.

"Hello?" Candace hears a voice behind her and nearly jumps six feet in the air. "I'm sorry," the small voice says, "but I've been here for about twenty minutes hiding, but then I heard you and wanted to see if you see what I see. My name is Anna, Anna Richards."

Anna is a diminutive dark-skinned older woman that Candace recognizes instantly. Many of the times that Candace had been to the prison to visit Raheem, Anna had also been there to visit her son. Candace remembers that her son's name is Rodrigo. Anna speaks with a slight Spanish accent, though she is clearly also a woman of African descent. Anna had once told Candace as they waited to be escorted to see their respective loved ones that her family is from the Dominican Republic. Before today, Candace had never known her name.

"Ms. Richards," Candace begins, "I just got here a few minutes ago. What happened?"

"I don't know," Anna responds. "I saw the CO out front slumped over and," she hesitates, "asleep or knocked out or whatever. I thought he might be dead which really scared me. I then walked back here to see if anyone knew what was going on. When I got back here, I saw all of the other COs in the same state. I have no idea what's going on. I just want to see my son Rodrigo."

Anna begins sobbing softly. She is clearly frightened. Candace puts her arm around her to assure her. "Come with me, Ms. Richards," Candace says. "We'll get this sorted out one way or another."

Candace walks them to the main door of the prison. She had never been through that door before, but she knows where it is because she had seen Raheem walk through it so many times. She doesn't think that she can open it, but hopes that someone on the other side, maybe another CO, can. Candace hopes that by speaking into the door's intercom or banging on it that someone will come and tell them what is happening. They are risking their visitation rights, but Candace thinks it worth it to get some answers and to get these unconscious COs some help.

Walking to the prison's main door, Candace finds the intercom exactly where she remembered it. She presses the button and speaks clearly with determination: "Hello? Is anyone able to hear me? I am here to see Raheem Gates, prisoner number B190607. There are unconscious COs out here. Someone needs to come see about them." Candace repeats this three more times, but no one responds.

After about five minutes, Candace and Anna become more and more frustrated and anxious. Candace decides to take a different approach. She decides to start banging on the thick glass window of the door and the metal parts of the door itself. Still, there is no answer. Growing tired from the effort, Candace turns her back to the door to check on Ms. Richards who is now seated in a chair next to the door. She then hears a very familiar and welcome voice.

"Baby! Is that you?! Boy do I have a crazy story to tell you!" Raheem says as he toothily grins at Candace from the other side of the door.

Thoughtfully regarding his top staff, President Douglas gestures toward Dr. Krauss and asks them "do you have any questions for him?" "Yes," Valerie starts, "Is there a way to identify the virus?"

"Yes, we think so," Dr. Krauss says. "The virus, in its current form, is the mirror image, structurally, of eumelanin which is the melanin molecule most responsible for skin and hair pigment. Apparently, the mutated virus attempts to seize control of the metabolic processes controlled by the brain and in the brain stem. If a sufficient amount of eumelanin is not at those cites, the virus is free to attack the brain and brainstem and take control of their metabolic processes. Because the original virus was designed to slow the aging process, the mutated version of the virus moves more aggressively to stop or drastically slow every bodily process thereby leading to the unconsciousness that we've been seeing. The end result is a near shutdown of the host, and a deep sleep occurs." At Dr. Krauss' words, a silence settles over the Oval Office occupants.

"So what you're saying then, Dr. Krauss," the President

says, "is that this eumelanin acts as a counter-acting force to the virus?"

"Why yes, Mr. President. That's exactly what I'm saying. When the virus attacks the brain and the brain stem, the eumelanin, when in sufficient quantity, attaches to the virus by bonding with it to prevent it from accessing the parts of the brain and the brain stem that control a human's metabolic functions. Remember, eumelanin and the virus, the Sleeper Virus, are mirror images of one another. They fit together like a lock and key. The virus is the key. Melanin is the lock. If there's no lock, or not enough locks, then the keys are free to attack the hypothalamus, pituitary gland, thyroid gland, and any brain cite where metabolism is regulated."

"Dr. Krauss, are you close to developing a cure?" the President asks.

"At present, sir, no. We're trying everything, but no cure is on the horizon, and we've been compromised in our main laboratory. Our top scientists have been stricken. We've lost internal expertise to do our research. We," Dr. Krauss stammers, "have only one scientist left in the United States, a dark-skinned Indian fellow, Dr. Singh, who possesses the core knowledge to find a cure, but he is just one man working by himself."

The President then inquires, "Okay then, Krauss, if there is no cure, is there a time frame for the Sleeper Virus to end its work and for the stricken to wake up?"

"Sadly, sir, we don't know enough about the virus in an unregulated environment. We just don't know. None of our previously stricken human hosts have not yet awakened. Some of them have been asleep for the last three months. This drug was highly experimental. None of this was predicted. The animal testing was fantastic. We thought," he stumbles as he speaks rapidly, "we thought that the human trials would go swimmingly. We thought that we were on the verge of a major break-through. We were wrong. We have no answers at this time, Mr. President, only warnings. We tested the virus in the U.S. in our subject cities. The virus mutated almost identically in all of our locations. Mr. President, as I said previously, we think that the virus may also be communicable by touch, mere touch. We know that it can survive within the oils and secretions of humans so long as those secretions persist. Once contracted, the virus rapidly moves into the bloodstream through the skin and starts to do its work—it looks for eumelanin, the locks, at the key metabolic sites in the body. Melanin must exist at a sufficient amount to avoid being comatose.

Whoever doesn't have enough melanin can expect to be stricken if they do not leave the United States immediately. The Sleeper Virus is fast acting. It doesn't incubate in a host. If you catch it, it manifests within the first few hours. As I said, we've lost almost all of our scientists and researchers. When internal alarms went off in our labs and offices, I quickly jumped into my specially made bio-hazard suit and haven't taken it off since."

The President critically regards Krauss. He has the unmistakable feeling that this man isn't telling them everything. He remembers that some of his staff have been stricken by the Sleeper Virus while in their biohazard suits. He wonders, how had Dr. Krauss avoided being infected? "How exactly does your suit work, Dr. Krauss?"

"It's state of the art, Mr. President. My air tank is, as you see, integrated into the suit. It's its own air producing system. It doesn't just store air, it produces it from CO_2. Proprietary technology in the tank allows my CO_2 to be made into O_2, all while allowing me to stay in this suit for up to thirty days if need be. The suit itself is especially attuned to block out all viral material and is impermeable."

"Proprietary you say?" President Douglas asks. "I want

it. Trevor, get NSA over to Krauss's main offices and assess the damage. I want this suit and everything else that they have. We'll need access to all of Dr. Krauss' offices. I want his notes, hard drives, materials, everything. Valerie, please draft an Executive Order giving us access to it all. This is a national emergency and we'll treat acquiring Pharmatech's information and technology as part of that."

"We have a team extracting data as we speak, Mr. President," his NSA chief said. Trevor is unusually adept at anticipating the President's needs, especially in critical times like this.

"Of course, Mr. President. You'll have it within the hour," Valerie King replies.

Dr. Krauss makes a look that indicates a note of protest to the conversion of his company's property by the federal government, but the grim looks on the President's and his staffs' faces persuade him to hold his tongue.

"Mr. President," Barbara chimes in, "we'll need a full information lockdown. No one outside of this room can hear this information yet, and especially not our enemies. Dr. Krauss cannot leave the White House." The President immediately takes her meaning and responds.

"Dr. Krauss, your company and the problem that it has created are now a matter of the utmost national security. You yourself will need to be quarantined and made available to our staff and scientists around the clock. I fear that we may be experiencing the same personnel problems that you are. I haven't gotten Mr. Campbell's full report yet, but I'm sure that it will be telling." The President motions to his Secret Service detail standing just outside of his office. He notices immediately that they were both non-White. "Take Dr. Krauss to a secure location within the White House and keep him there. Make him available to our scientists provided only that they present the necessary security clearances."

"Yes, sir!" the officers respond. They move toward Dr. Krauss and walk him out of the Oval Office.

*   *   *

After spending half of the morning meeting and interviewing Dr. Krauss, President Douglas still has not had his scheduled security briefing yet from Trevor Campbell, his National Security Agency director. After placing Dr. Krauss in quarantine, the President is more than ready to hear from him. Trevor is youngish, about thirty-five. He had not worked on the President's campaigns or come with his initial team from Atlanta. He is Washington, D.C. born and bred. His family had attended Howard University since, literally, the end of the Civil War. He had also attended Howard undergrad, though he'd gotten into Princeton and Yale. Trevor often proudly recounted that he is a fourth generation Howard man. He majored in finance and international affairs graduating summa cum laude in three years. He joined his father's fraternity and had often playfully chided President Douglas about never having pledged the black and old gold while he was at Harvard. Later, Trevor had gained a doctorate in world affairs from Harvard where he and the President met, the President himself working on his law degree at that time.

Like the President, all of Trevor's working life had been spent in the federal government, first at the State Department, and next at NSA as a policy and security expert. Trevor is the kind of man that could have made a fortune in private industry, but he had chosen a life of service instead. The President had thought him invaluable during his first term as he served as one of the President's top foreign and security advisors. In his second term, the President had elevated him to the top job at NSA.

"Trevor," the President says just after he closes the door, "give it to me straight."

"You may want to sit down, Barron," he says, using his first name when it was just the President, Valerie, Barbara and himself.

The President sits behind his desk, Resolute. Whatever he is going to hear, he wants to hear it in the strongest place possible. As his hands touch the wood, its hardness anchors him. Its smooth permanence somehow reassures him. This desk had been at the epicenter of some of the worst times in the country—the Cuban Missile Crisis; 9-11; the Vietnam War; the War in Iraq; and much more. It had stood the test of time not unlike the Presidency and the United States itself. Whatever he is about to hear, the President is determined to remain strong and implacable in the face of it.

"Mr. President," Trevor says as he recognizes the austerity of the moment, "we have a problem of unprecedented scope and depth. Nothing like it has happened in our or anyone's history. Our earliest estimates show us that, excluding Alaska, at least eighty to eighty-five percent of all White people in the continental United States, that is to say, the insufficiently melanated—IMs—have been infected and therefore physically affected. Many are being found deceased due to accident or unconsciousness due to the Sleeper Virus. No persons of color, the sufficiently melanated-- SMs--have yet been found unconscious, though a good number have also been reported as casualties due to accidents incidentally caused by the IMs." Trevor stops speaking to allow what he's just said to resonate with the President and his other staff. He takes a sip of water from a glass that sits on the table in the center of the room.

"IMs? SMs?" the President mutters to himself, that's how we're now distinguishing the afflicted and the non-afflicted? He thinks, "I know that's what Dr. Krauss calls them. Are those the best terms for our understanding, Trevor?" he asks.

"I believe so," Trevor responds. "The military loves simple labels and these will help them wrap their minds around who to help and who to conscript for help. As you know there were plane crashes, thousands of car accidents, explosions and many other kinds of accidents including train collisions. We've verified about a dozen serious chemical spills on land and in some of our waterways. The Ohio River in West Virginia has been contaminated. Many of those affected were killed by accident. Those in our embassies and outside of the continental United

States have not been affected. That includes the State of Alaska. Because of the short airborne life of the virus, we think that its ability to remain airborne longer than forty-eight hours is limited. But in the water supply, it could cross our borders. Canada is locking down any and all trade from the United States as we speak, and has closed its borders. Mr. President, the Canadian military is now manning its border against us. The Mexican border is closed too, but they seem to be a lot less aggressive about enforcement in comparison to the Canadians."

"What are our European friends saying, Trevor?" President Douglas asks.

"It seems to be a mixed bag, Mr. President, depending largely on what European delegation has been comatose. For example, the Turkish embassy here has not been affected. But the English, French, German and Spanish embassies have had most of their staffs become unconscious, that is to say, all but their sufficiently melanated staff members—their SMs."

"I don't know if I can adjust to calling people SMs and IMs, Trevor," President Douglas says.

"Sir," Janet Taros, the Homeland Security chief says, "do you have another suggestion? White and Black aren't the most accurate terms for this kind of crisis. More than White people have been infected and lost consciousness." President Douglass reluctantly acknowledges the truth of what his Homeland Security chief has just said. "Okay, that's what we'll go with officially, for now," he adds.

"And you can see the implications, Mr. President," Valerie King says. "Every industry is impacted by this crisis. For the foreseeable future, almost all U.S. based commerce have ground to a halt. We can't reopen the stock exchanges because there aren't enough people to run them. All of them are closed for the foreseeable future. We've got SM expertise to do that work, but we don't have enough people to fill all of the necessary positions to run them. That's true almost everywhere except, maybe, for our military. Our military nationally can still fulfill most of its commitments, but state-by-state, we're hurting. Nationalizing all of the state, city and local police forces helps, but that's still a short term fix for a longer term problem," Valerie says.

"Mr. President" Janet says, "It may become necessary for you to exert more authority than you already have in order to stabilize the country, especially with respect to law enforcement. I know how you feel about that, sir, but I would place our country's overall security above your personal discomfort on this issue."

The President considers what his top staff has just told him and sees Trevor and Valerie's quiet but pointed agreement with what Janet has just said. What his Homeland Security chief suggests is exactly what so many of his opponents had accused him of wanting to do when he became President. How little they understood him and his motives, they might never know, but now faced with the very real possibility of a total collapse of governmental and societal order, the President knows that this step might soon become necessary.

"I will take your recommendations and counsel under advisement. Right now, though, I'm not convinced that we know enough to take such a drastic step. What happens if our White, I mean our IM citizens, wake up in a day or a week from now and see their police have all been federalized and the equivalent of martial law enacted? Do we really want to have to answer those questions and deal with the inevitable fallout?"

"We understand your point, Mr. President, but honestly, you seem to be looking at the issue from a political point of view rather than that of exigent circumstances," Trevor says. "These are the most exigent of circumstances. Some leeway can be had.

Regardless, Congress stands at the ready to help you with these prickly Constitutional issues. It's your call, sir."

"Ah, yes. Congress. Where are we with that? What's the count?" the President Douglas asks.

"Congress," Valerie says, "is a literal shadow of its former self. The Secret Service has accounted for members' whereabouts. All of the non-White members, the SMs, are alive and well. There haven't been any comas among them. But the IMs, including Speaker Johnson, that were in the United States, have all been found unconscious."

"All of them?" the President asks, his voice cracking with stress.

"All of them," Valerie confirms. "Because both houses were in session, almost all of the lawmakers were in town except for those on specific missions away due to their committee assignments. They've all been found, most of whom were in their Congressional offices. Most were unharmed. A few were found at the bottom of staircases. No deaths, though, that we can tell. Speaker Johnson hit his head something terrible on some marble steps, but he'll survive it, if and when he wakes up, he's probably concussed."

"What about their families," the President asks, "what is the state of their families?"

"We're looking into that, Mr. President," Barbara says, "but our resources have suddenly become very limited. Just two days since the outbreak, we're down to only SM agents in the Secret Service. And we're pulling in every retiree and trainee that we can find to fill in the gaps."

"Understood. Please continue," the President says, now sitting straight up, his elbows on his desk and his fingers crossed in front of his face.

"Again, Mr. President, every industry has been affected. In most cases, non-IM expertise for all of our industries exists, but the issue is numbers, quantity. Most manufacturing can continue, but missing bodies means missing hands. And for the foreseeable future, there won't be much to export, or for that matter, people to handle our normal imports."

President Douglas lets everything that he has heard this morning settle over him like an uncomfortable, heavy, itchy blanket that he cannot shrug off. He offers up a silent prayer that he hopes God hears. His need for strength and clear thinking during this crisis are greater now than at any time in his life. He wonders, what, if anything, has prepared him for this moment? This isn't politics. This is survival. How might their enemies react? Their allies? The President understands that his actions in the next few hours might well determine whether the United States of America continues to exist and the form of that existence.

"Valerie, here are my comments for this morning's statement. Please review them quickly and make your usual notes and edits. I want to deliver them in the next sixty minutes before rush hour, if rush hour even exists anymore. And one last thing, please be ready to advise me on what it takes to institute martial law nationwide, and how to enact it. You have one hour to update me."

"One hour, Mr. President," Valerie acknowledges as his top staff gathers their belongings, exits the Oval Office, and leaves the most powerful man in the world alone to consider his and his country's fate.

CHAPTER VI

Raheem stares at Candace with a silly, toothy grin through the thick glass of the main security door separating the visitors' area from the inmate section. He had been walking from the cafeteria with yet another cart full of breakfasts for the still locked down inmates in his section of the prison when he hears loud banging on the prison's main inlet door, and persistent, yet muted yelling on the other side of it. He is surprised yet ecstatic at the source of the raucous cacophony. Of course it is Candace, he thinks. She had never been known to take no for an answer to anything. Raheem can't believe his good fortune at seeing the love of his life right now.

"Candace, baby, how the heck did you get here?" he asks.

"Better question," she counters. "What the heck is going on?"

"Oh, that," Raheem deadpans. "Honestly, your guess is as good as mine. We woke up, and we are missing some COs and the White COs that were already here, are all unconscious. We only have one CO running our whole block. He put Carlos and me on breakfast duty. He won't let anyone else out of their cells. It's just us. I was just about to deliver this next set of breakfast."

"Raheem, I haven't listened to the news yet, so I don't know what's going on. It was an easy ride over here. I didn't see anything out of the ordinary. But I get here and all of your COs in the visitors' section are unconscious. I'm really scared. What's happening?" Candace asks.

Raheem places both of his hands on the glass that sits between him and Candace. He invites her to place her hands where his are. The door and the glass are thick. They muffle their voices, but they can still hear one another clearly, especially since they are so close.

"Candy," Raheem says using his nickname for Candace, "I don't know what this is. The world seems to have stopped. But as far I'm concerned, I'm still getting out of here and will be with you and the kids soon. Keeping you all at the center of my heart has been what's kept me focused and grounded. I don't see any reason to stop doing that now."

"But Raheem," Candace says, "what if the world has changed? What if what's happened keeps you in here longer or totally takes you away from us?"

Raheem looks around to see if anyone is close by. Of course not, he thinks, everyone in this part of the prison is either in their cell or unconscious. Carlos is already back at their cellblock handing out breakfast. "Candy, come hell or high water, I'll be leaving here soon, either on my release date or soon thereafter. Nothing will keep me from you and the kids. Nothing," he says solemnly.

Candace looks at Raheem and some knowing passes between them. It's as if an electric charge shoots from him to her that causes her to relax, but most importantly, to trust him. She'd actually had this feeling before, but it usually came when they were tightly embraced. This is new, she thinks, but pleasant nonetheless. Candace offers Raheem a slight smile before speaking. "Rah" she says, "I trust you. You're right, you're on short time. Please don't make any mistakes and get home to us as soon as possible."

"Zero mistakes," he says. "Zero mistakes. This is all gonna turn out for our good, Candace. You'll see. But hey, who is the lady sitting there next to you?"

Candace had all but forgotten about Anna Richards, the older woman here to see her son, Rodrigo. "Oh!" Candace exclaims. "This is Anna Richards, Ms. Richards, she's here to visit her son Rodrigo."

Anna stands up slowly and clears her throat. "I didn't want

to interrupt you two. I appreciate you asking about me, Raheem. Do you know my son? Rodrigo? I just need to know that he's okay. He's on short time too. Really shouldn't have even been put here."

"Ms. Richards, I sure do. He's my bunkmate's, Carlos,' good friend. They play chess and checkers a lot together. Carlos looks out for him. Rodrigo is fine. We've already delivered breakfast to him. I'll check back on him and tell him that you came to see him, no problem."

"Thank goodness," Anna says. "Please give him my best. And tell him that I said 'no mistakes' too," she says echoing the same advice that Candace had just given Raheem.

Raheem chuckles at that. "No mistakes, indeed, Ms. Richards. I'll tell him. Candace, I need to get back now. Other guys need to eat, but uh, I see how you came to see me. We'll address that at another time," Raheem says winking his approval. Raheem turns and begins to move his breakfast cart back towards his cellblock. He mouths the words "I love you" to Candace and she in turn lightly places her full lips on the glass to form a kiss. In that moment, Raheem considers leaving the prison right now, but then immediately remembers his promise to Candace: no mistakes. Raheem catches the kiss out of the air, places it on his heart, but keeps moving. No mistakes, he thinks, no mistakes.

*   *   *

Major, formerly Captain Jill Williams, checks her pack one more time. She has her main flight uniform plus a spare. She has the box that contains her new maple leaves signifying her promotion to Major. Before her emergency landing in San Francisco, she had been at least two to three years away from being promoted to major. Now, back in the Air Force full time, her superiors immediately promote her and tell her that she's in charge of all new pilot training. All of that training is now to be run out of Andrews Airforce base. Such combat training normally happens out West in Colorado and Arizona. But now, with the smaller numbers of pilots for the American combat fleet, General Martin has moved all pilot training closer to home near Washington, D.C.

Unfortunately, Major Williams' new assignment is now on-hold, perhaps permanently. North Korea has massed its troops on the border that it shares with South Korea and has declared war against it. The official intelligence says that they are acting recklessly by trying America's resolve in light of the loss of nearly two-thirds of its population, a fact that is now well known. Clearly, the North Koreans see this as their opportunity to reclaim South Korea for itself without American intervention. They also calculate that China will not stop their aggression. Of course, Japan, having no army or navy, has no ability to check North Korea's aggression. North Korea's leader, Kim Pao Il, is a maniac, perhaps even more so than his father had been. The unofficial intelligence is that this is China's play with tacit approval from Russia.

American security officials believe that this is China's plan. They are the not-so-secret hand behind the throne that is testing the U.S. in its moment of greatest crisis. Apparently, China and most of the U.S.' enemies believe that with the absence of most of their White citizens, the country is vulnerable and unable or unwilling to stand with its allies. From Major Williams' perspective, they had badly underestimated the resolve of their Commander-In-Chief, President Douglas. She is here to demonstrate the high cost of that mis-calculation.

Later that day, Major Williams stands upon the deck of the USS Ronald Reagan aircraft carrier. It and its carrier group are now making its way to the Korean peninsula. It is to be joined by the USS Abraham Lincoln and its coterie of attendant ships, including three more destroyer class vessels. The President had made the decision for this show of force. Soon, they will make a show of force against the North Koreans. Major Williams hopes that this show, without exerting military force against North Korea, will be enough to turn them back from the border. If not, she realizes, her country will go to war to protect South Korea, even if that means that China is implicated.

They have enough pilots to fight, and just enough sailors to man both carrier groups, but their line is thinner than she and most other officers thought sustainable for a protracted conflict. Regardless, America is still America, the most powerful nation in the free world with or without two-thirds of their citizens. Recalling that her great nation had been built on the backs of their Black and Brown ancestors, Major Williams takes a bit of lukewarm comfort with her as she contemplates.

"Major Williams," a voice says behind her. Turning, she sees that it is a young Admiral, impossibly young, no more than thirty-five years old at the most, who is the commander of this aircraft carrier. It seems that so many, like herself, had been promoted in such a short amount of time. Such is the necessity of the times, she thinks.

"Yes, sir, Admiral Jones?" she hesitates, "yes, Admiral Jones. Major Jill Williams reporting for duty."

"It's good to see you, Major. All of the other pilots are now here. They're in the briefing room. I have your orders, Major. They've come directly from the White House." The new Admiral hands Major Williams a closed envelope that she accepts. She opens it. Her orders are simple in their communication: make a show of force against the gathering North Korean army. Engage the North Koreans only in self-defense or in defense of the South Koreans.

Not so simple, Major Williams thinks. War has a way of complicating matters and moving in unexpected ways. She flashbacks quickly to her bailout in Iraq over Bagdad in one of her many missions there—that was supposed to have been simple too. Nothing could have been further from the truth.

"Where do we go, Admiral?" she says.

"Right this way," Admiral Jones says.

Admiral Jones leads Major Williams down three flights of very steep steps, through a narrow corridor and into a ready room jam-packed with pilots—some old, many young, the gap between them cavernous. She is a student of air warfare and can speak volumes about the history of the use of American aircraft to fight in war. Major Williams has a particular fondness for the history of the Tuskegee Airmen and their fighting during World War II. Her Grandfather Don had been a pilot in the all Black corps of fighters. The scene before her would have been unremarkable to her grandfather, but for her it is the first time that she has been in a room of all Black, Hispanic and Asian pilots, but they seem to all be held together by one central commonality: they are all American, and they are all ready.

"Good afternoon," she begins, "I am Major Jill Williams. I am your flight commander on this mission. That mission is to first provide a show of force against the North Koreans before they cross their border into the DMZ. If they ignore the warning of our presence, we will strike certain pre-approved targets. We are not here to incite a war, but we do have the right of self-defense and defense of our South Korean allies. We don't yet have the list of approved North Korean targets. They should arrive right before take-off directly from the Pentagon. We have one-hundred pilots on this mission, sixty of which will be flying combat and the remaining forty flying support. There will be three combat groups: Alpha; Beta; and Gamma. I am leading the Beta group. Captain

Smithers, who you see standing to my left, will lead the Alpha group. And Captain Eugene, to my right, is leading the Gamma group. We'll go out with Alpha leading and Beta and Gamma following. Take off is in two hours. Please report to your squad leaders immediately after this briefing. Dismissed."

"Excuse me, Major Williams?" a young Air Force lieutenant raises his hand hesitantly.

"Yes, Lieutenant, what is it?" Major Williams responds with a slight note of irritation in her voice.

"Ma'am, please forgive my interruption. I wanted to ask you where our White pilots are? We know what's happened to most of the White folks in the States, but our White pilots stationed abroad and in the other carrier groups have not been affected by the Sleeper Virus. Are they fighting with us, or are we alone?"

Major Williams had hoped that she would not have to deal with this question. The answer is complicated. She isn't sure that she understands it either. However, she had an answer for the Lieutenant and for the others in the room.

"Lieutenant, there won't be any White pilots on this mission unless something happens to all of the rest of us. The President has ordered strict segregation of the White and non-

White groups. To the best of our understanding, each of us that's been in the States for the last week or so might be, and very likely is, a carrier for the Sleeper Virus. We cannot afford to have one more White American, one more IM, be infected by one of us. For now, all of our IM Navy and Air Force personnel are stationed within the Nixon carrier group at the President's orders. They'll back us up with heavy artillery if need be, but won't get involved unless directly called upon by the President. Does that answer it? Alright then, dismissed."

The room of pilots breaks up with the groups of twenty going to each of their squad leaders. Major Williams surveys the nineteen men and women that stand before her. She recognizes some of them either from her own flight training, or from the commercial airline ranks. She senses no trepidation in them, but this would be the first combat mission for many of them. Most had not seen actual combat or had seen it many years ago. However, she can tell from their steely-eyed dispositions that each one of them knows what is at stake: the salvation of an important ally, yes, but also, quite possibly the salvation of their own country. They are the first line of defense for their own homes in this place four thousand miles away.

After dismissing her squad, Major Williams makes her way to the officers' mess. She wants a cup of coffee and hopefully, a quiet corner where she can be alone with her thoughts. In warfare, she knows full well that anything can happen. The North Koreans might back off, and they could all draw down, or it could all go south--literally--in a hurry. Whatever happens, she is determined to maintain her command and fulfill the mission. In her reflections, Major Williams remembers a line from her favorite poem, one she had learned under stress while pledging her sorority in college:

"Out of the night that covers me,
black as the Pit from pole to pole, I
thank whatever gods there be for my
unconquerable soul."

Reaching the mess, Major Williams gets her cup of coffee and spies a chair in a corner with her name on it. Sitting down, she reflects on her wife and their children. Just like her squad, she is fighting for their lives. With America in its current condition, they are all ripe for an attack to themselves and their allies. This could be their first of many such displays of strength, she thinks. If it is the first, she is determined to make a strong show of it, and of what America can still do. Her ancestors hadn't built their nation to suddenly lose it when the responsibility of it has suddenly been thrust upon them all, she thinks. She and her family can count back to almost the year when their common enslaved ancestor traveled, forcibly, from Africa to the Carolinas where he had been enslaved and sold to a plantation in South Carolina. Major Williams' family can count back nine generations, and based upon a little modern research, knows all of the names of their ancestors counting back to the first. It had been an oral tradition, but now with modern ancestry research tools, her family has verified that tradition with the actual written records including the bills of sale for her enslaved ancestors.

Sipping her coffee slowly, Major Williams thinks about her family's history and her country's future. What has happened to their White fellow Americans is unexpected, highly unfortunate and has put their country into crisis in a manner never before seen. In spite of all of that, Major Williams is confident. The pilots on this mission are the best-trained in the world, and though few, are well- trained and competent. She does not expect it, but as Crazy Horse once said, today is a good day to die.

Raheem stares out of his cell. It is the morning and his door is open, wide open. It had been and remained that way almost since his lone Black corrections officer, Roscoe, discovered two days ago that he is all alone in this job and that no one is coming to relieve him. On the first day of this crisis, Raheem and Carlos discover that every cell block looks much like theirs' does. The White correction officers and prisoners are all unconscious. The only COs left are either black, Hispanic or Asian. The warden has not shown up to work and neither have any of his administrative staff.

Raheem, and by extension, Carlos had been drafted by Roscoe to help feed the inmates in his cellblock. Raheem is seen as a leader, but he resents, a little bit, being cast into the role of guard. He is no one's guard, he thinks. He is still as locked down as all of his fellow inmates. He and Carlos are not special, Raheem thinks, but perhaps slightly more trustworthy than some of these killers and hard core crooks.

He had only initially agreed to help Roscoe because he didn't want a single blemish on his prison record. He has a six month exit date he means to keep. If that means helping the prison be a prison, then so be it, Raheem considers to himself, but he does not like this turn of events at all. Raheem worries that somehow this crisis will lengthen his time in prison and away from Candace and his kids. He wonders how desperate he might become should he remain here with no release day in sight. He wonders.

Today, at his and Carlos' bequest, Roscoe has been allowing prisoners out of their cells about ten at a time. Raheem assures Roscoe that he will be responsible for them and will get all back into their cells for about two hours of exercise and recreation. Roscoe is hesitant at first, but he also understands that keeping the two-hundred fifty or so inmates in his cellblock locked down for twenty four hours without release can lead to catastrophic results. Roscoe is, as he has always been, concerned about the welfare of his inmates. "Alright, Raheem," he says. "We'll try this today, but you and Carlos are a) in charge and b) responsible for whatever happens. Take ten at a time to the yard and to the exercise room. Each group of ten will have two hours. Before I release another ten, you'll need to put the previous group back in lock up. I won't release a new group until everyone is accounted for. Deal?"

Raheem and Carlos agree. He knows everyone on his

cellblock and they all either respect or fear him. He is confident that they'll listen to him when it's time for each to go back into their cells. He hopes that he won't have to enforce the rule, but is prepared to if necessary. He also hopes that their current way of doing things will not last too much longer. At this point, he and Carlos realize, they're essentially keeping themselves locked up just to maintain order. Eventually, Raheem knows, that will have to change.

Seeing Candace a few days earlier had done little to assuage Raheem's anxiety. In fact, the opposite had occurred. Knowing that folks, White folks, were knocked out all over the prison and apparently all over their city for some as yet unknown reason terrifies Raheem. All of this, he knows, could impact his due date to leave and already has impacted his role in the prison. He hadn't liked prison, but he had liked his role. He is respected, has favor with the warden and most of the guards, and no one messes with him. He has privileges and had earned many good behavior credits. His only focus is in completing his term, getting out, getting a job and getting back to his life with Candace and the kids.

This gums up the works, Raheem thinks, as he prepares to

get up to make the next round of food deliveries for the inmates in his wing. Roscoe has become the de facto warden after he rounded up the ten other COs, who like him, were all men and women of color. Being the senior CO, he gave them instructions on how to carry out their duties and used Raheem and Carlos as models on what to do and who to pick.

"Hey, Raheem," Carlos says as they go about their next breakfast round, "how long do you think this is gonna last?"

"No idea, man. None. We've been going like this for a few days now. I don't know when it's going to change. And let me tell you something, Roscoe doesn't either. We've got no information coming into or out of the prison. No internet access--nothing."

"I was thinking the same thing, Homes. Eh, you know we could probably just walk out of here, right?"

And there it is. He knows that Carlos has been thinking about making a hasty retreat. Hell, he had too especially after seeing Candace. Raheem knows, however, that the better play is to stay put and let things here develop. It would be a crying shame, he thinks, to leave now and have the authorities after him in few days as a prison escapee. That could mean ten years or more added to his already too long sentence. Hells no, Raheem decides, he isn't going out like that. His plan is to stay right where he is, help Roscoe and the other COs, and keep cool until further notice.

"Carlos, we need to sit tight. This is not the time to make a bad decision. New guards or staff could be here any day. If we leave now, we'll be hunted, found and put under this joint. They'd probably ship us to a federal penitentiary for sure. No thanks. I've got Candace and my babies to think about, and you have your own family to consider as well. You don't have that much more time in here either. Follow my lead, bro, something good will happen soon, I promise."

Raheem understands Carlos' thinking very well. Carlos has more time left than him, not that much more, but more. He had gotten caught up in a grand theft auto ring and received a lengthy prison sentence as a result of it. He has a wife and a family too. He misses them terribly, but he has eighteen months, with good behavior, left to go on his sentence. He knows that he can walk out of their prison right now and no one would even try to stop him. Now, with the door all but literally wide open, the temptation to leave is almost unbearable. He could be a patient man when he had to be, but he feels Raheem was asking too much.

Sensing the thoughts in his friend's head, Raheem said

"Carlos, I feel you, I really do. But now is not the time to give up hope. Now is the time to have faith. Look at what's before us. No guards, basically, and no supervision. Yes, we can roll out any time we want to, but we'd do so and always be looking over our shoulders. That's no kind of life. Let's do it the right way. Trust me, man. We're going to be okay."

"Raheem," Carlos says, "they've got a week. Then I'm outta here."

"Fair enough, bro, fair enough," Raheem says, and he thinks that he just might join him.

*   *   *

The Oval Office is eerily quiet in the early hours of the new day as the sun makes its first peak over the horizon. The President sits in his chair behind his massive desk. He is all alone but for his thoughts. A shroud of calm and peace seems to drape about him, but mere looks are deceiving. In truth, he is the essence of exhaustion and concern. By late last night, the full scope of the problem before them is starting to take shape.

Millions are either missing, unconscious or confirmed

deceased. Billions, if not trillions, of property damage has been done. Looting is now widespread. All federal, state and local personnel are stretched thin unto breaking. Their allies are restless. World markets are crashing, and their borders are not secure. That is a singular, recurring thought for the President: for the first time in over two centuries, American borders are not secure.

In spite of his exhaustion, though, the President's mind is as sharp as ever. Two terms as President have honed his thinking and his ability to problem solve faster and at heights previously unmet. The fire of the Presidency is like that, he muses. It is similar to the high heat process that purifies gold. Though many days in office had caused him to feel a bit singed from time to time, on balance, he thinks, he had mostly shone forth. A famous former First Lady had once remarked that the Presidency doesn't make you who you are, it reveals who you are. Exactly right, the President agrees. That is exactly right, and his own First Lady would wholly agree with that sentiment.

The number one problem, according to his thinking, is the safe securement of all of their unconscious citizens. He had directed Homeland Security to launch an immediate search and rescue mission for all of their unconscious citizens—the Sleepers.

The President does not like the term 'Sleepers.' He thinks it a bit derisive and not nearly descriptive enough of the actual condition with which millions of Americans are presently suffering. Now, however, it serves as shorthand embraced by the nation's military. The President realizes that probably since its inception, the U.S. military had described friend and foe alike in one word quips meant to solidify, if not belittle, the identity of the subject of the used term. Sleepers is as good as any other word, the President thinks, but he still does not like it.

Thankfully, the head of Homeland Security had not been affected by the virus. As part of that effort, the President issued an Executive Order to immediately federalize all police regardless of locale. Those police had permission to deputize anyone that they think can help them, particularly with regard to their search and secure efforts of the Sleepers. Help is not voluntary, it is mandatory.

The number two problem, and it closely follows the first problem, is the securement of the nation's borders. Allies and enemies alike, by now, know what has happened and know who is most affected. One industry that they can still count on is the twenty-four hour news cycle. It hadn't skipped a beat since the beginning of the crisis or now. In truth, CNN, MSNBC and the other major networks did not seem that affected. One exception was FOX News. No one seemed to be home over there, and their broadcasts were spotty at best. Mostly, they seemed to be off the air until further notice. They are trying to get back on the air, but there didn't seem to have been enough people of color, SMs, to operate FOX after the Sleeper Virus struck, either behind or in front of the camera. Regardless, the President's daily briefings in the White House are now filled exclusively with Black, Brown and Yellow reporters.

Several days into the crisis, the President beams his daily briefings to Europe and Asia. As a part of these briefings, he takes questions from reporters in the White House briefing room and from reporters based outside of the country. Internationally-based reports, American and non-American alike, pepper him relentlessly with questions about the status of the Sleepers, containment of the virus, running of the country, border security, status of the military, property damage, the federalization of the police and the fact that the United States looked more like an occupied military regime than a democratic republic right now.

The President understands their alarm and attempts to

answer their questions as openly and honestly as possible given their crisis. The President senses a growing distrust from his foreign-based fellow Americans. He has told them that he has no estimated time for their travel back to the United States. He has no idea about viral containment and certainly has no good estimate for a cure. Since all air travel into and out of the country has been halted, he notes that there is no safe way back into the country. The President daily asks for patience in his briefings and tries his best to assure everyone that progress is being made and will be made. There is little else that he can do to assuage their doubt and fears, but he continues to try.

As with much of what has happened, the problem with border securement isn't an expertise problem. There are soldiers, pilots, ship operators of every color and ethnicity available for the work. There are even persons of color to operate the U.S.' massive nuclear arsenal if need be. The issue is the amount of persons to do this work. There just aren't enough hands to do the heavy lifting. If there had been enough people of color—SMs—to do all of the work, the President knows that he never would have had to federalize the nation's local and state police forces thereby pulling them altogether into one cohesive force to keep order in society.

At present, President Douglas works with his newly-constituted Joint Chiefs of Staff, General Phaylen Martin, to come up with some short and long term solutions. General Martin had answered the call the day before to head up the Joint Chiefs and to be the Pentagon head. He quickly assembled the highest ranking and most qualified persons of color for all the military branches, including the Coast Guard, to formulate their plans.

General Martin advises the President against making any big changes militarily and to take a go-slow approach for at least the short term. His reasoning centers on the fact that even with the absence of their IM population, the military is pretty well-staffed with SM personnel. Before the Sleeper Virus struck, active SM military personnel constitute about thirty-two percent of all armed forces. SM reserve personnel is less but stands at a solid twenty-five percent. The President has already made all reservists active. Together, the current military makes up close to about fifty percent of what they had been before the Sleeper Virus. Also, since there are no domestic or international flights within or without the United States for the foreseeable future, the President has conscripted, by Executive Order, all commercial pilots into the Air Force. Most of the pilots had previously served and needed a refresher. Some needed actual training for potential combat missions. Even with these measures, though, they are still short on pilots. President Douglas hopes that their enemies do not know how short that they are.

The President is worried, too, about the nation's cyber security. He has no doubt that enemies and allies alike will vigorously test their government and commercial digital vulnerabilities. There is beneficial but unexpected help for this issue that the President is glad to have. When the Sleeper Virus struck, the CEOs and senior executive staff of Google, Apple, Microsoft, and several other large computer, software and internet companies had all been out of the country for an annual show-and-tell technology retreat. This is Silicon Valley's once per year field trip to France to meet and discuss the world's latest technological advances. This conference is attended, in fact, by all of the world's leaders in digital based tech.

Though they cannot yet come home for fear of being afflicted by the Sleeper virus, they can access their home networks and their remaining staff to instruct them on proper protection of their companies and other classified governmental and non-governmental sites as well. The President advises these leaders at length that their services and their companies are now in service to their country, at least temporarily. All agree and have their teams step up to protect vital U.S. interests. Unlike some other industries in the U.S., the tech industry in Silicon Valley is very diverse. People of all hues and cultures work there, especially in locales outside of the United States. When the Sleeper Virus hit Silicon Valley, only thirty percent of its work force is directly affected. The remaining SMs, who have expertise and numbers, are able to continue almost as if nothing has happened.

Looting had, of course, begun. The President, through his National Security Advisor Trevor Campbell, gave law enforcement strict instructions to focus on identifying and cataloguing the IM population, and protecting them where necessary instead of stopping looters. The President had determined that these businesses' property is not as important as their unconscious employees, and all other unconscious citizens. As ordered, all IMs are to be transported to local hospitals until a plan to either revive or store them can be worked out. Each hospital listed as a location for IM gathering is staffed with civilian and military medical personnel. The President reluctantly allows the use of deadly force against anyone found to be harming or doing injury to an IM. He hopes that the looters get the memo and only take property from stores. No one will stop them, yet, so there is no reason to harm anyone.

Stepping out onto the porch, the President breathes in the chilly February air. He sees the sun make its full rise. With its rise he hopes that some good news comes with it. He and the nation need to hear something good. In the last few days news of IM abuse has surfaced. Abusers that could be caught have been caught and locked up until further notice. Some had been shot on sight by police and even concerned citizens. There is a feeling of lawlessness and even vigilantism. The lack of adequate courts and law enforcement personnel has, the President knows, added to the sense of lawlessness.

Gun stores throughout the country had been raided, mostly, by the new federalized police though some had also been raided by regular citizens before law enforcement could lock them down. The President's first order right after he federalized the police was to secure each and every gun and ammo store that they find. A small handful of the stores had been owned by SMs, but even those had been conscripted. Also, the President placed military personnel at the nation's gun and ammunition manufacturers two days ago.

Unfortunately, though, some of the gun and ammo shops were laid bare before the new federalized police or military could get there. Perhaps about ten percent of these shops were missed by U.S. forces. It isn't clear who is raiding these shops, but the President suspects that it is a mixed bag of folks--SMs--trying to protect themselves, protect their IMs who are their family members, and the worst of all categories, those seeking to arm up to take advantage of the current situation.

The President and his team understand that given the temptation for mischief, they will have to re-establish the courts as soon as possible. It is one thing to arrest or even shoot perpetrators in the act. It is another, however, to have a reliable judicial system. This is key to the maintenance of society, the President believes, a society that can last.

As the President contemplates all of these issues, the phone on his desk buzzes. Picking it up he hears his secretary say "Mr. President, I have former President Arthur Gates on line six for you."

"Arthur Gates? Are you certain that it's him, Margaret?" he asks. President Douglas is more than surprised because had assumed that former President Gates, his predecessor, is among the afflicted and is a Sleeper. The President hadn't sent anyone to look for Gates because he is no longer an official part of government. The President wonders, had he been out of the country? "Yes, Mr. President. It's him," his secretary responds. "He uses his presidential security code to verify. I'll patch him now."

Waiting just a moment, the President hears the clear, unmistakable southern drawl of the country's former President: "Barron, it's me. It's Arthur. How are you holding up?"

Incredulously, President Douglas says, "Better yet, Mr. President, how are YOU holding up?"

"Yeah, about that," President Gates says. "The strangest thing has happened. I'm not quite," he pauses "myself these days."

"Yourself?" The President asks. "We can probably all say that to one degree or another, Art. Where is Anne, your wife? And your daughter, Zoe?" President Douglas asks.

"Anne's asleep, Barron, unconscious. Zoe and her husband were overseas when it happened. They're still in England." President Douglas hears former President Gates stifle a sob but waits for him to continue speaking. "And I'm not exactly who or what I used to be any more. I was with Anne here, in New York, when it happened."

"Arthur, what exactly do you mean by that, you're not what you were?"

"I'm BLACK, Barron. I'm Black. Black as you. Blacker even. After I found Anne unconscious, I got a massive headache that knocked me out--literally. I woke up about sixteen hours later, rubbed my eyes, looked in the mirror, and saw a different man. From head to toe and everywhere in between. EVERY where in between," President Gates says emphatically. President Douglas understands his point.

"Arthur, have you seen anyone? Has anyone seen you?" the President asks.

"Not as of yet," President Gates responds. "We're in New York. There are no flights out. I don't want to leave Anne. I need to get her to a hospital. Two of my four guys in my security detail, Black guys, are still with me. I need to get the other two to the hospital too. I imagine that their families are likewise unconscious," he says.

Immediately realizing the stroke of good luck that had just landed upon him, President Douglas begins to think and speak quickly. "Okay, Art, listen to me. I'll have some Secret Service come and get all of you. We'll bring Anne back to D.C. with you and place her with our other key Sleeper personnel. We'll move your Sleeper Secret Service agents to close proximity with their families, who are presumably unconscious. Arthur, I need you in Washington, and I need you as part of what we're doing. We don't have all of the answers yet, but we're working hard to get them. Can I count on you?"

"Barron," he says, "Mr. President," he corrects himself, "you know that you can. I serve at the pleasure of the President."

"Okay, I'm sending a team to you by helicopter right now. We'll bring you all to the hospital at Andrews to start with, V.I.P. status to be sure. I need you to come see me at the White House right away." The former and current Presidents say their final good-byes, and then hang up. President Douglas, though still incredulous at the conversation that he had just had, is glad to hear that his friend is still among the land of the conscious. He wonders what it means that his friend, the former President, a visually obvious White male, who should himself be unconscious, has not only been stricken by the Sleeper Virus but has, apparently, been transformed by it. This is a new wrinkle, President Douglas thinks, and one that stretches the tendons of his believability beyond that which had already been stretched.

If this has happened to President Gates, perhaps he is one of many. Perhaps his transformation is one that others of their citizens are experiencing. If that's true, President Douglas reasons, then those folks must be quickly identified, re-oriented and given help to them and their loved ones.

President Douglas knows that he needs more answers. He had already suspected that Dr. Krauss had not told him everything about the Sleeper Virus and his own involvement with it. Krauss may be the only person on the planet who fully knows what is happening, he thinks. President Douglas decides to see him immediately to get the answers that he needs, even if he has to wring them from Krauss' neck.

The President walks down the narrow hallway that leads to one of the most secured parts of the White House usually reserved for dignitaries. This wing is subterranean and is rarely used. It is meant as a sort of safe house that had been added in the nineteen sixties.

The Secret Service brought Dr. Josef Krauss here at the President's direction right after their first meeting in the Oval Office. The President is unnerved by his call with the former President. He is safe and awake, but as he had said, not quite himself. President Douglas needs answers to this condition and whether, perhaps, more people have been transformed as he had. The possibility of there being thousands, perhaps millions, of transformed Americans gives the President hope that perhaps some of their IMs might be reclaimed as fully conscious and functioning people.

Arriving to Dr. Krauss' room, he finds him still in his bio-hazard suit sitting at the desk in the room working on a computer. A laptop had been provided to him. Since arriving to this location, he had been in constant contact with his researchers both in the U.S. and abroad to appraise them of conditions here, and to see whether any of his researchers are close to a cure. Upon hearing the President enter the room, Dr. Krauss looks up.

"Hello, Mr. President. How are things?" he asks.

"Things are not good, as you well know," the President replies. "Krauss, I have some questions. First, can the Sleeper Virus transform people from one color to another?"

The President watches Krauss sigh and push back from his desk. "You know, Mr. President, I wondered how long it would take before you would become aware of this. The answer to your question is no, not exactly."

The President feels himself become immediately irritated. Normally, his trademark cool would temper his responses, but not today.

Moving quickly toward Krauss, the President grabs him strongly by his suit and raises him up out of his chair, pressing him solidly into the closest wall. "Krauss", the President says through gritted teeth, "exactly what do you mean by 'not exactly'? And don't feed me any of your half-story bullshit. I need to know everything."

Krauss' arms flail beside him as he sputters and coughs inside of his suit. "Mr. President," he coughs out, "Please! You'll rip the suit! You'll rip the suit!" he exclaims.

"I don't give a damn about you or this suit!" the President shoots back. "I need answers. You need to start talking now!" The President lets Dr. Krauss go for a moment and allows him to collect himself. When he lets him go, Dr. Krauss bends over at the waist and places his hands on his knees. He is badly shaken.

After several more deep breaths, he begins to speak slowly. "Mr. President, towards the end of our trials, as we realized that the captured viral material had begun to mutate, we saw some increased pigmentation in our lighter-skinned subjects. We hadn't seen it in any of our animal testing, but yes, there were ten

incidents in which subjects, who had taken Zoesterol, became

darker. At the time, no one understood why this had happened.

The change was irreversible. You can imagine what would have

happened if we had allowed this news to get out. So, we hid it

from the FDA and hid the subjects from everyone, including their

families. We put them all on private jets out of the country and

placed them in our lock down research facility in Munich—it's not

unlike this place, actually."

"What about now, Dr. Krauss, any theories?" the President

asks, taking a step back from him. The President also eases the

intensity in his voice.

"I was just discussing that very issue when you walked in,

Sir. Our current theory is that those persons afflicted who go, as

it were, from light to dark, are persons who are able to generate a

sort of anti-body response to the Sleeper Virus. But they are also

persons whose bodies have the ability, on demand and under stress,

to produce sufficient melanin to prevent them from becoming

made permanently unconscious. It's almost like a reflex action

built into their bodies. But the production of melanin does not just

happen internally, it also happens at the upper epidermal level, the skin. The genes that produce melanin to this degree would almost assuredly have to be contributed from a non-Caucasian ancestor, an SM rather than an IM."

The President stands in silence for a moment absorbing what he has just heard. He remembers reading about Thomas Jefferson and the children that the he'd fathered with Sally Hemmings. Those children, it is said, were able to enter White society as adults because they could pass as White. It is possible then that Jefferson's descendants, and many families like them, carry the genes necessary to produce melanin and survive this virus. The President is heartened by the possibility that modern day Americans like Jefferson's descendants are alive and awake albeit darker than they were just three days ago. If that's true, he thinks, we might not be in quite the dire straits that it has appeared to be.

"Dr. Krauss, about what percentage of the U.S. White population can we expect to be transformed by the Sleeper Virus?" he asks.

"Sir, I can't give you an exact percentage. But we think, and this is only a theory, we think that about fifteen to twenty percent of the White population should manifest this change."

Fifteen to twenty percent—the President muses. That could

do it. That could be enough folks to help keep this thing together.

"Dr. Krauss, keep doing what you're doing. We need a cure as soon as possible. I'll require a daily briefing from you and your efforts. You're the closest thing to an expert that we have. If you need anything, let my staff know." As the President exits and makes his way back up to the Oval Office, he knows that all of Dr. Krauss' communications are being monitored. He'll know if Krauss lies to him or tries to keep anything else hidden. For now, President Douglas thinks, he needs to get his stop staff onto a new mission: find as many of the transformed IMs as possible and get them involved in the maintenance and preservation of their country.

*   *   *

An hour later, the President sits at his desk in contemplation of the day and waits for his top staff to rejoin him. Trevor Campbell and Valerie King hurriedly enter the Oval Office and stand directly in front of him with, apparently, urgent news.

"Mr. President," Valerie says, "We have some bad news. North Korea has declared war against South Korea. They've amassed troops at the border and say that they will strike in the next twenty-four hours."

CHAPTER VII

Leaving the hospital, Donnie decides to start in the center of downtown Chicago, somewhere close to Michigan Avenue and the Magnificent Mile to begin his search for unconscious people. There are many large buildings downtown for residency and work. He thinks that if there is a large concentration of unconscious people outside, this will be it. Donnie never thought that he would use his new car like this, but he's grateful that he can help.

He goes over the scene in his mind at the hospital. Emergency staff and, apparently, volunteers from the hospital assembled outside to intake drop offs like Donnie's two people. Steven, the maintenance guy at the hospital, had been drafted because they were short-staffed. Donnie then remembers the message blared from his favorite Chicago radio station about some sort of conspiracy with White people and the unconscious. As he drives on, Donnie turns his radio on to the station that he had last heard.

"FAM, THIS IS WKYS IN CHICAGO. WE HAVE CONFIRMATION OF WHAT WE'VE BEEN TOLD. YOU CAN CHECK OUR TWITTER AND FACEBOOK FEEDS IF YOU HAVE INTERNET. THAT MIGHT BE SPOTTY THOUGH.

INTERNET SEEMS TOUCH AND GO ALL OVER THE CITY.
ANYWAY, WE'VE GOT ACTUAL PICTURES OF FOLKS,
WHITE FOLKS, UNCONSCIOUS ALL OVER THE CITY,
WELL, AT LEAST THE WHITE PARTS. THEY'RE NOT
DEAD. I REPEAT, THEY'RE NOT DEAD, UNLESS, THAT IS,
THEY'VE BEEN INVOLVED IN SOME SORT OF ACCIDENT.
WE DON'T KNOW IF THEY CAN WAKE UP. WE'RE
GETTING CONFLICTING REPORTS ON THAT. LOCAL LAW
ENFORCEMENT IS TELLING US TO TELL YOU TO GET
EM OUTTA THE ELEMENTS—TAKE EM TO A HOSPITAL.
AND OTHERWISE DO THEM NO HARM. CHICAGO PD CAN
SHOOT ON SIGHT IF THEY SEE ANYONE HURTING OR
LOOTING FROM ANY OF THESE UNCONSCIOUS FOLKS.
YOU KNOW WHAT THAT IS. BE SMART, FAM."

Donnie lowers the volume on his radio. He wants to take a moment to consider all that he's seen and heard thus far. What the DJ has just said comports with what he has experienced. His office is empty except for himself, the only Black employee at his firm, at least on his floor. He had taken two unconscious White folks to the hospital. All of the workers that he saw were either Black or otherwise persons of color. This seemed to be happening all over the country based upon the news reporting and had definitely impacted Chicago and surrounding areas.

Donnie soon turns onto Michigan Avenue and begins a slow crawl down the Magnificent Mile. There is no traffic to speak of. He sees cars parked along the avenue, but no cars or buses are in operation. As he approaches the Nike store on Michigan, he sees them. About one dozen people are laid out in a strangely orderly fashion right in front of the store. A separation rope extends from the front door by about thirty feet. Donnie realizes that today must have been one of the company's famous new shoe drops, and that these persons are would be customers. They must have been here before the sun came up, Donnie thinks.

He also sees about a half dozen conscious folks, various persons of color, bending over and checking the unconscious people. Donnie stops in front of the Nike store and puts his blinkers on, something that he would never be able to do on any other regular day. He gets out and walks over to one of the unconscious people and looks down at him. He is male, White and about twenty-two years old. He isn't dressed adequately enough for this cold February day, Donnie sees, and Donnie decides to pick him up first and get him to his car. He grabs the man by one of his cold hands and prepares to carefully lift him and then walk him to his car when he feels a strong hand on his shoulder.

"Bruh, what are you doing?" Donnie hears. He turns around to see a large Black man of about forty looking intensely at Donnie. His voice is full of warning. Donnie decides to speak quickly.

"Sir, my name is Donnie. I just left the hospital on E. 51st Street. I dropped off a couple of folks just like this. The hospital asked me to find more and take them there."

The man releases his grip on Donnie's shoulder and a look of recognition crosses his face. "Man, I would do the same thing but I don't have a car. I've just been finding these folks all morning and trying to help 'em as best I can. I've had to put hands on a couple folks with bad intent. This shit is crazy." Donnie relaxes a bit and is glad that he did not get cross-wise with this large gentleman.

"What is your name, sir?" Donnie asks.

"Clarence, my name is Clarence," he says. "Here, let me help you. Is that your car? Looks like you can carry a few. I can help with that." Clarence then easily picks up the young man that Donnie had intended on helping. With little effort, he puts the man in the front seat of Donnie's car and straps him in. Donnie then identifies three more unconscious people to put into his car, and Clarence obliges him by helping him to get them into his car.

"Clarence, I appreciate the help. I'll be back right here just as soon as I get these four folks dropped off. Will you still be here?"

"Yep, I'll be here until these dozen or so folks are squared away. When you get finished up, I'll roll with you to find some others. Deal?" Clarence says, now showing an incomplete, toothy grin.

"Deal," Donnie says, now totally comfortable with his new compatriot.

*   *   *

Leaving the San Francisco airport, Sabrina and Isaac ride at a slow crawl from the airport's entrance to the 101 freeway. Cell service is spotty. Isaac's GPS on his phone is intermittent, a casualty of the cell service outages. Sabrina feels fortunate that she is able to speak with her mother in the airport when she did.

Their vehicle, a late model SUV, itself has GPS, but it also seems dependent on the same cell service upon which Isaac's phone is based. "I think that we should drive over to the Cabrillo Highway on the coast" Isaac says. "If the radio reports are to be believed, we'll run into a lot of trouble crash-wise by traveling either on the 101 or interstate 280. What do you think, Sabrina?"

Sabrina isn't sure. This was no time to take a scenic overview of California, she thinks. Either the 101 or the 280 would be much faster, but if there are crashes on either that they can't get past, they'll either have to get out and hoof it or get to another car down the way, neither option providing much relief or comfort. Looking at Isaac, Sabrina realizes that she'd be responsible for herself and literally pushing Isaac to L.A. They are several hundred miles away from home, she knows. "I think that you're right, Isaac. It's a longer route but probably the safest in terms of our ability to drive it. If the radio reports are accurate, the Cabrillo Highway is the best way to go. That means, of course, that we'll have to figure out a route to it without GPS or a map." Isaac chuckles at that and says, "Just head west and turn left once we get to the highway— seems simple." Simple enough, Sabrina thinks. "We'll see," she says.

Isaac touches the map icon on the screen in the dash of their SUV. "Let me see if I can key in a route. Who knows? It might work this time, at least long enough to show us the right route. If it does, I'll take a picture of it with my phone and we'll have it that way." Sabrina is impressed with Isaac's ingenuity. He definitely reminds her of her dad, who studied civil engineering while in college. "That's a great idea, Isaac. Gives us a little more to go on other than just *drive west*." Isaac immediately takes her meaning and feigns offense. "You've cut me to the quick, dear Madam" he jokes. "I would have thought a fine, educated young woman such as yourself would have already sorted this out," he says placing his right hand on his chest to signify his faux offense. They both crack up just then. It is a much-appreciated moment of levity before they begin what they both suspect could be a grueling ride home.

Isaac finishes keying in the first part of their destination to the Cabrillo Highway. The GPS doesn't respond. It looks like one of the screens on a computer that has received its commands but is waiting to execute. A spinning circle spins endlessly in the center of the screen. Sabrina decides to exit the highway and drive due west on the local streets until she can determine better where the next highway is. They exit into the neighborhood of San Bruno, a neighborhood of mostly modest looking homes, but Sabrina and Isaac both correctly guess that real estate here is in the $1,000,000 territory and above. The streets are clean and the homes well-maintained.

"Isaac, look," Sabrina says as she makes a right from the highway. "I see them, Sabrina" he says. As Sabrina drives down San Bruno Avenue, they see several people laid out on the sidewalk and even in doorways. Sabrina points to a young-looking couple that had been pushing a stroller that were half in and half out of the door way of a coffee shop that sits on the corner of San Bruno Avenue and another street. "Holy crap, Isaac! That's a baby in that stroller," she says. "I need to check that out. Need to see if the baby is okay."

"Okay, Sabrina," but be careful. "We still don't know what's going on. We could become affected too." Noting Isaac's caution and the worried look on his face, Sabrina reconsiders getting out of the SUV, but her concern for the baby overwhelms her concern of her and Isaac's safety. She parks the SUV on the corner right next to the coffee shop. Placing it in park, Sabrina then looks in every direction around them. She doesn't see any activity.

The only presence of any other humans are she and Isaac and the several dozen or so folks laid out around them on the sidewalk.

Sabrina cautiously exits their vehicle and motions to Isaac to lock it once she's out. She still hasn't taken a step forward after closing her door. She hears the click of the lock go down when Isaac locks the door. She hopes that she has not made a mistake. If something bad happens to her, she knows that Isaac is in trouble too. He may not be able to drive himself back to L.A. She needs to be doubly careful, she thinks.

Taking a deep breath, Sabrina walks directly to the baby stroller that sits right outside of the coffee shop. The people who look to be the baby's parents are a youngish, thirty-something couple, White, and dressed in sweats. It is a chilly day in the Bay Area, about forty-five degrees. The sun is up, and it is bright. Sabrina wonders how long they have all been here. She looks at her watch and sees that it is close to 11:30 a.m. They've probably been here a few hours, she thinks, as she approaches the stroller.

Sabrina looks in the stroller and finds a sleeping baby. By her dress, she correctly guesses that the baby is a girl. She appears to be about three months old. Sabrina reaches into the stroller and picks her up. Sabrina sees that she is wrapped in a bright pink blanket and has on a onesie. The blanket has the name Gina embroidered onto it. "Little Baby Gina," Sabrina said. "Are you unconscious like your parents or are you just asleep?" Sabrina does not know which, and she is no doctor.

As she holds Gina in her harms, Sabrina walks over to her parents, or who she thinks are her parents. The father is half-in and half-out of the entrance to the coffee shop. The mother is all the way out and lays right next to Gina's stroller. Each has a coffee cup lying next to them, both having spilled their contents onto the sidewalk. Mom is pretty with bright golden hair. Dad has dark hair and has long thin limbs, a runner, Sabrina guesses.

"Okay, Gina, what are we to do with you? We can't leave you here, and we can't take your parents with us." Sabrina looks over at Isaac ensconced behind the heavy frame of their SUV. The look of worry is still there, but he wordlessly communicates to Sabrina his recognition of their dilemma. Leaving the parents where they are is one thing, but leaving this baby is quite another. Sabrina places Gina back into her stroller and rolls it over to the SUV. Isaac unlocks the driver side door and she opens it.

"You see what we have here, right?" Sabrina says.

"Yep. We're in a damned if we do, damned if we don't

situation. Cannot leave the baby here," Isaac intones.

"Exactly. What are our options? Take the baby to L.A.? What if the parents wake up later today or tomorrow? Now we're kidnappers as well as car thieves," Sabrina says.

"There's another option, Sabrina."

"And what is that, Isaac?"

"We take the baby to the nearest hospital. There's gotta be people there working just like there are people at the airport working. We're probably in an emergency services and personnel kind of situation. They can take the baby and we can be on our way."

Sabrina bites her lip as she considers Isaac's proposal. She still doesn't feel good about separating Gina from her parents. They probably will wake up, she thinks, and then absolutely lose their shit when they see that Gina is gone. She knows that she would if placed into the same situation.

Sabrina opens the left side passenger door. Gina's stroller is formed into two parts: a detachable basket and a collapsible base with wheels. She detaches the basket from the base and places it on the seat directly behind her and secures it tightly. Sabrina had never done this before, but it seems straight forward. She then collapses the base and puts it into the trunk of the SUV. Once Gina is secure, Sabrina walks back over to Gina's parents. She pulls he father fully into the coffee shop and sits him upright onto the closest wall. Next, she partially lifts Gina's mom up by her torso and drags her into the coffee shop sitting her next to dad. Sabrina walks over to the counter and looks for a pen and pad. Securing one, she writes a short note telling Gina's parents what happened, where they are taking Gina—"the nearest hospital"—and Sabrina's contact information. She writes this note twice, and places one each into the pockets of Gina's parents. As she does this, Sabrina tries not to notice the half dozen collapsed patrons, including staff, in the coffee shop. Before leaving, she gives the shop a quick look over to make sure that none of the collapsed, unconscious people are in a precarious position. Seeing none, she exits the coffee shop after giving Gina's parents her notes.

As Sabrina walks swiftly back to her and Isaac's SUV, she hears the click-clack of the locks popping up. Opening the door, she sits down and begins to speak when Isaac cuts her off. "Already on it, Sabrina. I've got the closest hospital dialed into the GPS. It seems to be working again right in this area." He points to the screen in the dash and she sees that they're 1.5 miles away

219

from the closest hospital. "Okay, let's go, Isaac. Hopefully, there will be folks there just like at the airport. We'll get Gina squared away and then be on our way. Look, I found this." Sabrina hands Isaac a driver's license. "Is this Gina's mom?" he asks. "I believe so," Sabrina responds. "It was in the clutch that she carried. I figure that we'll give it to whatever doctor or nurse we find. I left notes with each of the parents too."

"That's good thinking, Sabrina," Isaac says with a slight smile. "You'll make an excellent mother someday, that is, assuming that you're not already one."

Sabrina chuckles at that. "No, not yet. My fiancé want a big family though. We'll see. I don't know which end is up right now though."

"Trudat," Isaac says echoing the slang of the early nineties. Gosh, Sabrina thinks, Isaac really is old.

Sabrina puts the SUV in drive and begins to follow her GPS' instructions to the hospital. "Let's get this show on the road, Isaac. Hopefully, we won't see any more babies."

"Or people," Isaac says. "I wish that we could stay and help them all, but we've got to get going."

"Trudat," she says and winks at Isaac, who smiles broadly at her.

*   *   *

It is a little past 3:00 p.m. and the sun is starting to go
down on this cold Chicago day. Donnie has dropped off three
more folks to one of the three local hospitals that he has visited
today. The scene at each is pretty much the same. Scores of
emergency personnel are at each place. Their primary work seems
to be the intake of unconscious people found on the street and in
their homes. The radio stations that he listens to have broadcast
instructions all day about what to do and what not to do with
any and all found unconscious persons. Donnie had seen and
heard about conscious folks finding their unconscious neighbors
and getting them to a hospital. He had also heard about some
unconscious people being badly used or killed before someone
could get them to safety. Donnie promises himself that if he sees
anyone harming any of the unconscious that he'll stop them and
get the person to safety.

After this drop off, Donnie turns out of the hospital's
parking lot and drives toward Michigan Avenue where he had first
seen Clarence. He drives back to the Nike store on Michigan and
sees him standing by the front door. There are fewer unconscious

221

people than there had been previously, Donnie sees. He looks exhausted. Donnie wonders if Clarence has been here all day keeping watch. That's exactly what it looks like to him.

"Just two more to go, Donnie," Clarence says as Donnie drives up with the passenger side window down.

"Wow, Clarence, you've really held it down today. Where are the others?"

"They've been transported to a few of the local hospitals. Somebody official came by here right after you left with some instructions. She put me in charge of protecting the folks here. Said she was from Homeland Security. Showed me a badge and everything. Tall Black woman. Very pretty. Looked like she was Amazonian or from Wakanda or some place. I'm waiting now for the next transport to pick up these last two, then we can bounce" Clarence says.

"Fair enough, C. Is it okay if I call you "C"?" Donnie asks.

"Sure, my man, no problem," Clarence responds. "I even had to fight off a few people to keep them from robbing or otherwise harming these folks. It was rough. Haven't had any trouble since then, though."

"Okay," Donnie says. "Would you like to wait in the car

with me? There's no point to standing out in this cold while we wait."

"Sure, Donnie. Thanks for that. It's been cold as heck out here all day. Let's put these last two unconscious folks into your car while we wait. Come on, help me with them."

Donnie gets out of his car and he and Clarence lift their first charge together and put him in to Donnie's car. He is a young White male, Donnie sees, no more than eighteen years old and thankfully very light. Their next charge is another White male, this one older, about twenty-five years old. Donnie wonders if either or both are high-end athletic show re-sellers like the ones he's heard so much about who buy exclusive kicks and then resells them at much higher margins on-line. Once the second unconscious male is placed into Donnie's car, he and Clarence also get in and warm their hands on the heater.

"Where you from, Donnie?" Clarence asks.

"Dallas. Born and raised. My family's been there for at least four generations. Since slavery is what they tell me."

"Huh. I've got some kinfolk in Houston, but not Dallas. Can't get them nigros to leave Texas for nothing. They absolutely love it there," Clarence remarks.

About five minutes after they get into Donnie's car, two

ladies pull up in a station wagon behind them. Both appear to

be Hispanic. "Hola, Clarence!" Donnie hears one of them shout.

Clarence opens his door and says "Hola, Senora!!" The woman

and Clarence give each other a deep, affectionate hug. "These the

last two?" She says to Clarence. "Si, Mami, they're it. Thanks for

all of your work today. This is my friend Donnie," Clarence says

motioning for Donnie to get out of the car.

Donnie gets out of his car and walks toward the back,

happy to be meeting more workers like him. "Hey, Ladies, como

esta? Crazy day, huh?"

"Hello, Donnie!" The first woman says, and gives him a

hug. She's at least fifty-five and somebody's grandmother, Donnie

thinks. "So glad that you're out here with us. We've been picking

up strays, our word for them, all day. Been taking them to the local

hospitals just like the radio said. Thankfully, we haven't had too

much trouble, except picking them up. Some are ungodly heavy."

"Hola, Donnie," he hears a small voice speak to him. In

the presence of this august grandmother, he'd nearly forgotten that

there is another woman with her. Donnie looks at her fully and has

to work to maintain his cool. This young woman is clearly some relation to the grandmother. She is about five feet, four inches tall, long black hair, full lips, light brown skin and the physique of a dancer. She is beautiful, Donnie thinks. Her big brown eyes provide the exclamation to her pulchritude.

"Oh, Donnie, this is my granddaughter Isabella. Isabella, meet Donnie." Isabella extends her hand to Donnie, all while looking up at him. Donnie feels lost for a moment but recovers enough to extend his hand and gently shake hers. He suddenly feels too warm and wonders if the scarf wrapped around his neck is too much. He should take it off, he thinks.

Clearing his throat, Clarence cuts into Donnie's thoughts and Donnie pulls away from Isabella. "And Donnie, this is Ms. Marquita, a life-long friend. When I called her and told her what was happening, she immediately came over and started to help me transport folks out of here. She's the reason that we can now leave. C'mon, D., let's get these strays into the back of their station wagon and get on to our next thing."

Donnie immediately complies, happy to be distracted from Isabella's eyes. They load the two unconscious folks into the back of Ms. Marquita's car in short order. "What's next for you, Marquita?" Clarence asks. "We'll get these two dropped off and then probably head in. It's getting dark and I don't want to be out here then. Isabella and I will head home. What about you?"

"Oh, we'll probably hit a couple more neighborhoods tonight. Donnie's been hitting downtown which is fine, but with his help, I'll probably hit some other areas like South Loop, Hyde Park and such. There's got to be a ton of folks not attended to in those areas. Need to get them out of the elements. It's gonna be another cold night."

"That sounds right, Clarence," Marquita says. "Be careful though. I'm hearing some disturbing things. Police have their hands full and they're super short-staffed as you might imagine. I've only seen Black and Hispanic officers today. So be careful," Marquita reiterates. "Oh and Donnie, when you and Clarence are done, you can come over for coffee and cake" she says with a smile and twinkle in her eye. Donnie looks at Isabella and sees that she has her head down, but also a small smile on her face. "Uh, thanks, Ms. Marquita. If Clarence thinks it's a good idea, we'll be over. Wanna go see," he hesitates slightly before clearing his throat "who else we can help first." Donnie hears Clarence chuckle. "Okay, Ladies, we might check you later. Get home safe. We'll be in these streets for a little while."

Clarence and Marquita hug their farewells, and they all get into their respective vehicles and start their drives to their separate locales.

"That was smooth, Donnie, real smooth" Clarence says chiding his new friend.

"What, C., what are you talking about?"

"Nothing, Donnie, nothing. Let's head down over to South Loop. Do you know how to get there?"

"Yep, I got it. Girl I used to date lives over there. I hope that she's okay."

"Don't take the expressway, we have no idea what's there. Take the street," Clarence says.

"Cool, I got it."

Clarence and Donnie begin the short drive to the South Loop neighborhood hoping to be able to help any unconscious people that they see. Both know that with the cold night coming, their efforts could save lives. Neither of them had a day that had gone as planned, but at close to sunset on this day, both had renewed focus and purpose. "Let's get it done, Donnie. Heaven only knows how many people need our help."

The largest hospital that is closest to Isaac and Sabrina seems to be the California Pacific Medical Center. Sabrina had been there a few times when her fiancé had applied for his hospital internships after medical schools. As a concession to her, Michael applied for an internship there to be closer to Sabrina, though he had really wanted to be in New York. He had gotten the offer, but she relented in her demand once she saw how much he wanted to go back home. He'd done medical school at UCLA to suit her and her career in L.A. She thought it would be tough for him to live so far away, but she had wanted to support him too. Their mutual faith and trust in one-another had paid off, at least until this calamity had struck, she thinks.

"It's just a few miles away, Isaac, but it's back in San Francisco. Thankfully, we don't need to cross any bridges or hit any high ways to get there. It's pretty much a straight shot from here," Sabrina says.

"If it's our best option, Sabrina, then let's go. We need to get baby Gina to some folks who can care for her" Isaac says.

Sabrina points their SUV toward the hospital, and drives

at a fairly brisk clip, slowing down only to avoid any accidents or people that she sees. She and Isaac decide not to stop again unless there is a child in distress. They see a fair number of unconscious folks laid out on the side walk, behind the wheels of their cars and trucks and a few in the street itself. In a few instances, Sabrina stops and pulls any street fallen unconscious folks from the street to the sidewalk out of immediate harms' way. She and Isaac had seen at least two of the unconscious in the street who looked like they had been run over. They also see a fair number of folks like them who appear to be picking up many of the unconscious and putting them into their vehicles. Sabrina hopes that their intentions are good, and that they're taking them somewhere safe like they're doing for baby Gina.

They soon arrive to the hospital a few minutes later. Baby Gina is no worse for wear and is still asleep. Now, Sabrina and Isaac both think that she's more than just asleep. She's unconscious just like her parents are. There seems to be light activity by the front most doors of the hospital, a sprawling complex. Isaac sees that there are more people going in and out of the emergency entrance of the hospital. "Look, Sabrina, over there by the emergency entrance. There's a line of cars pulling up to it. It looks like folks are delivering the unconscious just as we are. Let's go over there."

Sabrina slowly pulls the SUV into the line that Isaac points out. She is again glad that he is with her, helping her sort this calamity out. The line is long and they're about the twentieth car in line. They see hospital staff going to each car with wheel chairs and gurneys, speaking with each car's driver and writing down information on clip boards. "This must be their intake for the unconscious, Isaac. We should be able to drop Gina here. But we'll ask some critical questions first," Sabrina says. "Fair enough," Isaac responds.

Remarkably, the line moves with unexpected alacrity. What initially looked like might take an hour or more, takes only twenty minutes for Sabrina and Isaac to reach the front of the line. Looking back, Sabrina sees that the line has only grown with it now extending at least thirty cars behind her and out of her sight as it bends around the corner.

A hospital worker comes to her window and motions for her to let her window down.

"Who you got, Ms.?" He says.

"We've got one, a baby. She's no more than three months

old," Sabrina says.

"A baby?" The worker queries. "Any I.D.? No parents? We've taken in a few babies, but they've been with their parents. Have any info on the baby's parents?"

The rapid fire questioning of the worker makes Sabrina's head spin. She thinks for a moment about why they hadn't also grabbed the parents. She remembers that she would have had to do so by herself without Isaac's help and thought the task too much for her. She now wonders if she should have just made the effort to keep the family together.

"The parents are at this address," Sabrina says telling the worker the address of where she found them. "Here are the names of the parents according to their I.D.'s. Can you match the baby to them when they get here or wherever they end up?"

The worker shrugs his shoulders. "We'll try, but as you can see, we've got our hands full just trying to get folks in here. We're short-staffed with at least half our folks either not here or collapsed behind a desk somewhere. About the best that we can do is get folks logged in and into a room with a bed. If we get too full, we'll load folks into our waiting areas. At least those have couches and chairs."

Sabrina looks at Isaac. He reads her concern and the question behind her eyes. "We can't go back, Sabrina. We've got to push forward. This has been enough of a," Isaac hesitates, "distraction. We need to press forward. Don't you agree?"

She does but she does not want to admit it. Sabrina looks back at the hospital worker. She gives him the remaining information to identify Baby Gina and her parents. Sabrina gets out of the SUV and pulls Gina's basket from the back seat. Sabrina sees that she is still asleep. She hands her to the worker and then gets her collapsed stroller for him. "Here, sir, you can place her on this. It clicks in. Where will she go now?"

"All babies go to the children's part of the hospital. Eventually, we're transporting all children to Children's Hospital right down the block. Actually, you could have taken her there first. There's a whole crew doing intake over there too. But we've got her now and will get her there."

"Hey, Roger!! Is that a baby?!"

The hospital worker, Roger, turns at hearing his name called. "Yeah, Tone, we've got another one. Want to take her?"

"Yep, I'm loaded without about four right now. Taking all to Children's. Already in a stroller? Great! That'll make it easier.

We're walking them down. No more transports," Tone says.

Sabrina sees that she and Gina will soon be parted. She places her hand onto Gina's stroller and says a prayer of safety and protection for her. "You promise that she'll be okay?" Sabrina asks Roger and Tone. "Yeah," Tone says, "she'll be fine. We've been collecting little White babies all day. We'll get her logged in. Roger, please give me the information on her parents so that we can get her assigned."

Roger hands Tone the information that Sabrina supplied him. "Just hold it up. I'll take a picture of it on my phone. There, got it. Okay, we're out." Tone pushes Gina away in her stroller. Sabrina watches him join with two more workers who are all either holding or pushing a number of babies and small children away from the emergency entrance.

"There's a long subterranean hallway that connects this hospital with Children's. They'll move them through there to keep them out of the elements. Baby Gina will be fine, Ms." Roger says speaking to Sabrina.

As Sabrina watches Gina and the other babies and children be wheeled away, she can't help but feel a sudden impulse to rush to her, grab her back and take her back to L.A. with her. She doesn't want to leave her. In the course of an hour, she had bonded with the child in a way that feels primal. Sabrina is not sure if this how mothers feel, but she knows that she feels something powerful for the child. "Sabrina, we need to go." The sound of Isaac's voice startles her. Sabrina looks at Isaac and sees his gentle, yet firm eyes. "Yes, of course. You're right. Let's go then," she says pulling herself away from the spot at which she had been watching Gina wheel away from her.

Sabrina gets back into the SUV and puts her seat belt on. The audible click of the belt seems to anchor her back into their present reality. There is calamity all around them. They are several hundred miles away from home. Isaac needs to get to his ailing and perhaps dying wife. She needs to get home and somehow get connected back to Michael. It's time to go. They've waited long enough, she reluctantly admits.

Wheeling out of the hospital's driveway, Isaac sets the vehicle's GPS to Los Angeles and chooses the Cabrillo Highway as their preferred route. "Well, alright!" Isaac says. "Looks like we've got a connection. That's great! Isn't that great, Sabrina?" Sabrina smiles weakly and looks at the screen to see what its instructions are. She needs to travel on their current route for about five miles, then make a left onto another street and then on to the highway after that. It looks pretty straightforward. In place of her worry about their travel, Sabrina feels sadness and a twinge of regret at having left Gina with complete strangers and without her parents. "Sabrina, you did the right thing. Gina is in better hands than ours right now. She can get the care and help that she needs. And they know who her parents are and where they are. It'll be enough, hopefully."

Of course, Isaac is right. That does not mean that she has to like it. "I know," Sabrina says. "I've never felt anything like this before. It's a bit overwhelming. Lord, please protect and keep Baby Gina. Amen."

"Amen," Isaac says in agreement.

Soon, Sabrina and Isaac make their way to the Cabrillo Highway. They had been right. It is virtually clear of traffic and they see no accidents, at least initially. Hopefully, Sabrina thinks, they'll get home quickly and without any more hiccups. Looking at the gas gauge, Sabrina sees that it's almost full. She soon hears Isaac's deep breathing and sees that he sleeps. Sabrina wonders for a moment whether Isaac has succumbed to the unconscious illness but sees him scratch his bearded cheek and roll to one side.

Chuckling to herself, Sabrina wonders at this God-sent man who had shown up at the right time to help her and receive help himself. Alright Isaac, she thinks, you sleep. I'll get us home. And then we'll see what all of this is really about.

CHAPTER VIII

President Douglas walks into the Situation Room in an agitated state. His volcanic interior matches his now volatile exterior. He is angry that his country finds itself in this unnecessary provocation with North Korea. He is furious at the Chinese President and chief Chinese ambassador to Washington for lying to him about their influence upon North Korea to help cause its provocation.

Before the threatened military assault on South Korea, he had been on the phone over the course of two days with the Chinese President and had met face-to-face with his ambassador to Washington, D.C., who like most of the personnel in the Chinese Embassy, are not affected by the Sleeper Virus. Both assured him of their concern in this situation and appealed for peace. It is laughable, President Douglass thinks at the time, and he believes that they are both laughing at him. President Douglas remembers the lyrics to a particularly edgy rap song by Ice Cube—Laugh now, cry later—and feels the heat of his determination rise against both the ruler of North Korea and China's President. They might be laughing now, but the President fully intends to cause them sufficient pain for years to come. North Korea may begin to experience some of that pain with the destruction of part of its army and key facilities if they don't back down, he thinks.

"What's our status?" President Douglas asks his joint chiefs. His tone is all business with none of the usual levity or caution for which he is known.

"Sir," the Joint Chiefs say, "both requested carrier groups are in position. Their destroyers have also been placed just off of North Korea's coast. Jets are on the tarmac, their pilots are all in place. Major Williams is awaiting your target orders. It's five minutes to the scheduled flights of the Alpha, Beta and Gamma combat groups. You have the command, Mr. President."

The President sits down in the large leather chair at the head of the table. The level of tension in the Situation Room is high. He is on edge and his generals are as well. Every face now wearing the general insignia is new, save that of General Martin. He is the quiet calm in the room, his face etched with the memory of wars gone by. General Martin looks at the President thoughtfully and makes his way to him until he stands next to him. Choosing the closest chair to him, the General sits down. Others in the room see this and edge away to allow them a private word.

"Mr. President," he leans in to say, "this is a tough situation. It's tougher than Bin Laden. The country's on the line. But, Mr. President, you were made for this. You're the President of this time, and not any of the guys or ladies who fought you for this job. You're it. Those other contenders," he says emphasizing the word 'other,' "are all asleep right now. But you, you're wide awake and ready. You're ready, Mr. President. You're ready," he says with finality. General Martin stands up and lays a reassuring hand on the President's shoulder, briefly. He then walks back toward the generals huddled around the main monitor. The President regards them for a moment, and then clears his throat.

"Ladies and gentlemen, let's proceed. Send the strike locations to Admiral Murray." The President had kept the locations secret until it was go time. "Tell Admiral Murray to communicate the locations to each one of the squadron commanders. If it becomes necessary, the squadrons will strike those locations on my orders. I also have another contingency in place should it become necessary to use it," he says. "But for now, launch the squadrons." President Douglas sits back in his chair and observes his generals and commanders who are now abuzz with activity due to his orders. He prays a silent prayer for his troops, their success and their safety.

*   *   *

Major Williams surveys the cock-pit of her F-22 Raptor fighter jet. This plane itself is new to her, but she'd flown one like it in the Iraq war. Looking around at the pilots in her command, she silently notes that about half of them had flown the Raptor, but the other half had flown it in simulation only. Computers are great for basic prep, she thinks, but how would they do in a genuine firefight of combat, she wonders. In spite of her fears, Major Williams realizes that everyone who can fly and fight must do so. Easily two-thirds of their fighter pilots are asleep or otherwise on stand-by in this conflict according to President Douglas' orders. She assures herself that everyone in her squadron is a skilled pilot and that would have to be enough. She trusts their training, if not the pilots themselves. The training is the thing, she thinks.

Major Williams stands in a hangar one level below the runway of the Air Force carrier. Near her is a large screen that displays information related to their impending mission. She and others stand nearby the screen expecting to receive their flight and combat orders at any moment. Three piercing beeps cut through the air announcing their orders. She soon sees the flight plan

240

and combat plan flash across the screen. Interesting, she thinks. The President's plan is bold, but measured. North Korea has an out in this if it chooses to take it. If not, she sees, their country will be badly damaged, at least its military installations will be. Though Major Williams had voted for President Douglas twice, she had sometimes questioned his resolve in the face of military opposition. But no more. These orders make it quite clear what he intends should North Korea push forward militarily.

Major Williams quickly reads the orders for all three squadrons and assembles its leaders to her to give the order. "Alright now, as we discussed. Captain Jones, take them out first—Alpha squadron, go!" Captain Jones gives her the thumbs up sign and turns to climb into his cockpit. Captain Jones will be the first to fly out. His plane is already situated on the upper deck ready for takeoff. Once secure in his cockpit, he takes off like a shot into the early morning pre-dawn sky. After him, all of the next Raptors in Alpha, about twenty in all, take off in rapid succession until Captain Jones' entire squadron is away.

Major Williams' F-22 Raptor now sits on the tarmac upper deck. She aligns her plane in the same place for takeoff as all of the previous now airborne Raptors. Engaging the launch controls, she shoots across the runway and is soon in the air and taking flight toward their destination. All of Beta squadron soon follows and assembles around her as the lead plane. Gamma squadron soon follows and forms up on Beta's right flank while Alpha is on its left. All three squadrons connect at a rendezvous point about one-hundred miles east of the North Korean coast. At that point, Major Williams gives the order to fly toward the DMZ.

"Mr. President," General Martin says, "we're ready. All squadrons have been assembled and are heading to the DMZ."

"Alright, let's see how far North Korea is willing to take this. If too far, we'll give them a show," the President says.

"Mr. President," an aid to General Martin says, "the Chinese President is on line one."

President Douglas pauses in thoughtful contemplation for a moment before speaking. "Tell him that I'm unavailable."

*   *   *

Alpha, Beta and Gamma squadrons speed toward the DMZ at a little under Mach one. They fly in tight formation only a few feet above the flight deck to avoid radar detection. Each Raptor is fully armed and lethal. These are the fiercest combat jets in the world and North Korea's leaders know it, Major Williams thinks. Their fighters don't lack for fire power or speed. Whatever North Korea's leader had been thinking in their provocation against South Korea, they had made a tragic mistake, Major Williams believes. If they don't back down, this will be a very bad day for their country. Major Williams wonders whether China will aid North Korea but quickly re-focuses knowing that such strategic considerations are above her pay grade.

Soon arriving to the border of the DMZ, all three squadrons slow to one quarter Mach speed and survey the land. As all of their intelligence reports had previously shown them, the North Korean army is amassed at the border between North and South Korea at the DMZ. The North Korean army seems to go on for miles away from the border. The satellite photos that Major Williams had received and viewed had not quite done the size of the North Korean army justice. What she sees looks to be about one million or more troops. This is how the ancient Persian armies used to do it, she thinks. In comparison, Major Williams' pilots are far fewer but mighty.

"Alpha squadron, make the first pass directly over the front of their forces. Gamma squadron, make the next pass," Major Williams orders. Alpha squadron moves into position as instructed and makes their first pass. Suddenly, the alarms in Captain Jones' Raptor angrily blare. "I'm being targeted, Major!" he exclaims. "They've got anti-air craft missiles down there. They've got me locked in!" As soon as he says that, Major Williams sees a missile fire somewhere within the North Korean army speeding up from the ground toward Captain Jones.

Major Williams yells into her microphone, "Evasive maneuvers now, Captain!" Quickly complying, Captain Jones rolls his Raptor hard right away from his squadron. He then climbs high out of view moving at at least Mach 2 or 3. Major Williams then sees the bright lights of his anti-missile defense measures, his flares, deploy. A moment later he hears the loud boom of the surface-to-air missile exploding. "The missile is destroyed, Major," Captain Jones says. "I'm rejoining the formation now."

"Outstanding, Captain. Glad to have you back. Alpha squadron identify and take out all surface to air sites whether mobile or stationary. Gamma provide support," Major Williams orders.

Alpha squadron moves into formation and prepares to attack. With satellite imagining, they identify five stationary missile launchers and fire on all five. Each site explodes in turn. The North Korean troops surrounding the missile launchers scatter. Major Williams imagines the panicked looks on their faces, but from this distance there is no way to know what they're really thinking or feeling. She wonders whether any of them have ever seen any actual combat before today.

Suddenly, Major Williams hears the alarms in her cockpit blare loudly. "Major! We've got multiple Migs locked in on us!" She hears one of her squadron pilots say.

Major Williams then exclaims, "Beta squadron! Break formation and return fire! Kill everything flying!" she shouts. The Major accelerates to attack speed and turns her Raptor to face the Migs firing on them.

*   *   *

President Douglas looks grim. He hears all of the communications happening between his pilots and sees what they see through their helmet cams. He and his generals expected some sort of response from the North Koreans, but they hadn't expected their use of sophisticated fighter jets, and particularly Russian based airplanes.

"They're using their Migs, sir. Our boys are taking fire from them," one of his generals' aids says.

"Are there any casualties thus far?" President Douglas asks.

"Not yet, sir. We're better than that," the aid replies.

"Admiral Bennington," the President says speaking to his newly minted Chief of Naval Operations, "I want you to fire on all of their air force sites. I want them completely destroyed. I don't want even one of their jets to have a home to return to." The Admiral looks at his aid and gives him the signal to proceed. The aid communicates the President's order to Admiral Murray, who is in charge of the attack on the North Korean forces. Admiral Murray communicates his ascent to the President's generals and admirals seated in the White House's Situation room with President Douglas.

"This is Admiral Murray," he says speaking to all of the ships in his aircraft carrier group. "All destroyers are to fire their full load on all provided aircraft cites on my mark—5-4-3-2-1 FIRE!!!!!"

At his command, all of the destroyers, six in total, fire substantial parts of their ammunition payloads on all of the North Korean air bases. They include bases at Kaech'on, Hwangju, Toksan, Orang and Chunghwa, North Korea. Within minutes, all are reduced to smoldering ash. This is a move of last resort, as the casualty count is high. President Douglas and his military staff know that North Korea has no possible answer for the devastation. Even with the help from their Mig fighter jets and depletion of the American forces, the North Koreans are completely outgunned. They have no suitable defense for the U.S. Navy's response to their air play against their fighters.

"All confirmed targets are destroyed, sir," Admiral Murray's communications officer says. "Washington asks you to stand by. There may be more targets."

"Copy," Admiral Murray says acknowledging the stand by orders.

President Douglas looks at the satellite images of the destruction that he had just ordered. "How many North Korean casualties can we expect?" he asks his senior military commanders.

"Our best estimates tell us about five-thousand, mostly military personnel," General Martin, his Army commander says.

"The strikes were near surgical perfection. By all accounts, we did not have one stray missile or munition. We have more available targets, Mr. President, if you're ready."

President Douglas takes a moment to ponder the issue. Should he order more strikes or wait and see how North Korea and its allies respond? Were their actions enough to send the necessary message of strength or would more be required? He is genuinely concerned for the welfare of civilian North Koreans and wants to avoid doing them harm. Making his decision, President Douglas says "Let's hold off for now. I think that we've done enough at this point. How are our pilots doing?"

"We've shot down five of theirs. All of ours are still in the air," Admiral Murray replies with a wide smile.

"Good. Can we spare a squadron? If so, I want one to do a fly over the President's palace headquarters. I want the North Korean president to get the entire message. We can go wherever whenever we want."

"Yes, Mr. President, we can send a squadron to his palace."

"Make it so, gentlemen. I'm expecting a phone call. I should be back soon," the President says as he exits the Situation Room and heads to the Oval Office.

*　　*　　*

As she hovers above the DMZ, Major Williams sees almost no movement in the North Korean ground troops. They remain on the border though, all of their forward progression having stopped. She and her pilots had done an excellent job at dismantling the North Korean fighter jets. She suspects that when the groups saw their planes being blown out of the sky, it had taken something out of them. She thinks that she can feel the despair wafting through the ether to meet them. All of the squadrons, except Gamma squadron, fly overhead in formation since the remaining North Korean jets had been either destroyed or retreated from the battle. Gamma squadron now speeds to the North Korean president's palace. If he's there, Major Williams thinks, his day is about to become considerably worse.

She knows that if there is no turn back by the North Koreans, their very next order would be to start firing into their troop formations. That would be a lot of lives lost. With their anti-aircraft defenses reduced to rubble and no air response on their side, the North Koreans' ability to survive, much less win, this conflict is substantially reduced. That's good news for depleted American troops, Major Williams muses. Without their sleeping comrades, a protracted conflict with North Korea or any foreign power is not to their advantage. Hopefully, someone in Washington, China, or North Korea would step back before this got any worse, she thinks.

*   *   *

President Douglass does not over-estimate the impact that their successful rebuff of North Korea at the DMZ has had. At the most, he believes, the assault buys them a little time. It shows their enemies and the rest of the world that they remain a powerful, responsive military power. It also shows them all their limitations. President Douglas and his generals are certain that their Chinese and Russian observers saw that only their SM troops engage the North Koreans while their IM troops did not. This happened because of an appropriate abundance of caution on the part of the President and his military commanders. They view their non-infected IM military as their last line of defense against hostile foreign powers. Of course, this approach makes sense to them, but it also provides their enemies a potential opening.

Internal estimates show President Douglas and his Joint Chiefs of Staff that they have about thirty thousand IM troops stationed in various locales worldwide, including in their various aircraft carrier and submarine groups. At least half of them are stationed on the ground in Europe, Asia, the Middle East and Africa. There are also SM troops with them, but they will be summoned home to help with the effort to maintain order. That's a huge risk. Those SM troops could become carriers of the Sleeper Virus and therefore unable to leave the U.S. again until a cure is identified. President Douglas sees that he has little choice. Their efforts to locate and make safe their fellow IM citizens is paramount, and all available hands are needed.

For now, their IM troops operating within the Navy will have to dock in Alaska and at other friendly ports around the world. They can re-supply there and conduct their missions as before the crisis. Their vigilance, President Douglas knows, is needed now more than ever. President Douglas feels a tinge of worry. He worries that the IM soldiers, almost all of whom have family in the states, could lose focus and become disheartened in their mission. The President and his generals don't have a plan to deal with that yet. They all know, however, that such a plan must be created. Anticipating the fallout from this problem is a no brainer. They cannot afford, as a nation, to lose even one IM soldier's loyalty and presence to their cause.

President Douglas knows that he may also have Russia to contend with. Since the crisis began, Russia had stepped up its military readiness efforts. The President's Joint Chiefs had been tracking their military movements along the borders of several European countries. President Douglas thinks that he'll soon be speaking to the Russian President. That call, he believes, will be unpleasant. President Petrov, or one of his minions, could press him for details about the country's current state that he isn't ready to divulge yet. On the other hand, President Douglas thinks, it might be better to fully disclose their situation to Petrov, if, for no other reason, than to dispel any of the crazier rumors that he had undoubtedly heard about. The internet is going crazy, of course with such rumors, but President Douglas is fairly certain that they aren't yet in the midst of the much anticipated zombie apocalypse. The President allows himself to chuckle at that thought, but then sobers at the realization that their current state of affairs is not much better than zombies running through American streets.

The large phone on the President's desk rings. He sees that the ultra-secure private line is lit. President Douglas picks up the phone and presses it to his ear. "Hello, Mr. President," President Douglas says to the Chinese President, "how can I help you?"

"Mr. President, we see what you've done in North Korea. As I'm sure you know, this is very distressing to us. North Korea is our neighbor and our ally. Obviously, we recognize that the U.S. has vital interests in South Korea. We do understand your concerns with," President Kao pauses, "North Koreas build up on their shared border with South Korea. However, we must insist that the U.S. relent and pull back. We see your actions as wholly undeserved escalation."

President Douglas clears his throat before allowing himself to speak. He feels his temperature rising and knows that his temper rises with it. Before speaking, he reminds himself of what's at stake for his country given its current state. "With all due respect, President Kao, what North Korea did, and what the Russians are preparing to do, is unwarranted, provocative and in violation of every international law and treaty. We believe that their actions are a direct result of the crisis in America. We believe that these actions are aimed directly at us and our allies together. We also believe, Mr. President that North Korea did not act alone, but serves as proxy to another. It would be a tragic error, Mr. President, for anyone to think that just because we are in the midst of a crisis that America is not strong, capable and willing to defend herself and her allies. That would be a mistake of the highest order."

There is a long silent pause on President Kao's end. President Douglas allows himself a moment to relish in his counterpart's silence.

"Mr. President," President Kao says, "I understand, and I can assure you that China has had nothing to do with North Korea's actions. They are our ally, yes, but we did not authorize or suggest their aggression towards South Korea. Please know that we are deeply concerned about happenings in your country and stand ready to help you with anything that you may need."

"President Kao, I appreciate your sentiment and your words. They are very gracious. For now, we have things under control. It would not be safe, however, to return any of your ambassadors, diplomats, or staff to you as we are seeking remedies to our crisis. I'm sure that they've informed you about what's been happening. We'll keep them in the loop as we continue to make progress."

"Very good, Mr. President," President Kao says. "We look forward to hearing from you soon."

Both men hang up. President Douglas leans back in his chair feeling satisfied. He hopes that this call is enough to chasten China's ambition in the face of their crisis. He knows, of course, that President Kao is lying about China's lack of provocation through North Korea. That is exactly what happened, though it could not be definitively proven yet. In time, President Douglas thinks, they'll have proof enough. Until then, China knows that it has its ambassadors and diplomats for the duration and that they can't be recalled yet without risking injury to their own populations. That is the unspoken truth between them. The Sleeper Virus affects all people lacking sufficient melanin, whether White or not, and some of the Asian population would undoubtedly fall victim to it. This is a card that President Douglas has, and he'd just played it. President Douglas is certain that the contents of this call were recorded on the other end and will be shared with the Russian President. He expects to have that call today too.

*   *   *

"Admiral Jones," Major Williams says, "we're seeing troop movement on the ground. They appear to be retreating, sir. The tanks have turned around and the troops are marching away from the DMZ. What do you want us to do, sir?"

"Our orders are to stay put and monitor. I'll advise if anything changes. Keep reporting back, Major."

Major Williams gives the signal to her squadron to do another looping pass over the DMZ. She has no idea how long that they'll stay in place. She's happy that they're no longer fighting MIG fighter jets and that North Korea's troops are in retreat. This had been her first military exercise since the first Gulf War. She is happy that they are successful and that none of their pilots had been lost.

Major Williams knows that they cannot afford to lose a single plane or pilot. Their nation's military force is dangerously depleted. She hopes that North Korea will be the only nation that tries them militarily. They had shown their strength, but also their weaknesses, Major Williams believes. China and others saw who fought and who didn't fight, she muses. Was not including their other IM pilots who had not been infected with the Sleeper Virus a mistake, she wonders. Time will tell. She hopes that President

Douglas and the Joint Chiefs do not squander this opportunity. Time will tell on that too, she thinks.

*   *   *

"Mr. President," his assistant says, "the Russian President is on the private line."

President Douglas sees the secure line lit up like a Christmas tree. He quickly wonders how this call with the Russian President will compare to the one that he just had with President Kao, the Chinese President.

"President Petrov, how are you?" President Douglas asks sounding almost cheerful.

"Mr. President," President Petrov says responding in a heavy Russian accent, "We have heard some rather disturbing things about your country, Mr. President. What is happening?"

There it was, the question. It was put up or shut up time for President Douglas, and he knows it. "President Petrov, honestly, we're experiencing something that we can't yet fully define or describe. I can tell you that we're doing everything that we can to get out in front of it, but we're still not sure when or how this thing will end."

"Excuse me, Mr. President," President Petrov interrupts him saying, "but you aren't really telling me anything that we, I, do not already know. We've got embassy staff, employees and agents in your country that we can't reach. We think that they're alive, but no one is responding to our communiques. This has become quite serious. What has your country done to them, Mr. President?"

President Douglas hears the heat and the volume rising in his Russian counterpart's voice. He decides in that instant to be more forthcoming. It's a high risk gambit, he knows, but also a necessary one to quiet Petrov's fears about his people.

"President Petrov," he begins, "first, I want to assure you that your people are alive and well, and all accounted for. More than a week ago we experienced the unthinkable. It seems that most, if not all of our white and fair skinned citizens were rendered unconscious by something that we call the Sleeper Virus. The virus acts upon the metabolic systems of insufficiently-melanated persons by drastically slowing a victim's metabolism down. A major side effect of the Sleeper Virus is that it immobilizes its victims into a deep and unshakeable state of unconsciousness or sleep. Given that your people, like most other Americans, are very fair and have low melanin content, they were caused to become unconscious too."

President Douglas pauses before continuing. He had just made a huge reveal to the Russian President and wanted to give him a moment to catch up. President Petrov had no   dark-skinned spies that he knew of, so this is the first time that he is hearing the truth of their situation.

"Mr. President," President Douglas continues, "We've secured your embassies in D.C. and New York. All of your people have been secured and are being safely held as VIPs in our hospitals. They are receiving around the clock care and monitoring. They are alive and we plan to keep them that way."

President Petrov takes a deep breath. "Mr. President, thank you for telling me what is happening. I need to confer with my staff. Please do as you say, and take care of our people. I will call you again soon."

The two men hang up. President Douglas hopes that he's done the right thing by revealing to President Petrov their true condition. There is much that he does not tell Petrov, but the Russians would be quick to surmise those things as well. One crisis at a time, President Douglass thinks, as he heads out of the Oval Office back to the Situation Room.

*   *   *

"General, give me a sit rep on North Korea's nuclear facility," the President says.

General Martin is startled by the President's request and he looks it as he begins to answer him: "Well, Mr. President, North Korea's main nuclear complex is in Yongbyon, north of Pyongyang. It's not currently a target on the list that we discussed. What might you be thinking, sir?"

"I'm thinking that we may need to hit the facility to drive home the message to North Korea, Iran, China, Russia and whoever else might be watching, that the state of our union, militarily, is as strong as it ever was. Also, that we still have the expertise and the numbers to protect not only ourselves, but also our allies. Besides, we know the North Koreans have been developing a nuclear arsenal. Why not take now to disrupt their program?" President Douglas queries.

General Martin clears his throat as he composes his response. He doesn't think that the President is being unreasonable, but he believes that he might be overreaching. Today has been a success. Several important messages had been delivered to their enemies and allies alike. North Korea had been roundly trounced and more importantly, embarrassed. They would not soon live this defeat down and China would think two, three, and four times before putting their hapless ally up to such a fool's errand again. At present, China is nowhere to be found on the battlefield. They are the proverbial hand behind the throne, but a strike against Yongbyon, North Korea's nuclear facility might wake the dragon, so to speak. Fighting North Korea is one thing, but fighting China is a different matter altogether. The better part of valor, the General thinks, would be to allow North Korea (and China) the honor of an unmolested retreat. That act alone could pay diplomatic dividends in the future. China, especially, understands that U.S. forces had all of North Korea in its cross-hairs.

"Mr. President, with all due respect, I don't think it wise to further attack North Korea. They've been beaten, routed actually. A strike inland at Yongbyon could lose us China's respect and turn this into something else. And look what we've proven: superior air power, naval power, and tactical excellence. Their hope, I'm sure, was that you'd never pull the trigger. Well, sir, you pulled the trigger and they heard and felt it. Going beyond what we've done today, I believe, would be the proverbial spike of the football. Beijing would frown upon that, and might dip its toe into the water more than it already has. No sir, I think we take this win and use it to shore up diplomatic ties with China as we burnish our swords against Russia and Iran, and any other would-be trier of American might."

"Are you my Joint Chiefs of Staff or my Secretary of State, General?" the President wants to know.

"Well, Mr. President, you don't have a Secretary of State right now. I've done that job and know it well. I certainly know this one too. So, I guess for the time being, given what our country needs, I'm both."

President Douglas ponders that for a moment. On the one hand, the North Koreans are utterly untrustworthy and might be inclined to seek some sort of revenge against South Korea or even the U.S. itself, given its embarrassment at their hands. On the other hand, they might be chastened against such a move—at least, China might be chastened. And with the Korean peninsula sitting on its southern border, the possibility of nuclear fallout would not bode well for South Korea or China, which is already dealing with massive commercial pollution problems.

"Okay, General, I'll take your advice. And congratulations, you're now our new acting Secretary of State for the next six months or until you find your replacement. You did a masterful job of convincing me, now it's your job to convince the rest of the world, and yes, you retain your duties as Joint Chiefs. Again all, congratulations. Fine job, thank you."

At that, the President rises from his chair and leaves the room. All of the Joint Chiefs rise as one and salute him. He returns their salute somberly, but also with a sense of pride at what they had just accomplished together.

CHAPTER IX

Sabrina looks down at the speedometer in her recently borrowed, if not outright stolen, SUV. She makes very good time, she sees. At this rate, she thinks, she and Isaac should be back in L.A. by early evening. Sabrina almost can't believe their luck or providence, her mother says. Isaac is fast asleep in the passenger seat and snoring a bit. Sabrina turns up the radio to drown him as she considers all that has befallen them and their options.

Isaac's wife is in some sort of home hospice, intensive care situation. He himself is only semi-ambulatory. There's no way that he could have made this trip on his own. He needs her to do the heavy lifting. She has no money, no cell phone and no credit cards. There's no way that she could have gotten home without Isaac. As Sabrina reflects, she is happy that they each found each another, and are able to meet their respective needs.

As Sabrina considers their broader situation, her mood darkens again. She had miraculously survived a near fatal plane crash. Most of the folks on her plane were in some sort of sleep stasis, from which they could not be awakened. In their drive around the outskirts of San Francisco, she and Isaac had seen many folks in similar straits as those who were at the airport. It seemed that only people of color were awake, though Sabrina is not completely sure that that is the case.

Sabrina is startled out of her thoughts when she hears Isaac cough hoarsely. "Sabrina," he says, "are we there yet?" Getting anxious, Isaac groggily scratches his salt and pepper beard. "Not quite, Isaac," Sabrina says. "We're a good one-hundred or so miles away according to the GPS. I'll let you know when we get there. You should keep resting."

"Okay, Sabrinnaaaaaa…" Isaac says as his last syllables trail off into a snore.

Sabrina is glad that Isaac is resting. He'd been through his own ordeal before meeting her and had told Sabrina all about it. Isaac had taken a brief trip to Dallas, Texas to visit with two of his three sisters. Isaac is the big brother to them all, one of which, Clarissa, had passed a year or so ago after a long battle with diabetes. Isaac and his sisters are very close. He went to Dallas to prepare them for the passing of his wife, whom they had all known from their childhoods together.

Isaac had met his wife when they were children. She had lived just two doors down from Isaac and his family from the time that both of them were in preschool together. They had been friends their entire lives. Love sparked between them in high school, but faded when each had gone to separate colleges. Isaac went to Morehouse, while Angela, his wife, went to USC when she elected to stay home. They had remained good friends during their college years, though, and love rekindled between them when Isaac graduated, came home, and started working.

Early in their journey along the Coastal Highway, Isaac told Sabrina that his parents had often teased him about the very high probability that Angela had chosen him from the get-go, and that he had been a little slow on the uptake. "Took you coming home from college to see it, huh, boy?" Isaac's father had said to him right after he admitted his intentions to his parents about Angela. "That's okay, baby, we knew, and we've known for a long time," his mother had said. "And we already love her. She'll be a wonderful wife for you and a great mother to our grandkids for us!" Isaac's mother had said cheerfully.

Isaac confided to Sabrina that he just wanted what his parents had had—a long enduring marriage, with healthy kids and future grandkids. Isaac came from a large family that had immigrated to California from Texas after the Civil War. At least, that's the history that he had been told and what had been passed down several generations. Once, when Isaac had the resources to research his family's history, he discovered that his family had indeed been enslaved in Texas, but had also seen time in South Carolina and Georgia. Unfortunately, his research had hit a dead end. Genealogical records of enslaved Africans aren't as complete as those for actual immigrant families to the United States. All indications were, however, that his family of Africans who were enslaved in the states had been brought to the country some time right before or some time right after the Revolutionary War.

Sabrina could hear the pride in Isaac's voice when he told her that story. Isaac told her that he did not see the fact his family had been enslaved as a blemish. Rather, he relished in the power of his peoples' ability to endure and to survive. Isaac told Sabrina that she and her family, of course, have a similar story of overcoming intense adversity. He notes further that he never calls Black people "slaves," but instead describes them as having been enslaved. "See, Sabrina," he said, "our people were not slaves, they were enslaved. One is a matter of identity. The other is a matter of condition. Our folks, who have been on this planet longer than any other Homo Sapiens, do not have a slave identity. Slavery is just something that happened to our ancestors. It is not who they were or who we are today. Plus, they survived it and made dang sure that we can thrive here, though the forces that be make it harder and harder to do so."

What Isaac had said before he dropped off to sleep had really resonated with Sabrina. Of course, she knew and read about much of what Isaac shared with her. Every student of Howard University is taught much of the same. But hearing it so personally put as Isaac had, Sabrina thinks, provides a clarity that merely reading or discussing it in class had not. Isaac personalizes our shared history as something that is part of his personal family, Sabrina thinks. That's powerful. It crystallizes their ancestors' experiences in a way that neither a book nor lecture ever could.

Sabrina glances over at Isaac, who is reclined at an appreciable angle in his chair. I sure am glad that we got this vehicle, she thinks. It's just the right amount of comfort and size that they need. She looks at the GPS on the car's screen and sees that they're about eighty-five miles away from his house. So far so good, she thinks. It had been smart of them to take the Coastal highway. Driving along it had been easy. Traffic had been sparse, and they saw few cars stopped on it from either accidents or unconscious drivers.

Sabrina hopes that the rest of their journey is just this easy. She doesn't know what to expect once they get to L.A. She'll pick up the local radio stations once they're there, she thinks. Perhaps they will have some useful information to share. She doesn't quite know what to expect in L.A. It is such a large city, she thinks, and there are a lot of people in it who are White. If what happened in and around San Francisco also happened in L.A., Sabrina pauses her thinking afraid to draw the obvious conclusion. The scope and scale of this disaster is overwhelming. She instead begins to think about seeing her parents and her brothers who she knows to be okay and waiting for her at their house. Soon, she thinks, she'll be home and she can't wait. As if in response, Isaac snores his reply as he turns over in his seat, still asleep. That's right, Isaac, soon. You'll be home and I'll be home, then we'll see what we can see.

*   *   *

Donnie and Clarence are exhausted, Donnie more so since he had done all of the driving for the day. The South Loop neighborhood was about what they had expected. There had been a number of people passed out on the sidewalks, in their cars, half in and half out of stores and restaurants and more. Donnie and Clarence did what they could to either transport or secure people that they found who are asleep. In one instance, they find about twenty people passed out in a restaurant. Walking in they see five other awake persons tending to them. "What's up?" Clarence asks them. One of the men, an apparent chef appraises Clarence and Donnie for a few long seconds before responding. "Nothing, you see what it is. One minute they were eating the food that we had prepared," the man says gesturing toward the four other similarly dressed men with him, "and the next, they were slumped over. We had to make sure a few of them didn't suffocate in their food. We're just trying to keep them safe until…" his voice trails off. "Until someone comes to get them somewhere?" Donnie queries. "Yes, until someone does something," the man says. "Hi, my name is Taylor, who are you?" the man asks extending a hand to Donnie and Clarence.

"Hi, Taylor," Donnie says. "I'm Donnie. This is Clarence. We've been finding and transporting folks like this all day and all evening. It's nice to meet you."

"I could tell that you weren't one of the marauder types," Taylor says. "We've been hearing some strange stories of what's been happening around the country, not just in Chicago."

"We have too, fam," Clarence says. "I did the exact same thing you're doing for a bunch of folks who collapsed right outside of the Nike store on Michigan."

"Yeah, me and my crew have been holed up here all day and evening afraid to leave. We don't want anybody to get hurt on our watch. But nobody's told us what to do," Taylor says. "It's just been me and my guys Hernando, Roberto, Alex and Michal. What can you tell us?"

Donnie and Clarence quickly give their hellos to Taylor's crew and then proceed to tell them what they've been doing, what they've seen, and what they've heard about nationally. "Yep, it's a national epidemic, fellas. No idea when, or if whatever this is is going to end. Seems like we have one-half or more of the population that's gone to sleep, and can't wake up. Only real thing that we've heard is to find these folks and get them transported to one of the local hospitals. But how long can that last?" Clarence asks rhetorically. "If it's nationwide, that means that millions of people are infected or affected, or whatever. The hospitals are gonna run outta space and soon."

The room falls silent at Clarence's last words. The men's realization at the size of the problem and its scope weighs heavy on each of them. "Is it my imagination," one of Taylor's guys speaks up "or does it seem like only White people are being knocked out?" Donnie and Clarence exchange a knowing glance. "It's not your imagination," Donnie says. "That's also what we've been witnessing. It seems like it's only either White or really fair-skinned people who have been affected. We've also seen some very fair-skinned Asian people knocked out too."

"Yeah, but it doesn't seem like any Black or Hispanic people are being hit with it, at least not yet," Clarence says. "Everyone standing here talking is either Black or Hispanic… seems like there's some kind of connection."

"So what do we do now?" Taylor asks. "It's obvious that this problem is way bigger than our restaurant."

"Normally," Donnie begins, "we'd start gathering these folks up three to four at a time and start transporting. But honestly, I'm dog tired. Been at this since about nine this morning. I need to rest and then start fresh in the morning. I just met Clarence today. It's definitely best to do this retrieval and transport work with a partner. Some of these folks are really heavy. So I'd say for you guys to secure your folks, sit them or lay them in a way that doesn't hurt 'em, and then go home and get some rest. Come back in the morning and start transporting them to the closest hospital. You might want to leave one person here to keep watch, but there's not much that you can get done tonight."

"That'd be me," Taylor says. He turns to his crew and gives them instructions to go home and to come back in the morning bright and early. "I'll stay the night in the manager's office. He's got a cot that I can lay on. I'll check on these folks every couple of hours to make sure that everyone's breathing."

"That's fine with us," Clarence says. "Good luck."

Donnie and Clarence shake hands with each of the men and leave the restaurant. "Think they'll be alright, Donnie?" Clarence asks. "Yeah, I think so. If they were going to do something to their unconscious, they'd have done it long before we showed up" Donnie says. "Yeah, you're probably right. Can you get me home? I'm tired too. We can run this back tomorrow. You can even stay at my place if you'd like. Didn't you say that you live out in the suburbs? Oh, and Isabella lives in my neighborhood, D," Clarence says with a sly smile.

Donnie is hesitant to accept, but quickly realizes that he might not actually be able to get home given all of the accidents that occurred on the highway into Chicago. He also sheepishly realizes that he would not mind seeing Isabella again, sooner rather than later. Something about her big brown eyes had moved him.

"Okay, Clarence, I'm game. I don't think I could drive more than another ten minutes, honestly."

"Great, D., that's great. My neighborhood is only about five minutes away. We'll be there in no time. It's one of those transitional neighborhoods that won't look like its ethnic history in the next ten minutes," Clarence says sarcastically pointing out that his Chicago neighborhood is one of the ones experiencing rapid gentrification.

Donnie chuckles at his new friend's tone. They'd only been working together for one day, but they were already fast friends. Donnie liked this man and actually looked forward to working with him again. He senses that Clarence feels the same. He's glad that they had found each other in the midst of this calamity. He hopes that they will both see it resolved.

* * *

Sabrina cannot believe what she's seeing. "Isaac! Isaac! Wake up!" she says, the alarm in her voice rising each time that she calls his name. Before her is a scene that she had sincerely hoped to avoid. The highway is cut off and appears impassable. At least ten cars and trucks clog up the road so thoroughly that she immediately knows that they cannot get their SUV through. So close to L.A., but yet so far, Sabrina thinks.

"Isaac, we're stuck. The accident in front of us is impassable. What do you think we should do?" Sabrina asks.

"Walk," Isaac says flatly.

"Walk?" Sabrina asks incredulously.

"Walk," he says again.

Sabrina looks at their GPS. She sees that they're about fifteen miles away from Isaac's house. Looking at Isaac she realizes that she'd be the only one walking and also pushing him the last few miles to his house. She also realizes that once she gets him settled, she'd have another five miles to walk to her house. Sabrina sighs a sound of resolution. She thinks back to her time at Howard when she pledged her sorority. This must be what her Big Sisters had meant when, on many an evening, they told her to "suck it up, Ivy!" Time to put on my big girl draws and do what needs to be done, she thinks. "Isaac, get ready. I'm getting your chair and wheeling us the heck up outta here." Isaac nods his approval and Sabrina swings out of the driver's seat. She retrieves Isaac's wheelchair from the back of the SUV and after a few grunts and groans, finally gets Isaac into his chair.

Sabrina, looking at the gnarled mess in front her, takes a moment to consider their options. "I think that we have room to get past this mess, Isaac. It's too narrow for the SUV, but there appear to be enough gaps to wheel you through."

"Looks like, Sabrina," Isaac says. "You sure the SUV can't make it through?"

"Positive, I'm afraid. One side of the highway abuts up to the hill. It's impassable. The other side drops down into the ocean off a cliff. Impassable. No, it's this or get back in the SUV and wait for help, which neither of us can afford to do. Plus, we have no idea when or if help will ever get here."

"That makes sense," Isaac says. "But it's a long walk with me in this thing. Think you're up to it?"

Sabrina squares her jaw. "Up to it? No, not really, but what other choice do we have. Come one, times a wasting. Let's go."

Sabrina gets behind Isaac's chair and starts pushing. He's

heavy. The wheelchair looks to be fairly new and is made from aluminum, she sees. That makes the overall job easier, but nowhere near easy. As Sabrina pushes Isaac up to the front of the carnage, she can make out more details. What she sees horrifies her. It also informs her. The crashed cars before her are filled with people who are either asleep or dead. The dead, she observes, are made so by their injuries. As Sabrina and Isaac roll by one particularly gruesome and mangled car, they see a family of four. The father, or the man that they take to be the father, is slumped over the steering wheel with a large gash over his left eye. The mother is slumped over, her air bag having been fully deployed. They can't tell whether she's alive or dead. Their children, though, appear to be asleep. They are fully strapped into their seats, but appear otherwise unharmed. All of the inhabitants appear to be White.

"Hold on a second, Isaac, I want to check on the kids," Sabrina says.

"Okay, Sabrina, but let's not dawdle," Isaac warns.

Sabrina appreciates Isaac's laser-like focus. It's what has gotten them this far. But she can't help but feel compassion for all of these injured folks and especially the children.

The car's tires are flat, no doubt from the impact of its

collision, Sabrina sees. She notes two large depressions on either side of the car. It looks to Sabrina like it was struck on its right side and then struck something else, in this case a large flatbed truck which is also crashed. Peering into the back seat, Sabrina sees the two children, a boy and a girl. The boy looks to be about ten years old. The girl, his sister, looks to be about seven. Sabrina tries to open the back door, but it won't budge. She moves to the other side, the girl's side, and tries her door. With some effort, it pries open and with loud effect. Sabrina sticks her head into the back of the car. By now, she knows what to look for—any sign of breathing. The girl is so small that at first she doesn't see her breathing, so she listens carefully. There it is, Sabrina thinks. She's breathing. The girl's breathing sounds haggard to Sabrina, though she's no nurse or doctor. Yet, it sounds more labored to her than it should sound. Sabrina feels for her heart beat, and it feels regular. Her brother's breathing and heart beat are both strong and robust. He must be an athlete, Sabrina surmises. At his age, Sabrina can already see the musculature that he'll have as a teenager and as a man.

"Sabrina!!" Isaac says. "Times a'wastin'!"

The sound of Isaac's baritone voice jars Sabrina back into

their current reality. It also presents her with a difficult choice.

Stay and try to care for each one of these accident victims or go,

complete their mission and figure out what to do with all of the

persons, like these, that they find. Making her choice, Sabrina

walks quickly back over to Isaac and starts to push him away.

She says a silent prayer for all of the people that they pass in this

accident. "Isaac, I've got to hurry and get you home. I don't think

that anyone but us even knows that these folks are here. We need to

get word to someone and get them some help."

"Totally agree, Sabrina. But we've got fifteen miles in front

of us. What do you plan to do?" he says.

"I plan to hustle, Isaac." At that, Sabrina breaks into a light

jog and begins to push Isaac ahead faster down the highway.

*   *   *

"Stop right here, Donnie and hold tight. I'll be right back,"

Clarence says.

Donnie watches Clarence exit his car and walk a short

distance up the block. It's dark, but Donnie sees a strange sight.

Two people are collapsed on the sidewalk about thirty feet away.

They're laid out right in front of an apartment building, Clarence's apartment building. There is also a car parked next to them on the street with its lights on. Donnie can make out the taillights from where he sits. He also sees two large men leaned against the car standing over the two collapsed persons. One of them is smoking. Clarence walks directly over to them. One of the men extends a hand to Clarence but the other one maintains his distance.

Donnie can't hear what is being said, but he can tell from the three men's interactions that they're discussing the two collapsed people on the sidewalk. At first, Donnie hears them speaking in low tones, but then their voices become elevated. He sees one of the men, the one who did not shake Clarence's hand, step close to Clarence. By his body language, Donnie sees that whatever he's saying, it's not friendly and is probably threatening. Donnie opens his door enough to cause the interior lights to come one. The two men talking and now arguing with Clarence look up. Without turning to look at him, Clarence says firmly "Stay in the car, Donnie. Close the door now." Clarence has an impressive command voice, Donnie thinks. He closes his door but continues to fix his eyes on his new friend.

The first man whom Clarence greeted steps between Clarence and the second man. It's clear that he's trying to calm the tensions between them all. Donnie sees Clarence relax his shoulders and step back. He then watches as Clarence opens his arms wide, gestures to the two collapsed people and at Donnie. He sees the dawning recognition in each man's eyes as Clarence continues speaking. After a short while, the men stop speaking. Clarence trots back over to Donnie's car and motions for him to lower the passenger side front window. "Hold tight, Donnie, I'm in the midst of difficult negotiation" Clarence says and then smiles broadly at him showing him all of his teeth. Donnie sees that one of his top teeth gold.

Clarence walks back over to the men. Each now extends a hand to him and daps him up. Donnie sees them step toward their car and get in it. Clarence gives them a half salute. The men slowly drive off. When they do so, Clarence motions to Donnie to drive up right into the space that was just vacated by the two men.

"What the heck was that all about?" Donnie asks as he gets out of his car.

"Oh that?" Clarence says. "That was just two of the toughest gangsters in the city of Chicago deciding to let me take custody of these two collapsed folks against the orders of their capo. They didn't want to at first. But I let them know about the work we've been doing and what's been happening all over the city. They had orders to find and take charge of folks like this for, I guess, negotiation purposes" Clarence says and then shrugs. "But you almost lost us the negotiation and our lives, Donnie, when you opened your door. Them dudes are straight killas, Bro. You gots to be more careful."

"Wow, Clarence, I had no idea" Donnie says.

"I know you didn't, D. And I told them that. They could see that you're a civilian. So no harm, no foul. The one that dapped me up first is actually my cousin. He had no reason to do us harm. The other one, though, is quite dangerous. His street name is Dark Knight, because well", Clarence says as his voice trails off. "You know what, never mind. Help me get these folks inside. We're gonna take them into my spot and deliver them to a hospital in the morning. Cool?"

"Cool, let's do it" Donnie says.

Clarence and Donnie then pick up each person, two women, and each puts one over their shoulder and carry them into Clarence's apartment building. Fortunately, they're relatively small and light. Also fortunately, Clarence lives on the first floor of the building so they don't have to take any steps.

"I'm the super, D. This is how I make my real money" Clarence says.

Donnie waits as Clarence fumbles with his keys to his apartment. Once the finds the right one, Clarence opens the door and ushers them inside. Donnie is hit with the strong smell of incense and fried food. Donnie had forgotten how hungry that he is. The smell of Clarence's apartment makes his mouth immediately water. "Clarence, do you have food? I'm hungry as hell. Completely forgot about that because I'm so tired" Donnie says.

"Man, my cupboard is bare. Was supposed to go grocery shopping today, but you know" Clarence responds. "But don't sweat it, D. I have a solution. Let's get these two fine folks situated first and I'll make it happen. Shoot, I'm hungry too. I don't care how late it is. I need to eat."

Clarence takes his unconscious person over to his couch and gently sits her upright on it. He motions for Donnie to do the same. Once both are on the couch, they check the breathing of their respective charges and confirm that both are indeed alive, yet unconscious. They are either White, or White mixed with something. "Donnie, this is Mrs. Henderson and her daughter Lila. They live right here in my building, apartment 3C. They've lived here for at least ten years. They are the only White folks, far as I know, who live in this neighborhood. I'm sorry that this happened to them. They are nice folks. We'll take care of them in the morning. For now, they can camp out here. They'll be safe and warm."

Clarence pulls out his cell phone and makes a call. He speaks in hushed tones but Donnie clearly hears the word "food". Soon, Clarence hangs up and looks at Donnie with a slight smile and a twinkle in his eye. "C'mon, Don. I got us some food, some really good food actually, and company, excellent company." Donnie doesn't know why Clarence emphasizes the word company, but he also doesn't care. So long as he can eat, he's happy.

Clarence leads them out of his apartment and out of his building. "We don't need to drive, Donnie. Just follow me", Clarence says. They walk about a block to the next block to the South of Clarence's apartment building. "We're here" he says. They stop in front of a small single family home with a small front yard. Walking to the front door, Donnie sees it open and standing in the doorway is Isabella. Donnie stifles a smile, but he sees that Clarence sees that he's pleased. He wonders if Isabella sees it too.

"Come in, gentlemen", Isabella says with a slight Spanish accent and big brown eyes.

"Don't mind if we do, Isabella" Clarence says. "Is your mom up? We sure do appreciate you both feeding us."

"Yes, she's up. We made dinner hours ago. It's more than enough for you two and several more. We figured that folks would be hungry."

Donnie smells the food as soon as he steps inside. His stomach audibly growls at which sound Isabella chuckles.

"Hungry, Senior?" Isabella says in a sing-song tone while chuckling.

Once inside, Donnie is better able to take in Isabella's form. When they had met on the street, she was fully bundled up with little to show except for her very pretty face and some of her hair. Chicago in February can be frigid and this day is no exception. Now, in a t-shirt and sweat pants, Donnie sees that she's curvy, has long black hair and very pretty brown skin. She looks to be about twenty-one. Donnie is afraid to ask her age just yet. He admits to himself that he finds her to be attractive but wants to play it cool.

Isabella walks them to their small dining room. There are two plates set up at the table in the room. There are also four large dishes with food almost falling out of them. Donnie sees a chicken dish, a pork dish, savory vegetables, a large rice dish and bread. He's so happy at the sight, he almost can't believe it. "Isabella, this looks and smells great. Thank you so much." Isabella flashes him a beautiful smile. "Thank you, Donnie, you're more than welcome" she says. Donnie catches Clarence looking at him with a knowing glance. He feels slightly embarrassed and looks away. So what if he likes her, he thinks. In his mind he wants to tell Clarence to shut up, but he refrains from doing so.

"Donnie, please sit here" Isabella says motioning him to the head chair.

Clarence chuckles audibly. "Careful, Donnie. She ain't never asked me to sit there" he says good naturedly. Clarence sits in the chair across from Donnie and makes a big show of it. "Seems like to me that I'm not the most important hombre here. Humph!" He says in faux offense.

"Oh, Clarence!" Isabella says. "You've been here a million times. You're practically family. You're certainly no guest. Donnie is a guest. We treat our guests" Isabella says pausing for effect, "differently."

Suddenly, Donnie begins to wonder just what he's stepped into. He hasn't had a serious girlfriend since college. He's dated a bit, but nothing that has been serious. Grad school had been a whirlwind of projects and internships. Socially, he had spent more time with frat brothers and fellow Black Greeks than in trying to pursue a relationship. Plus, he thinks, post college relationships are harder. College had been much easier and, he believes, much less based upon materialistic nonsense. Donnie sees that Isabella clearly likes him. He wonders whether he should return her affection given their present circumstances.

As near as Donnie can surmise, they're in day one of what could be a long catastrophe. He knows that there won't be any such thing as going back to work, at least for a while. Given how large Chicago is and its outlying suburbs, folks like him and Clarence will be busy for quite a while. Donnie has no idea how long this might last, and he realizes that he has more questions than answers. As if on cue, Isabella hands him a plate full of food. "Eat, Donnie. You can worry about tomorrow, tomorrow." She places her hand on his and looks at him fully and with palpable compassion. Donnie feels his heart flutter. Isabella lightly squeezes his hand and then let's go. Donnie picks up his fork and starts to dig in. "What are we, savages?" Clarence says. "Let's pray first, bro." Donnie puts down his fork and bows his head. As Clarence prays, his thoughts are of Isabella and how she had just looked at him. "Okay, D., now let's eat," Clarence says. Donnie digs in and loses himself in the delicious food and good company.

*   *   *

Sabrina is very thankful that she had worn her athletic shoes onto the plane. Though her feet are burning from the ten or so miles that she's already walked and wheeled Isaac, she knows that they'd probably be numb and damaged by now if she had on her pumps which are in the bag that she lost. She had been able to jog for about five miles, but gave that up for a brisk walking pace. Her arms and her back are burning, but she's determined to press on. She needs to get Isaac home and needs to get home herself. She and Isaac had hoped that they might get a ride at some point, but no rides were forthcoming.

After the multi-vehicle collision that had stopped their progress, there had been virtually no other cars on the road. Isaac's GPS in his cell phone works intermittently. At last check, it placed them a solid five miles from his house. At one level, Sabrina is tired, dog tired. At another, she is more determined than ever to complete this task. This is the kind of thing that she had always been good at—completing hard tasks regardless of personal discomfort. Her family called it the "diligence" gene. She has it. Her mother has it. Her oldest brother has it. Neither her father nor her other brother have it. Sabrina is happy to be able to tap into this drive and press forward.

"Yikes!" Isaac says. "That's a pretty big hill coming up. Do you want to take a break, Sabrina?"

"Hell no," she replies. "I pretty well know the route from here. That's the last big obstacle to getting you home. It's either flat or down hill after this. I'd rather give it everything now and then coast for the final few miles. It's all good, Isaac. I've been training in Muay Thai for a few years now. This is just something to do."

Sabrina begins the ascent. She guesses that it'll last for about a mile at about five degrees. Her father had taught her and her brothers how to gauge landscapes on the many vacations that they had taken by car. He used to make a game of it for her and her brothers. Sabrina had almost always won because she had careful eyes, her father used to say, and somehow geometry had always made sense to her.

As she pushes Isaac further and further up the hill, she begins to build momentum. This reminds her of the many times that she had pushed a weighted sled with her personal trainer. She knows that it's easier to keep going than it is to slow down, or worse, stop and start back up. She can run a mile in her sleep any day of the week but doing so with a weight up hill is something else entirely. Still, Sabrina determines to try to do so quickly.

She begins to pick up her pace, extending her strides at first as she continues to walk. Feeling her momentum gather, Sabrina then begins to run. She sees the hills summit and is determined to get there. Sabrina calculates that she's already gone about a quarter mile. Realizing that she takes it up a notch, Isaac exclaims "Sabrina, wow! You're really moving. Please be careful, though. I don't want to take a tumble."

"I won't let you fall, Isaac," she says through short breaths. "But let me focus. This hill is the last hard part of this trip."

"Okay. You go, girl. I'm truly impressed."

Sabrina presses on and even impresses herself with her pace. She thinks that she can keep it. She's afraid of slowing down even a little bit. She knows that her grit and determination are what are fueling her. Her body hurts, but it still complies with her mind's commands. Sabrina now counts all of her Muay Thai and Cross Fit classes worth it, though she hated them at the time. For two years straight, she had trained particularly hard. At the time, she had no idea why she trained so hard, other than being the right size in her wedding dress. A couple years of that craziness got me here, she thinks. Moving forward, she starts to feel the wind at her back. Sabrina smiles, though her calves and hamstrings are burning, because she feels her second wind coming.

A few minutes later, Sabrina is about two-hundred yards away from the crest of the hill. "Almost there, Isaac," she says. "Yeah, I see, Sabrina. You're really doing this thing." As soon as Isaac says that, Sabrina almost buckles over and collapses. She recognizes the problem right away: Charlie horse! Damn it! Not now! "Sabrina, what happened?!" Isaac yells out. "Are you okay? You almost stopped." Sabrina is in too much pain to speak. She decides instead to keep her hands gripped on the wheelchair's handles and keep walking, though that walk has morphed into a limp. She grunts loudly, but still utters no words. Sabrina sees that she'll be able to rest at the top. She feels the knuckle-sized knot of muscle in her left calf, but instead of stopping to rub it out, she keeps walking but accentuates the flex in that calf to get some relief. Little relief comes, but Sabrina keeps moving.

They soon see the crest together. Sabrina and Isaac also see that from here, on this highway, their path is mostly downhill, and also flat. According to their GPS and what Sabrina knows about their location, she estimates that they're now about two miles from Isaac's house. "Sabrina, you did it. Please take a moment to rest." Sabrina gratefully obliges and stops pushing. She locks the back wheels of the wheelchair. She then bends over deep at the waist to stretch her legs, both legs. While bent over, she vigorously massages her left calf for a few minutes. She knows what to do. She's been here before. "Do the right one too," Isaac says. "We can't afford for you to have any more Charlie horses," he says. Sabrina knows that he's right, and she complies.

"Isaac, we're almost there," Sabrina says. "Only about three miles from your house now. I know where we need to get off and I know your neighborhood. I had friends who I went to school with who grew up there. I estimate that we should be there in about thirty or thirty-five minutes with no more stops."

"Thanks, Sabrina, I'm grateful to you. Is there anything that I can do for you?" Isaac asks.

Sabrina thinks for a moment. "Actually, there is. Let me call my family. I'll try to have them meet me at your house. That would save me a trip. Plus, we don't yet know what condition the city is in."

Isaac hands her his phone. "Happy to oblige," he says.

Sabrina takes it and dials her parents' house number. "Mom?" She says. "Hey, Mom, I'm, we're fine. I've almost got Mr. Isaac to his house. Can you please have Solomon and Xavier meet me there? Great. We should be there in about thirty minutes. Please tell them to hurry. No, we're fine. No problems whatsoever. See you in a few."

Isaac looks at Sabrina with a sly grin and twinkle in his eye. "Well that was a lie," he says good-naturedly.

"No need to worry her. She'll get the full story when I see her."

"Understood, Sabrina, understood," Isaac says. "Now, let's go."

Sabrina grips the handles of Isaac's wheelchair, and they go.

*　　*　　*

Donnie honestly doesn't know what day it is. The last five days have been like a blur. What he's sure about is that he and Clarence have been gathering up unconscious folks every day since the first day for what feels like a month. It's been less than a week, but given their long days, their time together seems much longer. By this time, he and Clarence are partners and best friends. He also knows that there doesn't' appear to be a real end in sight of this work or the calamity that caused it.

The President and his officials have been speaking multiple times per day, but Donnie does not feel any more knowledgeable from the first day to this one. Clarence thinks that some sort of virus is involved, but that it impacts only White folks or folks of a certain melanin content, he says. Apparently, Clarence believes that this all may be some sort of divine retribution for the centuries of oppression and control by Europeans and their offspring. He also believes that the Ancient Egyptians were the first people to ever create electricity. So, there's that, Donnie thinks. He decided days ago to take Clarence and his various hotepian theories with a sizable grain of salt.

Donnie also knows that he is totally and completely smitten with Isabella. How could he not be? He wonders. She feeds them daily, making sure to put extra food on his plate. The food is delicious. She calls and texts him multiple times per day to see where he is and check on his welfare. Clarence has noted often and loudly that Isabella, his play niece, ain't never done the same for him. Isabella usually cuts him a sharp look at his protests and then hands Donnie another plate.

"Any more of this, 'Bella, and I'll actually begin to gain weight instead of lose." When Donnie said that to Isabella a few days ago, she locked eyes with him, bit her full lower lip and pressed into him. Clarence wasn't in the room. In fact, he was back in his apartment leaving Donnie alone at Isabella and her mom's house. Isabella looks up at Donnie and kisses him before he can draw back. Up to this point, Donnie had decided to keep his romantic distance from her, though he was clearly attracted to her. The smell of faint burnt cinnamon and flowers overtakes him, and he kisses her back vigorously. That was three days ago, Donnie thinks, and they've been affectionate toward one another ever since.

Donnie feels lucky to have Isabella's attention and help. She is a phenomenal young woman, he thinks, and under any other circumstances he would avidly pursue her. He feels a bit conflicted because he does not know if and to what extent the current catastrophe has drawn them together. There is a sizable part of him, however, that does not care. That part tells him, "Donnie, go for it, life is short, get in where you fit in."

Looking across the table at Isabella, he is now full from having just eaten after yet another sixteen hour day of unconscious human retrieval and hospital placement. Isabella's hand holds his. "Bella," he says. I need to get going back to Clarence's place. It's time to get some rest for tomorrow."

"Not tonight," she says. "You're not sleeping there tonight."

"Bella…" he begins to protest, but she has already stood up, still holding Donnie's hand, and pulls him up to her. "Tonight," she says, "you're staying with me." Donnie feels all of the protest drain from him. He allows Isabella to lead him down a darkened hallway to her room. She opens the door and invites him in. He goes in and closes the door behind him. Donnie eventually goes to sleep and gets some of the best rest of his young life.

CHAPTER X

President Douglas takes little time to revel in his victory against North Korea. In the middle of the first night of real rest that he had gotten since the Sleeper Virus struck, he is shaken awake by his personal assistant. Though it's the first thought that occurs to him, he knows better than to strike out at the person grabbing his shoulder and insistently whispering his name—"Mr. President! Mr. President!" Carlyle's whisper sounds more like a hiss, a most unpleasant hiss at 3:06 a.m. The President asks, "Yes, Carlyle, what is it?" "Sir," Carlyle hisses again, "they're all waiting for you in the Situation Room. Russia."

'Russia,' the President thinks. That's the only word that Carlyle says but it's enough. He had hoped that North Korea might be the only military test of his country during this crisis, but he suspects that his hope is ill-founded. He is very aware of Russia's, and in particular, its President's ambition for conquest. President Douglas had long ago marked President Petrov's sense of menace that seemed to ooze from his every pore. The President had met with the Russian President a half dozen times or more during his Presidency. In that time, he had never seen or sensed even one ounce of goodness in the man. Instead, he had only observed

Petrov's great potential for harm to the world. With the U.S. in crisis, the Russian bear is loose, President Douglass thinks.

As he dresses, the President recounts all of the times over his term in which Russia had tried American cyber defenses. In both of his elections, a large foreign power had attempted to disrupt and upend his Presidential election. President Douglas knows that Russia had been the major culprit because his spy agencies had told him so. As a result, he had worked hard to secure all of America's national elections, even going so far as to nationalize all election procedures in the United States. Unfortunately, the Republicans, by their filibusters and control of the House, had defeated his best efforts to secure their elections properly. Most of what he'd been able to do had come by executive order, but those were limited.

The President continues to dress quickly, pulling on a pair of near-by trousers, a white collared shirt, and his favorite loafers. He is as ready as he's going to be, he thinks. Walking quickly to the Situation Room he wonders what he might find. Entering the room, he sees his worst fears realized. "Mr. President," the Joint Chiefs says, "Russia has mobilized at the borders of Ukraine and Belarus by land, and Poland and Romania by sea. Indications are that they plan to invade at any moment. Petrov has expelled our ambassador from our embassy in Russia. Also, he's demanding that we turn over our embassy immediately and has Russian troops stationed outside of it poised to enter. What are your orders, sir?"

*   *   *

Jerome and Elena had taken to keeping the televisions on in their home twenty-four-seven, something that they never did before the Sleeper Virus hit. They and their kids want to remain updated on the latest news and information. After the near all-out war with North Korea and their country's recent military actions there, they are almost afraid to turn their televisions off. The news, over the last two weeks, had been the most consistent part of their daily lives. By some miracle, all of the major news networks, except Fox, had managed to stay on. Networks like CNN and MSNBC were helped by their foreign press offices that had remained operational and, obviously, not been afflicted with the Sleeper Virus since they were outside of the United States.

Jerome stirs as he hears the familiar tenor of the President speaking. He cracks open his eyes to peer at the glowing screen in front of him. He has no idea what time it is, but he knows that something important must be happening. He turns his neck to look at his clock. It reads "5:03 a.m." Great, he thinks, another early morning. Since he and Darryl had been newly assigned to IM recovery in Cincinnati, he had put in many twelve to fifteen-hour long days, and usually started working at the crack of dawn or several hours before that. Their new jobs required the utmost trust and integrity. Unfortunately, there weren't enough trustworthy hands to do the delicate work required. In essence, they were too good at their jobs.

This is his first day off since their efforts began. In truth, he is not truly off, he is just being allowed to report in at 8:00 a.m. instead of 5:00 a.m. He listens to the President speaking. It is not good news. "Today, my fellow Americans, Russia has done the unthinkable. They've amassed their troops at the borders of Ukraine and Belarus by land, and at Poland and Romania by sea. President Petrov has expelled the American ambassador to Russia and is attempting to take over our embassy in Moscow, a direct violation of international law. Russia seeks to take advantage of our crisis and re-build the Soviet empire. This is unacceptable. We are working with our allies now to provide a solution. We do not intend to foster war, but if war must come, we will fight. We cannot allow Petrov or anyone to act as Hitler once did in Europe. Though our enemies think of us as weak, we will show them that we are STRONG."

The President emphasizes his last spoken word – strong - with a resolve that Jerome had never heard before. In previous addresses like this one, he had seemed more tired than forceful. This morning, though, the President looks and sounds remarkably vigorous and resolved to him.

Jerome feels Elena begin to stir. She brushes his leg with her right foot and murmurs. "What is it, J?"

"It's the President," Jerome replies, "I think he just declared war on Russia."

*   *   *

The President meets with his top general and asks, "What are my options?" If his Joint Chiefs are tired of hearing that question, he is certainly tired of asking it.

"Mr. President," General Martin begins, "our options are few. We have three nuclear subs in the area, the sixth fleet is close by and the second and fifth fleets are within two days travel of the hot zones. Having said that, given Petrov's notable instability, we think, well, I think that striking Russian forces directly could trigger," General Martin pauses to give added weight to his words, "a missile attack of some sort, probably not nuclear, by Russia on our own soil or at least on the soil of one of our closest allies."

The President looks at General Martin with a mixture of shock and anger. "Wait a minute, General. You're telling me that you, all of you," he says as he sweeps his hand toward all of his Joint Chiefs, "think that it's even a possibility that Russia could strike here? Could hit us?"

"We do, Mr. President. It's no secret that we've lost two-thirds of our population and that that two-thirds is the most integrated segment of our population, our military and its support operations most especially. Not only have we lost soldiers, we've lost pilots and specialists of every kind and stripe. We won in North Korea, but we were also exposed militarily by North Korea. We pulled together what we could to fight them and won, but we have bigger problems. We have service men and women, White service men and women that are serving but can't come home for fear of being struck by the Sleeper Virus. They're stuck either in other countries or on boats or subs. They're still loyal, but how long can we count on that if we don't find a cure soon? It is for these reasons, Mr. President, and I hesitate to say this, please know that, but we recommend that we do nothing about Russia—at least not at this time."

Nothing, President Douglas thinks. The word has such finality. To be a word that represents the absence of weight, its heaviness seems to press against him and everyone else in the room. To the President, it is the heaviest and worst word that he's ever heard.

"Nothing," the President begins, "is what you've given me. Nothing is what I have, and nothing is what you expect me to do?!" President Douglas is nearly yelling by the time that he finishes his question, and his face is flush. The faces before him, though all Black and Brown, are all ashen. Several of his Joint Chiefs can't seem to look him in the eye. The President sits back in his seat and cups his hands. Composing himself, President Douglas begins to speak again. "Ladies and Gentlemen, I do not accept your proposition. 'Nothing' is unacceptable. We can't just let fifty plus years of history with our allies go down the drain because of our crisis. But tell it to me again, General Martin. How is a Russian missile attack of our Homeland, in the view of you and those in this room, a possibility? How did you arrive at that conclusion?"

"Sir, we did not arrive to it quickly or lightly. Petrov fashions himself a chess player and a bit of a strategist. Though a megalomaniac, he is shrewd. We see North Korea as the first provocation specifically designed to draw us out, test us and see what our weaknesses are. We see Russian aggression as one more test, but this time to see if we'll over-extend our already thin resources. We don't think that the four countries being threatened are his goal at all, but instead we think that we, and perhaps Great Britain, Germany or France are the prize. It is based on that analysis, Mr. President that we consider doing nothing vis-a-vis responding in the way that he expects as our best option."

"I would also say, Mr. President," General Martin says "that Russian forces themselves will probably not land here. We think instead that they could invade by long range attack and/or by proxy. Given that most Russians are rather melanin deficient, we think that they'd be afraid to come here themselves. They know what's happened to their now unconscious embassy staffs both here and in New York. We can see them collaborating with Iran or others for whom melanin deficiency is not a problem. We already know that they've tried to affect several internet-based attacks to some of our power plants, communication networks and more.

That's why we moved to close off the internet to them and all others."

"And by nothing, Mr. President," General Martin continues, "we don't mean literally nothing. We think that we should order all our fleets home to guard our two coasts. This includes all our submarines. We can use the Canadian Navy to re-stock and re-supply all our ships until we get a handle on the Sleeper Virus. We think that a show of force in American waters will be sufficient to ward off any Russian aggression directly towards us." General Martin concludes his summary and looks intently at the President. Gone was his momentary flash of anger, the General observes, replaced now with the look of cerebral thoughtfulness that he had come to expect from his Commander-In-Chief. The President, General Martin thinks, is every bit the strategist that Petrov is, and more so. General Martin believes that in a battle between Petrov's ego and President Douglas' pragmatism, pragmatism wins.

"General Martin, Joint Chiefs," President Douglas says, "I get it. I don't like it, but I get it. Over-extend and we're exposed to something far worse, a possible attack of some sort--if not us then someone close to us like England, France or Israel. Do nothing, draw back even, and we live to fight another day, hopefully a day when the cure presents itself. How much time do we have? I need a few more moments to consider our options."

"Mr. President, not much," General Martin says. "If Petrov invades any of the four countries, we expect it to happen within a day or two."

"Alright, General, you'll have my orders by this afternoon." The President stands, salutes his Joint Chiefs and exits the Situation Room. He considers a remembered quote from one of his favorite authors as he walks down the hallway towards the Oval Office: "Sometimes the hardest thing to do is to do nothing." Hardest damn thing indeed, President Douglas thinks, hardest indeed.

*   *   *

Returning to the official residence at just after 5:00 a.m., the President is alert and feeling a bit anxious. He finds Helen, his wife up, wide awake and reading. She looks up at him when he walks in, a smile trying to hide the concern on her face. He smiles in return and walks over to her and lightly kisses her cheek. "What is it?" she asks.

"Remember Russia?" he asks in a flat tone.

"Of course," the First Lady says. "It's that Euro-Asian country with delusions of grandeur run by that maniac that I don't like." Helen had never been a fan of the Russian President. Being highly intuitive, she felt that his thin veneer of charisma masked an enmity that was unnerving to her. She had made it a point, when on official visits of state, to spend as little time in his presence as possible. The President knows how she feels all too well, as she had been quite vocal about him never trusting the Russian President.

"Well," the President begins, "Petrov has forgotten himself. He has placed his troops and navy at the borders of four European countries, recalled his ambassador from Washington, kicked our ambassador out of Russia and demanded the turnover of our embassy in Moscow." He let what he had just said dwell with his wife for a moment before continuing. "The Joint Chiefs have a recommendation, but I don't like it. If I follow their advice, the world may never be the same. But if I act in haste, we leave our country open to possible, if not probable, military invasion of one sort or another."

"Ah," she says, "they told you to do 'nothing.' Is that General Martin's personal recommendation?" she asks.

"I think so. If I'm reading them correctly, they're more afraid of an attack on the Homeland by Russia or China, or one of their proxies than they're letting me know. They didn't exactly say to do nothing, though. Their precise recommendation is to: a) not respond militarily to Russia in Europe; b) recall all of our forces that we can recall, including our naval and submarine fleets for stationing about our Atlantic and Pacific borders. I don't like that approach, as I told you. But the generals are right that we are stretched thin. Fully responding to Russia would make our already thin ranks even more so. I think that Petrov saw exactly how we are constituted in our response to North Korea. We won, but there was a cost—valuable intel to all of our other enemies. They now know things about us that we'd rather they not know. For example, Petrov knows what we can and cannot do in the air and in the water with our much-depleted force numbers."

The First Lady lets out an audible breath of air and looks at her husband intently. "Well, Barron, what are you going to do?" This is her way, he thinks. She'd listened and then usually cut to the chase of the decision that needs to be made. The President looks over at the clock on his night stand. "5:10 a.m." it reads. It is still entirely too early in the morning, he thinks, for this level of stress.

"I don't know yet. I need to hit the gym, get a shower and a cup of coffee. I need to clear the cobwebs out." Helen knows her husband's process better than he does himself. While he was gone the previous day, she had put his Secret Service detail on notice that the gym should be opened and made ready for him. She had also made sure that his favorite navy suit was out and ready along with a starched white shirt and laid out two ties for him to choose—a pale blue striped tie and a bold red one. She thinks that the pale blue one is the better choice. Since the crisis caused by the Sleeper Virus, he had seemed to be on television every single day multiple times per day. She thinks that for his skin tone, the color red tends to wash him out on camera. Blue is a better, cooler look for him, Helen believes. "Your clean gym clothes are in the top drawer. Please put them in the hamper when you get back. I'm going to go check on the kids. They're not up yet, but I want to check."

As the President makes his way to their prodigious closet, Helen gets out of bed and puts her robe on. Except for her room, the private residence is quiet and dark. She sees the outlines of several Secret Service agents at their assigned posts—all standing and all quite awake. It's eerie to see their statuesque forms in the dark. They look perfectly still to her. "Ma'am," one of the statues says said as she walks by. She gives a breathless "good morning" and hurries on to the children's rooms. Connor and Grayden, their sons, are fast asleep in their beds which face each other. Connor, the oldest, is a few inches taller than Grayden. Both are athletes, basketball players like their father used to be. Helen hears Grayden snoring. Seeing them okay, she silently exits their room. Closing their door, she walks slowly back to her room. Sleep will not return to her for a while, she thinks. Helen knows that her husband has yet another world-altering decision to make today. She does not envy him, his position, or his responsibility. Reaching her bedside and having no hope of falling back to sleep, the President's wife puts her hands together and repeats the words that had so often before given her solace and comfort. "Our Father, which art in Heaven, hallowed by thy name," she says and then quickly finishes her much-practiced prayer. By the time that her prayer is over, she feels sleepy again and crawls into bed to lay down. Soon, she is dreaming of the soon-coming spring.

*   *   *

Right before leaving the bedroom, President Douglas lightly touches his wife's shoulder and whispers a soft "I love you" to her. She had fallen asleep again and he did not want to disturb her. Twenty-seven years into their marriage and she never ceased to amaze him. At moments like this, he feels the most grateful for her. This job is their job together. He holds the primary responsibility, but they carry the burden together. He is lucky to have chosen her, or had she chosen him, he wonders. He also believes that he is divinely blessed to have her.

More than luck had been involved on that fateful day on Yale's campus. The first time that he had even seen her, she had looked somehow placed before him, like he was supposed to see her at just that moment. That's the right word, he thinks, she had looked placed, as if he was supposed to see her there, like she was supposed to be there to speak and spend the rest of his life with her.

The President continues to reminisce about that day as he makes his way to the Oval Office. He expects to see his top security advisors there waiting on him. He is not disappointed. "How is everyone?" he says entering the room. The looks of his top staff are grim—and tired. They are all tired. They are easily as tired as he is, and they all have families as he does. No one is sleeping much. Each knows that their advice and his decisions are critical to America remaining a viable nation. No one has a time line for the wake up of their fellow unconscious Americans--the IMs. A cure doesn't seem imminent. Even if a cure comes soon, the geopolitical realities that countries like Russia and China are forcing upon them could become irreversible. A full shake-up in the current world order seems likely.

"Mr. President," Trevor says, "there's been no change. Russia is still amassing its troops in key strategic locations on the land and sea borders of the four countries. There does not seem to be any further troop movement though. They seem to be in a holding pattern. However, Israel, Germany, France and Great Britain are on high alert and have called in all of their military personnel. It's a show of force, but some Israelis are claiming that it's time for them to strike Iran. Iran has in turn aligned itself with Russia and has put its military on high alert. Fighting in Syria has been ongoing. The Syrian President seems to be planning a massive push into occupied parts of his country against the Syrian rebels. We're concerned about another whole scale slaughter of Syrian civilians should he proceed. It's a lot to contend with, we know, Mr. President. Those are all of the facts as we understand them."

"Thank you, Trevor," the President begins, "you're right. That is a lot. I fear, though, that we may be only at the beginning of it all." The President pauses before speaking again. He wants to survey the room. He looks for fear and doubt amongst his team. What he sees instead is caution, resolve and courage. "I don't like any of our options. I really think that we've been caught with our figurative pants down. North Korea undressed us. It showed our enemies and allies how thin we are. There was no way to hide that, I know, but I don't like it just the same."

"We're caught between the proverbial rock and a hard place with no good options. But our number one priority at all times," he continues, "is to protect the Homeland. If there is a good chance that we might be struck or invaded, we have to make that our first priority. It would not do us or the world any good to stop a Russian breach into Eastern Europe only to face a massive attack or invasion in our own country." The room stands in rapt attention to his next few words. "Therefore, I am authorizing the effective pull back of our Navy to our own waters in the east and west. I want all of our carrier groups and submarine groups to create a nautical barrier that communicates our resolve to protect and maintain our country. We have no idea yet when our IM citizens will rejoin us.

Hopefully, it will be soon. Until then, we must protect the country. This is our first and only priority right now."

There is an audible sigh of relief as the President finishes speaking. Clearly, he sees, his top staff isn't too keen on the idea of going to Europe to fight Russia and whomever else that they might encounter. "Valerie," he says, "please alert the Joint Chiefs that I'm implementing General Martin's recommendations. I'll need him to patch me into the Admirals of all the carrier groups. I want them to hear it straight from me."

"Understood, Mr. President. I'll arrange that right away," she says.

Good, he thinks. His next most unpleasant task would be to call the leaders of each of the threatened countries and then to speak to his country's greatest allies to assuage their growing doubts and fears about U.S. commitment to them as U.S. allies. President Douglas has no doubt that American members of the foreign press will try to absolutely crucify him for his decision. Those members, though, have the benefit of not having to deal directly with the crisis at home. If there was ever a time for the President to remain unconcerned with public opinion, this is it, he muses. Still, he isn't looking forward to making his dramatic announcement followed by his briefing with the press. Perhaps chewing glass would be more pleasant, he thinks.

*   *   *

Jerome and Darryl are about halfway through their shift working swiftly from house to house in the Indian Hill neighborhood of Cincinnati when they hear the news come over Jerome's walkie-talkie. "The President is calling all of our fleets and non-White soldiers home immediately. He's stationing our White soldiers on warships that will be stationed off of our Pacific and Atlantic coasts. Subs are coming home too." The voice that they hear is that of their commanding officer, Captain Hinton. "You sure that's true, Captain?" Jerome says into his walkie. Captain Hinton barks back, "Do I sound like I don't know how to listen to CNN, Middleton?! Of course, it's true! At least, that's what's being reported. It's on MSNBC too. In fact, it's everywhere. Now get back to work. I knew that you'd want to know. Hinton out."

Jerome looks at Darryl with an incredulous look. "Don't look so surprised, Rome," Darryl says. "What did you think would happen? If I were Russia or China, I'd try us too. If they are ever going to have a chance at getting out from under the American imperial shadow, now would be the time." Jerome marvels at how prescient Darryl can be about these kinds of things. He is far more than what he appears to be, he thinks. He seems to be learning something new about his friend every day in the midst of this crisis. The more their circumstances have changed, Jerome thinks, the more Darryl seems to add layers and reveal a complexity that Jerome had not seen all the years that they had ridden their trash truck together.

"Maybe", Jerome says, "I'd just like not to have to put on a soldier's uniform in addition to all of my other duties. Do you think that they'd reinstate the draft, Darryl?"

"They might, but I think we'd have to be in all-out war for that. No, this seems like a show of force by the President of a different kind--more preventative than anything else. It says to me 'look, we see what you're doing, but attacking the United States is not an option—don't try us.' It's the smart play. We can't afford to be sending our military all over the world to stamp out 'Soviet' aggression wherever we find it. I think that those days are over." Darryl clasps his hands in front of him like a philosopher who has just taught a master class on strategic military maneuvers. Jerome is impressed.

"Darryl," Jerome begins, "how do you know all of this? How are you able to see around these corners like that?"

"I read, my Brother, I *reads,*" he says in a faux urban street accent that makes everything that he's just said, suddenly, very funny to Jerome. *Art of War, Patton, How Wars are Won, The 33 Strategies of War*—they're all staples in my library, Rome. And speaking of Rome, the Romans were the toughest, baddest military in all of pre-modern warfare. Military students today are still required to study them. I mean, Hannibal of Carthage was a bad boy too, but you get what I'm saying."

Jerome chuckles and says "Okay, Darryl, let's check in on our crew. We've got about forty workers going through all the homes in this part of Indian Hill. Lots of people have been found, most of whom who are in pretty good shape. What's the count thus far?" Darryl looks at his iPad which houses the official and most current count of people afflicted with the Sleeper Virus in their area: "By my count today, we've found four-hundred and five Sleepers—of that number about ten fatalities. The fatalities are all either from accidental falls or exposure. No one was intentionally killed as near as I can tell from the reporting. I've got pictures of all the fatalities except for two of them. Same address for those two though. I suggest that we go over there and take a look for ourselves."

"Sounds right, D.," Jerome says. "I don't want to miss any cause of death. The Captain will not be pleased if we do."

"Right," Darryl says, "like two days ago when Captain Hinton chewed the leader of Team Norwood up one side and down another for missing those five bodies and mis-reporting their cause of death. I thought the poor dude would fall to pieces right there, but he managed to hold it together."

"Exactly. We can't get caught slippin' like Norwood. Hyde Park must remain perfect in our Sleeper reclamation efforts. Are you with me?" Jerome says almost comically but also seriously.

"You know it, Rome. Now let's get to that house and make sure that everything is everything."

Jerome puts his police-issued SUV in gear and heads to the home of the two fatalities. He hopes that their cause of death is accidental or natural, and not caused by anyone seeking to take advantage of their crisis. He can only hope.

CHAPTER XI

"Right here, Sabrina. This is it" Isaac says as Sabrina wheels him onto his street. Isaac points to his house, a good-sized yellow two-story in the Baldwin Hills neighborhood of L.A. As they move forward toward it, Sabrina hears her name being loudly called. She looks up to see her brothers, Solomon and Xavier, sprinting towards her and Isaac.

Solomon, being the biggest and oldest, gets to her first. She collapses in his arms. Solomon picks his sister up gently. He sees the exhaustion on her face. "Oh, Sabrina," he says, "I'm so glad that you got here safely. We have been worried sick."

Xavier, Sabrina's younger brother, gets behind Isaac's wheelchair and continues pushing him towards his house. "Hello, sir" he says. "Thank you for taking care of our sister."

"Ha!" Isaac says nearly laughing. "It was mutual. She took good care of me. Got me here and everything. I'm impressed!"

"Mr. Isaac," Solomon says, "we've checked on your wife. She's fine. She's had around the clock care. No one has forgotten about her. Last we checked, she was awake and calling for you."

"The Lord is truly faithful," Isaac says. "Please get me inside."

Xavier moves quickly to wheel Isaac into his house. He has to stop at the steps leading to his front door, but carefully eases Isaac from the wheelchair and braces him as he makes a slow ascent to his front door. Sabrina sees them disappear inside.

"You can put me down, Solo," Sabrina says using her brother's nickname. "Okay, sis," he says slowly releasing her.

"How the heck did you get here from San Francisco?" Solomon queries.

"Luck, determination and some combination of Muay Thai and Cross Fit," she says.

Solomon chuckles at that. "Okay, sis, I see you. Proud of you too. We didn't know if you'd made it off your plane or not. We were all in near hysterics before you called to let us know that you were okay. I started to come get you, but Dad didn't want us to leave L.A. We didn't know if we had been invaded or what. It was all so crazy."

"Still looks crazy," Sabrina says. "Wheeling Isaac from the highway into the city," she hesitates before continuing to speak "we saw craziness."

Solomon shakes his head in agreement. "Yeah, that's the best word to describe it. There are so many people here. Of course, there are lots of unconscious White folks literally everywhere. While we waited on you, X and I helped to grab folks off the streets and out of their cars and just move them to some safe areas, mostly hospitals, but wherever the mayor and police told us to. There's been a lot of looting, but it looks like that might be ending here soon. Surprisingly, all the gangs have called truces and are helping the police secure folks. It's a sight to behold. L.A. is remarkably calm in my opinion. It's been amazing seeing so many Black, Brown and Asian folks working together. Inspiring, really," Solomon says.

Sabrina takes a moment to consider what Solomon has just said. Walking into L.A. from the highway had been unnerving. She had seen many accidents along the walk to Isaac's house. She had also seen many casualties and evidence of where casualties had occurred. Sabrina and Isaac also observed that there is a lot of activity in the city. Folks, mostly Black and Brown had been bustling about attending to the unconscious of which there are quite a few.

"What's the latest news, Solo?" Sabrina asks.

"Oh boy, it's a lot, sis. For starters, the government looks dang near shut down. President Douglas has been keeping us in the loop with near round the clock press conferences. It's clear that whatever this is has occurred nationwide. Definitely, all the big cities are hit, rural areas are hit, and everything inside the continental U.S. got hit."

"Alaska? Hawaii?" Sabrina queries.

"No, they seem to be okay. Our fleets outside of the U.S. are all operational. And all of our White Americans outside the U.S. are okay too. This crisis seems to be limited to folks who were here today. That's it. But that also means that White folks can't come home yet. We don't know what it is. But rumors are spreading."

"Rumors? What rumors?" Sabrina says with a puzzled look on her face.

Solo sees that his sister is close to passing out and thinks better about telling her anything else until after they get her home and she can get some rest.

"Hey, Solo, let's go, bro" Xavier says as he exits Isaac's house. "Isaac is straight. He's sitting with his wife now. Her home healthcare worker is here and taking care of her too."

"Cool," Solo says. "Let's get baby sis home. She's through."

"I'm not through, punk" Sabrina says in mild protest to her brother.

Solomon chuckles as he guides Sabrina into his big wheeled Jeep. "Your car is ridiculous," Sabrina protests as she struggles to get into the elevated back seat. Solomon partially lifts her into it, recognizing that his sister's strength has all but left her. He marvels at what she had been able to accomplish with Isaac, and decides to keep his snide comments to himself, at least until after she's had a chance to recover.

Once Sabrina is secure, Solomon and Xavier scramble into the Jeep. Their house is only two neighborhoods away from Isaac's house. They'll need to avoid a few accidents along the way, but the ride shouldn't take more than fifteen minutes. After about a minute Solomon and Xavier hear their sister snoring softly. "She's spent, bro" Xavier says. "That's facts, X" Solo replies. "Mom and Dad will be happy to see her. Can't wait to get her there." Xavier nods his head in approval at Solomon's statement. "Once she wakes up, we'll have a lot to discuss. There's lots to do right now" Xavier says as Solomon carefully wheels them through the city to their parents' home.

Donnie stirs to the light sound of Latin music wafting
its way into Bella's bedroom from the kitchen. He smells the
distinctive scent of breakfast food being conjured – bacon, eggs,
chilaquiles and pancakes, Donnie's favorite. Donnie cracks an
eye open and sees Bella still sleeping next to him. Ah, he thinks.
Bella's grandmother is up and making breakfast. Donnie wonders
if she knows that he's here. Just then, Donnie hears loud laughter
between Ms. Marquita and Clarence. Yep, she knows, Donnie
thinks since he didn't go home to Clarence's last night. He feels a
tinge of worry at what Ms. Marquita might think, but decides not
to dwell on it.

"Good morning, sleepy head," Isabella says to him in a
mostly whisper.

Donnie looks at her and smiles. "Good morning, Bella," he
says.

She reaches out to him and pulls him close to her. Donnie
feels that she's still naked. He is too. Bella places her full lips onto
his and kisses him deeply. He catches the faint whiff of morning
breath from her and smiles, because he knows that he has it too.

"Um, I need to go brush my teeth. I'll be right back,"
Bella says as she turns from him to exit the bed. Donnie watches
her voluptuous form as she dons a nearby robe. His eyes stay fixed
upon her as she quickly, silently exists the room. Oh boy, Donnie
thinks. He hadn't expected any of this to occur, but he's glad that
it did. A lot had happened since the first day of the crisis. Donnie
thinks that while a lot around him has changed, he's changed too.
Donnie knew that he'd really liked Isabella before last night. Now,
after having spent the night together, he feels an attachment to her
that he did not expect. He wonders what she may be feeling and
plans to ask her sometime soon.

Donnie is startled when he feels Bella slide into the bed and
under the covers next to him. He had gotten lost in his thoughts
and had not noticed when she came in and took off her robe. She
nuzzles into him, the smell of fresh breath covering the small
distance between them. Bella kisses him softly, but Donnie resists.
"I need to go brush my teeth too," he says. She kisses him again
and he doesn't resist. "I've got enough fresh breath for the both
us," she says. After another long kiss Donnie asks, "Um, is your
grandmother okay? Does she know that I'm here?" Bella chuckles.

"Of course, she does. Who do you think gave me

permission to have you over? My abuela knows all, sees all. You're fine. Just relax. We can get breakfast after."

After what, Donnie wonders, but it does not take long for him know what Bella means.

*   *   *

Sometime later, Donnie re-awakens with a monster appetite. He sees that Bella is no longer in the room. He hears her soft voice through the door. She is speaking with her grandmother. He does not hear Clarence's voice. Donnie looks at his watch and recoils in horror…oh crap, he thinks. It's after 10:00 am. He should have been gone hours ago. Clarence must have left without him, he decides.

Donnie looks around the room for his clothes. He sees them neatly folded on a chair near the bed. Gingerly, he gets up and dons his clothing. As he straightens his shirt he hears Bella's grandmother, Marquita Fuentes, call his name.

"Donnie, Donnie," she says. "Come get something to eat."

The smell of breakfast still clings to the air. Donnie's hunger is now ravenous but thinks he'll miss this meal to catch up with Clarence. Donnie opens Bella's door and walks to the kitchen. He sees Mrs. Fuentes and Bella sitting at the small kitchen table, both nursing cups of coffee.

"Come, Donnie, have a seat," Mrs. Fuentes says. "Bella has been telling me all about the work that you do as a stockbroker and financial analyst. When do you think that you'll get back to that?"

Donnie is struck by the question. It's the same one that he'd been considering for the last few days. More than two weeks into the crisis caused by the Sleeper Virus, Donnie's job had been and is to work with Clarence to secure as many unconscious White and fair-skinned people that they can find. They had not been deputized by the Chicago Police Department, but they had signed on as independent contractors to do much of the same work under their guidance. This is an arrangement that both men prefer. Donnie believes that he'll soon be able to get back to his stock broker job. Clarence, as a former felon, has an innate deep distrust of the police, all police, and never wants to become one.

"I honestly don't know, Mrs. Fuentes. I plan to go back by my office sometime soon, but other than that, I don't know when the financial markets will re-open or even what they'll look like when they do re-open. I suspect that when the markets re-open, it'll be all hands-on deck, and that includes me. I don't even know how to get paid for that job anymore. There's no one there."

Mrs. Fuentes deeply furrows her brow as she looks at Donnie. She crosses her arms and draws a deep breath before speaking. "I think that it's important, Donnie, that you not lose sight of what it is that you really do. It seems to me that some kind of normalcy will return, whether a cure is found or not. In that normalcy, skilled, educated folks like you will need to step up and do what you do. Bella is about a semester away from graduating from college. Those all seem to be suspended right now, except for the HBCUs that I've heard about, but I'm telling her, just like I'm telling you, that she needs to finish and contribute, especially if the Sleepers remain, well, asleep. What do you think?"

Donnie marvels at the wisdom of this almost seventy-year-old woman. She is beautiful, and Donnie can readily see that she was every bit as gorgeous as her granddaughter is when she was younger. Donnie glances at Bella and sees her looking intently at him. It occurs to him in that moment that she is as much interested in his response as her grandmother is. Donnie remembers an oft handed comment that his father had once made about how a woman chooses the man, and not the other way around. He wonders in that moment if this is part of the choosing. Donnie decides to choose his words carefully.

"I think that we really can't predict an end to this crisis with the Sleepers. I believe that the government, or what's left of the government, is working on it. I believe President Douglas when he says that we must remain one nation and that we all have work to do on that. I'm happy to see so many folks pulling together to help make that happen. I think that our countrymen who are afflicted by the Sleepers Virus would be fairly impressed with what we've done so far, not that we've been perfect. I definitely want to get back to my regular job and hope to do so soon. But I have to be honest, Mrs. Fuentes," Donnie pauses "I think that I've fallen in love with Bella, and I don't see my life ever being the same because of that."

Donnie hears Bella audibly gasp and sees a mix between knowing and amusement on Mrs. Fuentes' face. "I see, Donnie, is that honestly what you feel?"

"Yes, I do. I'm young, but I've only ever felt this way once before in my life, in college. That didn't work out, but I know that it was love," Donnie says.

"Bella, how do you feel?" Mrs. Fuentes asks.

"Abuela, I've never been love before. I've had boyfriends, but never this. I love him too. I think I've loved him from the first day that I met him. He's all that I think about and, other than you, all that I care about."

"Well I'm glad that that's settled," Mrs. Fuentes says. "I've been watching you two circle each other for the better part of two weeks wondering when you might both realize what this is. In these uncertain times you would do well to hold onto what you have and nurture it. We don't know what this country might become in the near future. Hopefully, you'll have each other. I approve."

At that, Mrs. Fuentes stands up and walks to her counter. She picks up a plate heavy with food and hands it to Isabella. "Bella, give this to Donnie. Take the plastic off first, girl. It's already warm."

Donnie hungrily takes the plate from Bella with thanks. He begins to devour his breakfast and is grateful for the food. Bella watches him as he eats in her intense, yet unobtrusive manner. His thoughts drift to when he might check in on his regular job and when he might actually go home to his apartment. He considers that he should do both soon. "Bella, I need you to pack an overnight bag for a few days. I need to get to my apartment and check in at my office. Is that okay?" he asks. "Yes, of course. I can be ready to go whenever you are."

"You know what," Donnie says "today is as good a day as any. Cool?"

"Cool," she replies. "Abuela?"

"Cool," Mrs. Fuentes replies.

"Awesome. We'll see you in a few days, Mrs. Fuentes."

"No, you won't," she replies. "And that's cool too."

*   *   *

"This car really is ridiculous, Solo," Sabrina says.

Sabrina's oldest brother, Solomon, chuckles at what she says. "Yeah, I know, big, bad and way too much. But that's just how I do. Now shut up and let me get you out of it, sis."

Sabrina's legs are both cramped and it's hard for her to move, let alone walk. She allows her brother to ease her out of the high back seat but won't let him carry her. "Let me try to walk. You both get on either side of me and I can make it."

"It'd be easier if you let one of us carry you, Sis" Xavier

331

says, but Sabrina would hear none of it. This is the trademark Clayton stubbornness, Xavier thinks, of which Sabrina had gotten a double dose.

Slowly but surely, Solomon and Xavier lift and hobble their sister to their parents' front door. As soon as they arrive to it, the door swings open and Sabrina's parents are there.

"Sabrina! Sabrina!" her mother shouts. "We have been worried sick about you!! We thought that you died!" her mother says throwing herself around her daughter. Sabrina's mother is not a small woman and stands at five foot eight inches. She is not as tall as Sabrina, who is tall at five foot ten inches. Like her daughter, she has been an athlete all of her life. Angela Clayton played tennis in college and has taught it for most of her adult life. She is fit, trim, and strong.

Sabrina feels her mother's strong arms pulling her in even closer as she feels herself become light headed from loss of breadth. "Mom," Sabrina gasps. "You're crushing me!" Mrs. Clayton eases her hug just enough to allow Sabrina to catch her breath, but not so much that Sabrina can move. "I just love you so much, girl. I was worried sick. You're my only daughter."

"Gee thanks, Mom," Xavier says sarcastically. "That makes Solo and me feel great. Thanks for that."

"I always knew she was your favorite, Mom" Solomon says with a wry smile on his face.

"Shut up, boys and let your sister get inside. She looks exhausted," their father Robert says. "Angela, please release our daughter and let her inside."

Mrs. Clayton begrudgingly complies with her husband's entreaties but holds onto Sabrina as she walks her inside. "Sabrina, your beds all made up. I want you to get into bed and rest. We'll talk about all your adventures when you awake. There's a small plate of food for you on the nightstand in your room. You must be famished. You should eat what's there for now and when you awake, we'll have a feast."

This is a big deal, Sabrina thinks. Even as adults, their parents forbid them from eating in their rooms. Her mother putting food in her room and allowing her to eat there is huge. Sabrina turns around to look at her brothers and gives them a smug look of triumph. Her brothers, of course, respond with the necessary hand and facial gestures to communicate their displeasure.

Once on her bed, Sabrina collapses into it. She allows its soft comforter and pillows to envelope and draw her in. Sabrina wants to completely give in to her exhaustion and fade away into oblivion. As she begins to contemplate the nothingness of her soon coming rest, her right eye slides open. She sees a plate with her favorite: her mom's grilled turkey and cheese sandwich. Sabrina can smell its savory aroma and feels the pang of hunger in the middle of her stomach. As a sheer force of will, she raises up onto her elbows and then sits straight up. Sabrina hungrily devours the sandwich, the potato chips and orange juice provided to her, miraculously, by her mother. She lays back down, now fully embracing the rest to come. Her last conscious thought is of her fiancé, Michael, and how she's going to get to him.

*   *   *

"Paging Dr. Fleming! Paging Dr. Fleming!"

Michael stirs from his sleep. He lays on a cot set up for he and the other doctors who have been working around the clock at the hospital since the Sleeper Virus caused this crisis. Checking his watch, he sees that he was able to sleep for about an hour. That's more than last time, sixteen hours ago, he thinks. Dr. Fleming rises, and puts his glasses and his shoes on. His clothes are already on. There is no time or ability for him to undress when he's able to rest. He knows that he has to move quickly when called upon.

Michael walks a short distance to the nurse's station to check in. "Hey, Gloria, what's up?" he asks.

"Dr. Fleming, we've got several Sleepers in emergency who have been wounded. Some appear wounded from car crashes, some," Gloria hesitates "seem wounded from deliberate bodily harm inflicted upon them. Police and good citizens were able to rescue them and bring them here. They need you downstairs to help operate."

Great, Dr. Fleming thinks. It is one thing to see a Sleeper who had been injured from accidental injury. It is another thing entirely to see one hurt or worse because of some evil person's actions. Those are the hardest to witness medically and to treat. Dr. Fleming thinks that he'll probably need some medical help himself to deal with his own growing trauma. He decides that he cannot dwell on that now. Now is the time to serve and help others through this mess.

"Thanks, Gloria. Tell them that I'm on the way."

Dr. Fleming finds the closest door to the steps and begins a quick descent to the first floor. It's six flights down, but he'd rather walk the distance than wait for an elevator. He thinks that the physical activity will give him the opportunity to clear out some of the cob webs of his previous nap.

On the way down to the emergency room, Michael's thoughts drift to Sabrina, his fiancé. He knows that she's okay. He knows that she survived her flight. He knows that she's making her way home to L.A. from San Francisco. Her brothers and parents, especially her mother, had kept him informed. The cell phone networks are janky and unreliable right now, but the internet is still up and he'd been getting their emails. He hopes that she doesn't encounter any problems and that she gets to her family safely. Michael also hopes that she gets to him somehow. He immediately dismisses that thought as both selfish and ridiculous. If anything, she needs to stay in L.A. and be with her family. That's the safest of all places. He wants her to be safe more than he wants her to be with him.

"Dr. Fleming, we're glad that you're here," Dr. Marshall says. "We've got multiple casualties, some of which are pretty gruesome. I know that you've just finished your surgical rotation. We need every qualified and mostly qualified pair of hands down here to help out. Since we've been in taking the Sleepers, we're pushed to capacity on staffers. Thank goodness for the volunteers that are rounding them up and helping us with intake."

"I've got you, Dr. Marshall. Happy to help. What do you want me to do first?" Dr. Fleming says.

"First, scrub up, then meet me in OR 1. We have a Sleeper with multiple gunshot wounds. I think that I can save her, which is why I'm even trying, but I need a second pair of hands. You up for it?" Dr. Marshall asks.

Hell, no I'm not up for it, Michael thinks, but the job is the job. "Yes, Sir, I'm ready. I'll see you in five minutes."

Michael dons a fresh pair of scrubs and washes his hands and arms thoroughly in preparation for surgery. A nurse meets him at OR 1 and puts the rest of the required surgical garments on him. He enters to see Dr. Marshall already there, in gloves and ready to go. Michael takes a deep breath and says a silent prayer as he walks the distance from the door to the patient who is laid flat on the operating table. He sees the patient's wounds and is struck by how young she is, no more than twenty-one. Any other day, he thinks, and this would not be happening to her or most folks that look like her. But neither today nor this week are like any other.

"Michael, are you ready?" Dr. Marshall says.

"Yes, Sir, let's proceed."

*   *   *

"Sis, here, drink this." Solomon hands Sabrina a cup filled with green tea and honey. "You've been asleep for the last ten hours. Mom thought I should come and wake you up. How are you feeling?"

There is genuine concern on Solo's face. Sabrina notes it and decides to claw herself back into wakefulness. "I'm fine. Still tired, but fine. What's going on?"

"Lots," Solomon says. There's been some looting in the city but police and citizens are trying to clamp it down. But L.A. is a big place, so there's no way to stop all of it. Also, it looks like there is some issue in North Korea. Europe now knows what's been happening here. There has been talk of shutting down the internet so that no one can do damage to our network and facilities that depend on it for operation."

Sabrina remembers that Solomon, her oldest brother, is a nerd and a techie. He had been a computer science major at college for two years before he'd dropped out and got a job programming and doing IT. He had wanted to stay close to his parents while going to school and working and had never looked outside of the city for either opportunity. Solo is truly a home body, she thinks, and again marvels at how different that they are.

"Solo, what do you think is going to happen?" Sabrina asks.

"My best guess, sis, is that one or more foreign powers is going to try to cause some major disruptions at some of our most sensitive locations. It's what I would do if on the other side. The problem is, we have so many things networked and connected that it would be fairly-easy to cause some major disruptions. That's the thing that I'm most worried about. I'm thinking about reaching out to someone in charge to see if I can help with that."

"I think you should," Sabrina says. "You'd be great at that."

"Aw, sis! You do care!" Solomon says and kisses his sister on her forehead.

"Aw, shut-up, Solo!" Sabrina says playfully before planting a solid punch into his right shoulder.

"Ouch, sis! You know that you're trained. Don't hit me, sucka," Solo says.

Sabrina starts the slow process of easing herself out of her bed and getting up. "Hand me my robe, bro. It's on the back of that chair." Solomon dutifully complies. "I'll meet you in the living room, sis. There's a war council gathering. We need to talk all about what happened to you and what to do next. See you in five," Solomon says and then exits Sabrina's room.

Sabrina puts her robe on and then sits on the corner of her bed. She's still groggy and would rather instead go back to bed. She knows, however, that she needs to satisfy her family's curiosity as well as her own. It's clear to her that they all know more than she does about what's been happening. She has questions about their city, their country and Michael. She knows that her fiancé is physically okay but has not spoken to him at all. Sabrina is unsure whether speaking to him is even possible. She is determined to try.

Walking into the living room, Sabrina sees her mother, father and both brothers gathered in the main sitting area. She joins her brothers on the couch, sitting between them. They're big men like her father and make her look small in comparison. Growing up with two large big brothers had always been one-part pain, to three parts joy. They had always been very protective of her to a fault. High school boyfriends were all but non-existent. The one brave soul who came to her home with any regularity, Derrick, had been the only one willing to endure the stares and threats of her brothers for the privilege of watching a movie, in full view of all, in this very room. Perhaps because Derrick had had sisters of his own, he understood Solo and Xavier's motivation. Their act did not seem to bother him at all.

"Sabrina, I'm really glad to see that you're okay," Sabrina's father, Robert says.

"Thanks, Dad. I'm still very tired, though. But I should recover quickly," Sabrina says.

"Oh, baby, we're just so glad to have you with us," Sabrina's mother says.

"Thanks, Mom."

"It's really whatever," Xavier says.

"Right. I mean, she cool, or whatever, but damn," Solomon says echoing the playful, silly sentiments of his brother.

"Boys, be serious, you know that this is nothing short of miraculous that we didn't lose your sister. You'd be crushed if we had."

The room draws silent at her father's admonishment. A heavy weight enters and they all feel it.

"Sabrina, there have been hundreds of people who have lost their lives in plane crashes around the country. There are potentially thousands who have died from automobile accidents. The authorities also know that many have been injured in some places that not a lot of Black and Brown folks live in. We may never be able to get to them all," Robert says.

"We've been doing our part to try to help, sis" Solomon says. "It is overwhelming though in a city as big as L.A. Xavier and I have been driving around picking up folks where we find them and transporting them to the local hospitals, which is what the mayor and others told us to do. Xavier has been volunteering at a hospital as well, working to intake Sleepers as they arrive."

"Yep, it's been a trip, Sabrina," Xavier says. "Most coming in are accident victims. Some, though, received intentional trauma after falling asleep. I've even seen some intentionally killed. Those are the worst."

Sabrina allows all of what she is hearing to sink in for a moment before speaking. "Wow is all I can say right now. What is our government doing?"

"Our government?" her father says. "Our government is doing all that it can. Congress is depleted, the courts are depleted, most, but not all of our police forces are depleted. I know that in some cities, the police are deputizing folks to get them to help. Haven't seen that here because of the diversity of the force, but LAPD has been asking folks to volunteer to help them out. I know that the gang unit has helped to organize the gangs, who were already helping, frankly, to maximize their efforts."

"Yeah, that's been some kind of freaky kismet to observe the Black gangs, the Chicano gangs, the Asian gangs and the police all working side-by-side to secure Sleepers and help to maintain the peace. And the gangs seem to be taking their new role very seriously, even to the point of rescuing Sleepers from others seeking to do them harm," Xavier says.

"What about Michael?" Sabrina asks.

"He's been worried sick, dear, just like we have," Mrs. Clayton says.

"Has he been able to call, Mom?"

"No, Sabrina, none of us have. Phone service has been spotty. Sometimes it works, sometimes it doesn't. The internet is up so emails are getting through. I emailed him the second you went to sleep. He should know that you're here safe. I know that he hasn't left the hospital but once or twice to get fresh underwear. He's sleeping at the hospital," Mrs. Clayton tells them.

"Sabrina, no one knows how long this crisis will last. We're all hoping for the best, but there is no good timetable," Mr. Clayton says. "All planes except for the military are grounded until further notice. Trains and buses too. There is no organized transportation right now."

Sabrina is quiet for a moment before clearing her throat. "Guys, I really need to see Michael. I want to travel to New York to be with him."

There it is, Sabrina thinks. A nuclear bomb. She looks at the terrified expressions on her parents faces. She looks at her brothers too. They're like stone. She can't tell what they're thinking or feeling. The silence in the room is deafening. Sabrina puts her head down and squirms.

"Told you," Solomon says.

"Yep," Xavier chimes in.

"We know our sister, Pops. It is what it is," Solomon says.

"She's more stubborn than her mother, damn it," Mr. Clayton says. "Sabrina, I can in no way allow this, but you're a grown woman. The only way to do this is to drive it. The whole thing. Three thousand plus miles away. We have no idea what's out there. You can't do this alone, honey."

"Why not? I got Isaac here by myself with no one to help. Why can't I do this alone?" Sabrina asks.

"Because you don't have to," Solomon says. "We'll take you. X and I already discussed it. We knew that you would try to do something like this. There's no way that we'd let our baby sister travel by herself all the way to New York, no matter how tough you are."

"It's settled then?" Mrs. Clayton asks.

"It's settled, Mom," Xavier says.

"Sabrina, when do you want to leave?" Solomon asks.

"Tomorrow? Does that work, guys? Sabrina asks.

"Tomorrow works," Solomon says. "We'll take my big ass ridiculous Jeep. We'll be fine."

CHAPTER XII

Had it only been thirty days? President Douglas thinks to himself. His logical mind confirms that it had been, yes, thirty days since the Sleeper Virus struck. However, his illogical heart feels as if it's been a year or longer since this crisis began. That is how much older President Douglas feels and that's how much he looks, at least to himself, though his wife lies and tells him that he has not aged a day. He knows better.

The country that was, just thirty days later, is different today—in some ways better and in some ways worse. In order to maintain it, the President had been called upon in ways that he did not expect or like. He, in turn, had to call upon others to help him safeguard the country against any would-be invaders, attacks and antagonizers. As it currently stands, the IMs are still unconscious. Neither Dr. Krauss nor any of their top researchers are any closer to a cure. They had identified and isolated the Sleeper Virus, but every attempt to dislodge it from the key systems that govern the body's metabolic processes had failed. Because the human body's metabolism is controlled by several systems operating independently, but also cooperatively, attacking the virus in one manner or in one place in the body does not work. A systemic approach is required. That approach does not yet exist.

Dr. Krauss has since described fighting the Sleeper Virus like fighting a cancer that had metastasized and attacked multiple internal organs at once. For now, thirty days after Sleep Day, recovered IMs are safe and being kept alive. Their housing, mostly in hospitals and warehouses, is not ideal, but the President and his team are working on a plan to provide a suitable long-term remedy if need be.

President Douglas having forsaken rest for the last month is tired. Sleep had escaped him and his staff most nights since the beginning of this epidemic. Helen is worried about him—worried enough to step up and be one of his most trusted advisors in the absence of others, officially in the White House. He had appointed his wife as an official part of his Cabinet because he trusts her implicitly, and to see her more. Because of all the upheaval to the country, his job now robs him of more sleep than even his previous tasks had. He is grateful to have her work shoulder to shoulder with him. It is all hands-on deck in the Douglas White House.

When the Sleeper Virus hit, there were twenty to thirty members of Congress, White members, who had not been afflicted because they are overseas. They continue to serve in their official capacities albeit from one of several American embassies abroad. Most are in either France, England, Brazil, Germany or Israel. The President coordinates a daily briefing with these members to keep them abreast of the country's progress. As a group, they had been more than a little hesitant to confer additional powers to President Douglas, but given the circumstances, reluctantly agreed to do so. Their chief concern, other than the country's welfare, is the location and welfare of their families. As with the families of the several hundred afflicted Congress persons, he had ordered them safely moved to secure hospitals on military bases within the first week after the Sleeper Virus took hold.

Thirty days into the crises caused by the Sleeper Virus, President Douglas pauses to reflect on all of the changes that are occurring albeit for the survival of the country. His entire staff is again full and completely reconstituted except for the persons of color who were already members. Every person lost to the Sleeper Virus has been replaced. The remnants of Congress, notably the White members now overseas, Congressional Black Caucus, Latino congressmen and women and the one lone Black Senator, had authorized extraordinary powers to the Executive Branch, temporarily, to keep things afloat. All had insisted, and the

348

President had readily agreed, that such new powers are temporary. No one wants a king, least of all President Douglas himself.

Even Supreme Court Justice Reynolds is now on board. When the virus struck, his wife had been afflicted. He had been inconsolable. After two weeks, the President sent over the Secret Service to his house to roust him and bring him to the White House. They sat and spoke together for a long time. Though Justice Reynolds is known for his conservatism and his silence on the Court, he had been loquacious in the expression of his grief and his fear for the country. Neither man had spoken together much before, but that day President Douglas had gained ground with him. Justice Reynolds promised him then that he would work with Justice Ortega to maintain orderly government so that the nation might recover. True to his word, the Supreme Court, with Reynolds now its acting Chief Justice, approved Congress' temporary powers act to the President.

Thirty days from Sleep Day and they had their 'shadow government,' one of the last things his former Chief of Staff had recommend before he was himself afflicted with the Sleeper Virus.

In North Korea the country had done enough to prove its military prowess, at least enough to keep Russia, China and all others at bay if only for a little while, President Douglas hopes. The North Korean President had done the U.S. a favor, President Douglas thinks. By provoking an attack on South Korea, the U.S. had been given a relatively easy opportunity to show its military might. It had also, however, shown its military limitations. When the Russians massed at the borders of Ukraine, Belarus, Poland, and Romania, there was little that the U.S. could itself do about it, being stretched too thin. Instead of engaging the Russians directly, the President had ordered that its fleets return to U.S. waters and form a barrier against any would-be foreign invaders on its east and west coasts. It had worked, at least, to assuage the fears of the President's Joint Chiefs.

President Douglas and his staff had also worked hard since Sleep Day to shore up their digital borders. Unlike some others, the United States' internet is wide open. That's a problem when a well-financed foreign power seeks to disrupt key systems and sites within the country. So much of the United States is networked through the internet that powers like Russia, Iran, and North Korea were able, initially, to cause major issues at refineries, power plants, mining sites and even gas stations. That was true before President Douglas issued orders to cordon off the U.S. internet to block out any and all foreign outlets. This decision, in particular, had been hugely unpopular amongst the SMs and overseas U.S. citizens, but it was a necessary one given the size of the threat and the damage that malicious nations had already caused.

True to the malevolent intent of its ruler, Russia invaded Ukraine and re-incorporated it into Russia. In response, France and Great Britain sent sea and air forces to Poland and Romania. President Petrov seemed to have gotten the hint. He withdrew all Russian forces from the remaining countries, but kept Ukraine as its prize. The West had lived to fight another day, President Douglas thinks. He knows, however, that he'd have to make things right in Ukraine one day. Though a fledgling ally, Ukraine is still an ally and deserves the U.S.' help.

Logistically, finding and cataloguing all the IMs is a daunting task that continues. Many millions of IMs live in the major cities. Finding them and helping the city dwellers had been easiest. By sheer volume, finding them all is a herculean task. To aid in that task, the President made, what in other times would be, a highly controversial, if not impossible decision. He issues Presidential pardons and grants clemency to all incarcerated non-violent offenders under the condition that they each report to an assigned governmental office for new work assignments. President Douglas also suspends the prosecution of drug-related crimes temporarily. The infrastructure to prosecute and hunt down drug offenders currently does not exist like it did at previous levels. He wants the pardoned offenders to know that he is serious about keeping his word.

Another logistical nightmare is getting the remaining SM personnel busy doing the IM search and rescue work to every place that the IMs are. Before the Sleeper Virus struck, the SM population had been concentrated in mostly urban areas. The IM, or Sleeper, population is for the most part, evenly dispersed throughout the country. There are states that had almost no SM population and therefore little ability to quickly identify and rescue the IMs. Places like South Dakota, North Dakota, Wyoming and the plain states are the most onerous places to be if you are an unconscious IM, especially if you became unconscious outside in the elements. The Sleeper Virus struck in February, in the middle of a very cold winter. Severe winter storms knocked out workers' ability to find and rescue many Sleepers there. Undoubtedly, many IM lives had been lost due to the elements, by accident, and simple starvation because of a lack of SM availability for search and rescue.

The President had sent as many resources to these locations as possible, while still maintaining the country's internal security integrity. For many towns in the heart of the country, such help had come too late. They discovered that whole towns had been wiped out by the combined effects of the virus and the inability to reach the IMs before they either starved, froze to death, or worse.

As he had promised, the President re-opens the markets three weeks after Sleep Day. Predictably, the markets tanked badly. The Dow Jones dropped 5,000 points in ten minutes; the NASDAQ likewise dropped 3,000 points. The President orders the markets closed after fifteen minutes, seeing that there will be no immediate recovery. Almost all the trading had occurred because of the skittishness of European and Asian investors, but the President also knows that there are companies and governments seeking to gain economic advantage against the United States in the wake of their crisis. He and his advisors correctly surmise that China, India, or the EU are using the American crisis, namely, the absence of two-thirds of their population, to supplant the United States as the leader of all world economies, and if possible, forestall the American dollar as the world's chief and singular currency. President Douglas warns those governments quite directly that any attempt to harm U.S. markets will not be tolerated. He further promises to keep U.S. markets closed if any foreign power attempts any more financial manipulation against the United States.

It is a bold threat but also one, the President knows, could prove hollow if he cannot get America's businesses back up and running again at something close to full capacity. To shore up his economic intent, the President re-constitutes all the senior officers of the Federal Reserve and appoints a new Fed Chair since all the previous members had been stricken by the Sleeper Virus. The Fed, like many other U.S. companies, had ample expertise to perform its daily and even long-range functions. What it lacked were the numbers of necessary persons to do the daily work. To handle these duties, the President taps--some say conscripted--whatever bankers, traders, and other finance specialists with the background and experience his government could find to handle the work load.

There is also a sense of empowerment amongst the SM population, the Woke as they've informally started to call themselves, that few, if any, had ever experienced before. Before Sleep Day, every major institution had been run, overwhelmingly, by the Sleepers. There had, of course, been SM participation, and some at the highest levels, but that participation had been too sparse. Now all of it is in the hands of the SMs. Though the problems are daunting and seem insurmountable, the spirit of the country is surprisingly hopeful.

Those previously held at the margins of society now feel as if their lives have greater purpose, and indeed they do. There is too much work for them all to do to be idle. As a result, unemployment is at near zero percent. Everyone that can work does work. If law enforcement has needs, they're free to conscript or strongly suggest the service of any and all eligible persons. All non-essential governmental services had been curtailed until further notice--the total focus had become the daily maintenance of the country and its conscious citizens, the SMs.

The President is also concerned about what to do about the schools. Few schools had re-opened since Sleep Day. If the nation is going to survive, he knows that the country needs to get back to the business of educating its populace. He has a plan for that and will announce it in this evening's broadcast. A solid education, both traditional and trade, he believes is key to the nation's salvation. How to implement his idea is the next big hurdle to surmount.

*   *   *

Raheem can hardly believe his good fortune. He stands in a crowd of other former inmates just outside of the Lorton Correctional Facility—his now former prison. Not thirty days before, he was counting down the days when his sentence would be up. He had had about six months left. Now, he stands with about six-hundred of his closest friends--his fellow former inmates— ready to be released. He also has an undetermined new job, and a full Presidential pardon in his hands. Not only is he going home, but he is doing so with the full faith and credit of the United States government. What a startling turn of events, he thinks, marveling at the rapid change of events since Sleep Day.

"See, Carlos, I told you. Follow me, be cool, and we'd find our way out of this," he says grinning widely at his now former cell mate and best friend in prison.

"You were right, Heem," Carlos responds in his thick Mexican accent. "But who knew though?" he continues. "We got a get out of jail free card all because all the White folks went to sleep. Who saw that coming?" He asks incredulously.

Raheem and Carlos got word about what was happening

on the outside about two weeks after Sleep Day had struck. When it happened, almost all the cellular networks had been knocked out except for the emergency network kept by the government. Roscoe, their jailer, hadn't been home that entire time since he had no relief. After the first week, Roscoe hadn't even bothered to close Raheem and Carlos' cell door anymore. They had proven themselves trustworthy and he knew that he needed them. Once the cell networks started operating again, word started to filter in through cell phones of the correction officers' and the illegal cell phones of some of the prisoners.

When Raheem and Carlos discovered what had been happening in the outside world, as well as all five-hundred plus of their fellow prisoners, there had been a general call to subdue (or kill) the guards and to beat a fast track out of the Lorton prison. Raheem and Carlos worked with the remaining Black and Brown guards, and some other prisoners, to maintain order. Raheem had not been sure whether he was making the right choice at the time, but he chose to err on the side of caution and order. Surprisingly, Carlos hadn't fought him on it, and worked just as hard as he did to help keep the prison together. A few days into the third week, a small battalion of military personnel showed up at the prison gates and informed the acting warden, Roscoe, of what was happening and what they needed.

They informed him that they wanted two dozen men between the ages of eighteen and twenty-five who are in good health and who had never been convicted of a violent crime. Roscoe is surprised by the request, but readily complies. Raheem and Carlos are outside of the age limit, a fact that Roscoe is happy about, else he would have had to turn them over immediately. The head of the battalion tells Roscoe that the men are earmarked for military training and will then be used to help guard the country's southern border with Mexico. This is in response to incursions into the country by several of the Mexican and Colombian drug cartels emboldened by the crisis caused by the Sleeper Virus.

Soon afterwards, word comes that the Administration will offer clemency and pardons to low level offenders and non-violent offenders. When the query for Raheem comes, Roscoe does him a solid. He changes his file so that it shows him as a non-violent offender even though he had been locked up for aggravated assault. Raheem is forever grateful to Roscoe for that favor. It meant the difference between him seeing freedom now with a job, and not seeing it for another six months with no job guaranteed. Candace,

Raheem's girlfriend, is ecstatic when she finds out.

"It's no problem at all, Raheem" Roscoe had said. "You did me that solid a few weeks ago and probably kept me alive in the process. Now that I'm warden, this is an easy payback. I couldn't have kept order without you. All the other prisoners respect you so much. Now farewell and don't hurt nobody," he says. Raheem daps Roscoe up before they part company, a thing that he would have never done just thirty days ago given the rules and ethos of most prisons in America.

The crisis caused by the Sleeper Virus had made kings of almost all in that it had given so many a fresh start from whatever had been their previous circumstance. Only the most violent prisoners were left inside of prisons like Lorton. Raheem is glad not to be named among them. "It's almost time for pick up, bro," Carlos says. "Where are you going?"

"Back to D.C., man" Raheem says. "Candace has a place for us there. We'll be in either North West or North East. I don't know which yet. You?"

"Me?" Carlos asks rhetorically almost comically. "I'm going back to Philly, bro. My family is there, all my homies. They tell me that the complexion of Philadelphia, literally, looks a lot different. I'll try to make a go of it there. Who knows what will happen with these new jobs or new government though. I hope that it's cool. I hope that it works. All my folks are really excited."

"I hope so too, Carlos." Raheem, however, is troubled. Everything is so new and so different than any of them had ever known. Being former military, he is more worried about the state of his country than most. He understands, inherently, what it means to be perceived as weak militarily. He hopes that President Douglas fully appreciates the challenges of their new situation. He isn't so sure though. President Douglas had never struck him as someone particularly thoughtful about or knowledgeable of the nation's military and how it's perceived and feared in the world.

Thinking about the next few hours when he is a free man again, though, makes Raheem smile. His girlfriend and the mother of his children, Candace, is on her way to pick him up. He can't wait. He told her not to bring the kids. They will make an overnight stop at a motel before they get home for good. He wants her all to himself without distraction for a few hours. Once he gets home he suspects that he will be busier than ever.

The President had kept his word about the pardons, sure enough, and now Raheem, and all others like him, have a mandatory job to report to bright and early in forty-eight hours. Raheem does not exactly know what his new job will be. He hopes that it's something that incorporates his military training. He only knows that he must report to the police precinct closest to his house in D.C. Since the police had been federalized, Raheem is unsure where he might end up.

Right this moment, he could have cared less. He is free. He is pardoned. For all intents and purposes, the last three years had been just a bad dream that Raheem wished had never happened. His baby is on the way and right on cue (beep! beep!), here she is.

Candace pulls up in their five-year old Honda Accord. As requested, she is alone, and man does she look good. Better, it seems, than when they first met. She purrs her hellos and Raheem all but rips the door off its hinges trying to get in. He sees some other inmates looking at her lustfully and immediately shoots them murderous stares. It was well-known to stay away from Raheem when he was imprisoned. The inmates remember this, and back off deciding the laces of their shoes are far more interesting than his girlfriend. He hops into the car and plants a long kiss on Candace's succulent lips.

"Sweetie, seeing you right now is the best thing that has

ever happened to me," Raheem says. We've got two days to get to know each other again. Please, let's go now." Hearing this, Candace pulls off with a near screech. Raheem smiles as his head hits his head rest. Looking at her more carefully, he sees that she's wearing a close-fitting trench coat, high heels, and apparently, nothing else save the bright red lipstick that utterly accentuates her voluptuous mouth.

Raheem realizes now, more than he had before, how much of a fool he had been to punch his boss and be away from this incredible woman and his family. "Candace, before we go too much further, I want to sincerely apologize again for putting you and us in this situation. I was hot-headed and dumb. I didn't think, and my actions caused us so much misery. I am truly sorry." Candace stares straight ahead without responding. Raheem sees tears beginning to form in her eyes.

Clearing her throat, she says, "Raheem, it's been very hard. It's just been me and the kids holding it down without you. I have been really mad at you, especially at night when I was all alone. I often thought 'how could he have done this to us?' half a million times or more. My friends and family said that I was crazy to wait for you. But I believed you when you said that you would get out as soon as possible. I've always believed you. I know that you love me and our family. I have long since forgiven you. I want you to know that. I will always love you. And yeah, I'm that ride-or-die chick brothas say that they always want. But peep this," Candace pauses, "I'm your ride-or-die chick" she says emphasizing the word *your*.

It is now Raheem's turn to tear up. He is a big man and normally too proud to cry. No one in prison had ever seen him cry or show so much as a soft emotional center. But now, he let his tears fall as he receives this awesome declaration of Candace's love and fidelity to him. "Candace, I need you to be more than my chick. I want and need you to be," he pauses, "my wife. Candace, will you be my wife?"

Candace laughs involuntarily. "Only if you'll be my husband," she replies as they pull up to their motel room. Raheem steps out and comes around to her door, opens it, and picks her up. "Baby, I can't wait. I'm carrying you across the threshold right now. And tomorrow, we're getting married at the justice of the peace." She giggles, hands Raheem the key, and they walk across the threshold, she in his arms, together.

Jerome is a changed man. The last thirty days had utterly, permanently changed him. He isn't the only one. Never had he worked so hard or done so much. He is no stranger to hard work, of course, but this work had been the most grueling. It had taken his crew the better part of two weeks to identify and catalogue every household in Hyde Park, Indian Hill, and Oakley. By the end of that time, their two-man crew of he and Darryl and ballooned to over one-hundred "searchers." By the end of the first week, Officer Johnson had placed Jerome as the head of all of the searchers in the three neighborhoods. Once identified and catalogued, all the neighborhoods' residents had been shipped to one of the major hospitals in Cincinnati—either Christ, Children's, Good Sam, or University hospital.

Jerome is also a full-fledged police officer now, along with Darryl. They both carry standard issue Glock nine-millimeter caliber semi-automatic handguns. By now, Jerome isn't going into houses himself. He and Darryl ride around the several neighborhoods for which they had responsibility all day, every day, checking on searchers' efforts and limiting searcher theft wherever and however possible. Because of his own example, theft from the homes and persons of the Sleepers had been minimized, but it had happened. If caught, a searcher was removed and given an immediate thirty-day jail sentence. One searcher, in the Oakley neighborhood, had been found harming a Sleeper. As it turns out, the Sleeper had been the boss of the searcher prior to Sleep Day. He had been harsh and unkind to this particular searcher, making her professional life a living hell for three years until ultimately, she was fired without cause. The searcher had not known that she was going into her ex-boss' house. When she sees him, she flips out and starts beating him.

Her fellow searchers pull her from the man, bind her hands and escort her outside. Normally, such behavior would have led to an immediate jail sentence of six months or more. But this searcher, Laila, is instead removed from the searcher ranks and sent home. It is generally understood that such incidents might happen; i.e., an SM working to identify a Sleeper might come across one that had been unkind or discriminatory towards him or her. The written protocol says to restrain and severely punish the SM who causes injury. But that rarely seems to happen. Only in the more extreme cases of rape or murder are SMs being so punished.

Such abuse is never allowed or approved of, but most SMs can identify with the weight of the emotional and psychological abuse heaped upon them in the now former America.

The Federal government forms a separate, non-military organization called the Searcher Corps. Its job, under supervision of Homeland Security, is to find as many Sleepers, alive or dead, as is possible. If found alive, an IM is to be shipped to a local hospital. If found dead, an IM's identification is to be recorded and that IM stored in one of the many refrigerated warehouses that are being built, by order of President Douglas, or converted from previous warehouses until resources can be put in place for their later burial.

Burials had been paused because graveyards in all the major cities are overflowing, so much so that new ones have had to be commissioned if burials are to continue. Out of earshot of President Douglas, his staff discusses and quietly begin preparations to cremate IMs by the many thousands, if it comes to it, to preserve resources and prevent rotting corpses from spreading disease.

The Searcher Corp, now its own organization, works as an adjunct to the federalized police. Members of the Corp, like

Jerome, work against time to identify and rescue the remaining Sleepers in and around Cincinnati. After two weeks of not being found and helped, IMs are dying generally from exposure, hunger, dehydration or other causes. Jerome knows that now, thirty days later, the prospect of finding any IMs alive who had not been previously found and treated are minimal. They have other problems too. Squatters had begun showing up in the homes of former IM residents, so they are also tasked with rooting the squatters out for now. This is, at times, even more disheartening than the early work that he and Darryl had been doing in finding the first Sleepers.

Most often, the squatters are SMs who had never had the opportunity to live in a house, much less a nice house. These squatters are mostly from the poorer neighborhoods in and around the 275 loop. As the President begins to issue his pardons en masse, families are coming back together in huge ways like many, including Jerome, hadn't seen in their lifetimes. Jerome, though, feels ambiguous about claiming someone else's house for his own, even if there is no near prospect of them returning. He and Elena had made a life for themselves in a good, working class neighborhood, and he is fine with that.

Sitting at a stop light, Darryl, who is driving their police SUV looks over to his left. He sees Officer Johnson, their supervisor, sitting in another police SUV. Officer Johnson motions to them to roll their window down. "Middleton, go see Captain Hinton. He needs to speak with you."

"Yes, sir," Jerome replies. He has no idea what this is about. Probably some new assignment. Jerome had thought that as his search and recovery duties wound up, that he might be re-assigned. He had already decided not to return to sanitation recovery, his job as a trash man. Jerome's trash collection days are over. Most of those duties are now being assumed by former inmates from the recently de-populated prisons, as well as all other daily essential services like mail delivery, recycling, basic manufacturing, and the like.

Arriving back to District 2, Jerome hops out of the truck. "Stay right here, D., this shouldn't take too long." Loosening his coat, Jerome walks in and heads straight for Captain Hinton's office. Since becoming a police officer, his pay had increased with his responsibilities. He had never thought of becoming a cop, but he appreciates the new work. He solves major problems every single day and feels the respect of the people that he helps, and even some of the people that he's helped to lock up.

SM on SM crime is minimal. What has kept them working the hardest is the crime perpetrated against the IM population, those unable to defend themselves, but even that had drastically decreased as IM round-up, at least in and around Cincinnati, is coming to an end. Looking through Captain Hinton's door, Jerome sees that he is on his phone. Captain Hinton motions for him to come into his office, and Jerome does so. Once in, he closes the door behind him and stands until the Captain gives him permission to sit down. Captain Hinton stands and paces as he speaks. Jerome tries not to listen but can't help overhearing parts of the conversation.

He's talking about the Sleepers, their placement, and also, their possessions. The Captain has a look of resigned concern on his face. He wraps up his call with a curt "goodbye, sir," and hangs up. Looking at Jerome for a moment, he addresses him.

"Do you know who that was, Middleton?" he asks gruffly.

"It sounded like the Chief, sir" Jerome replies.

"It was indeed the Chief. Do you know what he said?"

"I do not, Captain," Jerome replies.

"He said," Captain Hinton continues, "that all of the IM

property and businesses are now confiscated by the government until further notice. They belong solely to the federal government. Also, much, but not all private property will be distributed to the SM population, under certain conditions. I'm putting you in charge of all that property distribution in the areas in which you've already covered—Hyde Park, Oakley, and Indian Hill. Your job is not administration, not directly anyway. Your job is enforcement, making sure the right stuff goes to the right people. We're not letting any squatters squat, as you well know, but anyone, whether squatter or not, can apply to live in any home that they wish that is not already housed by another SM. Obviously, there are going to be some rules and some preferential treatment. For example, officials like you and I get first dibs, first choice. Also, a single individual will not be allowed to take a mansion so long as there are families out there that need a place to live. And whatever is in the house, for example, cars, jewelry, cash, whatever, goes to the new occupant, no questions asked. Those possessions will need to be registered, so as to be newly assigned."

For Jerome, this is a lot to take in. "May I sit down, sir?" Captain Hinton gave him the go ahead and he sits. This is the signal that he had been waiting for. It had occurred to Jerome that there might come a point when the SMs, the Woke, would decide that all that lay before them now belonged to them, to us, he thinks. But Jerome also understands that this is no mere land and property grab. The government has no answers and no cure for the Sleeper Virus. Right up to President Douglas, no one knows when, if ever, that the Sleepers will wake up. "Captain Hinton, is there any change in the prognosis of the IMs? Is there a cure on the horizon?" Jerome asks.

"No and no, Middleton." No one has said anything to me about a cure or a change for the IMs. They're being herded up, they're being kept alive, and unmolested. Meanwhile, Washington is still functioning. And from what I hear, even bigger changes are on the way. We're part of the change, Middleton, get into it" Captain Hinton says.

"Okay, Captain, when do we start?" By "we," Jerome means him and Darryl.

"There's no 'we,' Middleton, just you. Congratulations, Lieutenant." Captain Hinton hands him a small case. Jerome opens it to reveal a new pair of lieutenant's bars. "Officer Isaacs is being re-assigned. We've got other work for him to do. I'll tell him so later today. Meanwhile, Lieutenant, pick a house, preferably in the Hyde Park area. You've earned it. And yes, that's an order. Dismissed!"

When Jerome gets back in the SUV, Darryl asks him "what the hells the matter with you?! You look like you've seen a ghost."

Composing himself for a moment, Jerome looks at Darryl and says "D., things have changed. First, I've been promoted to Lieutenant. Second, I've just been given a new house with all the property inside, yes, one of the IM houses. Third, the government doesn't seem to have any reasonable expectation that the IMs will wake up anytime soon if ever. Last, I think that you're being reassigned, and I have no idea where."

After Jerome speaks, they sit there in silence together. For long minutes no one speaks. The only sound that can be heard is the sound of their engine running. Even their own breathing is muted. Both men have friends and family that are IMs and who had been afflicted by the Sleeper Virus. Because of their positions, they are able to find and keep track of their friends and loved ones. Both men had been to see about them in their respective places. In fact, they often see other SMs visiting their IMs whether family or friend, and doing little things to care for them. Some SMs even pinned notes to their IMs for them to read when they wake up, whenever that is. Their lives are interwoven. To them and many other SMs, there is no Black nor White, only family.

"Darryl, Elena and the kids are going to be devastated when I tell them this. We've all been holding out hope. It's only been thirty days!" Jerome exclaims.

Darryl clears his throat before speaking, "Jerome, you're right. But practically, those homes are just sitting--and the property that's in them. If the Sleepers don't come back, should we just let it all sit?"

"D., I know that you're not saying that this is right?!" Jerome fairly exclaims.

"No, not right, but perhaps," he pauses, "logical and even necessary. We've got SMs that need new homes. We've got SM squatters. In my opinion, the government can only do so much for so long to keep the squatters out. Should keeping the squatters out become a full-time job or do we make the property available in a responsible manner? Add to all of that that we'll soon be flooded with new immigrants any day now."

"New immigrants? Where did you hear that, Darryl?"

"Trust me, Jerome, I hear things. Like I hear that I'm being re-assigned as well as you, and not to your assignment either. I'm just saying, with the SM populations being moved around and with the new SM immigrants coming, housing is an issue. We have housing. We should use what we have. And besides, it's not like our entire country isn't the product of the largest land grab in mankind's history," Darryl concludes.

That last comment rankles Jerome. They had had many geo-political conversations during their years delivering trash. Darryl is decidedly pro Black, and unapologetically so. His view of the world and of the role of government is quite a bit different than Jerome's. Admittedly, though, Darryl is far better read, although he hadn't spent one day in college, and thinks more deeply about these issues than Jerome does and anyone, in fact, that Jerome personally knows.

"Is that what this is about?" Jerome says. "They steal it first, so we'll steal it last? You've got as many IMs in your life as I do! Hell, your son is married to an IM. You've got half IM grandkids. I'm disgusted that you would even suggest such a thing," Jerome said.

"I don't think that you're hearing me, Jerome, and I know that you're not seeing the big picture. I get that you're upset. I am too and for all the reasons that you are. The big picture, though, is that we, all of us, are trying to keep our country. Whether we're keeping it just for ourselves or for the IMs as well doesn't really matter. We've got real enemies who would love to take advantage of this crisis and try us. If we're going to get past those threats, as Americans, we've got to do things differently, and strengthen all those that can be strengthened that are here and coming."

They both allow what Darryl has said to settle over them before continuing. Jerome is not angry with Darryl. Not really, he thinks. He is disappointed, but it's no one's fault. It is the virus' fault. The damn Sleeper Virus had come in and wiped out two-thirds of their population without warning, and they are who and what is left. Jerome knows that, for the most part at least, Darryl is right. If the country is going to move forward as a country, hard choices are going to have to be made. Not at all did Jerome want to be part of those choices, but being a part of them he is, and will be again.

"Darryl, please cover the rest of my shift for me. I'm clockin' out early. I need to speak with Elena. I'll see you in the morning. Maybe." At that, Jerome hops out of the SUV, gets into his car, and drives home.

*   *   *

The President almost can't believe what he is hearing. He sits in a wide black leather chair at a long meeting table in the West wing of the White House. On one side of the table are a bank of monitors, each showing the face of the top leaders from Germany, Great Britain, Spain, France, Italy, Greece, and Holland.

"Mr. President," the Prime Minister of Great Britain says, "we seven have conferred extensively on this issue, and we've decided. We will begin deportation of our melanated populations today. They'll travel by boat since air travel to the United States is still restricted."

"Explain to me again, Prime Minister, why you are forcibly removing your melanated citizens," he emphasizes, "from your respective countries. Don't all of your actions break all international law and the laws within your own countries?!" The President's voice is raised now, for the first time since this 'discussion' began, he is clearly showing his irritation and outrage.

"Mr. President," the Prime Minister begins, almost hesitating, "the travails of the United States have affected us all. No, the Sleeper Virus has not affected us directly, yet, but the fact that your White population is unconscious has. Our White populations have reacted with great anger and virulence toward our Black and Brown populations because they fear them. They're worried about them becoming carriers for the virus as, apparently your SM population is or may be."

"Truthfully," he continues, "their existence in our countries, and some more than others, has always been a bit strained. But now, when false rumors of the origin of the Sleeper Virus have spread, the demands that something be done about them, even a violent solution, have exploded. Our SMs are being targeted everywhere. Nowhere is safe for them. And our police are overwhelmed with trying to quell the violence against them. Some of our SMs have begun fighting back and even killing the IMs. We don't want to respond in the manner of the Russians who have simply rounded up and locked up their SMs and Muslims whether SM or IM," Great Britain's Prime Minister says.

"Instead," he continues "we think the most prudent and most humane thing to do is to send them to the United States. You're an all SM nation now. No one knows when your IMs will wake up, if ever. You can absorb them better than we can retain them. For us, it's more violence and upheaval. For you? Well, it appears to us to be more of the same, that is, your own kind. Besides, these new immigrants will help re-supply your lost population. It's, how you Americans say, a win-win."

The President recognizes that there is some wisdom and truth to what the Prime Minister says, even if it is cynically and racially derived. The notion, however, of expelling millions of people from their home countries, the only countries most had ever known, seems barbaric and smacked of something colonial to him. But he is right about one thing: the violence in all of their countries is escalating rapidly. The SMs there are being attacked but they are also fighting back, in earnest. This could not last, they all know. At some point all the respective countries' militaries would step in, and they would step in on the side of the IM populations, not the SMs. When that happens, it would mean mass arrests, incarcerations and perhaps executions of the SMs in Europe. So that is the choice facing the President: rebuff these leaders and refuse to receive their SM populations, thereby subjecting them to more inevitable violence and death, or receive them and guide them into an unknown and uncertain future.

"About how many people in total are we talking about?" President Douglas asks.

The British Prime Minister looks down at some papers on his desk. "One moment, Mr. President, I have the total number here. Ah, here it is: sixty million, total. About twenty million of that from Great Britain; ten million from Germany; ten million from France; two million from Holland; and the remainder fairly split between Portugal, Italy and Greece."

Sixty million people, the President ponders. They had already begun to receive Canada's SMs who, though not forced out, received strong encouragement from their government to leave. This is probably what had given this group of leaders the gumption to even suggest such a thing. But maybe, the President thinks, this could work in their favor. A total of sixty-five million new people could greatly help the country in its transition. At least seventy to eighty percent of the newcomers are themselves highly-functioning and productive members of their countries. Though not a favored option, he thinks, it could work out in the U.S.' favor. The President and his team had previously determined that theirs' is not an expertise problem. Theirs' is a population problem—there are more jobs to do than people to do them.

"Gentlemen and Lady," the President begins "before I tell you my answer, I want to share a few things." He sees the French and Spanish Presidents shift uneasily in their chairs. "History will remember this moment. It will record that you made this decision as ONE NATION and that you chose homogeneity over diversity. It will record that instead of fighting the good fight of governing all your people, you specifically chose one group, the Whites, over all others. The narrative that the good British Prime Minister utters is, as he well knows, one of convenience. The truth is that you would rather not deal with your SM populations. Even before Sleep Day happened, stories of widespread animosity and violence toward people of color had become more and more commonplace in each of your respective countries. It is known, for example, in Russia that tourists of color are prevented from, and should not travel beyond Moscow's city center. So it's unsurprising that you, and Russia most especially, are giving in to your populations' xenophobia and racism." The President lets that resonate for a moment as he clears his throat and sips from a glass of water.

"But be that as it may, I must take the world as it is and not as I would like for it to be. So, yes, send us your tired, your poor, your huddled masses yearning to breathe free, the wretched refuse of your teeming shore. Send these, the homeless, tempest-lost to us. And be sure to tell them that they're coming" President

380

Douglas pauses "HOME." The President's emphasis on that last word clearly rankles his listeners and he does not care. They know what they're doing, and they do not care. If an all-White Europe was what they want, an all-White Europe is what they shall have. "Trevor," he says looking at his NSA director "please assemble the Joint Chiefs in the Situation Room. We'll be sending two battle groups to ensure safe passage of our soon to be new American citizens."

CHAPTER XIII

Dr. Krauss rubs his chin and looks at himself in the mirror. It had been more than a few days since his last shave. Since returning to his native Germany, he had had little time to do much of anything except run experiments with his army of fellow researchers at his company's German lab facility.

Being released to leave the White House by President Douglas had been more difficult than expected. Neither the President nor his top staff, particularly NSA Director Trevor Campbell, had wanted to let him go. Dr. Krauss had assured them, however, that their best chance of finding a cure was with him and select staff working unhampered in a facility of his choosing. He had chosen Germany because he would have access to the world's best minds. Information sharing, he had told the President and his staff, would be the easy part. Coordination and collaboration is what is most difficult. That collaboration would be hampered if he remained on U.S. soil, tethered to his bio suit, and without ready access to his staff. Reluctantly, they had agreed and let him go.

When he is released, Germany takes extreme measures to get him back into the country. Instead of by plane, he had been carried across the Atlantic Ocean in a U.S. destroyer. The ship travels to the North Sea about one-hundred miles from the German coast. Several German military vessels meet the U.S. ship. Dr. Krauss is then placed into a small single engine vessel used to travel the remaining several hundred yards to the closest German vessel. Before entering the ship, he is stripped of his bio suit which is left in his small boat. He is then ushered into the hold of the ship, thoroughly washed and irradiated. The process is wholly unenjoyable and uncomfortable for Dr. Krauss. He is a small man to begin with, and the jostling that he experiences during his washing and irradiation is jarring, in spots painful and more than a little humiliating.

Once dressed and somewhat recovered, Dr. Krauss begins the painstaking process, begun in Washington, of putting his best team of researchers together. Fortunately, he has the benefit of the world's foremost international minds except for the Americans afflicted by the Sleeper Virus. He is responsible for the coordination of researchers in about ten countries including Germany, China, Japan, the United States, Great Britain, South Africa, India, France, Pakistan and Saudi Arabia. Notably absent from the discussion are researchers from Russia. The official communique out of Russia is that they did not have the resources or expertise to share to help look for a cure to the U.S.' Sleeper Virus problem. The unofficial word is that Russia does not consider it to be in their own best interests to have a fully populated and operating United States of America. They are betting that an unpopulated U.S. is a weak, if not toothless lion.

Since returning to Germany, about two weeks after Sleep Day, Dr. Krauss and his team make some progress, but not much. To their credit, he and their team had successfully identified the virus and genetically mapped it. The Sleeper Virus, however, is sublime in its structure and its operation. Because it itself began from altered genetic material that later mutated, it seems to be able to alter its own structure incrementally to defy isolation and treatment by gene therapy, specially designed drugs or even the injection of more eumelanin, whether that eumelanin is in human form or synthesized. Also, it hides by the most ingenious incubation process that Dr. Krauss or anyone on his team has ever seen. They observe that whenever the Sleeper Virus senses itself to be under attack, it attaches to a nearby organ and alters its external structure to mimic the cells of the organ to which it is attached. This viral adaptability happens, they observe, without any change to the internal structure of the virus itself. It is aggressive. It is intelligent. It's not finished adapting or mutating.

Thirty days into the search for a cure, Dr. Krauss is not encouraged even though there's been progress. Finding a cure for a complex disease is never a mere academic exercise. Under these conditions, such a find is particularly onerous. Their work has world altering implications. If they are successful, the previous world order could be re-established, at least in the United States. If they are not successful, the world politically and racially will never be the same, and what it then becomes, no one really knows.

The eyes in the mirror looking back at him, already old, look older. At seventy-two, he had been living twenty-hour days. Sleep is spotty and rarely comes easily. For the last two weeks while in Germany, he had been sleeping in his office. This is the first time in a week that he had decided to come home to his spartan apartment in Berlin for a quick shave and a decent shower. He hates the showers in his lab's facility. The water pressure is always too low, and they never seem to get hot enough, ever. This morning, he treats himself to his custom high-pressure nozzles and a clean change of clothes. Dr. Krauss feels a little guilty because he knows that none of the other researchers are going home, but he needs this brief break. He thinks that he'd be the better for it. He is right.

In about forty-five minutes, give or take, he'd take the short walk to his office and get back to work. On the docket today, he must review the results of the experiments performed in all Eastern labs--China, Japan and India. They are responsible, chiefly, for finding a synthetic answer molecularly similar to the eumelanin that is easy to produce and effective. At the end of the day, the goal is to wake up an already unconscious subject. To do that, his research team's thinking goes, they need to find a way to speed up the metabolic processes of the subjects.

When they first start this work, conventional methods are applied to sometimes disastrous results. They had injected adrenalin into unconscious IMs. The adrenalin shots are meant to speed up their hearts. Such an approach might kick start consciousness as a response to what is, essentially, a mild heart attack. That does not work. In their initial experiments, ten IMs go into full cardiac arrest, five of whom lose their lives. This is a disastrous result. Next, Dr. Krauss tries shocking several IMs awake thinking that shocking the entire body, instead of just the heart, could cause consciousness, even if only briefly held. One person actually wakes up for about ten seconds, becomes unconscious again, and is thereafter completely unresponsive.

386

Three others failed to wake up or respond. Dr. Krauss and his team don't kill anyone with their electric shock experiments, but neither do they move any closer to a cure. Dr. Krauss and his team wisely decide that continuing this experiment, though not yet fatal, is too dangerous.

At about sixty-five days removed from Sleep Day they are honestly, Dr. Krauss is loath to admit, no closer to a cure. The world's best minds, save the Russians, are working as quickly and as thoroughly as possible. While they've all learned more, they're no closer to a breakthrough than they were on the first day. True to his word, President Douglas has provided every resource available to Dr. Krauss and his team that he requests. They know enough to be able to identify the Sleeper Virus' molecular structure, but beyond that, little else can be ascertained. The Sleeper Virus, at this point, is completely unpredictable in its responses to their attempted treatments. They are stuck.

Finishing his personal preparations for the morning and looking freshly cleaned and shaven, Dr. Krauss walks the short distance across his building's court yard to his lab offices. He hopes that after his four-hour respite he will hear something encouraging about the research from the night before. Today is a report day. He has a scheduled call to the White House in a few hours. He does not want to report that no new progress has been gained. Dr. Krauss considers this entire debacle to be his fault. He understands that the U.S. Government and President Douglas do too. The pressure to find a cure for his and his company's mistake is immense.

Entering his laboratory, Dr. Krauss notes that it seems bright if not cheery. He sees that the place is abuzz with activity. Several high-level members of his team are meeting in the glass-walled conference room. They gesture wildly and seem to be arguing. Dr. Jessica Lundgren, his lead researcher in Germany, points her right index finger in the face of another older, male researcher named Dr. Alex VanBuren. Jessica and Alex hate each other on the best of days. In these days and times, their animosity is in full throat and is prone to chaotic outbursts. This makes sense given that they had once been briefly married.

"That's what I'm talking about, Alex!" Jessica exclaims. "Your native inability to see anything but your own narrow minded, myopic perspective! Your stupidity is mind numbingly transparent!" Jessica exclaims. In retort, Alex draws in a breath and bellows "you stupid bitch!!! The only reason that you're even working here is because your father helped start this goddamn company!!" he swears in obvious exasperation.

A desk separates the two researchers by about three feet. Jessica is a diminutive but agile thirty-three-year-old blonde woman, and a former member of Germany's Olympic Tae Kwon Do team. She'd also studied Brazilian Jiu Jitsu for several years. She hadn't competed since her teens, but she is still renowned in the martial arts world for having won the Silver medal, losing only by 0.5 of a point to the then reigning champion from South Korea. Her ex-husband never stood a chance.

From a standing jump, she leaps the distance between them in a blur. Her left leg extends to the side, and her left foot catches him squarely in the front of his mouth. At the painful blow, Dr. VanBuren steps back, his mouth now a bloody mess. Though he holds one hand up to stop Jessica's assault while holding his mouth with the other hand, Jessica easily finds his sternum with a front kick buckling him and then connects with her left elbow to his nose breaking it. He collapses with a thud, a bloody mess teetering somewhere between consciousness and unconsciousness. She isn't even breathing hard.

"Jessica!!" Dr. Krauss exclaims. "My God, woman, you nearly killed the man."

Jessica stands over the heap that is Dr. Alex VanBuren, ready to strike again should he stir. "No one calls me a bitch to my face and goes untouched, Dr. Krauss. No one." Her eyes are a sparkling emerald that remind Dr. Krauss of the lakes of his home town. She is stunningly beautiful with the kind of looks that give away none of her lethal ability. It occurs to him that Dr. VanBuren should have known better than to fire any of his trademark sexism at Dr. Lundgren, and that perhaps he more than deserves this thrashing.

"Jessica, please remember that you used to be married to the man," Dr. Krauss says. "Lewis, Garth," Dr. Krauss says as he motions toward two of his other researchers in the conference room, "please take Dr. VanBuren to the medic and get him patched up. We'll need him later today." Lewis and Garth immediately comply and lift a groaning, bloody Dr. VanBuren up from the floor between them and out of the conference room. Dr. Krauss stares after them as he considers what he should do or say next.

"Everyone, please leave the room. Jessica, Dr. Lundgren, please stay," Dr. Krauss says.

Within seconds the conference room is empty. "Jessica," Dr. Krauss begins "you cannot beat up my researchers, even the ones that you don't like, even your ex-husband."

"Uncle Josef, I'm not sorry. Alex has been highly insulting towards me and others on the team. He levies his insults when you're out of earshot while smiling in your face. Also, he's been more hindrance than help on this work. With his research team he has not allowed any of his researchers to expand beyond his narrow directives. He's working as if there is some personal glory in this for him instead of what this really is, the end of life as we have all known it, in the United States at the least."

Dr. Krauss looks at his niece and goddaughter intently considering what she has said. There is more than a little truth to it he knows. Alex is a pompous, sexist man. Dr. Krauss has known this for a long time, from the time that they were both young students together at university. He is also, however, brilliant, especially when focused and engaged. Dr. Krauss doubts now that he will be of any further good use, given how Jessica has so thoroughly embarrassed and hurt him.

"So now, Jessica, what do we do? VanBuren is a top researcher. He's irreplaceable. His team needs leadership, and we need results," Dr. Krauss says.

"I'll take his team, Uncle, and guide their research. They'll have more leeway with me to be creative and think outside of the box. My team is responsible for finding the virus' weaknesses. His team is responsible for developing a vaccine that prevents the unconsciousness caused by the virus. Both goals are related. I can handle both," Jessica says.

Dr. Krauss has no doubt that this is true. Jessica is brilliant in her own right and has every right to feel confident. Though young, she has already produced great results for the company. She worked on the team that created the initial unmutated strain of Zoesterol. Years ago, while Zoesterol was still in development, she had been the first to identify the drug's first mutation, an early form of the Sleeper Virus.

At the time, she had been rising fast through the ranks of Pharmatech and was well-regarded by her colleagues. Everyone knows who her father is, Dr. Benjamin Lundgren, the co-founder of their company with Dr. Krauss. They also know that she is Dr. Krauss' niece and goddaughter. When he and her father tried to dissuade Jessica from coming to work for Pharmatech, she had insisted, of course, on doing exactly that. They told her that a cloud might forever overshadow her being related to the two founders. Jessica had promised to never make their family relations an issue and to come up through the ranks the good old-fashioned way. True to her word she rose quickly by working harder, longer and better than almost all of her peers. Today, she is a standout researcher and manager and one of Pharmatech's best and brightest.

"Okay, Jessica, by virtue of knocking out the other key researcher on my team, his team is now yours. And no pressure, but the fate of the world is basically in your hands, so do a good job," Dr. Krauss says with a heavy amount of his trademark snark.

"Uncle Krauss, I promise to make you," she hesitates, "and Dad proud."

* * *

Darryl looks at his watch wondering what time it is. He feels the first mild breeze of spring dance across his skin as he lays in the brush of his assigned post. His eyes peer wearily through his infrared goggles as he searches for human heat signatures, specifically the signatures of Mexican Cartel militia.

He had been assigned to the advance team that is to scout the town of Brownsville, Texas. It had been overrun by two formerly dueling Cartels, now united with the singular goal of acquiring U.S. real estate in the wake of the crisis caused by the Sleeper Virus. When they attacked, many of the residents had been able to escape to locales further north. But a few had gotten caught and had been taken hostage. The hostages include SMs and worse, unconscious Sleepers unable to defend themselves.

The government believes that about thirty-five SMs and about fifty-three IMs had been kidnapped and are now in the Cartels' possession. All are American citizens. The federal government considers the Cartels to be terrorists and refuses to negotiate with them for the release of the hostages. Unofficially, President Douglas had communicated to his military commanders that he wants the Cartels driven out and every American citizen liberated. Darryl's is the first wave of that liberation team, he knows. For now, he is hunkered down in his post, peering through his infrared sights for any movement.

After three hours in the same position, lying on his front, his left arm begins to fall asleep. He loses circulation in it quickly. He slowly, quietly stretches his arm to make it straight. With his right hand, he moves his rifle onto his shoulder in a still position. He can now massage his left biceps and triceps to stimulate circulation and hopefully bring feeling back to it. It is at moments like this that Darryl most missed his time working the garbage truck with Jerome, and even the IM recovery work that they did together.

They had been good company for each other and constantly in motion. Jerome, after a while, had become his best friend, and he had grown close to his family. In Cincinnati, they had been all that he had. Being a bit of a loner, single and with but one child, now grown, the Middletons had been a welcome respite to the mundanity of his formerly ordinary life. It is that singleness, however, that had made him perfect for this new life as active military and a trainee in the Army's Special Forces. It seems that everyone new is a trainee of one thing or another. It also seems that trainee is just a title that hides what they all are--actively engaged and on mission.

"Command," Darryl whispers into the mic of his com device.

"This is Command," Darryl hears.

"What's the sit rep?" Darryl asks.

"No change. No movement," Command says.

"New orders?" Darryl asks.

"Sit tight, Sgt. Isaacs. There's no change from headquarters. Sit, observe and report. We'll advise if there's any change. Command out."

Sgt. Isaacs sits tight. An hour later he massages his right arm when he thinks that he sees something. His scope is trained on the northwest quadrant of a four-story building at the edge of town. Command believes that there may be Cartel members, hostages or both either in the building or somewhere close to it. It is quick, but he had been looking at a bank of windows for the last four hours when he sees a flash of light come from one of them. He is certain that he sees it. Electing not to call it into Command, he waits. About a minute later, there it is again, the same flash of light.

The light is stark against the landscape because it is night, and all the electricity had been cut to the town by the Army. Any light being used would have to come from either lamps or flashlights. This is no flashlight. That is lamp light, shown only because someone moved a curtain or blind--twice.

"Command," Darryl says. "I've got lamp light flashing in the northwest quadrant of the town hall building in sector eight. Orders?"

Darryl hears only the static from his microphone.

"Command?" He again offers.

"Hold, Sgt.," he hears. About thirty seconds later Command says "Sgt., we're going to assault that building. We believe that the hostages are trapped down in its basement. That light flash, we believe, came from one of them to alert their position. We don't know how he or she made it up past the basement, but we're sure that they took a hell of a risk to do so. We're moving in five minutes on my mark. Are you ready?"

Hell yeah, I'm ready, Darryl thinks as he finishes rubbing out the sleep in his right arm. Hell naw, I'm not ready he next thinks as he realizes that this is his first fire fight, and he is still just a trainee. "I'm ready, Command. Orders?"

"Will advise right before mission. Command out."

Great, Darryl thinks. The next few minutes are the longest of his life as he waits for his very first mission orders to assault the Cartel. All in all, he'd rather be slinging trash cans and have his old life. He had asked for this, though, and Darryl knows there is no turning back. His country needs him now more than ever. All systems go, Darryl thinks. Ready.

Dike Omowale is frustrated and in a rush. The more that

he rushes, the more frustrated that he becomes. He is missing his

favorite pair of socks that he is sure he washed. He remembers

washing them, folding them, but he does not remember putting

them away. He'd left that to his wife, Adanna.

When they had lived in France, Dike and Adanna had each

been employed to teach in the new immigrant school for western

Africans. Not being married initially, they lived apart to honor

both of their families, which was common even for modern day

Ghanaians who had immigrated from their native country. It is

only after they received notice from the French government that

they would have to leave Ghana that they decided to marry. The

French had given them two clear choices: go to America where

their futures are very uncertain, or go home to Ghana where their

professional options could be considerably less. Though uncertain,

America had seemed like the better choice. It appeared wide open,

full of opportunity (and peril). The Sleepers had not yet awoken,

and no one has a time table. Without them, Black people like

Adanna and Dike had, frankly, more to do and little to oppose them in their ambition. America it is then, Dike and Adanna decide. They had chosen together.

Of course, they are saddened and outraged that they even have to make such a choice. They are being summarily kicked out of France with no choice in the matter. They had each come to France on education and work visas. They had been exemplary students at home in Ghana and in France. Dike and Adanna liked France and had been part of a vibrant middle class West African community there. They had each faced their share of racism in Paris, but on balance it was a livable and workable life for them both. Before the Sleeper Virus struck triggering the hyper xenophobia of France's White European citizens, and much of the rest of Europe, they had even imagined a life together in Paris instead of returning to their homeland. All of that came to an abrupt end when the French President announced that all Africans, Muslims, and people of color, and even some eastern Europeans are to be expelled. They are told that they have three days to prepare to leave France and return to either their native countries or go to America. Transportation for either would be coordinated by the French government.

For the first day after the French President's announcement, there had been riots in Paris, massive riots. Particularly in the Muslim community, its persons of color rioted for half a day in front of the French parliament building until the French riot police are ordered to disperse the crowd. At first, tear gas and rubber bullets are used. Then, the unthinkable happens. Live ammunition is fired into the crowd killing over two dozen people and injuring scores more. The French President then goes on television that night denying responsibility for the killings and puts the fault for the police-induced murders squarely on the shoulders of the rioters themselves.

It's the shot heard 'round Europe. At this point, ninety plus some odd days into the crisis caused by the Sleeper Virus, every European nation expelling its SM population believes that it has the green light to use force, and deadly force if necessary, to ensure that all of its SM populations are removed.

Dike and Adanna hadn't needed to be told twice. They register for travel to the United States along with most other persons of their community. Their reasoning is that if the U.S. recovers, they would already be there and have the opportunity to create the lives that they had imagined for themselves in France and perhaps become citizens. Whatever crisis the U.S. experiences, they had reasoned, would be better than what they could do in Ghana or any other country.

In spite of the crisis, the United States remains a resource leader and consumer in the world. Also, the President of the United States had explicitly asked for every able bodied person of color to come join the SMs in the U.S. and their rebuilding efforts there. He had also promised American citizenship to every immigrant within six months to a year of their arrival, so long as they work and are productive. Dike, Adanna and many others like them had not needed to hear more before making their choice.

Traveling to New York had been like an out of body experience. The French would not use their own ships for transport due to fears about contamination from the Sleeper Virus, which was a ridiculous notion since none of Europe had been infected. The French, Dike and many other non-White Europeans believed, are either irrationally fearful or are using the threat of the Sleeper Virus as an excuse to purge most European countries of their darker countrymen and particularly, their immigrant populations. Many like Dike and his wife Adanna think that the latter is true.

In response, the United States commandeers all of the sea worthy cruise ships docked in Florida and the Caribbean to take the trip to France, Spain, England, Portugal, Germany, Italy, Greece and other expelling European countries. Only Norway, Sweden and Switzerland, of the major European countries, resist the call to expel their African, Arab and immigrant populations. These countries' leaders express their horror at their neighbors' mistreatment, particularly France, and all had gone on television to denounce them as xenophobic, myopic and racist, but to no effect. The expelling European countries are decided.

Once at their respective locales, the ships are loaded with scores of Europe's SM people and taken by military escort to New York City, Ellis Island. When they come, President Douglas wants each new SM immigrant to see Lady Liberty as they ride by Ellis Island. All new SMs from Europe are processed centrally in New York City. The President, having a strong sense for the dramatic and of history, relishes this new moment in forced immigration to his country. In years to come, President Douglas wants this expulsion to be a reference point for each new SM immigrant received.

On their ship, Dike and Adanna are given a honeymoon suite on a very nice, very large cruise ship that had been used, they see, as one of the flagship vessels for the Disney cruise line. They are grateful for the journey as they hadn't had time to take a proper honeymoon since their wedding. The day after they are married, they pack what few belongings they have for their journey to America. Had they had many possessions, most of them would have been left in France. Their American handlers had instructed them to bring only what they need. They would be re-supplied once they come in country, they had been told.

The trip to America lasts four, mostly restful days. The ship is meagerly staffed and not to the level of most vacation cruise ships. The food supplied is bare bones and meant only to sustain them for the trip. Still, Dike and Adanna have a suite of ample size and comfort. They try their best to enjoy one another and the time that they are afforded. They know that there is no telling what their lives might become once they reach, apparently, their new country and home.

As they travel, Dike and Adanna see that they are part of a long line of ships following one another across the Atlantic. They also see that several impressive looking American war ships line the route that they take. Adanna feels safe, and though she had never been to the United States, she feels as if she is going home. She does not tell Dike what she thinks because she feels silly. To her, it makes no sense. She tells him, however, when they arrive and see Lady Liberty for themselves that no matter what happens, they had a new life and a new country and would make a strong go of it.

Grabbing their now few belongings, Dike and Adanna disembark from their cruise ship. They are guided into a large holding area that once served as a warehouse for goods coming to the country by boat. There look to be a few thousand people gathered, almost all from someplace else. There are large signs posted along the high walls of the warehouse that had the names of major U.S. cities on them. Dike and Adanna see signs that read NYC, Wash., DC, Boulder, LA, San Francisco and many other, apparently, large U.S. cities. Adanna and Dike wear plastic tags that identify their professions as teachers. They had received the tags, which now hang conspicuously around their necks, the previous day while still on their ship.

Each tag that they wear has the words "TEACHER" emblazoned on them in bright red letters. In the center of the

404

warehouse is a large sectional ringed table. In each section there is a uniformed official seated at a computer. Dike and Adanna feel their cell phones buzz in their pockets and pick them up to see the message. "Table six" both phones say. "Looks like we need to go to Table six, honey" Dike says to Adanna. "Let's go then," she responds.

They know which table is number six because it has a large number six placard taped to its visible side and hangs from it. Dike and Adanna walk briskly to it, pulling their luggage with them. The official behind the desk looks up at them as they arrive. "Cards, please," she says. Dike and Adanna remove their cards and hand them to her. On the back of each is a large QR code printed in the center of the card. The official scans each and returns them to Dike and Adanna. "Alright then," she says in a heavy New York accent, "you're both assigned to Washington, D.C., Howard University. The government is placing teachers in our major cities, and D.C. is number one on the list. The gathering spot for the transport to D.C. is right over there," she points to the large Washington, D.C. sign hanging down from one of the large warehouse walls. "You should be leaving in about an hour. Please don't wander off. Another official will re-scan your cards before you get on the bus or train. Good luck. Next!" Dike and Adanna thank her and move to the next part of the warehouse as instructed. Adanna grabs her husband's hand and squeezes it. He squeezes back and looks at her encouragingly. "Here we go," he says. She smiles and thinks to herself, yes, here we go.

*   *   *

Arriving in D.C. had been a heady experience for Dike and Adanna. The city bustles with Black and Brown folks all around them and an energy that neither had ever felt in Paris. It is the energy of renewal and hope. It is not, as Dike had expected, the energy of fear which he had personally felt when they had been summarily ushered out of Paris, out of France, out of Europe and across the Atlantic under military escort to an uncertain future.

Adanna had said to him then, just before their arrival, to keep heart and keep faith. Dike well remembers those words that his wife had spoken, and how they had made him feel. He feels encouraged by them. Right now, though, he feels the familiar frustration of not being able to find his favorite pair of socks for his first day of work at Howard, the university at which he had been assigned to teach. Adanna had already left for work. Asking her to help him find his favorite pair of socks is a no go. To add to his frustration is the home that they live in. It is far larger than any either he or Adanna had ever had. In fact, it is three or four times larger than any that they had ever had. Usually, having such room is a wonderful luxury. Today, however, as he is trying to get ready, it is a nuisance. Adanna, if she were here, would be laughing at him he thinks.

Finding another pair of socks, he finished getting dressed, grabs a to-go cup of coffee and leaves their home. According to their neighbors, they live in a wealthier part of D.C. called Brookland. Their neighborhood sits on the western edge of Catholic University which, like Howard, is also being repurposed for the country's new educational objectives. What they know is that they had a lovely new home and it is close to their jobs and the Metro subway system.

Almost immediately upon arriving, Dike and Adanna are both given jobs at Howard. Dike works as a college professor in mathematics, while Adanna also works there, but as a physics teacher in the high school which is being housed, temporarily she is told, on the campus. Their large home comes, in part, due to their new status as teachers, something that the President had promised to elevate in their new America. When they arrived to their home, it had been fully furnished, something that they had not expected. The previous couple that had lived there was an IM couple. The husband was an investment banker, his wife a well-respected socialite and philanthropist. Their home had been well-preserved and in good condition. When they arrived to it, they met another uniformed official named Keisha Reigns who had previously worked in the IM Searcher Corps in this part of D.C.

Keisha is a short, plump woman in her mid-forties. She has a wide smile and a bit of silver hair in her immaculately coifed afro. She greets them cordially and helped them to get settled in their new place. She told Dike and Adanna that she had personally inspected this house and found the IM couple that had resided here. She had taken personal care of them and made sure that they were properly packed and transported. In fact, Keisha, tells them, she had been responsible for IM recovery in this whole neighborhood.

The day that the Omowales arrived, Keisha provides them with a tour of the neighborhood, keys to their home, and a brief history of the city in the immediate days after the Sleeper Virus struck many of its residents. D.C. and its surrounding area known as the DMV had been particularly hard hit. There were, before the Sleeper Virus struck, millions of IMs that were affected. By any socio-economic measure used, IMs in the DMV were the predominant social caste in the area. As a group, they were wealthy beyond almost all imagination, and were the captains of industry of every industry that the city offered, especially within the government. As part of that, Keisha explains, they owned much of the best property in the city and its surrounding area. Before the Sleeper Virus struck, there had been over seven million people living in the DMV. After the virus struck, that number dwindled down to about four million.

Since the new SM immigrants started to come into the U.S., D.C.'s, and many cities' like it, had swelled in population. Sixty million or more SM immigrants or more had landed at the port of New York, most of whom were being shipped to different cities for varying jobs. President Douglas had indicated to the new immigrants that they would be free to either take an assigned job needed to be done in either the private or government sector or that they were free to find their own jobs in this new environment. Many seek their own way and are generally able to secure employment relatively easily. Most, however, either take a recommended job in the government or private sector. Work is plentiful.

Despite the loss in population, there is a hopefulness in the people. Dike, himself, is one of those who carry that hope. He had a new job as a college professor and believe that almost anything is possible. As he ponders that, he walks in front of the building in which he is about to teach on Howard's campus. His first class, Calculus I, is to a group of new college freshmen. Normally, such a class was a weed out class, but the new Dean of Howard's Mathematics Department tells him and his fellow colleagues that no student is to be weeded out. Instead, each will be helped and each will learn the material sufficiently to pass. The country desperately needs newly educated minds to do all of the work that is before them.

Dike walks into the massive auditorium in which his first class will take place. It fits about five-hundred students. All five-hundred chairs are taken. As he enters, the room immediately becomes quiet. All eyes are on him as he makes his way to the front where the large white boards are. He places his brief case on a stool near the boards and takes out a black dry erase marker. Facing the class, he utters his first words in an American classroom in a French/West African accent that he hopes his students can understand: "Good morning, students. My name is Professor Dike Omowale. You may call me Professor Omowale or Professor O. I am here to teach you the wonders of mathematics. Specifically, today, I am here to teach you the wonders of Calculus I."

*   *   *

If Darryl is just a trainee, he thinks, then he is drastically underpaid and needs a stiff raise, should he survive this venture, because this here, he further muses, is veteran's work. He now stands at the corner of the town hall building joined by four of his fellow Special Forces trainees and one commanding officer, Lieutenant Clark. "Rooks!" Lt. Clark says. "This is the plan. We're assaulting the building from the first floor. Another group is coming in from the roof. Our task is to get to the basement clear it out of any Cartel members and secure the hostages. We're going in weapons hot!" He repeats it again, "weapons hot" in rasp that sounds more like a snarl than a language.

"On my mark, Rooks. We're going into this side door two by two with me in the lead. Understood?"

"Understood!" Darryl and his fellow armed soldiers whisper into their coms.

"On me," Lt. Clark says.

The door that they need to breach is, of course, locked. Darryl applies silent explosives to it to remove it. Once applied, Darryl and his fellow soldiers move an appropriate distance away from it prior to detonation. When the explosives detonate, they sound like a muffled puff of smoke. After the detonation, the door remains exactly where it had been. Its hinges connected to the door sill are completely blown off. Darryl and another soldier grab the door, and move it to the side. The inside of the building is completely black. There is no light going into or out of the building.

"Cameras," they all hear Lt. Clark whisper into his mic. By cameras he means for them to don their night vision goggles that are attached to each of their helmets. Darryl's night vision goggles are already on. He stands right behind Lt. Clark, ready to make the initial breach into the building. Lt. Clark stands in front of the door portal, his backs facing them. He gives the hand signal indicating that he is moving forward. Darryl stands to the lieutenant's left, his partner, Miles, stands on his right. He and Darryl and the other trainee's file into the building, knowing exactly what to do. This is a building breach operation that they had trained for at least fifty times or more in their short time together. As they move forward, their small unit takes a conventional lead two-by-two formation.

Darryl and his unit move swiftly. The first floor is completely darkened. There is no light coming from any room or crevice. His unit makes almost no noise. The only noise that he can hear is the very light breathing of his fellows into their coms. Other than that, their feet leave no impression that they are even there. About mid-way through their search of the first floor, Lt. Clark raises his right fist for the signal of full stop. He crouches down into a firing position. Darryl and the rest of the unit does the same thing. Lt. Clark points toward a door and turns his hand down to indicate that this is the door to the basement of the building. Lt. Clark whispers one barely audible word into his com—"flyers"— this means that another Special Forces unit has just landed on the roof and would be making their way down.

Noiselessly, Darryl and his unit stand from their crouching position and begin moving toward the basement door. It is closed and it has the ragged look of a poorly aged, well-worn portal. Darryl sees the lieutenant pull a small container from one of his many pockets--a small can of oil. The lieutenant applies liberal amounts of the oil to the hinges at the door. Finishing, he slowly pulls the door open. Darryl and his partner peer through the portal into sheer darkness. They crouch for a moment listening, just listening. From here, they take the point of their procession. The stair case is not, however, broad enough to support more than one of them descending at once. Darryl gives the signal to his partner that he will go first.

Carefully, painstakingly, he descends the stairs as quietly as possible. Though the stairs are old, they do not creak. Darryl expects to take fire at any moment, but none comes. Reaching the bottom, he sweeps the area visually in all directions. His goggles register no movement, his ears register no sounds. Finishing his sweep, he clucks his tongue once into his mic, his signal for his unit to follow him. Two would remain at the top of the stairs for cover, the rest will follow him.

The basement of the town hall is cavernous. Rooms sit along the perimeter of the basement, but its center is an open expanse. In the far northwest corner of the basement, about forty yards away, Darryl sees a sliver of light coming from beneath a door to a room there. This is the only indication of possible life observed thus far. Lt. Clark, back at the point, gives the signal for forward progress toward the door. Moving forward, Darryl and his unit spread out from the close formation that they employ on the first floor. In this more open space, they need to make themselves less of a target.

Suddenly, to his left, Darryl sees a shape move. Looking more closely, he identifies a man sitting on the floor, a guard, holding a shotgun. He sees the man lift his head toward them. Darryl is close enough to him to smell that the guard had not had a bath in several days and that he reeks of some hot spice. Darryl fires one shot at the guard before he can raise an alarm with his converted special ops M4, equipped with a modified suppressor that makes his shots sound like whispers. When the guard hears the whisper, it sounds to him like death whispering his own name.

Moving forward, Darryl and his unit make it to the door. If one guard is posted outside of this room, it is reasonable to believe that at least three or more persons, kidnappers, are on the other side of the door. Darryl knows what their tactic will be. Lt. Clark will toss in a flash bomb grenade, Darryl and his partner will take out the lights, and their two fellow soldiers behind them will identify and kill the kidnappers. This should all take about seven seconds, Darryl thinks, at the most.

On cue, Darryl's partner opens the door, and Lt. Clark tosses in the grenade. Darryl immediately hears loud yelling in Spanish. There is a single source of light about ten feet away in the center of the room, an oil lamp that Darryl snuffs out with one shot. It is a great shot. He avoids breaking the bottom of the lamp which contains the oil and shoots out only the wick that is lit, thereby avoiding a fire. He then hears four whisper shots behind him in rapid succession and the awkward thud of falling bodies. Soon gone are the yells in Spanish. Four shots, four bodies, and now complete silence. It had taken only four seconds, a new record. Darryl smiles mirthlessly to himself. He and his unit will be bragging about this for weeks, he thinks.

"Light," Darryl hears Lt. Clark say. In response, Darryl and his unit produce glow sticks and crack them, which causes them to light up. The room is soon aglow with the eerie neon glow of their glow sticks. Once lit, they can make out the faint outlines of the room, and they see its other occupants. Six SMs, sufficiently melanated, sit on the concrete floor with their hands tied behind their backs, their eyes and mouths also covered. Other than their confinement, they are all alive and seem to be in relatively good shape. In another area of the room, two IMs, lay prostrate next to one another, side by side. Lt. Clark crouches over them taking their vital signs to see if they are still alive. Darryl can tell by the smell of decomposition in the room that at least one of them is dead.

"Those two are dead," one of the formerly imprisoned SMs says in a hard to hear rasp. "The Cartel members tried to forcibly wake them up. When they couldn't do that, then they started doing," he paused, "things to them. It was horrible. I couldn't watch. They both died a couple days ago."

"Where are the others?" Lt. Clark asks.

"I don't know, sir," the SM responds. "Gone, sir. Four or five other Cartel members began moving the IMs out of town through an underground sewage line a few nights ago. They knew that you guys were coming. They wanted to make sure that they got the most valuable prisoners out before you attacked. They talked only in Spanish, but I knew what they were saying. They tried to get me to admit that I knew Spanish, but I didn't break."

Now Darryl knows that they has a different problem--IMs spirited into Mexico to God knows where. They are unable to get here in time to save these two poor souls though they would liberate their fellow SM Americans. Regardless, he strongly doubts that either the President or the government will let this slide.

Mexico would have to be dealt with. Great, he thinks, but before he goes into Mexico to fight, somebody would have to take "trainee" from in front of his name or they are going to have a massive problem with he and his fellow trainees.

CHAPTER XIV

The President stands on the stage in the largest auditorium at the Howard University School of Law. He waits patiently as important dignitaries and thought leaders file in. He sees all of the members of the former Congressional Black Caucus assemble. They no longer use that name, because they in fact are the Congress, or at least what's left of it. He sees various scientists and medical professionals enter. He even sees authors and artists make their way in. He had requested that Valerie King, his Chief of Staff, assemble a meeting of the best minds in the United States. As these things now go, all of the best minds are with him within the remaining Blacks, Hispanics and Asians—none of whom had been afflicted by the Sleeper Virus--the SM population.

When the auditorium is full, the President taps the mic to ensure that it's on. He clears his throat and then begins to speak.

"Good morning. I am President Barron Douglas, and I will be facilitating this discussion. We asked you to leave your cell phones and smart devices outside because we are seeking to have total and complete privacy. You may see that several members of the press are here, but not in their official or professional capacities. They are here to contribute. This meeting is about how

419

we, the SMs, take our country forward and not lose what we have and what we've been fighting for. It's been three months since Sleep Day, and none of us has hardly had a moment to breathe. From the engagement with the North Koreans to the defense of our border with Mexico, each of us has had to step up in ways that we hadn't thought possible. But stepped up we have, and will continue to do.

Today, our enemies know that we remain in command of our massive arsenal and that we have the expertise to defend ourselves and our closest allies if need be. What they may not know is that we're still missing the requisite numbers that we need to 1) maintain a strong international presence and 2) maintain our commercial advantage in the world. The bottom line is that we need more skilled people to make the United States as powerful and robust as possible. Not only that, we also have to plan for the future, a future that may or may not include our IM brothers and sisters."

The participants in the room gasped collectively as he says that. He is not surprised by their response. Up until now, all official communication from the White House had been that a cure is being worked on and is forthcoming, and that the IMs could soon be revived. This had certainly been the President's hope. However, he had recently learned from Dr. Krauss and his team that the Sleeper Virus continually replicates inside of its host, and therefore cannot be flushed out of the victims' various systems. The scientists working to find a cure for the Sleeper Virus also learned that it had a way of lying dormant in healthy cells when antibodies came against it. It could even mask itself like a chameleon and take on the form of cells of vital organs to which it is attached to avoid detection. Thus, an IM, once revived, might still be infected even if revived. As of this date, no one had been successfully revived for any appreciable amount of time, and several IMs had been accidentally killed by the effort.

"Let me be clear, ladies and gentlemen," the President continues, "there is no cure and as of now, no prospect of a cure forthcoming. The Sleeper Virus is too sophisticated, and we don't know enough about it yet." A participant in the front of the room near the President sobs. The President understands the reason. Since Sleep Day, the President is himself reminded daily how much the lives of IMs and SMs had been integrated and intertwined. One group had held the superior societal position, IMs, but they were just as dependent on their SM brethren as their

SM brethren were dependent upon them--and in the running and maintenance of a country? Both are critical even if one had never been treated fairly or equally.

"So what do we do? Do we concede defeat to one another or to our enemies and devolve our country into fiefdoms or *worse* to be plucked off by any invader? Or do we set a new course, one that includes the growth of this great nation and its continued union?" Now the President speaks in steely tones and in a familiar rhythm learned while sitting at the feet of great men that he had known and listened to for most of his life.

"I have outlined five key objectives that require our most immediate attention, and I would like to share them with you. Now, I'm not sharing to dictate. I'm sharing to collaborate with you on how best to meet them. Each is for our good and the good of the country. In my view and that of the Administration, we need to do all of the following things. First, we'll shore up and equip our military with the necessary number of skilled operators for all four military branches and the Coast Guard. Second, we'll ensure that all of our major industries are operating at maximum capacity, research and development and production. Third, we get our kids and college students learning again in the highest quality schools and institutions, unlike anything that this country has ever seen. Fourth, we build our infrastructure and get us connected physically and digitally like never before. And finally, we grow, grow, grow!!!"

The President's four points flash on a large screen which serves as a backdrop to the President. After he speaks, the room is silent. It is so silent, in fact, that President Douglas begins to wonder whether anyone has actually heard him. He taps his mic again to make sure that it had been on.

"Mr. President," someone in the back of the auditorium says haltingly. "Mr. President, what you're suggesting will require a massive government commitment and a massive redistribution of wealth from the IMs. Sir, our Constitution as written won't allow for that. What exactly are you suggesting, sir?"

The President looks at the speaker thoughtfully. He is familiar with who he is and realizes that he had been one of the right leaning Black journalists who had editorialized against the President's health care initiatives, infrastructure program, high speed rail program, jobs programs and, in fact, *every* program that the President had ever tried to create and initiate.

The President clears his throat. His next words would be history defining. At the least, they are the words that could utterly make or break the country, and *himself,* he thinks.

"Brian, who created the Constitution? What did they look like? Did they look like us? Were people who look like us even considered when the Constitution was drafted and ratified? I'll spare you from having to answer. No, the Founders did not look like anyone in this room. But yes, your ancestors were considered when it was written: they were considered to be three-fifths of a person because they were not regarded as human but as property. They were regarded as property by the ancestors of the IMs who now lie unconscious and have been so, with no end in sight, for ninety some odd days."

"So what are we now to do? We have a country to run; defenses to shore up; allies to support; financial markets to empower; land to manage, et cetera, et cetera. Is the right course to hold all of everything belonging to the IMs in trust for a day when they will rejoin us? Or should we put their vast wealth to service for the good of the country?"

President Douglas draws a deep breath before continuing. "We have mouths to feed. We have children and young adults to educate. We have a country to re-populate. We have new SM immigrants cast out of their home countries—Canada; England; France; Australia among others—that need to be Americanized and helped. These immigrants no longer have homes. Do you remember these words: *Give me your tired, your poor, your huddled masses yearning to breathe free, the wretched refuse of your teeming shore, send these, the homeless, tempest-tost to me, I lift my lamp beside the golden door!* Are we not still that lamp? Or have these words lost their resonance?"

"Simply put, if America has a chance to be America, we must use every resource and every person in America to get the job done. There are wolves at the door, ladies and gentlemen--wolves. Those wolves would like nothing better than for us to be bitterly divided and unwilling to do the hard work to re-build this still great nation."

"So yes, I am proposing some radical changes, in the short term. Let me be clear. I have no desire to become a king or even 'President for life.' Having said that, I do not think that we're ready for new elections in 2016. I propose, therefore, that we rescind the term limits amendment—the twenty-second amendment. At present, we no longer have a true two-party system.

We are functionally only one party though I realize that there are Black and Hispanic conservatives. Their numbers are too small and their organizations are too," he pauses, "un-organized to proffer much of a candidate. In any respect, the branch of government that deserves the most attention is Congress. Therefore, I propose that we have elections for Congress in the next three months for all of the populated states. This should happen as soon as possible so that we can show the world our political viability and our ability to continue as one nation under the existing laws of our land. We shall exclude the de-populated states. In fact, the land of those de-populated states should now become federalized, temporarily, until such time as they can be re-populated."

The President is all the way into it now. He looks at his Chief of Staff for some encouragement and finds none. The decision to have this discussion is his alone. She had argued against it, but he had insisted. This is, he believes, the most direct way to save the country as is. "This is not a time for half measures, Valerie, this is the time to be bold," he had said with far more confidence than he currently feels. But regardless of how he feels, now is the time to press forward.

"I'm not asking for a blank check. We'll put a lot of people to work. We'll end unemployment in our lifetimes. We'll advance clean energy. We'll make healthcare available to all at low or no cost. And we'll educate and train our people to be the smartest, most talented and most entrepreneurial human beings on the planet."

"So I *am* asking," he emphasizes, "for your help to enact my agenda to re-build our country and re-build our population. Anything less, I strongly believe, could end our way of life as we've known it."

He steps out away from the podium and stands in front of it. The President wants to show himself fully to this audience. It would be their leadership that either moved or devolved their country. This is not the time for petty politics but for a full, open-eyed accounting of what is required. Everyone here would have to sign on and agree. Only by whole agreement might they have a chance.

"Who's with me?" he asks. By the time the last hand goes up, the sound in the room is a roar of agreement.

*　　*　　*

The rest of the day had gone very well. The President had managed to put together a plan with the help and buy-in of all of the thought leaders in attendance at Howard's law school. Afterwards, members of the audience half-joked that this had been America's second constitutional convention. They hadn't been too far off the mark. They weren't about the business of creating a new Constitution, but there are going to be some changes to the one that they have and some new laws that would enable the Executive branch to move more efficiently about the business of executing the nation's laws. Also proposed are new Congressional limits to its authority and control so that government would not be needlessly be obstructed as it had in recent sessions of Congress.

After the day's events, the President returns to the White House. He reclines slightly in the seat of his limo. It would be a pretty speedy ride back to the White House, but he still has about ten minutes to review the list of the most sought after items coming out of this Convention's discussion that he would take to Congress. 2016 Presidential elections will be postponed, indefinitely. The 22nd Amendment would be rescinded immediately thereby allowing him to serve beyond a second term. Congress, however, would institute term limits in the House and the Senate: no more than two consecutive terms for a Congressman and no more than three terms total; in the Senate, no more than two terms ever, whether consecutive or non-consecutive. Also, Congress would work to immediately create legislation that would limit the effect of the old Supreme Court's rulings that allowed unlimited amounts of money into political campaigns. If any of the old IM billionaires who funded many of today's political campaigns ever wake up, the President thinks, they would be without the ability to pump hundreds of millions of dollars into any election or any candidate again.

The U.S. would federalize large swaths of land, principally land that has very low SM populations before Sleep Day. Currently, there are whole towns and some small cities that are virtually empty either due to low or no SM population to begin with, or because they are being abandoned for the larger cities where jobs and services are being doled out. SMs are being asked to populate key cities—Boston; New York; DC; Baltimore; Charlotte; Atlanta; Miami; Tampa; Dallas; New Orleans; Birmingham; Houston; San Diego; L.A.; San Francisco; Chicago; Cincinnati; Detroit and Seattle. The plan is to focus resources in these key cities for the remaining SM populations and then as those populations increase, re-populate the smaller cities.

All concerned understand that they would need new adult bodies--fully functioning people, and that they cannot wait for new babies to handle all of the work that needed doing now. To get these people they would do two things: first, release all non-violent offenders from prison, and second, allow new SM immigrants into the U.S., especially those being expelled from their home countries. The United States would take them and use them to rebuild their technical and physical infrastructure. The President plans to provide Presidential pardons and clemency to many thousands of non-violent offenders with certain pre-conditions and then put them to work at a living wage on one or more of the several projects that would be initiated. Because they are so few relative to their need, there is more work than there are people to do the work. That work is in the public sector and in the private sector too.

In education, the President wants the nation's colleges and universities to be put to good use. Many of them would now become the sites of the elementary and high schools in the key cities. Centralization is key. If this next generation is to be well equipped, it would require the best educators. New teachers from top universities will be paid well and given a choice of prime IM property to move into for their service. The old paradigm of low teacher pay, the President argues with other members of Congress, must end. He wants the most experienced and best qualified minds to teach this new generation of woke citizens and to be well compensated.

The President also makes innovation a key feature of his agenda. At present, Howard University is probably the most populated of all the universities in the country. It had already been a top-ranked research facility. He wants it to become the new M.I.T, since that institution is no longer open. Billions would now be allocated to technology innovation, and Howard and schools like it would lead the way in the United States and eventually, the world. To augment its status, the President proposes a new Innovation Corridor be built in D.C. and other key cities in which HBCUs exist close to the university where new innovations would be created and where its students could participate and help lead.

The President and his staff want not just Howard to prosper, but also all of the other Historically Black Colleges or Universities (HBCUS) that are already up and operating, most of which are operating at maximum or near maximum capacity. They wouldn't need much ground level work, but would require more resources to advance their respective missions. They would also need greater expertise. They would shift the SM expertise at the nation's top schools to a select group of HBCUs. Since many of the IM majority colleges and universities will not be used or rather will be used as centralized schools for a city's SM population, the SM professors of those institutions can be re-allocated to varying colleges and universities around the country for that purpose.

Some schools like Harvard, Emory, LSU and others will become the elementary and high schools for a city's SM populace. The President and the attendees of the Convention thought it prudent to centralize the location of primary and secondary education. The school age populations in most of the large cities are small enough to centrally locate the elementary and high schools in all of the cities save D.C., Atlanta and New York.

In D.C., the plan is to use George Washington University, the University of the District of Columbia, and Catholic University as the new primary and secondary schools locations. Residents living outside of the city will be asked to move back into the city to bring its population back to pre-Sleeper Virus levels. The prevailing thinking is that each city center needs its best expertise in close, collaborative association with most of the city's residents.

Plus, as services are distributed, it will be better, logistically, to have would-be recipients closer for easier access.

In New York City, much the same will be done. Three or four universities are to be chosen to be the new primary and secondary educational hubs for the city populace. And in all of the target cities, universities will be used as the central locales for primary and secondary educations. For now, university resources would be allocated to the top five to ten HBCUs since 1) they already had faculty, students and resources in place and 2) they are the most ready jump off points to a new emphasis on education enacted by President Douglas.

The only exception might be California. California is unique. It is already a state whose majority of residents are SMs. Thus, the largest California universities--USC, UCLA, Cal Berkeley and Stanford--two or three of the existing California schools will be used strictly as universities for the West Coast and IM students out west seeking to attend university there. Other smaller California universities can be and will be used as centralized locations for elementary and high schools where necessary.

Though the loss of the IM population is a near insurmountable blow to nearly every American institution including the economy, justice system, education system, and many others, losing two-thirds of the population also presented some keen opportunities for the remaining woke population. For example, the United States, virtually overnight, moves from being a top consumer of the world's natural resources to a middle of the pack consumer of those resources. As a result, energy consumption is less, and food consumption is less, much less. The President argues passionately amongst the Convention attendees that now is the time to address their long term energy needs, energy creation, farming, and food production. His goals, he argues, are to entirely change the way that the United States creates and uses energy. The President wants to go almost green entirely.

With not a little hand wringing, the attendees agree with the President that eighty percent of all private farming should now be federalized since food production had now become a strategic issue. Relatively few SMs are engaged in the massive farming structure that had existed before Sleep Day--at least not nearly enough to sustain the massive quantities of food needed to be produced for the country. In fact, major corporations own and manage almost all farming that had occurred in the United States. The President explains that his goal for a federal takeover is, hopefully, a temporary one. He agrees with the Convention attendees that almost all land used for farming would be sold back to private citizens once they have an opportunity to develop an infrastructure to handle and control its management. Suddenly, the existing SM farmers had become experts and would be used to manage the food production now in governmental hands. Hopefully, the President says, they would soon become the captains of tomorrow's private farming industry, thereby alleviating government ownership.

The President wants innovative food production to occur as well. Because he is asking SMs to move as closely to the various city centers as possible, he and others think it prudent that food production be done closer to the city population too. In fact, proponents amongst the attendees argue that city farms should be created for the production of locally grown produce that will be free from pesticides and genetic manipulation. The city populations will learn to farm, thereby ensuring that that the knowledge is transferred to many others.

Ideally, in time, a city might become its own source of food production and every day residents will learn how to do so for their own needs and the needs of their neighbors. It is probably too much to hope for, the President thinks, but he is optimistic about the possibility of breaking free of the old system of mega farms to grocery to consumers. He has a vision of direct growth to consumers' waiting hands. It is worth a shot, he calculates. At the very least, he reasons, a significant percentage of food production occurs in the proposed city farms to augment production by the large now-government farms.

Energy production is one of the most robust discussions to be had. In fact, they all agree, it deserves its own day or week or month or year. But they do not have a month or week to merely discuss it, the President knows. Energy is as much a strategic issue, militarily, as it is a vital life issue. There are one-hundred and twenty-two nuclear power plants in the United States, all still in operation and under guard. But the current population needs, maybe, fifty of them to be operational. Important questions about their use or non-use need answers. For example, what should be done, safely, with the remaining seventy-two non-used nuclear plants? Also, what should be done about future energy production?

Should the country remain an oil based energy producer, or should it greatly expand into renewable energy sources? These are all questions President Douglas considers and plans to put to this group.

President Douglas is emphatic that now is an ideal opportunity for the U.S. to free itself from crude oil consumption and exportation. He does not want the U.S., in its new form, to be subject to a potential oil embargo or the price fluctuations in the oil market because of their population reduction. Currently, oil is sold at close to two-hundred dollars per barrel, and a gallon of gasoline, in an unregulated market, sells at close to seven dollars per gallon. The President had foreseen that possibility in the first week after Sleep Day by tapping the strategic oil reserve and, in the short term, federalizing the gasoline production industry in the U.S.

The President's vision is expansive. He does not want to stop at mere reductions in crude oil production and use. He wants massive wind farms established on new federalized lands for the production of electricity. His aides calculate that several million acres of existing farm land could be taken off line for use in wind farms. The President tells the convention members that his Energy Secretary will, under his orders, spend billions to create new wind and solar farms for energy production. This will be part of the largest infrastructure project in the nation's history. It will be so large, in fact, that every American that needs a job will have one.

There are other incentives for such work including housing, training, and education. The President notes that for energy production and conservation, every idea is on the table. He wants innovation and development unlike any that mankind has yet approached. He also wants the United States to lead it. It is for their sakes and their descendants' sakes, he reasons. "China won't lead here. Neither will Russia or India. We must lead as we always have," President Douglas tells them. "Is there any argument to be made that the state of the world depends upon us? As our ancestors built this country," he argues, "so we must again lead the way for the rest of the world."

Energy is a key a point of the President's infrastructure initiative. He wants new roads and bridges to be sure. Along with massive new wind and solar farms, he wants a new electrical grid with an all new electric infrastructure. Solar would, of course, figure prominently. All new homes and buildings would now, due to new proposed regulations, have to reach a minimum of thirty percent energy production for the life of the home or building in years one and two, and eighty percent energy production for the lives thereof by year five. He is almost shouted down by some of the Convention attendees for the ambition of this proposal, but again, he argues passionately that such energy independence is now a strategic concern. "Besides," he quips, "the American people, the SMs, need to engage in such an ambitious project to ensure that existing knowledge is being transferred to others, and that new discoveries are found as a result of the problems that they are sure to discover and solve."

A massive infrastructure program, the attendees agree, is the best first place to begin to reach one-hundred percent employment of the citizenry. Everyone that can, will participate and learn new skills, especially those currently unemployed or previously unemployable. The President wants to use the existing system of private companies and a job bidding process instead of federalizing construction. Wealth still needs to be created, and the free market system maintained. He is not the would-be socialist that his conservative opponents had claimed. He wants, regardless of their accusations, wealth to be accessible and enjoyed by all that work for it.

Housing presents a thorny and controversial issue. It is perhaps the one issue that could still get him impeached by the SMs themselves. His idea is risky, but it is necessary to share it, he thinks. The President and the Convention attendees are well aware of what is happening in the country. The homes of IMs, whether they had been officially removed or not, had become the homes of many squatters. There are many SMs who had previously been relegated to substandard housing in ghettos. Consequently, IM homes and buildings are being taken over by such SMs. Frankly, there is no one to stop them. As soon as one home or building is cleared out, another SM family comes in right behind the one cleared out. Besides all of that, precious police resources are being used for such clearing out when they could hardly be spared.

One attendee, an elderly Black woman, asks some poignant questions: "Why should we stop them? Isn't home ownership one of the main ideas behind the founding of this country? Why shouldn't we instead promote such ownership in this *new* America?" she says emphasizing the word "new." President Douglas observes many heads shaking in agreement at her comments and subtle but unmistakable sound of "Amen" from several in the gathered audience.

Regardless of the robust arguments against such ideas, her questions sink in with several of the other attendees that are on the fence. Attendees ultimately realize, the President included, that the government holding IMs' property in trust is not the best use of that property. No one knows when they might wake up, or even if they will survive their virus-induced unconscious states. Besides, some argue, building new housing now is not a good use of their time and resources, especially when more than sufficient housing exists at the ready for immediate occupation for those who need it. Since almost all surviving IMs had been found and moved, letting their homes and buildings sit unfilled seems an unnecessary waste especially when the lives of millions of SMs can be immediately improved by their use. This is especially true, President Douglas reasons, for the new SMs coming to the States, it seems, every day.

A decision is finally made and agreed to by the Convention attendees. They agree to allow any SM to claim an unfilled home or condominium. There will be certain pre-conditions to fulfill. First, the size of the home has to fit the needs of the SM and family. A single SM cannot claim a mansion-sized house, for example, without having a family to fill, at least, fifty percent of it. The attendees express a strong desire for new home owning

441

SMs to be reasonable. There will be plenty to go around, they recognize. No one would need to be greedy. Also, existing squatters will have to file the necessary paperwork for any home in which they currently reside to effect a proper transfer of title. The President wants all title transfers to be legal and all such titles to be searchable through a national database.

President Douglas clearly understands the underlying Constitutional issues with this agreed-upon taking of the property of others who, technically, are not dead. Without some form of compensation to the aggrieved party, it is illegal to assume the property of an IM. It is decided that to overcome this problem, any and all transfer in titles to property both real and personal, would be provisional for a period of time, and then made permanent after a sufficient period. Provisional titles to property will be granted, but they are immediately reversible should the IMs regain consciousness in six to twelve months. Once the year is up, the titles become permanent.

Thus, an SM family that claims an IM's home and property is taking a risk. If an SM claims a property, that SM would have to give up all claim to any existing title on their dwelling and take a provisional title belonging to an IM. If that IM wakes up within the year provided, that SM has to vacate upon demand--or some reasonable time thereafter--and return all private property owing to the IM or pay the reasonable costs for the value thereof. The President and Convention attendees do not want to encourage a free for all amongst the SMs for IM property.

The conservative voices amongst them are loathed to give any property away whatsoever, but even they recognize the practical issues related to leaving so many useful, high value properties empty and unused. One item that the conservatives fight for passionately and win, is a mandatory home ownership course required of every SM head of household that had not previously owned a home. Many think that provision is silly, including the President, but it is a minor concession and perhaps one that may reap future positive dividends.

In the few weeks since the crisis in North Korea and the debacle with Russia's attempted massive land grab, security had become a bit less of an issue for the President and the country. The one exception had been the brashness of the Mexican drug cartels. They are seeking to make physical inroads into the United States by taking over towns in Texas that had either low SM populations and/or low security forces. Given their apparent lack of fear of the

Sleeper Virus, their goal seems to be the actual taking and control of land inside of the United States.

Once notified, the President dispatches the Army to root out the cartels. Cartel members had been killed, but not before they had injured and killed several SM and sleeping IM civilians and had taken hostage some IMs who they ferreted back across the border into Mexico. Special Forces followed the kidnappers into Mexico, retrieving most of the IMs taken, but some had been killed or otherwise gone missing.

In response, the President indefinitely closes the Texas and California borders into Mexico and assigns troop regiments to man the borders. He uses the Coast Guard to prevent any ships or boats coming from Mexico onto U.S. shores. He also legalizes nationwide marijuana use and production. This is seen as an economic crippling measure to the Mexican cartels since their number one cash crop is marijuana. Going forward, in President Douglas' Administration, the government will regulate and tax it. Overall, drug use will be de-criminalized except when used in the commission of a crime. President Douglas and others in government believe that these moves coupled together will deal an economic blow to the cartels and to the worldwide drug market.

The international drug market had already been spiraling by the absence of the IMs who were the biggest source, by far, of the demand for the consumption of drugs in the United States. If they ever regain consciousness, President Douglas thinks, America's drug policy will look very different than what it had been.

When speaking about the prison industrial complex, President Douglas emphatically states his goal: "It ends forever in this country. We cannot afford, as a nation, for all of the talent of our citizens to be housed away from the rest of us. I propose that we de-criminalize, forever, marijuana use. In fact, we should grow and regulate it right here. No other country need ever import the plant into the United States. And instead of criminalizing all other drug use, we will treat those addicted as having a disease—they will receive treatment, not imprisonment. Starting very soon, we'll release all non-violent offenders from prison upon condition. Each will be assigned a job paid for by either government or private enterprise. The formerly incarcerated will have the opportunity to have their records completely expunged after a year, provided that they stay out of trouble and perform their jobs well. Going forward, we'll never be the type of country that disproportionately imprisons one group of people over another ever again. Those days are over" he says to an uproar of applause.

Once the applause subsides, President Douglas continues speaking. "We will also require training and education of the soon to be released prison population. They will work and go to school. They have something that we need, he says: able bodies. We have something that they need: a chance to rejoin society and advance their own lives."

The President again sees the majority of heads nodding at his comments with only a few crossed arms and frowns, notably, from the more conservative members of the Convention. Thankfully, President Douglas thinks, they are in the minority here. He sees that he has won the day for almost all of his hoped for changes. These changes are necessary, President Douglas further argues, because liberating the million plus imprisoned SM men and women might prove the difference between maintaining the nation, and not being able to do so.

Previously, the President had re-opened the stock exchanges one week after Sleep Day, and that had been a mistake. The markets tanked in the U.S. and nearly caused a worldwide collapse. All of the Asian and European markets had followed the U.S. exchanges with stunning thirty percent or more losses. It had been a disaster. In a single day, trillions of dollars had been lost. This happened in minutes, not hours. In response, President Douglas had closed the U.S. markets and had not yet re-opened them. In fact, he is not planning to re-open them until after the results of the Convention are fully ratified, workers are put into place within the most needed industries, and he can assure the other major world markets of their solvency.

To help solve the labor issue, long term, in which the country finds itself, the President proposes an amendment to the Constitution: all large companies doing business in the United States, regardless of whether such companies are headquartered in the U.S. or not, would now have to hire employees in proportion to U.S. demographics tied to the most recent United States census. The census would now be taken every five years instead of every ten years, given that technology had advanced far enough along to manage such a huge undertaking. The President has no doubt that such an Amendment, once ratified, would be fought for in the courts for years to come. Regardless, he wants a baseline standard to avoid the type of calamity in the work force that they are currently experiencing.

If the IMs wake up some time after this amendment passes, the President will undoubtedly be accused of a hyper affirmative action push or of socialism. If that happens, he thinks, He will remind his detractors that they all but died and that the SMs protected and safeguarded them while they remained unconscious. President Douglas recognizes that this is not necessarily a winning strategy, but one that reminds the IM population who stewarded the country in their absence.

In the interim, President Douglas also wants a moratorium on all income tax, especially as his would-be jobs program for released inmates is initiated. He reasons that the government is or would soon be in possession of trillions of dollars or more of IM assets and personal property. Monetary assets held in U.S. banks had already been frozen by the I.R.S. at the President's orders two weeks into the crisis. By holding these items in trust and using them to fund government and private projects, the government can and would fund almost all of the necessities of the nation. "In six months," he argues to Convention attendees, "we can provide a low flat tax on all income that graduates based on income levels. For now, we should use this money to keep things afloat and get society moving again." Few argue against having a short term income tax moratorium. It is, after all, for the good of the country. The President observes a collective glistening in the eyes of the conservatives in the room as approval when he announces his short term, no income tax mandate.

The President also wants and formally proposes something that he could never get under a GOP led Congress: a massive jobs bill for the country's citizens, now SM population. He proposes the broad outlines of the bill to the attendees. It will include public works, infrastructure and training at levels not since after World War II, tax breaks, and education subsidies and grants to get people working and educated in the United States. Since the European borders are now closed to the SM American population, the President insists that any and all manufacturing be brought home. He wants home-based manufacturing for all things in the U.S. The foreign companies that had factories or businesses in the U.S. whose borders had closed to SM Americans, would have their facilities taken over, at least temporarily, by home-based American companies, unless and until the border restrictions are rescinded. This includes Canada, though the Canadian prime minster had seemed more open to resuming normal trade relations with the U.S.

President Douglas also suggests to the Convention attendees that new strategic partnerships should be created in light of the rebuff of their former European and Canadian trade partners. He suggests that manufacturing sites in the Caribbean and in Africa should be created as the U.S. shifts away from Europe and possibly China. Trade relationships with China, President Douglas recognizes, are an open question. It had not yet closed its borders to the U.S., but the President and his staff had heard rumblings that although the Chinese considered themselves to be "melanin sufficient," they did not want to take the risk of being infected by the virus, thereby potentially infecting their European counterparts. The President, therefore, believes that their longstanding trade partnership with the Chinese could soon be coming to an end. America therefore needs a plan in case China, like Europe, bows out of its relationship with the U.S.

Next, the President speaks about crime, and he emphatically says to a stunned audience, "Rescind the Second Amendment." He pauses to let his words take their desired affect before beginning again. The baritone of his voice holds their attention as he speaks again. "We've had far too many unnecessary deaths to gun violence. Within a week of Sleep Day, we confiscated and cleaned out every single gun shop that we could find. That was among my first orders. Also, all gun manufacturers have been federalized and shut down except for the few that the government uses the most. With our unstable population numbers, I don't want a single person to die from a handgun or otherwise. I realize that we cannot go into peoples' homes and confiscate their guns. And really, I don't want to do that. However, we will provide great incentives for every person that turns in their guns-- and every gun that they find--including personal and real property. Also, all ammunition will now be federalized, permanently. That means we own the ammunition makers too. We're going to make the acquisition of guns and ammunition outside of specific police and federal responsibility near to impossible. We're going to dramatically decrease the loss of life from gun violence. Our new America will be a gun free zone as much as is possible. If citizens don't like it, they can leave. We're getting out of the gun business in this country." Pausing for a moment, the President sees that the conservatives in the room are positively livid and look like they might mount a protest.

Continuing on, he says "Not only that, I want sentences for those involved in gun violence to do an automatic twenty-five years of hard labor with no possibility of parole. None. If the penalties are not high enough it won't be taken seriously," he concludes. President Douglas sees out of the corner of his eye the group of conservative attendees gathered to his right. They are clearly unhappy. Their ringleader looks apoplectic. "Mr.

President!" He soon booms out, "You are completely and utterly changing the fabric of our country! Who are you to demand such a thing?!" he exclaims. A chorus of "Amens" and "here-heres" echoed his comments.

The President turns fully from his position on the stage to face his conservative opponent. "Mr. Robinson," he says, "we have just lost two-thirds of our population. We have no idea when or even if they will return. We have been able to save millions of them, but we know that millions more may never be found and are lost to us. When and if they do regain consciousness, their numbers will have shrunken so much that, as a group, they will never control the levers of government again. We're *already* a new country whether they ever re-join us or not. While I appreciate your reminding us all of our historical traditions, one of the most shameful of those traditions has been the irresponsible way in which we have regulated, or in this case, not regulated the acquisition and use of guns amongst our private citizens. The NRA, for all intents and purposes, is dead. It will never have the power or sway amongst our elected leaders again. It will never be so powerful as to decide elections and public policy ever again. You asked 'who am I'? Here's my answer: I'm the guy that happens to be the President, who happens to be conscious, not unconscious, and who sees the opportunity that we *all* have," he says with emphasis, "to build a fairer America and one that fairly reflects our values and input. In one fell swoop, Mr. Robinson, we have become the wealthiest nation of non-European derived people in the history of the world since the Ancient Egyptians and since the Moors controlled North Africa and parts of Europe. I think that means something, and I think our approach to solving some of these age old problems that Black and Brown people have faced should be different. What, good sir, do you think?"

The President allows his question to linger in the air as Clarence Robinson, his conservative opponent, stands with his hands in his pockets looking down at his feet. His supporters look thunderstruck. The President allows a slight smile to dance at the corners of his mouth, his hands clasped in front of him in a cupped position, waiting. "Mr. President," he hears Clarence say, all of the boom now lost from his voice, "if the White people…if the IMs

wake up in the midst of this 'new America' or is it *New Egypt*,"
he says mockingly, "how will you and we handle this whole scale
shredding of the Constitution as we've known it and their reaction
to that?"

"Mr. Robinson, as I've said, the Constitution stays. We
remain a nation of laws. Changes will be made—some temporary
as I have clearly articulated, and some permanent. We did not ask
our fellow citizens to be stricken by the Sleeper Virus. But now
we must care for them and for the nation that they've left us." Mr.
Robinson then sits down, his opposition stilled for now, and the
President prepares to present the next topic.

President Douglas begins to speak about his plans for one
of the country going forward. Since the cities would now become
the epicenters of their remaining population, the President wants
the most advanced high speed rail to link them. This would be
their first massive public works projects that would keep many
employed for years to come. He wants the major cities linked,
and the mid-sized and smaller cities too. "Our expectation is that
our population will grow again, wildly. With ninety-five percent,
or more, of our population gainfully employed, families should
have all that they need to grow and thrive. And with that growth,

we'll be able to back fill the cities and towns that have been all but evacuated," he says. "Now, therefore, is the time to build our high speed rail system to connect our nation like never before. And who knows," he says almost joyfully, "such a network could one day replace our commercial air travel system."

A tremendously daunting problem is up next for discussion: i.e., the almost six and a half million Americans living abroad most of whom are IMs. At least ninety percent of that number are IMs who could not return home for the foreseeable future. Some had permanently repatriated abroad so that returning home would not have been an option in any event, but most are temporary workers or vacationers. Several thousand had even been caught on cruise ships in international waters when Sleep Day occurred. They are now docked in varying countries across the Caribbean and South America.

These IMs are, understandably, very upset at their status and feel that they are Americans without a country. Those who had permanent homes in the U.S. are demanding the protection and securement of their physical assets--their homes and personal property. The President well understands and appreciates the problem, and also, that there are no easy solutions. These IMs cannot return, perhaps ever, and holding their property in abeyance forever is not possible. Perhaps some of their physical assets can be sent to them, but the real estate, obviously, is not movable, President Douglas reasons.

As a solution, he recommends all of the following: all real property--homes, buildings and land--belonging to the IMs are to be held in trust and not transferred to any squatting or otherwise SM. These properties will be held in trust for either: 1) a year or 2) until it is safe for IMs living abroad to come home, whichever occurs first. Should the year period lapse, then that property will be made available to SMs by lottery. However, an IM may extend the trust by another year if a cure for the Sleeper Virus has either arrived or is imminently forthcoming.

All personal property belonging to the IMs, including bank accounts, valuables, and the like, are to be returned forthwith to the IMs who are abroad at their own expense. If any such property cannot be found to be returned, it will be considered lost and its value deducted one- hundred percent on their next filed tax return, whenever that occurs. Speaking to Convention attendees, President Douglas says that "We recognize that these are not fully equitable solutions, but that they represent the best possible recourse to

456

protect IM assets while acknowledging practical concerns of return."

President Douglas almost hesitates to broach the next subject. Clearing his throat, he begins to speak in a measured tone. "On top of the American IMs living abroad who have not been touched by the Sleeper Virus," he begins, "we also now have a new SM population, former IMs who have become SMs. These are IMs who have the ability, via their genetic predisposition, to produce melanin on demand, for example, as when the Sleeper Virus attempted to attack their metabolic systems to put them to sleep. Simply put, as the Sleeper Virus attacked their bodies of these IMs, their bodies went into a type of stasis that looks very similar to the slumber of those afflicted by the Sleeper Virus. But they don't stay asleep. Instead, they've typically awakened in twenty-four hours, sometimes more, sometimes less, and awakened looking quite different from their normal selves. I know that some of you have either seen this with your own eyes or heard the rumors." President Douglas hears a smattering of yeses and affirmations confirming his statement.

"Remarkably, these persons, in so far as we have seen, have all awakened with darker skin, and usually much darker. Our

457

scientists tell us that this seems to be a natural by-product of the melanin production to combat and seize the Sleeper Virus. For obvious reasons, we no longer regard these new SMs to be IMs anymore. They're awake, they're alive and moving about in our country as you or I am. They're pretty easy to spot. Though now possessing darker skin, the color of their eyes are usually quite light, for example, blue and they've retained their typical Euro American features." President Douglas thinks to himself that having seen a few of these persons himself, it is a little jarring to see persons who otherwise look perfectly Euro American with very light eyes and yet have dark skin.

These new SMs represent about five percent of the total IM population, about five million people. Most of that population is located in the southern states, which makes sense, as their ancestors would have mixed more frequently with a person of African descent at some point in the early history of the country. Importantly, these new SMs, because they had lived as White Americans for all of their lives, had never known the "separate but unequal" treatment experienced by most persons of color in the United States. Thus, a good seventy percent of the new SM population, at least, are high functioning members of society and have the ability to help with the restructuring of the country and its forward motion.

About half of that population, though, had been very conservative Republicans or Libertarians. Some had been virulently racist until they woke up the day after Sleep Day dark brown or black as any Sub-Saharan African. The President can only imagine the psychological trauma that some of the new SMs must have experienced upon obtaining consciousness from their metamorphosis to see the remainder of their household unconscious, or other family members, most notably their children, Brown and Black like them.

The Convention attendees all agree that the new SMs should be included amongst the ranks of the rest of the SMs. Their property rights would not be impinged, and they would have access to any suitable empty property as any other SM would have. They might have to assert those rights over an SM squatter, but the law will be on their side. The attendees also agree that it is good that the new SMs are among them. There is a ton of work to do, and their experience and expertise would be invaluable.

None of what had been discussed or agreed to answers the current issue of IM health and their storage. Millions had been lost since Sleep Day, either to lack of care, injury, exposure to the elements and even murder. The President, in one of his first acts in the first few days after Sleep Day, ordered anyone caught harming an IM to be shot on sight by the now federalized police officers. In these early days, President Douglas had wanted to instill as much fear as possible against those SMs foolhardy enough to harm any IMs found. But at the thirty day mark, the President explains, finding any IMs alive, even with their vastly slowed metabolisms, is a near hopeless endeavor. Though unconscious with significantly slowed metabolisms, they still needed nourishment and hydration. Few humans could live thirty days or more without both.

Three months later at the time of the Convention, the President explains, all found IMs are identified, catalogued and are being housed and cared for in large hospitals in the larger cities. This situation cannot last forever. Eventually, those hospitals would all have to be freed up for SM use, especially as SM populations grew. The President has ideas about what to do next, but he pitches the question to the attendees for their input. He decides to listen before weighing in.

One attendee, a renowned physician, submits that the current system of intravenous nourishment seems to be working, on the whole, with the now housed IM population. He warns, though, that the current system can only be temporary as each IM now requires a person to attend him or her. He suggests that a robust, automated system of care needs to be designed and implemented. The current system, he advises, requires hundreds of thousands of dedicated personnel to care for about one-hundred fifty million people. The ideal system, he postulates, would be fully automated and require only a few thousand to care for the population and perhaps, in time, only a few hundred or a few dozen.

Another attendee, a logistics expert with one of the country's major consumer goods companies, suggests that the IMs should be centrally located for any and all care. "Mr. President," she begins, "I hate to use the word *storage*, but that's exactly the concept that I'm going for. If we store the IMs in one place or in a few places that are close together, the delivery of everything that they need can take place much more efficiently. Also, their care, overall, can be highly regimented and made uniform. If the idea is to protect our IM population, find a cure to the Sleeper Virus and help them when they start to regain consciousness, a single location is the way to go."

Other attendees questioned who would move the IMs, when they would be moved, and where the central location would be? The President demurrers as to the last question. "A study would have to be done to scope out where, in the country, the entire IM population might be moved," he says. The President suggests, though, that in-place automated systems should be created and that the IMs will be moved into the interior of the country to several of the soon to be abandoned cities. The cities, themselves, will be transformed into housing centers for the IMs until a more permanent solution can be created, if necessary at all—the President holds out hope that either a cure would soon be found or the IMs would regain consciousness, soon, on their own.

In any event, the President notes that plans for a massive IM move and care needs to be put into place immediately. It would have to be a military-led and executed operation. He expects the cities to be newly populated with SMs coming into them and with an expected new SM immigrant population. The cities' hospitals and the space that they occupy would have to be freed up to meet the needs of the new SM populations. Of all of the institutions affected by the Sleeper Virus, the nation's military branches are the least affected, and thus the most capable of handling the monumental task of collecting and moving the millions of unconscious IMs.

By midnight that night, all of the Convention attendees know that this is just the beginning of the discussion and much more work remains to be done. The President is satisfied, though, that he has most of what he needs to take to Congress and the American people. He encourages the attendees to continue meeting for the rest of the week and form committees on the broad outlines of what had been discussed and agreed to today. It is Monday, and the President wants all recommendations delivered to his staff by Thursday of this week. By Friday, he wants a comprehensive package to deliver to Congress, for ratification in the next week. All attendees think that doable and agree to the deadline. If the conflict with North Korea and Russia had taught them all anything, it is that time was of the essence, and therefore gridlock could not be tolerated. America, the *new* America, had to show itself strong, nimble and ready to govern at home and worldwide where it could.

CHAPTER XV

Sitting in the Oval Office with his now complete senior leadership team, President Douglas is a mostly happy man. He has the final report from the Convention attendees in his hands and he likes what he sees. All of the big ticket items are here. Literally, everything that he has asked for he has gotten. The attendees had even provided more recommendations that hadn't occurred to him, but that he supports nonetheless. They also provide some sunset provisions to the President's authority so that he would not, as they write, make him a "king." The report begins with a letter to the President from the Convention attendees that he studies carefully.

Dear Mr. President,

You have asked us to provide you a list of recommendations to move our country forward beyond the terrible tragedy that has been wrought by the Sleeper Virus. We mourn the loss of our American brothers and sisters—our family. We remain hopeful that the survivors will re-awaken and soon join us in the work of our country.

Going forward, there is much work to be done to maintain our momentum and protect America. Our near war with North

Korea has greatly chastened us as a nation and placed us on our guard. To avoid war and to protect our Homeland, we make these several recommendations, several of which give you many, important enhanced powers as our Executive. But make no mistake, Mr. President, we are not making you our King. Your powers rest with the People and belong thereto. And while our recommendations enhance your authority, those enhancements are deemed to be temporary, and not permanent.

Having said that, sir, we, the Conference of New American Leadership, place our confidence in you and our existing leadership to protect our country and right the ship of our prominence in the world. In addition to our collaboration earlier, you will find additional recommendations not previously discussed. Our hope is that you will approve of all of the recommendations as is knowing that 1) time is of the essence and 2) we, as you, have the best interests of our country at heart.

Very Respectfully Submitted,

The Convention of New American

Leadership

President Douglas allows the words of the attached letter to resonate in his mind a moment. The Convention attendees had given themselves a formal title: The Convention of New American Leadership. He thinks it appropriate, if not a bit grandiose. What seems implicit in the title is the fact that they are a new party with which to contend. He appreciates, though, their forthrightness in declaring their agreement, but also their reservations. They do not want him to become a king, but they understand that some of his actions would appear king-like. This will be temporary, the President promises himself. He has no desire to assume the mantle of king of this or any other country.

The President turns the page and begins to delve into the details of the recommendations. During that week, a sub-committee had gotten together to discuss the issue of culture. Apparently, there had been great argument as to whether or not culture would even be discussed.

The naysayers are soundly beat back on this point. The prevailing attendees began to outline some measures that should be taken to alter and permanently reverse the negative stereotypes that had too long penetrated popular cultural norms.

They wanted, for example, education in the schools to move away from a euro-centric emphasis to that of an SM emphasis, whether African, Native American or Asian. Slavery would no longer be given short shrift, but the truth of its horrors would be brought to full light in the classrooms as well as all of the atrocities visited upon the major minority groups in the country. These events would be viewed as a testament to the survival of not only Black Americans but of all SM groups that survived some form of indentured servitude or abuse in the country, particularly the Native Americans. A new point of emphasis would be strength through survival.

Media images of SMs would also change. By no longer being relegated to the margins of society, the attendees argued that their images should reflect that and show them large and in charge. This would be good for the country and its standing in the rest of world. To that end, the attendees recommended a large, coordinated public relations campaign showing SMs positively and in full command of themselves and their country.

These attendees had no recommendations for religion but stated that the longer that they would be bereft of the presence of the IMs, the more that they expected religion, and at least religious imagery, to be altered to fit the world and spiritual views of the SM population. The only partial recommendation on this point by the attendees is that the separation between church and state should remain, and that the American people should sort out their own religious or anti-religious choices.

As another recommendation, the attendees want the government to sponsor and advance the arts like never before. Creating a new and substantial artistic culture, they argue, would further the formation of a new national identity, one distinctly different than that had before Sleep Day. This new identity would, they hope, do battle against the "prison culture," the "misogynist culture," the "poverty culture," the "anti-education culture," and all other faux, negative cultures that most SM ethnic groups had experienced. This made perfect sense to President Douglas, and he is glad that they had thought about it. He would add to this new push in the arts, a PR program that would push themes of uplift, scholarship, service and national unity, things that in this search for a new national identity, they were all in sore need.

The Convention attendees also recommended that as cities fill up, Congress and the Senate should be fully re-constituted as soon as practicable. This would present a slight problem, the President thinks, because several of the states had become de-populated due both to the loss of the afflicted IMs and the President's request that all remaining SMs move to a city on the

list of cities being actively supported by the federal government.
"The will of the people," the report reads, "must be preserved
and maintained even in these dire times. You have said to us,
Mr. President, that you have no desire to be our king. Prove it by
ordering Congressional and Senate elections ninety days from
now." President Douglas does not know whether elections in ninety
days might be possible, but he is willing to try. He believes that in
order to maintain the confidence of the people, the United States,
in all respects must operate in a manner that the Founders intended.
Of course, they had certainly not intended *this* turn of events nor
foreseen them, but surely they had always intended order and the
manifestation of the peoples' will through free elections.

There are myriad other additional recommendations in
the report from the Convention that had not specifically come up
during their discussions with President Douglas. The President and
his team read them carefully. They agree with, if not like, most of
them. There is one, however, that gives President Douglas pause:
the Convention recommends that abortions be restricted unless
the health of the mother is impacted or in the case of incest or
rape. Their thinking is that with the immediate de-population of
the United States and with no foreseeable cure for the IMs, re-

establishing a solid population is paramount. This next generation of Americans will have to be robust and plentiful to carry on their work and the maintenance of the nation. The President, they note, had already discussed with them that there would be a push for families to *go big* and have, at least four children per household. This recommendation, they postulate, is a natural extension of that push.

The President and his top advisors debate this point for the better part of a day. There certainly is practical application for a moratorium on abortion, at least in the near term, but two points stick out: whether anyone in government has the ability to order such a moratorium given the Supreme Court's decisions and the fact that his and most of his advisors' political careers had been staked out in the pro-abortion wing of the party. The President wonders to himself whether his party even still exists. To him, it seems that they are all just survivors of the Sleep Virus trying to keep and run a country.

President Douglas acknowledges to his team that he doesn't think that there exists a political solution to the morass, short of a Constitutional amendment that specifically out-laws abortion save for a few exceptions. He might, though, as the Chief Executive forbid any doctor or health care workers, all of whom at this point had been federalized, from performing any abortions unless it meets the criteria of one of the exceptions. He can, as a short term measure, forbid any and all healthcare providers from performing abortions for a period of time. He suggests one year. His advisors suggest ten. They settle on three.

The Convention attendees, as a last, and most interesting item, request that President Douglas maintain it as a separate arm of the government operating as a consultant and idea generator until such time as the government is fully reconstituted. They think it prudent that they remain part of the national discussion given their expertise and experience. As part of that consultation, they want the President's leave to create a set of national plans that would out live them all--namely, a five-year plan, a ten-year plan, a twenty-five year plan, a
fifty-year plan and a one-hundred year plan. Such plans, they argue, would be strategic and place the U.S. on more solid political and economic footing rather than the year-to-year political squabbling of pre-Sleep Day. The President nods his approval to himself. Strategic planning at a high level in the private sector and government, he thinks. It could work. It might have to.

*   *   *

Jerome walks hand in hand with Elena to their polling station in Hyde Park, Cincinnati. It is set up on Hyde Park Square, just a few blocks away from their house. It is August, it is hot, and the mosquitoes are out. They had both doused themselves and the kids in repellant that they all hope protects them. Their children, Micah and Sarah, are excited. They are old enough to grasp many of the changes that are happening, it seems, at break neck speed around them.

From their perspective, their world had been flipped onto its head. Most of their friends had become unconscious due to the Sleeper Virus, all but the Black and Brown ones. Micah and Sarah mourn them as if they had died, but they know that they aren't dead, just unconscious. When their father became a federalized police officer, they made sure that they had the names of their friends and their addresses. They wanted him to personally go to their houses, find them, secure them and keep them safe. Jerome promised them that he would do so. The list included about ten families, eight of which had lived in Hyde Park, one in Indian Hill and one in Kenwood.

Jerome and Darryl found every family and Micah and Sarah's friends all unconscious except for one, the family in Indian Hill. Their Indian Hill friend, Chase, his sisters and their mother, had all become colored, that is, transformed. They had become SMs. This meant, of course, that when the Sleeper Virus attacked their bodies, their bodies had responded by super-producing melanin to protect them from its affects. They had all learned about the transformations caused by the Sleeper Virus. Since it acts on a molecular level, altering a victim's metabolic processes at a molecular level, only a molecular response can stop it, the melanin molecule.

Micah and Sarah had also insisted that their father take them to see their friends once they were secured. He took them to the hospital at which they are stored—Good Samaritan. It is heart breaking to see their friends in their unconscious states, not moving and not speaking. Micah moves to each one, in turn praying for them. Sarah says her own words and kisses each one on the cheek. Sarah attaches letters to each of them reminding them of who they are and where they live. On the ride home, they ask their father what the latest news is on a cure. Jerome doesn't know and he hasn't heard of anything new. But as soon as something changes, he says, he will be the first to tell them unless Twitter gets to them first.

That time seems as if it were years ago instead of a few short months. They watch their parents walk ahead of them down towards the Square. Their neighborhood had steadily become more populated over the last few months ever since they had moved into their house, their new big house. When they first move into it, they are the only family on the entire street. As more people get qualified, though, they start moving in until one day, Micah notices, Hyde Park seems nearly as populated as it had before Sleep Day had struck.

He and Sarah had attended a private school in Hyde Park, and when their parents allow them to, they would meet with friends after school on the Square for ice cream or even lattes. Even before they had moved there, they had been pretty familiar with Hyde Park and its constituents. Today, walking toward the Square they see a similar number of people, cars, bikers, and walkers as they had six months ago. If Hyde Park had been a ghost town, Micah thinks, it hadn't remained that way for long.

Sarah notices her parents' excitement. Today is the day that they, and the rest of the nation, would be voting for their new

Congressional representatives. The President had been all over the television and social media touting the need to get government working again for the people. The new Congress would be smaller given that about five or more states had been de-populated and their land federalized, but it would fairly represent the will of the people in the other populated areas. Though it is early August, she and Micah had already gone back to school. They are now taking their classes at the local university—U.C., the University of Cincinnati. Xavier University is also being used for the overflow from U.C. As in most cities like theirs,' elementary, junior and high schools had been moved out of their regular locations and centralized on two campus'—U.C. and Xavier. Neither can really be used as separate colleges anymore because the SM college populations are not large enough. Besides, SMs from Cincinnati going to college are all going to either Howard, Morehouse, Spelman, Stanford, or any of the other HBCUs or California schools. The President had been super funding those universities since they already had professors and infrastructure in place to teach their kids.

When Sarah and Micah begin attending U.C. for school, they are immediately fast-tracked for early graduation. President

Douglas had stated that he wants kids who can go to college by the age of sixteen and graduate from college by the age of twenty. The country needs them, he says, and the sooner that they are prepared the better.

Micah and Sarah see that their parents' polling station is just ahead about a block from them. Several passers-by walk towards them, each smiling and wearing an "I VOTED TODAY" sticker somewhere on their shirts. The kids know that their parents would each be sporting a brand new sticker on their own shirts. "Hey Dad," Micah says. "May Sarah and I go and get an ice cream while you two vote?"

"No, Micah. We want you both to join us. Pick a parent and you'll vote with that one," he replies.

"I pick Daddy!" Sarah says before Micah can speak up. As in their races, she usually beat him to the punch here as well.

"Fine," Micah says. "I wanted Mommy anyway. Punk." He glowers at his sister which is confirmation enough that perhaps he had really wanted to vote with his father.

Walking into the polling station, Jerome and Elena expect to see a somewhat disorganized mess. They find anything but that. The poll workers are in place, the machines are up, and the ballot

counting machines are in place. "Jerome and Elena Middleton,"
Jerome says. He smiles at his wife and squeezes her hand as if to
confirm that they are really here. "Yes, Mr. and Mrs. Middleton,
here are your names. What is your address?" Jerome tells the poll
worker, an older Black woman, their new Hyde Park address.
He is pleased to see that she reads the address that he had just
shared. "Do we need to show I.D." Jerome asks? "Why no, sir, Mr.
Middleton. Confirmation of your address is I.D. enough. Here are
your and Mrs. Middleton's ballots. Thanks for voting."

Jerome and Elena accept their ballots and lead their
assigned child to a ballot booth. Sarah sticks her tongue out at
Micah as she and her father walk into a booth together. Micah is
pretty easily provoked, and she loves doing it. Walking into the
ballot box with her father feels like a dream to her. Never had she
sensed as much hope and purpose amongst the grown folks as she
does today. The country is different, but it is theirs, *all* of theirs.
In listening to the adults talk, she and Micah hear their excitement
mixed in with a touch of melancholy. There is still ample concern
about the IMs and what might happen to them. Some, in truth,
hope that the IMs never regain consciousness.

For them, life had never been so good. There are new homes, cars and jobs aplenty. It seems that overnight poverty had fully dissipated in the SM community. Gone were the days of driving while Black, workplace discrimination, glass ceilings, dubious accidental police shootings on unarmed Black men, a presumption of incompetence, and all of the hallmarks that marked racism and discrimination in American society before Sleep Day. While there is widespread concern for the IMs, there is also a collective sigh of relief experienced by the SMs that their day-to-day lives are no longer defined by the societal control of the IMs.

Sarah, begrudgingly, can relate. School had not always been the most pleasant of places for her. She is smart and pretty. Her grades had often been better than her White female peers. That sometimes brought on ugly looks and comments. She hadn't always felt welcome at their school. She prefers not to think about why she had sometimes been ill-treated, but she thinks she might know. She is both Black and *not* rich, but middle class. Her father had driven a trash truck and her mother, when she worked, had been a nurse. Her school had been predominantly made up of rich, White kids who were extremely privileged. Those children had been expected to be smart and to succeed. She had not been expected to be as successful as them. When she had proven herself every bit as talented and smart as her peers, it seemed to grate on some of them. One girl had even said to her one day: "You know, Sarah," her White classmate Emily had said, "I wish that slavery still existed. That way, I'd never have to see you again." Sarah wasn't the type of girl to be violent, but in that moment, she felt like punching Emily for all that she was worth. She hadn't though. She had merely told her teacher and her parents. Emily had never spoken with her again.

When Sarah told her father what had happened, he went through the roof, his usual calm demeanor gone. He calls the school and demanded accountability for Emily's actions. She is held accountable, but the sting of the incident stayed with Sarah for a long time. She would often later see Emily though they no longer spoke to one another. Ever. For Sarah, every "A" made and every goal scored is a little bit more of her claiming herself back from the hurtful words that had seemed to take so much. Sarah had included Emily's name and address on her list of friends to check on by her Father. He understood the significance of that gesture and checked on them as requested. Emily and her family are one of the ones that her father and Uncle Darryl had found unconscious.

Jerome secured them, carefully, and shipped them to a hospital for safe keeping. When Sarah had prayed for her friends, she had prayed for Emily too.

"Okay, honey, my ballot's all filled out," Jerome says. "Take a look."

Sarah looks at her father's ballot as he pushes his chest out in obvious pride. She doesn't really recognize any of the names, but she surmises that her dad probably knows everyone that he chose personally. His ballot selects two new Congressmen and two new Senators. Given the demographics of Ohio, and the fact that Cincinnati, Columbus and Cleveland are still heavily populated, most of the Representatives and Senators would be Black, a few would be Hispanic. In states like California, the reverse is true, given their population differences.

Micah and her mother come out, it appears to Sarah, both glowing and floating. Micah's arm is wrapped around his mother, as they seem to share some private secret between them.

"J., you ready?" Elena asks calling her husband by her pet nickname for him.

"Yeah, baby. And I see that these two are at it again." He nods toward Sarah and Micah who are once again making strange faces at one another. "Why don't we grab that ice cream now?" Sarah and Micah clap in glee, bouncing up and down in place. It is decided.

Headed out of the polling station, Jerome takes a deep breath. "Elena, smell that. Take a big whiff. What's that smell like?" Jerome asks.

Elena breathes in heavily. "Change," she says, "and freedom".

*   *   *

CNN, MSNBC and the new FOX networks all provide rolling, up to date coverage on the Congressional and Senatorial races. The commentators note that these races, besides being the first of their kind in the nation's history, are also unique in their tone. The former partisanship is all but absent. The Republican Party still exists, but it is a sad shadow of its former self. Because it had rarely taken the presence of minorities in its party seriously, the removal of the IMs had left it virtually, but fully empty. Most races either feature one candidate who runs unopposed, or two democrats opposing one another. Debates are civil and not personal, the commentators remark. All participants seem more interested in the actual survival of their country instead of their own political gain. Since Congressional term limits are in full effect, everyone seeking office understands that they have a finite amount of time to work and make a difference.

The commentators also remark about how the political landscape had changed so drastically. Because of the federalization of some states, votes would not be taken from them. They had been essentially de-populated. There is really no precedent for this in the history of the United States, but few doubt that there would be any challenges filed in federal court, if only because the courts themselves are not fully populated.

The commentators note that as soon as the elections are over and Congressmen and Congresswomen installed, the President will move to re-constitute the Supreme Court and all other federal courts. It would be a massive undertaking. The Supreme Court, it is said, can be filled with qualified candidates, but the federal court system is massive, even though the new federal court system would serve fewer states and a smaller overall population. Filling all of the vacancies would take time, provided that the IMs remain unconscious. If they regain consciousness between now and then, the commentators note, then some different

issues might arise including the existence of a new Congress

and new Federal judges. It had been six months since Sleep

Day and there is no known change in the status of the IMs. The

commentator on MSNBC notes that the President would begin

phased evacuations of the IMs from the city hospitals. Those

spaces are now needed, he says, due to the rising populations in the

cities.

The President and his staff watch all of this with

mounting interest. They are witnessing history. A new House of

Representatives and a new Senate for what seemed like a new

America. The President had cast his ballot that morning. The

District of Columbia, by Executive Order, would now have one

voting Senator and two Representatives. His vote, along with all

other District residents, actually counts for the first time, he muses.

At least now, "taxation without representation" is no longer the

rule of the day for D.C. residents.

"Robert," the President says speaking to his new White

House Communications Chief, "how are we looking? Are all of

our sponsored candidates making the cut?"

"It looks that way, Mr. President, except for a few races in Missouri, Texas, and Arizona" he says. "But even where our folks are not getting in, some similarly situated like-minded pol is winning. It's a wash, sir."

President Douglas smiles. This vote, he thinks, isn't just important for public relations purposes, but for actual governing. He has an ambitious plan that needs to be executed, preferably, before the IMs wake up. He had begun to think now of the Sleeper Virus as a true mixed blessing if he could enact his agenda before they could arise to fight against it. Truthfully, he doesn't want the IMs unconscious forever, just long enough to make his ideas happen. In truth, except for health care and a small handful of other ideas, he had never had much latitude in enacting a coherent agenda. The conservative IMs are too plentiful, too steadfast, too well-organized, and too belligerent. If the President said "White," he thinks, they'd say "Black," even if "White" had been their original idea. If he had agreed with them and said "Black," they'd switch back to "White." It had all turned into an absurd political show, he thinks.

But now, the President is about to get the Congress that he wants, one that has the political power and will to back most of his initiatives. President Douglas knows, however, that even with an all SM Congress in an all SM country, time is ticking. They are all still Americans and that independent American streak cuts across all lines of religion, ethnicity, gender, and age. He has to quickly show that his ideas are the best ideas, or he'd be set upon by his critics, just as he had been before Sleep Day, and still was with American media that maintains their posts outside of the country.

When the President announces the recommendations from the Convention to the American public and the overseas public, the response by the American IMs living outside of the country had been predictably brutal. Of course, they accuse the President, and by extension, the remaining SM population, of trying to take *their* country from them. The President and his ambassadors, try their best to explain their decisions to them. However, his attempts are not well-received. Instead, in some quarters, American IMs who cannot return to the country openly discuss acquiring a military that might invade the U.S. or at least put fire to some of its cities, thereby destroying vast segments of the country. The President warns that any American caught fomenting or planning violence against the country would be treated and tried as traitors in absentia and eventually hunted down.

The President is loath to have such a trial, but believes it necessary if pushed. Once the government begins placing the property of IMs in trusts as promised, much of their protests stop. Many of the IMs find homes in Europe and in Canada. Typically, they avoid other countries that have high populations of people of color. England, France, Spain, Canada and Holland are particularly welcoming of the American IMs. Some even travel to Alaska given that it had not been infected by the Sleeper Virus. The President and the country feel especially loyal to the IMs that make Alaska their home, because it means that they had not given up on being American. The same could not be said for some.

Today, the communications room of the White House buzzes with activity. The President, his staff, and several aides are in the room reviewing results, listening to the cable news reports and discussing post-election results and strategy. "Fox News sure does look different, doesn't it," someone in the room remarks. "It sure does," another responds. There is no mistaking the changes on television these days and not just in the news.

For the first few months of the Sleeper Virus, television had been pretty consistently available and looked just like it had prior to Sleep Day. Recently, though, it had started to change since

SMs had taken over the studios in Hollywood and elsewhere in the country. New programming starts to show up that features lots of folks that had worked in Hollywood for years and lots of new folks not previously known. The usual bevy of comedies and dramas are being made, but their tone is different. It is as if, suddenly, writers had learned how to write authentic stories of SM life in America, whether for African Americans, Hispanics, Asians or Native Americans. The images now being produced about SMs are overwhelmingly positive, except, of course when bad guys are shown, but even they seemed richer in texture and more complex—more *Stringer Bell* and less *fit the description* generic caricatures.

Radio had changed too. There were not nearly as many radio stations as before, and they all seemed to follow an urban format or something similar. New music, reflective of the times, was being created that mirrored the new energy in the nation. A lot of the music, especially hip-hop, sounds almost happy, an emotion that modern hip-hop often poorly reflected. It reminds the President of much of the music that he had grown up listening to. In fact, artists like KRS-1, Rakim and Public Enemy experience a bit of a resurgence in this new era. He only knows that because he catches his sons listening to a "hot new artist" that sounds suspiciously like one of his favorite rappers, KRS-1. His sons had been mortified to learn that they were listening to and enjoying someone from their father's generation. He had merely chuckled and asks for the CD so that he could later play it for himself.

The President hopes that every positive political move that they made moved them closer to national and international stability. He scores these elections as a "win." They would show the world that they are still one nation, and what's more, the legitimate and natural heirs of the new nation, if that's what it comes to. Hopefully, it would not come to that. The nation wants the surviving IMs to be alive, whole and conscious. If that did not happen, the President is determined to protect and maintain the nation that they now have.

He also wants to grow it in every possible and responsible way. He wants to re-grow the middle class, grow technology, grow energy conservation, grow infrastructure, grow transportation, grow American manufacturing, and yes, in spite of the Sleeper Virus, grow international relationships for America worldwide. He plans to use the Caribbean extensively for their and his country's benefit and then to expand that same outlook and approach to Africa.

Around midnight the final results start to come in. All of the votes had been counted. A new Congress had been elected. All of the available seats in the House and Senate had been filled. Swearing-in ceremonies would occur in the next thirty days, and the business of the country could begin again. The President sincerely hopes that that new business advances the new nation that they had all inherited.

*   *   *

Mary stretches her long arms down her body as she yawns. She cracks her toes too for good measure. Peering through her window she sees that the sun is just beginning to peek out over the tree line in her backyard. It's early, she thinks. She feels the ragged exhaustion of having spent too many nights up worrying and planning in a seemingly endless cycle.

This is the day that all of her planning and worrying is realized. Her feelings are a mixed bundle of sadness, resolve, and not a small amount of joy. She also feels a nagging pang of guilt. Her psychiatrist describes it as "survivor's guilt," the kind of guilt that survivors from wars that are normally relegated to soldiers get.

She is no soldier, but she had experienced it all the same. Mary feels guilty for having survived.

Logically, she considers her feelings to be ridiculous. Yet they're with her pretty much all of the time, tormenting her. Looking down at her arms, she is at once thankful for her new brown hue, but conflicted too. Like so many of the new SMs, she had never truly known what might be in her family other than a European lineage. She had known as far back as her great grandparents, but there are no records of her family before them. Even when she had tried, several years ago, to research her family's history through a paid ancestral subscription service, she could never get past her great grandparents on either side.

Now she thinks that she knows why. Someone in her family had been a person of color, perhaps several someone's, and judging by her new hue, a person of African descent. This, of course means but one thing, at least one of her American ancestors had been enslaved. She is sure of that fact since both sets of her grandparents had come from the South, Georgia and South Carolina, respectively. If anyone in her family had known it, that fact had been well-hidden, so well-hidden in fact that at least two generations had lived as if they are one-hundred percent White.

490

But DNA does not lie, Mary thinks. Her skin is as brown as it is because she possesses the DNA necessary to produce melanin, a lot of it. When her body had needed to, it had responded and kept her awake, and ultimately alive. Mary realizes that if she had used one of those paid DNA services like several of her African-American friends had, she probably would have discovered that she had some lineage somewhere in Africa, most likely in the west of that massive continent. Looking back, Mary thinks that this would have been information worth knowing. Of a certainty, she knows it now anyway.

When the Sleeper Virus had attacked her, it knocked her out just like it had every other White or light-skinned person. In her case though, her sleep had been temporary. She had awakened sixteen hours later with a bad headache and a bad bruise on her temple marking the place where she had fallen. She is one of the lucky ones though. She had fallen at home. She had been about to go into her garage and get into her car, but when the Sleeper Virus struck, she fell right at the door leading to her garage, so she remained inside of her locked, safe house. Many like her had not been so lucky, and many had been killed on accident or because of some evil done to them when made unconscious.

Mary and her husband Doug are childless. He had worked full time at a company that he'd helped to build in Chicago. Mary is an accomplished physician and geneticist. She works at a hospital in Schaumburg, right outside of Chicago. On Sleep Day, Doug had gone to work early. It was supposed to have been a day of heavy meetings for him. His business was entering a complex deal that Doug swore was about to take his company to the next level. When she wakes up, Mary's first thought, other than her throbbing headache, is of Doug. She calls his office as soon as possible. She does not reach him. She calls and keeps calling. She calls every number that she has for him. She never reaches him. That had been the hardest day for her since she had awakened. It had been the worst.

Mary remembers the panic and the loss of that day ruefully. When she sees herself in the mirror for the first time, she screams and nearly falls again. As badly as her head had hurt, this had been worse. The face that stares back at her is hers, at least, the eyes are hers. The skin and the hair though, are someone else's. Where once her White, admittedly darker-toned, skin and light auburn hair were, in their place is skin the color of cocoa and hair the color of ebony. Mary notices too that her skin seems smoother and that

492

there are fewer lines etched across her face. She looks ten years younger, much younger, at least, than her forty years say that she is. She remembers a line overheard from one of the Black nurses at her hospital made in jest, "Black don't crack," and wonders if this is what the nurse had been talking about.

When Mary had awakened she'd made every effort to get to her husband. After making every call that she could and sending every email that she could, she resolves to get in her car to go find him. She had needed to see him and tell him what had happened to her. She does not know the cause, but as a geneticist, she understands that her transformation had happened at a genetic level. She surmises that something had triggered the hyper production of melanin in her skin. Her complexion had always been swarthy, a fact that she greatly enjoyed during summer time, but this reaction is much different. To her knowledge, there had been no strange solar event that could account for her transformation.

At first, she believes that what had happened to her was only skin deep. Post her transformation, she hadn't felt sick or otherwise nauseous. In fact, she had felt strangely revitalized and full of energy. Though she does not yet have access to any of her instruments for internal checking, she senses that all of her organs are working normally and all of her metabolic processes properly engaged. Other than her skin and hair changing, she feels, mostly, like a super energized version of her former self.

In the hours past her first waking up, realizing that she is unable to drive due to a likely concussion, Mary had turned on the television to see what else might be amiss. Television is strange. First, not all of the live news channels are available, notably Fox news. Second, the news channels that are available seem to only have persons of color doing the news. They speak about some occurrence happening on a national scale affecting millions, but details are sketchy. Mary picks up that there had been mass accidents, including U.S. planes falling out of the sky with some crashing into heavily-populated areas, thousands of car accidents and many casualties. The President had come on television many times to reassure the country that what had been happening is not a terrorist attack, but that the full details as of yet are unknown. To say that this is spooky, Mary thinks, is a major understatement.

Those early days after the Sleeper Virus had struck had been heady and uncertain times. The last three to four months had been a whirlwind of activity. She had managed to find Doug a few days later, slumped over in his office with his phone to his ear. By this time, Mary had prepared herself for what she might find. She finds his partner too in the adjoining office. In fact, when she'd arrived, she had found three or four other African and Hispanic Americans looking for their loved ones just like her. Two of them she had known as the spouses of her husband's employees. They look at her at first with shock and surprise, but then with looks of knowing and understanding. No words are shared between them, but they embrace one another and Mary silently sobs her fears, loss, and frustration into the arms of a big Black man who is the husband of Doug's administrative assistant. His name is Michael. He helps Mary wheel Doug out of his office and puts him into her car. Michael then carries his wife into his arms and puts her into his car. He promises to follow Mary home so that he can take Doug inside. Doug is a big man and far too heavy for Mary to manage by herself. Mary is grateful for the help, as apparently there would be no help coming from the police or emergency services. They are each busy trying to maintain order and rescue accident victims from the carnage created by the Sleeper Virus. For a little while it seems at least Mary is on her own.

Today, months later, Mary is hopeful. Because of her expertise, she had been tapped to head up the recovery of Chicago's and the surrounding area's IMs. By her estimate, she had recovered between seventy-five and eighty percent of the IMs who had been struck by the virus in and around the city. She realizes that her recovery efforts have helped save many, many lives. In the first few days after the virus strikes, there had been horror stories of abuses perpetrated upon unconscious IMs before Chicago police, the army, and many volunteers had shut that down. The President had been quick to act to rescue the IMs in major cities like Chicago, L.A., Dallas and others, but some of the smaller cities and towns had been missed due to a lack of resources. As a result, many IMs had died, mostly due to starvation and the elements but also, some due to killing and abuse by others.

Standing up, Mary stretches her diminutive frame and heads to the shower. She quickly showers and dons her most comfortable warm-up. She had packed the night before, but is only taking a small duffle bag for her trip. She had been advised that though she might be gone for a few months, she needn't take a lot of clothing. She would be sufficiently outfitted with proper gear, she had been told. Mary therefore takes only her favorite underwear, some books and other knick-knacks that hold sentimental value between her and Doug. Her next assignment is to be her ultimate assignment.

Because of her exemplary work in Chicago, she had been tapped by the White House through the Department of Homeland Security to help plan and execute the collection of all sleeping IMs and their transport to several centralized locations in the Mid-West and West. Ultimately, the goal is to house and keep the IMs alive until either they wake up or a cure is found that will revive them. Mary wants to work on the cure too, but first things first. Her job is to lead the transition and storage of the IM population. She hates that word, storage. But practically, what they are doing is storing their fellow citizens until they are cured and revived. Mary had been over the ethical conundrum a million times in her head—"do no harm"—she reminds herself. Besides that, she feels that this is the best use of her time and talent while her husband is still unconscious.

Mary readies herself to leave and make her way to Midway airport. A private government jet awaits her transport to Washington for her final instructions. She is being provided with a team of fellow doctors and care practitioners, all vetted by her and the Secret Service. The locations of the future homes of the IMs is a secret that requires the highest security clearances. Everyone working on the project has to have cleared a thorough background check and already be trained as a health professional. Mary is well aware that many of the medical schools had been emptied to find suitable persons to help work on so massive an undertaking. The transport, storage, feeding and continual care of millions of their fellow Americans is no small undertaking and requires herculean amounts of work, logistical coordination, accessible infrastructure and dedication. For Doug's sake, Mary hopes that she is ready. For all of their sakes, she hopes that the country is ready.

EPILOGUE

TWENTY YEARS LATER

Director James Cooper glides noiselessly in his shuttle pod at three hundred miles per hour. He had received an emergency text on his private line about an hour ago at three a.m. He reads its contents and is out his front door five minutes after that. Now, speeding in these caverns, he wonders what he might do if the text is true and accurate.

The underground cavern in which he now travels is buried five hundred feet below ground, far enough to avoid any other construction above, and far enough to keep it and its occupants secret and protected. President Douglas, as one of his last acts in office, had commissioned its building. That had been more than twenty years ago. The country and the care of the IMs had changed dramatically since then. Officially, it does not exist. Unofficially, its workers and staff refer to it as the Hive.

The country had needed a place to house its IM population--about one hundred and fifty million, give or take. This location, somewhere between South Dakota and Wyoming, is extremely

499

stable and about the size of the state of Ohio. It is divided into one-thousand sections, each housing about one-hundred and fifty thousand IMs. Each IM housing unit is wired, temperature controlled, clean and all but fully automated using a massive central computing system and robots to care for its occupants. Nutrition, healthcare and every necessity to keep each IM alive is delivered on a schedule and by automation. Once the system had gone live and the last of the IMs had been delivered, their care is all but assured. The Sleeper virus keeps them asleep and strangely non-aging, an aspect of their extremely slowed metabolisms. All they have to do is keep them fed, hydrated and safe, a simple idea in theory but massive to execute with so many people.

But not so simple today, Director Cooper thinks as he speeds his way to Section 556. The monitor in his shuttle pod tells him that he is now just five minutes away from arrival. Few human workers ever come this far into the Hive anymore. He, himself, had not been here for a year or more. The status of each and every IM is comfortably viewed from his pad device, watch or cell phone or from the control room at the top of the Hive. Now, only about twenty human workers work in the Hive in total and only come this far for emergencies which are rare. The Director thinks about the subterranean river that had broken into section

149 a few years ago and had drowned ten thousand sleeping IMs before the robots had sealed the hole and pumped the water out. Every section of the pod could be isolated to protect every other section so the water leakage in section 149 had been cordoned off and kept separate from every other section of the Hive.

Director Cooper's right hand, Andrea Smith, awaits him when he steps out of his shuttle pod. "Director Cooper", she says. "Good evening, Sir. I'm so sorry to have disturbed you."

"It's okay, Ms. Smith, I told you to contact me immediately if anything happened. What's happened?" he asks.

"I think I better show you, Sir", she says. Director Cooper follows Andrea Smith from the platform holding his shuttle pod. She traces a path down a narrow hallway that leads into a large expansive chamber the size of a large college football stadium, large enough to contain one-hundred and fifty thousand unconscious human beings. A control panel stands just off to the left of the entry into the chamber. A mechanical system had been constructed that holds each IM in a separate robotic enclosure encased in a fluid filled, clear enclosure. The enclosure is called an IM pod. Each pod is attached to a robotic arm, each of which is completely filled with a life preserving fluid. The fluid consists of mostly water, saline, an anti-microbial mix and everything necessary to keep the skin and hair healthy. Each IM is outfitted with a breathing tube that ensures a constant rate of breath. Monitors are attached to every IM that registers the heart rate, blood pressure and any hint of distress or disease.

Ms. Smith steps to the monitor and punches in an access code. She then looks at her phone. "556102309", she says as she punches in the numbers. Immediately pressing the enter key, robotic arms before them begin to dance and whirr with motion. Soon, IM pod number 556102309 is before them. In it, a blond blue-eyed girl of about ten lays suspended with her pod attached to a robotic arm. She stirs in her pod, opens her eyes and looks directly at them.

"As you can see, Sir, she's awake. She's been awake since about five minutes before I called you", Ms. Smith says.

"Five minutes", Director Cooper almost exclaims, "why the hell did it take you five minutes to call me?!"

"Because, Sir, I wasn't sure what I was seeing. I was asleep too when my phone buzzed. And I wanted to re-check the data to make sure. I haven't told anyone else."

"Good", he says, "and don't. I'll handle this. Ms. Smith, this stays between the two of us. Understood." It is not a question. She nods her affirmation, turns toward the exit and walks out of the chamber. Director Cooper waits until he hears her shuttle pod whisk away before moving. He steps to the monitor and types in his access code. The previous screen is erased and his screen replaces it. In the left hand corner of the screen is a digital button with the word "PROTOCOL" emblazoned onto it. Director Cooper presses that button and a text box appears. He types in one word— "Omega". Another box pops up that asks the question—"Subject or All?" He pauses for a moment thoughtful contemplation. Readying himself, he types the word "All" and presses the enter key.

He looks at the girl before him. She is pretty, he thinks, and young. Before his next thought, her eyes close and she is asleep. Director Cooper checks her vitals to make sure that she is unconscious. Satisfied, he leaves the chamber and gets into his shuttle pod. Speeding back toward the cavern's entrance he wonders what, if anything, he is going to have to do about Ms. Smith.

~ END BOOK ONE ~